...ok her face into h...
...between us."

She searched his eyes for more. Something to say that he trusted her, something to say that she could trust him. There were lies between them, and a son.

"Connor will be part of my life, Kat." Her heart tripped, seeing such love in his eyes. "If I'm wary and cautious, it's because I'm not taking any chances when it comes to Connor."

Kat thought about that a few seconds. "I understand. I'm relieved that you feel protective about him. He deserves…"

"The best in both of us."

* * *

The Secret Heir of Sunset Ranch is part of The Slades of Sunset Ranch: The sun never sets on love and redemption for these rich Nevada ranchers!

A

THE SECRET HEIR
OF SUNSET RANCH

BY
CHARLENE SANDS

Published in Great Britain 2013
by Mills & Boon, an imprint of Harlequin (UK) Limited,
Eton House, 18-24 Paradise Road, Richmond, Surrey TW9 1SR

© Charlene Swink 2013

ISBN: 978 0 263 90491 8

51-1113

Harlequin (UK) policy is to use papers that are natural, renewable and recyclable products and made from wood grown in sustainable forests. The logging and manufacturing processes conform to the legal environmental regulations of the country of origin.

Printed and bound in Spain
by Blackprint CPI, Barcelona

Charlene Sands is a *USA TODAY* bestselling author of thirty-five romance novels, writing sensual contemporary romances and stories of the Old West. Her books have been honored with a National Readers Choice Award, a Cataromance Reviewer's Choice Award, and she's a double recipient of the Booksellers' Best Award. She belongs to the Orange County chapter and the Los Angeles chapter of RWA.

Charlene writes "hunky heroes with heart." She knows a little something about true romance—she married her high school sweetheart! When not writing, Charlene enjoys sunny Pacific beaches, great coffee, reading books from her favorite authors and spending time with her family. You can find her on Facebook and Twitter. Charlene loves to hear from her readers! You can write her at PO Box 4883, West Hills, CA 91308, USA or sign up for her newsletter for fun blogs and ongoing contests at www.charlenesands.com.

This book is dedicated to my late father, Charles, who proudly served in the army during World War II, and to all the other brave military men and women, both past and present, who have served or do serve our country with honor.

One

Justin Slade was home. It'd been three days now.

His Ford F-150 truck barreled down the highway with enough horsepower to match the equine force of Sunset Ranch's best thoroughbreds, radio blasting Luke Bryan's latest country hit. It was beat-tapping music. At any other time, Justin would be pounding the dashboard in sync with the rhythm.

But today, he wasn't enjoying the music, the blue Nevada sky or the morning weather, which was clear and crisp enough to remind him winter was on the distant horizon. His gut churned in half a dozen ways as he faced what he was about to do. The marine in him hadn't a doubt he was doing the right thing. He had to come clean for Matilda Applegate's sake and for…Brett.

He punched the off button on the radio and Luke's voice disappeared.

Appropriate silence filled the air.

A cold shiver of dread hung around him like an invisible cloak, refusing to be shrugged off with upbeat music or good weather. Brett Applegate was dead. It was Justin's fault, and Brett's aunt, his only living relative, needed to know the truth.

He pressed his foot to the pedal and glanced around the outskirts of Silver Springs as a sultry female voice on his GPS gave him the coordinates. Gravel spit under his tires.

The deserted road narrowed and a knot in the pit of his stomach begged for this to be over. He'd been on dangerous missions in Afghanistan that hadn't caused him this much anxiety. Guilt and apprehension sucked as constant companions.

Justin popped two antacids into his mouth. He'd been living on the darn things lately.

"In fifty feet, turn right," the GPS voice instructed.

Justin made the turn and drove his truck down a dusty dirt path that wound its way toward a one-story ranch house matured by frigid winters, hotter-than-hell summers and a string of bad months in between. Seeing Brett's home in such a state of neglect was a sharp shot of reality, testament to the economic misery the Applegates had suffered over the years. Brett had always said his uncle Ralph would've gotten heartsick seeing what had happened to his once-proud home.

As the truck ambled closer, Justin caught a glimpse of a disabled car near the house, the back tire flatter than a flapjack, and a woman bending over, her head deep in the bowels of the trunk. Her jewel-pocketed derriere pointed skyward, drawing his immediate gaze. Hell, it was a beacon for any man in his right mind to stop and help out.

Justin pressed on the brake, keeping his eyes trained on a sight he hadn't seen in a long time: a gorgeous, perfectly shaped female ass. It was enough to get his juices flowing. Heck, after nine years in the marines, it didn't take much. But hot damn, the view was fine.

He swallowed and climbed down from the cab of his truck. His boots ate gravel as he neared the back of her car. The woman's silky blouse climbed her waist while she continued to search the trunk, and his eyes locked on to five inches of soft-as-butter, creamy skin.

"Sweet heaven, what else is going to go wrong?" Her

voice flowed over him like smooth bourbon. He grabbed a peek of that exposed skin again.

Man, oh, man.

He cleared his throat. Darn his mama for teaching him gentlemanly manners. Forcing his gaze away from her beautiful bottom, he focused on her curly, platinum-blond hair.

"Excuse me, miss. Can I lend a hand?"

She jerked up and hit her head on the inside of the trunk. "Ow."

She scowled as her hand went to her head, rubbing away the pain. "Oh, I didn't see you—"

Their gazes locked. Her hand froze in her shoulder-length platinum locks. Her brows pulled tight and her lips rounded. "Oh."

She was a stunner.

A twinge of recollection jarred him out of his lusty thoughts.

He remembered those deep jade eyes, that pouty mouth and Marilyn Monroe hair only a few women could pull off. He would've bet his last dollar he'd never see her again. And now, here she was…in the flesh.

On Matilda Applegate's homestead, no less.

He didn't much believe in coincidences. And this one was too big to ignore. His gut churned again, begging for another antacid.

Maybe he was wrong. It had been over a year and a half ago. Maybe she only looked like the woman he'd met in New York City that one weekend.

Justin removed his Stetson and her eyes flickered at the gesture.

"Sorry if I startled you, miss."

Seconds ticked by as she took note of his shiny black boots, new jeans, silver belt buckle and tan shirt opened at the collar. She studied his face and gazed deeply into his eyes. With her hand in her hair, her fingers wove through the silver-blond strands as if she was fashioning some new upswept hairdo. With her arm raised and bent at the elbow, she tilted her head to one side and gave him thoughtful consideration. The move exposed the delicate softness of her throat. A breathless sigh escaped from her mouth.

That bit of body language was unique to the woman he'd known. Sexy. Not forced. Genuine. A jolt hit him smack between the eyes.

It had to be her. He thought back to that night at the Golden Palace Bar.

"I don't date soldiers," she'd said as he stood by her table.

He'd taken a seat and smiled anyway. "But you'll make an exception for me."

"B-Brett? Is that really you?" The hope in her voice confused him and then another jolt hit. Oh, man, this wasn't possible. "I don't understand," she was saying. "We were told...we were told you were dead. Killed in a gun battle. Oh, my God, your aunt Mattie will be so happy. Was there a mix-up? What happened?"

He pulled oxygen into his lungs, then looked away from her puzzled face and squinted against the bright afternoon sunshine. *Jerk.* He hated himself for the lie, and for the hurt he'd cause when he told her the truth.

"I'm not Brett Applegate," he told the blonde.

She pursed her lips and inclined her head, studying him. "But I remember you. Don't you remember me? I'm Katherine Grady. I go by Kat."

Hell, yeah. He remembered her. But he didn't have a clue why the heck Kat was here, looking gorgeous, in front of the Applegate home.

Silently, he cursed the bet he'd made with Brett Applegate. Justin never thought he'd lose an arm-wrestling match to his buddy. He never had before. But damn if Brett hadn't bested him three out of five times right before they'd been selected to accompany a high-powered general to a three-day summit in Washington, D.C. After they served out their mission, the general granted them weekend leave in New York, before they were to head back to their forward operating base in Afghanistan.

The price of the bet? Reversing roles for the weekend.

They'd emptied the contents of their pockets, and good ole Brett had jumped at the chance to live in Justin's skin for a few days. He'd waved Justin's gold credit card in his face and scooped up all seven hundred-dollar bills Justin had dumped onto the bunk. "Gonna have me some fun being you," he'd said, grinning like a fool.

For his part, Justin had blown Brett's spending cash on a bottle of house wine at the hotel and afterward Kat had taken him to her tiny fourth-story walk-up. He'd been looking for a good time. He thought she was, too. They'd clicked. And then things got complicated.

"I remember you, *sugar.*"

Her eyes softened. "No one else has ever called me that."

Justin winced at the sweet tone in her voice. "My name isn't Brett. I'm Justin Slade and I live about twenty miles north of here. Brett and I served together on a tour of duty in the marines."

Her voice dropped off. "You're Justin…*Slade?*"

He nodded.

"*Sunset Ranch,* Justin Slade?"

He nodded again.

"But, we… You told me your name was Brett Apple-gate. You were a marine heading back overseas. You told me all about this place…. You—"

He grimaced. He was the worst kind of heel. He'd taken advantage of a woman's trust, something he'd never done before. He swallowed down regret and then softened his voice. "I lied."

She condemned him with her eyes. He didn't blame her. It was an idiotic bet and a fool thing to do.

Slowly, her hand went to her mouth. Slender fingers covered her lips. She began shaking her head. "Oh…no. No, it's not true."

"Maybe we should go inside the house and talk. I'll try to explain. Is Matilda Applegate home?"

She closed her eyes and kept them closed as if she were silently praying.

He spoke firmly. "Kat."

Her eyes popped open and she blinked a few times. She spoke quietly. "We can't go inside."

"Why not?"

The front door creaked open and an older woman with hair the color of a sunburst stepped onto the front porch, holding a baby boy dressed in brown corduroy in her arms. The woman moved slowly, but with precision as if she calculated each step she took. Her light blue eyes were the most vital thing about her, painted with black eyeliner and deep-sea blue eye shadow. Blotchy face powder accented rather than hid the wrinkles on her face. But the kindness in her eyes was authentic and aimed straight at him.

"I thought I heard voices. Who have we here?"

The baby took a peek at him and then whipped around to grab at her neck with a death grip, his little legs kicking at her hips. She squeezed him tight, and whispered reassurances in his ear. "Now, now, Connor baby. Don't be afraid."

Kat cleared her throat. "Aunt Mattie, this is Justin Slade."

The woman's brows drew together as she tried to place him. "Slade? The name sounds familiar."

"I was a friend of Brett's. I came here to talk to you."

* * *

Katherine Grady knew how to handle a lot of tough situations. She'd grown up the only daughter in an abusive household. She'd moved from one women's shelter to another with her mom, running from a belligerent father and trying her darnedest to keep her mother from falling apart. There was nothing pretty or heroic about living hand to mouth. About never knowing if they'd have to pick up and run or have enough food and shelter for the month.

Kat learned how to survive from early on.

What rattled her more than anything was fear of the unknown. How could she fight something she couldn't see coming?

This was one of those times.

Usually she hid her emotions well—thanks to all that training from her youth—but right now fear tightened her throat and sped up her heart. Her body shook so hard her knees wobbled. Could it be possible? The man she thought was Brett for all this time was really Justin Slade. *Gracious.* She couldn't wrap her head around the bald-faced lie she'd been told. It was a lot to absorb all at once. But Kat's emotions didn't matter at the moment. Her concern was for Mattie. The older woman couldn't afford a setback in her recovery.

Mattie invited Justin inside and he didn't hesitate to approach the front door. He held the screen open and allowed them to step inside first and then followed behind. The door slammed shut as it was prone to do and Kat jerked, her nerves worn thin by something much bigger than that familiar sound. Funny, how just a few minutes ago, her biggest problem was a tire that needed changing.

But the scene that was about to play out in the parlor of Aunt Mattie's modest home could very well kill her with grief. Kat didn't know how to stop it or protect her from the truth.

"Have yourself a seat, son," Aunt Mattie said. "I'll take a seat, too, if you don't mind. Little Connor here is quite a handful, tiring me out. He's weighing nearly twenty pounds now, isn't that right, Kat?"

Kat's stomach ached. She gave a hesitant nod. Justin waited for both of them to take a seat. Kat perched uneasily on a colorful floral chair and Aunt Mattie lowered herself onto her brushed suede recliner that must have once been a lemony yellow. Justin finally sat on the sofa and set his tan felt hat next to him. He kept darting glances at Connor.

"Pardon the mess," Aunt Mattie said. "Kat here is doing wonders fixing the place up on a scant budget. She's got quite a flair for it, wouldn't you say?"

Justin scanned the room politely. Kat wondered if a man's eye would notice things like handmade pillows in contrasting colors, small scatter rugs that tied the room together and flower vases and pictures placed strategically to enhance the modest three-bedroom home. When Kat had first arrived, with Mattie's illness sapping her strength, the place had been a wreck. In the two months she'd lived here, she'd managed to stage the living spaces to bring new life to the house. Her arrival, or rather Connor's arrival, had brought new life to Matilda Applegate, as well.

"Looks nice and homey," Justin said.

She still couldn't believe this man sitting here being polite to Mattie had lied to her about who he was. Why?

She understood lies to some extent. She'd had to lie her way out of a few tight spots in her life. She could abide them, if it meant keeping your nose clean or protecting someone you loved. But why would Justin Slade lie to her about who he was back then?

Her teeth clamped down so hard, pain shot to her head. Any second now...

"You say you knew my nephew Brett?"

"Yes, ma'am. We met in the marines. When we found

out we were practically neighbors, coming from this part of Nevada and all, we got friendly."

Connor was beginning to relax. He turned around in Mattie's arms and plunked his little bottom down in her lap. Tears welled in Kat's eyes. This was a special moment, a brief but monumental span of time when Connor's sweet brown eyes locked onto Justin's for the first time. The gravity of the moment sent Kat's mind spinning. *Her son meeting his father.*

"Oh, look, Connor's warming up to you. This is Brett's boy. Going to have his first birthday before you know it."

Kat lowered her eyes, the weight of the situation crashing down on her shoulders. She had to think fast. To find a way to protect Mattie.

"He's your boy?" Justin asked her.

"Yes." Kat rose quickly and moved over to Mattie. "Let me take him, Aunt Mattie. Your arms must be tired from holding him most of the morning."

"Kat was trying to fix the flat," Aunt Mattie explained to Justin. "The roads here are murder on the tires, you know. My arms are getting a bit tweaked. I'm not as young as I used to be," she said as she handed Connor over carefully. "Though there's nothing in this world better than holding our little Connor."

The baby was on his best behavior, not fidgeting as he was prone to do when he was around strangers. Connor clung to Kat's neck and she kissed his soft little cheek before turning to face Justin. "Aunt Mattie is recovering from a heart attack. She took the news of Brett's death *very hard.*"

Aunt Mattie interjected, "I think I would've died, if it hadn't been for Kat and Connor showing up when they did. That little boy was like an angel coming down from heaven to save my life."

Justin rose. His gaze switched back and forth from Connor to Kat. The suspicion she'd known would come lit up his eyes. "Brett never said he had a son."

Aunt Mattie chimed in. "That's because Brett never knew about Connor. Kat came here looking for Brett, to finally tell him about his baby. But it was too late for Connor to meet his daddy. Kat's been living here, taking care of me ever since."

Justin's eyes rounded on her. "You never told *Brett* he had a son."

The lines around Aunt Mattie's eyes crinkled with worry. "Oh, dear. Did I say something wrong?"

"No, it's okay, Aunt Mattie," Kat told her softly. "Justin was a friend of Brett's. He might as well know the truth." She stared at Justin, hoping to get her point across. Now that it had sunk in that she'd been deceived, she didn't want to transfer the damage to Mattie. Her emotions rolled through her like a tornado, but she kept up appearances rather than hurt Mattie Applegate any further. "I met *Brett* in New York and we spent time together. After I learned I was pregnant, I tried to reach him overseas. But I never heard back from him. So, I stayed in the city and worked, raising my son until…well, until the day I decided to come to Nevada to try to find Brett here."

Justin glanced at the little boy in her arms and then focused back on her.

Kat stilled her frustration at the man who'd deliberately lied to her. She continued quickly, "I didn't find Brett, but I found Aunt Mattie." Kat turned to face the older woman. "Meeting Connor was the best medicine for her. Her health has improved so much even her doctors can't believe it. Isn't that right, Aunt Mattie?"

Aunt Mattie leaned forward in her recliner, nodding and making the sign of the cross across her chest. "It's a miracle, is what it is. Connor is a gift from God."

Justin squeezed his eyes shut for a second and then

glanced at Connor with a proprietary look that curdled Kat's stomach. "He is at that."

The older woman began to rise. "Where are my manners? Would you like some pie? I can my own peaches and Kat made peach pie this morning. We'll put on a pot of coffee, too. And then we can talk more about Brett."

"Sorry, I can't," Justin said firmly. "Please don't get up. Thanks for the offer, but I'm short on time today."

Mattie's face crumpled with disappointment. "You'll come back, though. I'd like to hear about your friendship with Brett."

Justin stared at Kat, condemning her with a solemn look. At least he caught the gravity of Mattie's situation and kept his lips buttoned. Kat was thankful for that. "I promise I'll come back." He walked over to Aunt Mattie and lowered down on one knee to gently take her hand. He focused his full attention on the seventy-year-old woman who had raised Brett Applegate since the age of five, after his folks were tragically killed by a deadly storm.

"That's good." Mattie's blue eyes glowed with warmth. She looked twenty years younger with that twinkle. "I'm very happy to meet one of Brett's friends."

"Nice to meet you, too, ma'am. Brett always went on and on about his aunt Mattie. Why, I'd say Brett's talk about your peach pie got all the men in our unit longing for a piece of that pie."

"Oh, that's nice to hear, son. Next time you come, I'll be sure to serve some up to you."

"Will do. I'll be by again before you know it. We'll have that talk about Brett." Justin grabbed his hat and walked to the door, glancing Kat's way with a pointed look. "Kat, if you come outside to lend a hand, I'll change that tire for you."

"Isn't that nice," Mattie said, settling back in the recliner.

Kat forced a smile. The authority in his voice told her the marine sergeant wasn't one to mess with. But the more she thought about Justin Slade lying to her, the more she couldn't tamp down a surge of anger. She wanted answers. "I'll be right there."

Once Justin left the room, she kissed Connor's cheek and placed him in the play yard that sat three feet away from Mattie's chair. Connor sank his butt down and immediately picked up a Baby Einstein musical toy. He pushed the button, something he'd just learned to do, and "Twinkle, Twinkle, Little Star" rang out to placate him.

"I'll watch him," Aunt Mattie said.

"Thanks. I shouldn't be long."

Mattie peered outside the window with a thoughtful expression. "He seems like a nice young man."

Kat practically choked out her agreement. "He does seem so."

Then she walked outside to confront Justin Slade.

She had no doubt in her mind the fudge was about to hit the fan.

Justin set the jack on the ground and began hoisting up the underbelly of Kat's ten-year-old Chevy. Kat kept a safe distance away, watching him work with rolled-up sleeves, his face tight, sweat beading on his forehead.

Looking at him now, she took a subjective view of what had happened in New York and understood why she'd broken her rule with him. Normally, she didn't date soldiers or any other man who might drag her down to the ditch she'd clawed her way out of. She was heading to the top and nothing would stop her. She'd gone the poor man's route once before with a young man, and that had gotten her nothing but grief. But Brett...or rather Justin, had had enough charm to persuade her to make an exception. She'd been so lonely, so desperate for a true friend. And he'd been that for two solid days. She'd opened up to him about her life and the recent loss of her mother. He'd listened. He'd understood. He hadn't pressured her for sex. He hadn't made a move on her that first night. He'd slept on her tiny living room sofa without complaint. They'd toured the city on a dime, and had laughs. The whole time, Kat knew the weekend was going nowhere. There wasn't enough charm in the world to get her to give up her dream. She wasn't going to fall for some down-on-his-luck and out-of-money hog farmer.

With the jack in place, Justin fastened the wrench he'd found in the trunk over a lug nut on the wheel. The nut refused to budge and Justin dug his heels in, determined. Corded muscles in his forearms strained and bunched with each powerful jerk he gave the wrench. A vein popped from his neck as he put the full force of his body behind each counter-clockwise turn. After he managed to loosen the first lug nut, he sat back on his heels, wincing against the afternoon sunshine, and then shot her a glare. "Is Connor my son?"

"Shh," she said, glancing at the front door. Hopefully, Mattie was dozing. "Don't let Aunt Mattie hear you."

Justin fastened the wrench to the next lug nut and turned it sharply to the left. The nut released. "How many men did you sleep with before and after you met me?"

One other, but she wasn't going to tell him that. She was certain Brett Applegate was Connor's father...or at least the man she'd thought to be Brett. "You lied to me. You told me you were Brett."

Justin finished removing the nuts from the wheel and rose, his grim expression aimed straight at her. He approached, taking slow predatory steps. "Just how hard did you try to reach Brett Applegate after you got pregnant?"

Kat visibly shook at his tone. He was determined to get to the truth. She wanted that, too, but protecting Aunt

Mattie came first. "We can't talk about this here. You saw Aunt Mattie. That woman has been through enough heartache in her life. Her heart is frail. I'm convinced she'll have another setback if she overhears any of this conversation."

He stared at her with the full force of his dark brown eyes. *Connor's eyes.* As if reading her thoughts, he spoke with a rasp in his voice. "That baby has my eyes and dark hair."

It was true. Connor looked enough like Justin to make those comparisons.

"Shh, Aunt Mattie loves Connor. He's given her new life. We can't…we can't have this conversation right now. If you're truly a friend of Brett's you know how much he loved her. He wouldn't want her getting hurt. And that's exactly what would happen if you—"

Justin took the hint and spoke more quietly now. "I don't plan on hurting Brett's aunt. But if that boy is my son I have—"

"Please…" Her nerves raw, she glanced at the door again. "Don't you get it? I'm not going to talk to you about this here."

"We're gonna have this conversation, Kat. Meet me at seven at my house at Sunset Ranch. It's twenty miles west of here."

Kat's body shook. She couldn't go to the Slade house. Showing up on Sunset Ranch would only complicate matters. And she wasn't going to tell Justin why just now. "I can't."

A vein throbbed against the side of his throat, looking ready to burst. "Why not?"

"I'll meet you somewhere else. Someplace neutral."

He folded his arms across his chest. "I'm listening."

"There's a little café in Silver Springs called Blossom. Do you know it?"

"I'll find it. I'll meet you there at seven."

"Eight. I have to put Connor to bed first. I read to him every night and we have a routine. He's a pretty good sleeper. It'll be easier on Aunt Mattie if he's already in bed when I leave."

Justin's eyes softened at the mention of Connor's sleep habits and for a second or two, she felt a sense of relief that her son's daddy wasn't lost to him forever. Then, Justin turned a sharp eye on her once again. "If you're not there, I'll come looking for you."

Really? Did he think she'd run out on him? "I'll be there. I want answers, too."

"You'll get them." Dismissing her, he turned around and walked back to repair the flat.

Her heart beating like crazy, she walked into the house. Mattie was indeed dozing. Thank goodness. Little Connor took one look at his mommy, rose onto his knees and then hoisted himself up by the wall of the play yard. He stood on planted feet, holding on tight to keep his balance. His eyes sparkled with pride over his newest accomplishment and Kat beamed with love and that same sense of pride.

Your daddy is alive, Connor.

He's also rich and powerful.

The implication made her dizzy. But Kat couldn't think about all of that now. She had Mattie's welfare to consider. There wasn't a doubt in her mind that Matilda Applegate would suffer heart failure if she learned the truth about Connor. Kat couldn't let that happen. Mattie didn't deserve any more heartache in her life. There was a tipping point, and this was it. Kat would do everything in her power to protect her. With her flamboyant red hair, and sweetly feisty spirit, the older woman had touched something fierce and protective in Kat.

She picked up Connor from the play yard and hugged him to her chest, stroking his soft dark curls.

It was only minutes later, after she heard Justin drive off, that she could finally breathe evenly again.

Two

Justin ground his teeth together as he drove off the Applegate property. Shell-shocked wasn't a strong enough term
for what he was feeling right now. He'd come to spill his
heart and guts out to Matilda about how Brett had died,
and instead discovered he had a son—an adorable dark-
haired, brown-eyed boy.

His son.

His mouth twisted. He had to be careful. He didn't know
anything for sure right now. The boy may or may not be
his child.

But he did remember Kat. So many things about her.
He remembered her beauty, her creamy skin, her pretty
green eyes and the way she accepted him inside her body
with tight, wet, welcoming heat. Though he'd spent the
weekend with her, they only had one night of sex. That
one night made up for the prior eight months he'd gone
without. Once they got going, there was no stopping them.
She'd had no boundaries, no fussy little complaints, no inhibitions when they were together. Her only rule was that
she didn't want any entanglements afterward.

She'd spelled it right out.

She didn't want a relationship with a soldier or a farmer.

In other words, he was good enough to bed, but that's
where it would end.

Justin had gotten the message loud and clear and after

leaving her without so much as exchanging phone numbers or addresses, he'd also understood better what Brett Applegate was up against with the fairer sex.

Eight o'clock couldn't come fast enough for him.

He downed two more antacids and pushed the button to lower the windows. Damn that fool bet. Reversing roles hadn't been one of his wisest moves, but now a child's life was at stake. If Connor was his, then he would move heaven and earth to make up for lost time with his son.

Stepping on the gas pedal, he peeled down the road. During scorching hot summers in Afghanistan he'd picture himself whipping down the highway with the sun at his back and the cool wind blowing his hair in ten different directions. Like now. He'd daydreamed about coming home to Sunset Ranch and working alongside his brothers, too. He'd clung to those thoughts as he battled both enemy and unyielding climate.

Justin pulled into the parking lot of the Amber Pail, a hot spot for Douglas County locals and a place he probably should avoid. But it was early yet and he needed to kill some time and think without his family around. He climbed out of his truck, plopped his hat on his head and kept his sunglasses on. He strode toward the entrance to the bar and had nearly made it inside, when a man's voice boomed out behind him.

"Justin Slade…tell me you're not planning on drinking alone."

Justin turned to find Sheriff Robbie Dunphy striding in his direction. Justin had gone to high school with the sheriff's younger sister, Tiffany. "Hey, Robbie. How's it going?"

Robbie strode up to face him on the sidewalk. He filled out his tan uniform, the buttons on his shirt ready to pop. He stood head to head with Justin, and as usual had a smile on his face. He hardly fit the bill for a stereotypical hard-nosed lawman. "I got no complaints. How about you? You acclimatin' to being home again?"

"I'm getting there. Nine years is a long time to be away."

"I got to thinkin' you might just make a career of soldiering, with you getting the Congressional Medal of Honor and all."

Justin clamped his teeth together. The medal was a source of pride to him but at the same time, it reminded him of his failures. He didn't think of himself as a hero, but as a soldier who'd done his job. Brett's death had hit him hard, and he'd decided when his last tour of duty was up that he was through with the military. "At one time, I thought the same thing. But looks like I'm home to stay now."

"Well, good." Robbie gave him a congenial slap on the back. "Come on, then, and let me buy you a welcome home drink. Amber's still here, working her ass off and brewing the best ale in the state. You gotta try her latest concoction, something she calls Nevada Punch."

What the hell. He couldn't very well insult the sheriff and tell him he wanted to drink alone. Maybe some hometown company would keep his mind off of troubling thoughts and help him pass the time. "Sure thing, Sheriff."

They sat at a table right smack in the middle of the darkened tavern. It was a throwback to the sixties, with dim yellow lights reflecting off a long mahogany bar. The second his butt hit the padded vinyl seat, Amber came striding over, her teased brown hair as big as ever, swept up in the back with bobby pins and a little black bow.

"You're a sight for sore eyes, Justin Slade." She gave him a motherly kiss on the cheek.

"Hi, Amber."

"I do believe this is the first time you've been in my bar legitimately."

"Wasn't old enough before I left for boot camp."

"I know it, but you've been here dozens of times. I used to open the back room up for my son and the rest of you boys to play pool. You remember that, don't you?"

He nodded, thinking back on that time. "I'll never forget that trusty old pool table." He'd lost his virginity on that pool table with Betsy Ann Stankowski when he was sixteen.

"I'm not hearing any of this," the sheriff said, leaning way back in his chair.

Amber waved him off. "Robbie, don't tell me you didn't know about the boys coming here. You didn't make any noise about it because your little sis would tag along with them sometimes, so don't you get all high and mighty now. For pity's sake, I never gave any of the kids liquor."

The sheriff shrugged off her reprimand. "Who's getting high and mighty? I'm here to buy Justin a drink. What'll you have, boy? Want to try you some Nevada Punch?"

"Sure do."

"It's on the house," Amber said. Then she pointed at the sheriff. "And your favorite iced coffee since you had the good sense to bring Justin in."

"Thank you, kindly," Justin said.

"You got a heart of gold, Amber Louise." Robbie sent her a grin.

She lifted her brows at the sheriff dubiously before she turned to focus on Justin. "It's the least I can do for you. Why, you're a hero, saving five lives like you did. You make us all proud."

Though he was uncomfortable with the praise she lavished on him, Justin thanked her. She meant well. Everyone meant well, but he didn't want free drinks, or meals on the house, or reporters poking around Sunset Ranch, hoping to get an interview with the hometown hero.

What he wanted was time to adjust to being home.

Kat Grady had thrown a wrench into those plans, pronto.

Amber served the coffee to the sheriff and her specialty beer in a tall pilsner glass. Justin brought the glass to his lips and took a gulp of the dark, rich ale. "This is pretty good," he said to the sheriff.

"Hits the spot, doesn't it? So what are your plans now that you're back home? Planning on working on the horse farm with your brothers?"

"Don't rightly know yet. Those two have the ranch running smooth as silk."

While overseas, he'd given it a lot of thought. He loved the land and raising horses, but when he'd returned home three days ago, he wasn't sure where he fit in the well-oiled machine Sunset Ranch had become. Logan and Luke had been at it a long time, and they had the running of Sunset Ranch, the lucrative Slade horse farm, and Sunset Lodge, an upscale version of a dude ranch, down to a science. Sure, Justin could work with them but not out of necessity. They didn't really need him.

And since Brett's death, Justin had been bouncing something around in his head that wouldn't roll away. The more he thought about it, the more it made sense to him.

But first, he had to deal with fatherhood.

He glanced at his watch. He had four more hours before his meeting with Kat.

"Well, if you're of a mind at all for public service, let me toss this suggestion out at you," the sheriff said. "There's a county commissioner's seat opening up next month. You'd be perfect for the job. Why, with your background, you'd have pull and influence enough to get a lot of things accomplished. Could do a lot of good for the citizens of Douglas County."

Justin couldn't believe his ears. "What?"

Sheriff Dunphy's eyes shone bright as he nodded encouragement. "Jeff Washington, our county assessor, well…he and I were talking about the vacancy and the upcoming special election yesterday. Your name came up first thing."

Justin began shaking his head. "I've been home three days, Robbie, and my name's coming up for a special election?"

"Well, no, not exactly. Your name came up because we've got to clear a date on our calendar. The county's planning on throwing a parade in your honor."

Caught off guard, Justin felt the blood drain from his face. He kept his mouth from dropping open, just barely, as humbling astonishment rolled through his gut, making him ready to pop a few more antacids. "I...don't know what to say. A parade?"

Wasn't that sort of thing reserved for Olympic champions and, well...Santa?

The last thing Justin wanted was a parade. He didn't deserve the adoration of the entire county. He'd barely made it home in one piece mentally, and the word *hero* was reserved for soldiers much braver than he'd ever been.

"Yes, we're all excited about it. But it's gonna take a while to pull it off. Douglas County wants to welcome their hero home in style. We've got three high school bands practicing, a news crew alerted and the county's Women's Association and the Boy Scouts working together to build you a float."

Holy crap.

A thought flitted into his head and he turned a suspicious eye on the sheriff. "You didn't just bump into me today, did you, Robbie?"

"Of course I did. I would never abuse my authority by having patrol cars give me your location or anything." The sheriff's wry smile said the exact opposite.

Robbie was a sly one, not as Gomer Pyle–ignorant as he had people believing.

Amber strolled over, carrying a tray with two dishes

of fried chicken, potatoes and gravy. She set the plates down on the table and smiled at him. "Here you go, Justin. Meal's on the house, too. It's my way of saying thank you for your service to the country."

Robbie Dunphy rubbed his hands together, peering at his plate with boyish glee. "Looks delicious, doesn't it, Justin?"

Justin stared at the food for a second and then raised his eyes to Amber, who patiently waited for his approval. "Sure does, Amber. Thank you."

"And while we're eating," Robbie said to Amber, "Justin's gonna think about becoming Douglas County's new district commissioner."

"That's wonderful. Well, you two take all the time you need."

After Amber walked off, Justin finished his ale and leaned forward in his chair. "Robbie, I know you mean well, but I'm not ready to make any decisions about my future just yet. The one thing I do know is that I'm not a politician. No way. No how."

He didn't want a parade in his honor, either, but Justin couldn't bring himself to call it off. There were already too many people involved. Douglas County had been good to the Slades over the years, and Justin wouldn't insult the citizens by telling them he'd rather be face-to-face with a rattlesnake than sitting on a float, waving to people who'd come out to pay him tribute.

It wasn't until he pulled through the gates of Sunset Ranch that Justin's muscles began to relax. Spirited mares and stallions dotted the pastures along the drive toward the house. The acreage was fertile here, the soil nurtured by runoff from the Sierra Nevadas and rain plentiful enough to keep the pastures green most of the year. Justin inhaled the scent of alfalfa and manure, of leather and earth, as he approached the one-story Slade house and parked the truck.

He'd always loved his childhood home and since returning he felt a greater appreciation for the freedoms and privileges life brought to him. He'd been in hellholes, seen danger and atrocity at its worst and survived, though not without some painful internal scars. The place he'd come from in the Middle East seemed far removed from life on Sunset Ranch.

Off in the distance he spotted two riders and immediately recognized one as his brother Luke. The woman riding beside him was his new fiancée, Audrey. The two had recently become engaged and were due to have a child of their own.

With Luke engaged and Logan's wedding fast approaching, Justin felt like a fifth wheel already. And he'd only been home three days.

He climbed down from the cab and gave a wave to Ward Halliday, who was standing next to his car over by the main corral. The ranch foreman had welcomed Justin on his first day home with a manly hug, making no mention of his war hero status. He'd only wished him well and told him he'd missed him. Justin appreciated how perceptive the man was not to make too big a deal out of things. "How's it going, Ward?"

"No complaints," he called out. "Molly's got beef empanadas waiting for me at home."

"Sounds good. Tell her hello."

Ward nodded. "Stop on by sometime. Molly would love to see you."

"I will."

Justin climbed the steps of the house and walked inside. From the foyer, he could see Logan leaning against his office door down the long hallway. He was drinking liquor from a tumbler and nodded for Justin to join him.

"About time you showed up, little bro. I've been fielding your calls all day. Come take a look."

Justin's boots clanged against the stone floor as he made his way toward the office where Logan conducted Sunset Ranch business. Logan worked at the house, while his fiancée, Sophia, worked at Sunset Lodge. The two were planning a big blowout of a wedding. But they'd waited for him to come home; Logan had asked him to be his best man on his first day back.

Luke, too, had decided to wait so that Justin could be in attendance before tying the knot with Audrey.

"Want a drink?" Logan asked.

"No, I'm good." He glanced around. Today, just like the other days since his arrival, he felt his father's presence in the room despite Logan's efforts to remove all traces of Randall Slade. Some things just died hard, he thought as he plunked down into a black leather armchair.

Logan sat down and faced him from across his desk. "You might, after you see these. You have seven phone messages flashing on the machine, and Ellie took all of these from the house phone." Logan handed over a stack of notes. "Looks like you have at least three messages from Betsy Ann Stankowski alone."

Justin's head shot up. "You don't say."

Logan gave him a knowing smile. "Maybe she wants to pick up where you left off before you enlisted."

Justin balked at that. Logan had caught them fooling around behind the barn once and when questioned, Justin had confessed Betsy Ann had been his first. His older brother had told him point-blank not to mess around with girls on the ranch or anywhere else. He was too young to know what he was doing and there could be consequences to pay. Yeah, well, years later, he hadn't taken that advice with Kat, and as a result, he'd fathered a child. *Maybe.*

"Betsy Ann and I were over way before I left town."

"You mean, you actually listened to me?"

Justin clucked his tongue. "Now why would I do that?"

A smile spread across Logan's face. "I didn't think so. Betsy Ann teaches grammar school and I hear her students love her. She's also made a name for herself as the president of the Douglas County Women's Association."

"Seriously?" Betsy Ann would always be stamped in his memory for granting him those painfully awkward, profound and awe-inspiring sixty seconds on the pool table. "She always did like school."

"Three messages in one day," Logan said. "She sure wants you for something."

Justin didn't think Betsy Ann had any lingering feelings for him. She'd dumped him like a hot potato in their junior year for some older guy. He'd bet fifty bucks that he knew what she wanted from him. If she was president of the Women's Association, then she was calling about the parade. Justin didn't want to open up that can of worms with his brother now. He had enough to contend with.

He scanned over all the messages scribbled down on notepaper, tossing them down one after another onto the desk. At some point he'd have to call these people back, but he wasn't going to do that today.

Logan spoke up. "Let me know if I can help. You shouldn't be bombarded by everyone you've ever known in a fifty-mile radius on your first week back."

"Thanks, but I'll take care of it."

"I also gotta tell you Luke shooed two reporters off the property this morning after you left. They want interviews with Sergeant Slade."

Justin jerked his head back and forth. "Man, I didn't think my homecoming would cause such a stir."

"Be patient," Logan said, leaning back in his chair. "You coming home a war hero is big news around here. Everyone wants a piece of you."

"Tell me about it. Robbie Dunphy cornered me today. He's got some wild ideas about my future. Don't even ask."

Logan's eyes lit with understanding. "Okay. Listen, Sophia wants to have you over to the cottage for dinner tonight. It'll be quiet with just us, Luke and Audrey. No phone calls. No one barging in or cornering you."

The cottage had been Sophia's home when they were growing up. She'd lived there with her mother, Louisa, who managed the lodge. But when it came out that Louisa and Randall Slade had been lovers, the whole thing went bad and Louisa packed up Sophia and left Sunset Ranch. Recently, because Randall had put Sophia in his will, she'd returned to the ranch for her inheritance and Logan had fallen in love with her. "Sounds good, but I can't make it. Tell Sophia I'm sorry. I have a…something to do tonight."

Logan's brows lifted. "A female…something to do?"

Justin glanced away. His brother was too damn perceptive. "Let's just say, it's important. I'll tell you about it once I figure it all out myself."

"All right, but you know that Luke and I are here if you need us. We have your back."

"I appreciate that."

Justin left Logan's office and walked to his bedroom in the opposite wing of the house. Baseball trophies from his Little League days sat next to a smattering of CDs and DVDs from his teen years on a bookshelf. Textbooks were stacked one on top of the other, and his old dial-up computer that deserved a spot on *Antiques Roadshow* was stored on the lower shelf. Justin grinned at the old thing, thinking how far technology had progressed since his childhood. When he'd arrived home, he made a vow to tackle this room and get it up to speed ASAP. But he hadn't brought order to the chaos yet. There was something mildly comforting in having things as they were… at least for a little while longer.

His brother Luke had seen fit to order the only new item in the room, a king-size bed to replace the single he'd had since he was a boy. When he sat down, the firm mattress supported his weight and he smiled as he stared directly across the room at the walk-in closet that had once doubled as a fort, a secret hideaway and an imaginary campground.

For the past nine years, he'd gotten used to close quarters with only the essentials of everyday life. Just a short time ago, his entire personal space on the outpost could fit inside that walk-in closet.

He closed his eyes for a moment. An image of Brett appeared. He couldn't force it from his mind.

He was holding Brett's limp body. His face was streaked with blood, clear blue eyes suddenly wild in the face of death. Crimson puddles pooled over Brett's belly. Justin's hand pressed down on the bloody seepage.

"Get out of here. I've lost this bet."

"Hang on, buddy. Stay with me, Brett. Brett."

Eyes devoid of life stared back at him. His friend's warmth turned to ice.

Justin lay there with him, clinging to his body.

Shedding tears.

Justin snapped his eyes open. His body jerked involuntarily and he bounded from the bed. He paced, pounding the floor with his boots, back and forth, back and forth, with his head down. Tremors made it hard to breathe. His heart raced.

Brett's bloody face remained.

He'd died four months ago and for all those months, the grief and guilt had been eating at Justin.

He forced his mind to turn to something else.

Connor's chubby cheeks and vivid dark eyes filled his thoughts. Images of the little boy, so small yet so mighty, slowed his racing pulse. His breaths came easier now.

Connor.

Justin thought of the boy with proprietary pride.

He had to find out for sure if the boy was truly his son.

"I'm going in to kiss Connor good-night," Kat whispered to Aunt Mattie from outside the bedroom door. "He'll most likely sleep through the night. Thank you again for watching him."

Aunt Mattie gestured with a wave of the hand. "Don't you worry about a thing. You have a nice visit with Cecelia now. Doris is coming for a cup of tea. We'll watch out for our little boy."

Kat tiptoed into Brett's old room—which she now shared with her son—and made her way to the snow-white crib on loan from one of Matilda's neighbors. She smiled at the sight of Connor asleep atop baby-blue sheets with cartoon monkeys printed on them. "You be a good baby now. Sleep tight," she murmured, placing an air kiss over Connor's cheek. "Mama loves you."

She lingered there a few extra moments, watching him breathe, in and out, his plump baby chest rising and falling. This little person, cozy in a terry-cloth sleeper decorated with brown footballs, filled her world with joy. She'd never get over the miracle of her unexpected but cherished son. It was hard to leave him, if even for a short while, but this meeting tonight had to happen.

Kat hated lying to Aunt Mattie. But she couldn't think of any way around it. At least a lie didn't feel so much like a lie if there was some truth in it. So Kat had told Matilda she was picking up a check from Cecelia Tilton for the baby clothes she'd put on consignment at her boutique. A month ago, when Kat had mentioned Babylicious, her budding online store featuring the fashionable and affordable baby clothes she designed, a very gracious Cecelia had offered her a place in her shop to help promote her work. Cecelia's home wasn't far from Blossom and this afternoon Kat had phoned the woman to make the arrangements.

Her conscience continued to nag her as she left the house and headed to Cecilia's. But half an hour later, as she drove away from the shop owner's home with a small check in hand, she felt a little better. Three hundred and forty dollars would go a long way in helping Mattie pay for her medications.

Kat shelved thoughts of business as soon as she pulled up to Blossom. Her heart in her throat, she shook off tremors of doubt, straightened her frame, held her head high and walked into the deserted café. Blossom was known more for their savory hot breakfasts and so-so lunch salads. Not too many patrons dared their blue plate specials at this hour of the evening.

Kat spotted Justin sitting in a corner booth with his head down, looking impatiently at his phone. Her tremors took on a different character as memories rushed in of that weekend she'd spent with him. She'd let down her guard for two days with a hot, charming, understanding man, who'd left his indelible stamp on her. She'd thought about him for weeks afterward but had convinced herself he wasn't right for her. *He* hadn't been enough. She'd wanted more out of life than he could offer. They'd ended things civilly with no illusions of anything else developing between them.

On a steadying breath, Kat lifted her chin and ventured farther into the café. But a piece of broken grout between the floor tiles trapped her four-inch heel, throwing her off balance. Flailing her arms, she managed not to fall flat on her face. But darn if the perfectly dignified entrance she'd plotted in her head wasn't shot to hell.

Justin saw the whole thing.

As she walked closer, he took in her clothes with his piercing gaze. She wore stretch blue jeans and a billowy white top tucked under a cropped jacket. A sterling silver rope chain made of entwined oblong circles dangled from her neck. On her wrist she wore a matching bracelet.

The clothes were her own designs and had been rejected by every major fashion house in New York City.

"You're late," Justin said, rising from his seat.

"Babies aren't predicable. It always seems to take longer than you think to put them down to sleep."

He gave her excuse some thought. Then his lips thinned. "I wouldn't know."

Oh, boy. Kat got it. He wasn't happy about the circumstances, but then neither was she. If they were going to accomplish anything, they would have to agree to civility. By this time of night, after a day of taking care of a baby and an aging woman, Kat was pooped and not up to verbal sparring. "I can leave and we can do this another time…when your attitude is better."

Justin swore under his breath. His mouth clamped down and he sent her a long thoughtful look. Then like magic, his demeanor changed before her eyes. His body visibly loosened up, as if on command, and he gave her a reluctant but gracious smile. "You're right. I apologize. Please sit down so we can talk."

Accepting his apology, she dropped into a cushioned seat facing him and set her purse down beside her. As she looked across the café table, a quick zip of awareness caught her off guard as she really, really studied Justin's handsome face.

My God…Connor looks exactly like him.

Yes, their hair and eyes were the same color, but Connor shared Justin's wide full mouth, too, and a deep dimple that popped out on the left side when they smiled. She couldn't begin to count how many times she'd kissed that disappearing dimple on her baby's face. Their skin tones were smooth and olive and she imagined Connor would easily tan golden-brown just like Justin when he got older. They shared the same hairline that cut a neat straight line across their forehead. Connor would have the same arrow-sharp nose, too, when he grew up.

Her son's adorable baby features were a precursor to Justin Slade's adult appearance.

His brows furrowed. "Who's watching the baby?"

"Aunt Mattie and Doris Brubaker are with Connor."

She went on to explain, "Doris is a neighbor. We're friends, and I asked her to stay with Aunt Mattie until I got back. They're having tea and I don't want to impose on them any longer than necessary."

"Okay. Let's get on with it, then. Ladies first."

"You told me you were Brett Applegate. I want to know why you lied to me." Then she added, "I would appreciate the truth."

"Just remember that when it's my turn to ask questions."

A waitress wearing a snappy blue outfit and white tights showed up at the table with a notepad. "Hi, I'm Toni, and I'll be serving you tonight. Have you looked at the menu yet? Just so you know, the blue plate special is—"

"Decaf coffee for me," Kat said. Her stomach knotted at the thought of food. "That's all I'd like."

"I'll have the same," Justin said, nodding to the young girl. "Thank you."

"No cherry pie or apple cobbler?"

They both shook their heads. "Okay, I'll be back with your coffee in a sec."

Kat watched the waitress walk away and then turned to Justin. "You were about to tell me why you lied to me that weekend."

The muscles in Justin's face pinched tight, a distant look in his eyes hinting at regret. "I lost a bet."

Kat blinked. "You lost a bet? What does that mean?"

He leaned forward, his elbows flat on the table. The material of his navy shirt pulled taut across his broad shoulders, and it wasn't hard to remember what he'd looked like with a shirt off. She could almost feel the sensation of touching his golden skin and ripped muscles under her fingertips now. "It means Brett beat me at arm wrestling. Best of five."

Kat didn't like where this was going. "So?"

"So, I made this stupid bet with him, because I never thought I'd have to pay up. He was egging me on in front of my men until I finally thought, what the hell. I'd never lost a match to Brett before. If he won, I'd have to trade places with him the next time we had time off. We'd switch wallets—and the cash and credit cards inside—and assume each other's identity with…" Justin's lips snapped shut. He ran his fingers over his mouth and winced.

Kat caught on. "With women?"

He gave her a slow nod.

"So, the weekend you spent with me was to pay off a bet? You used me…lied to me…had no intention of ever telling me the truth?"

Something hard flickered in his eyes. "I didn't use you. If you remember correctly, I didn't pressure you for anything. And you made it clear you wanted no ties to a hick from a small town, remember? We didn't exchange so much as cell phone numbers when I walked out your door."

That was beside the point. He'd been amazing that weekend and by the time the second night rolled around, Kat couldn't imagine not sharing her bed with him. He'd been compassionate and kind and patient and just what she'd needed at that moment in her life.

Maybe he'd assumed more than Brett's identity that weekend; maybe Justin had taken on Brett's personality, as well. That weekend helped heal some of her old wounds. She'd needed a strong shoulder and an understanding heart. It hadn't been all fun and games between them, it had been unexpectedly more. "I'd put it a little gentler than that, Justin. But yes, it's true. I couldn't get romantically involved with a man that wouldn't—"

"Serve your purposes?"

She tried harder to explain. "Didn't fit into the life I wanted. Don't forget, you lied about who you were and that might have altered my decision about the weekend."

"You mean if you'd known I was a loaded Nevada rancher, you might have taken me to bed one night sooner?"

Her cheeks burned. His accusation was a hard slap to her face. He wasn't going to get away with it. "You have no right to judge me. You have no idea who I am and what I've been through. I didn't ask you to come over to me at that hotel bar."

"Why wouldn't I want to meet a beautiful woman? It was obvious you were waiting for someone. You kept checking your watch. I figured some jerk stood you up. And I was right. He didn't give a crap that your mother had recently passed away, did he?"

That jerk had been Michael Golden, the heir to the entire Golden Hotel chain. It was a blind date. Later, she'd found out from her friend that he'd been called out of town suddenly and hadn't gotten word to her. She'd been waiting for him more than an hour when Justin strolled up to her table.

The waitress walked over and set their coffee cups down. Taking one look at the intense discussion at the table, she lowered her voice. "I'll be in the back if you need anything else."

Justin gave her a sharp nod and she strode away.

Steam wafted up from Kat's ceramic mug of decaf and she moved it out of her line of vision. "I told you that night, I didn't date soldiers."

"We told each other a lot of things."

"But what I said to you, what I confessed during those

two days that we were together was the truth. You can't say the same, can you?

He pursed his lips and hung his shoulders. "No."

She leaned back in her seat and stared at him.

He stared back. "I'd like to know something. How hard did you try to find Brett?"

Her lids lowered. "I wrote to him and he never answered back. I don't know if he ever received my letter."

"*One* letter was all he was worth to you?"

"I didn't say that."

"We were stationed in a forward operating base in De-laram, the third battalion of the 4th Marines. I know I mentioned that."

"All I heard you say was Afghanistan. I didn't want to know the details. I didn't remember anything else. It doesn't really matter now. Clearly, it wasn't Brett I slept with that night. It was you. But I didn't know that because you lied about your identity."

Justin shook his head. "I didn't know we'd conceived a child."

"Obviously," she said. "I wasn't planning on having a child, either, but I wouldn't trade having Connor in my life for anything." A surge of emotion brought tears to her eyes. "My son is everything to me."

When she'd finally looked Brett's family up and come to Silver Springs to do the right thing, Aunt Mattie had given her the news of Brett's death. Brett had died in action, and Kat couldn't help but think if she'd tried harder to find him, he wouldn't have taken chances. Maybe he wouldn't have died at all and maybe Mattie Applegate's heart wouldn't have been broken. Now Kat understood that wasn't the case at all because if her letter had reached Brett, he would've put two and two together and shown it to his buddy. He would've known the baby she carried wasn't his but Justin's.

It was a sad set of circumstances and she'd lived with the guilt of not trying to find Brett sooner. But in the end, she had done the right thing. "I know there were some things I could have done differently. I…didn't." She shrugged a shoulder, not knowing what else to say. "I just didn't."

Justin peered deep into her eyes. "There are things I would've done differently, too, had I known. Tell me one thing. Do you believe that Connor is my son?"

She didn't hesitate. She'd always known exactly when she conceived her little boy. "I know he is."

For a moment tears welled in Justin's eyes. The hard planes of his face softened and his shoulders fell with relief. As he took it all in, he began nodding and Kat saw his expression transform suddenly. Determination set his jaw. "It's been a year and a half."

"Yes. Almost."

He blinked and then blew breath from his lungs.

Just then the waitress walked into the room and said, "I've got to start closing up, but you can finish your coffee. Don't mind me."

She glanced at the two cups that had gone untouched and then looked away.

Justin pulled a twenty out of his wallet and set it down on the table. Then he rose to his full six-foot-two height and reached for Kat's hand. "Let's get out of here."

"Where?"

"Doesn't matter. We need to finish this conversation."

Reluctantly, she took his hand and let him lead her out of the café.

Three

His hand across her lower back, Justin guided Kat out of the café. Darkness and the chilly night air surrounded them and Kat shivered. "Get your coat," Justin said.

"I didn't bring one. Why, where are we going?"

"For a walk. Give me a second." He marched to his truck, ducked inside the front cab and came up with a leather bomber jacket. It was worn, its soft leather cracking a bit and the lambswool lining thick enough to warm a body in a snowstorm. "This will do," he said. "You gotta know these nights get cold."

"I didn't think I'd be spending a lot of time outside this late."

"It's not late and we've hardly gotten started."

He wrapped the jacket around her shoulders and she fit her arms through the sleeves. The jacket was two sizes too big for her, the shoulder seams going partway down her arms and the hem nearly touching her knees. Watching her platinum curls bounce off the collar, he gripped the lapels and drew her closer. Her eyes, big and green and surprised, snapped up to his. She was unique, a throwback to a classic fifties movie starlet with that ice-blond hair, an innocent expression that proved deadly and a luscious mouth painted pink and rosy.

"Warm enough?"

She glanced at his mouth for a split second, a tempting little look that pulled his groin taut.

"Uh-huh."

He hesitated to let her go.

Moments ticked by as they stared into each other's eyes. His grip tightened on the fabric, his knuckles grazing her torso just an inch from the two full ripe breasts that had given him a sliver of heaven once. He hadn't forgotten.

He heaved a big sigh and let go. Immediately, she tugged the jacket tight across her chest and crossed her arms.

Justin put a hand on her back again, guiding her down the street. "When I drove up, I saw a town square. There's a gazebo we can use. Or we can just sit in my truck with the motor running and the heater on."

She shook her head at that notion and he was glad of it. Kat warm and comfy in the cab of his truck wouldn't serve either of them well. The last time they'd been alone together in close quarters they'd had a marathon of combustible sex. Justin still felt the pull of attraction to her, but the stakes were too high now for any wrong move.

They walked south with light from the streetlamps leading the way. A few people were out for a brisk stroll, and Justin and Kat both smiled cordially or nodded their heads in greeting while they pressed on. The gazebo was visible in the distance, marking the center of the town square. They walked past park benches and down a garden path until they reached it. Luckily, they had it all to themselves.

Justin led her to a wooden bench that was painted white and she sat down. Behind her, past the lattice, flood lamps lit the surrounding shrubs, giving off enough faint light so that they could see each other's faces. Justin paced for a second, pulling in his scattered emotions.

"Tell me about Connor."

Kat's face beamed immediately and her voice took on

a whimsical, loving tone. "He's an amazing little boy. He was born healthy and strong. His Apgar rating was ten."

"What's an Apgar rating?"

"It's a test they do at birth, named after the doctor who invented it. It measures things like heart rate and breathing and muscle tone. Ten is the highest score a baby can get."

Justin nodded. Unfamiliar pride pierced his heart.

"When I brought him home from the hospital, he took to breast-feeding right away. He's a good eater and a pretty sound sleeper. You have to know a few little Connor tricks to get him to take a nap and I'm learning just like he is, every day."

"What kind of tricks?"

"Well, first I give him a bottle. And then I sing to him. If that doesn't work, I show him a *Sesame Street* video clip on my phone. He's crazy about some of the characters. And once he's mellow, I hum to him, some of his favorite baby tunes. When I get him to sleep, sometimes I just watch him breathe and thank my blessings for him every minute of every—"

Kat stopped talking abruptly. "I'm…sorry."

Regret pumped through his veins. "So am I."

"It's done, Justin. We can't change the past."

"I'll never get those months back, Kat. I lost all that time with Connor."

Sympathy settled in her eyes. "I know that. I can't imagine what that's like. But if you had known, it's not like you would've seen Connor that much. You were serving in the military."

"That's not the point. He has a family here and I would've done what I could to spend time with him. To acknowledge him, even if I couldn't watch him grow. But that's all going to change starting right this second. I'm going to be a major part of his life now. He's going to know I'm his father."

"No, Justin." Kat's green eyes sharpened. "You can't do that to Mattie. It'll kill her. If you take that baby away from her, she'll die. I swear to you, she'll go into cardiac arrest."

Justin took a step back, noting the warning in her voice. Was she serious or overstating the facts?

"You have no idea," she continued. "When I got here two months ago, she'd just been released from the hospital. She'd had a major heart attack after she learned of Brett's death. She had no reason to live. She'd lost fifteen pounds, and as you can see, she's a small woman to begin with, and she didn't want any part of rehab. She was living in the house alone. I saw the hopelessness in her eyes, Justin. It reminded me, of…well, of my own mother. When I told her my story, about how I met Brett and conceived his child, she…she made a remarkable comeback. In just the few months I've been here, she's put on weight and her whole outlook has changed. Her heart is still damaged and she has to take it easy, but the doctor has told her over and over that our little Connor is her antidote to heart disease. You have to believe me. You *cannot* tell that woman that Connor isn't Brett's son."

"That's hardly fair, Kat. I've already missed out on so much with Connor. And it's not fair to the boy to deprive him of his real father."

"Do you want to be responsible for putting Aunt Mattie back in the hospital…or worse?"

Damn it. His gut told him Kat was telling the truth. The blow was hard to take. He didn't want to deny his son a father a second longer. But he'd seen Matilda Applegate with his own eyes. She was frail and weakened. She certainly looked older than her seventy years in body, but when her gaze lit on Connor, it had a youthful spirited glow. He hated to admit it but that woman's life revolved around that little boy.

Every day of Justin's life, Brett's death gnawed at him.

He'd vowed that once he returned home, he'd come clean and speak with Brett's aunt. Telling Mattie the truth about Brett's death would go a long way in clearing his conscience. It had taken Justin three days to build up the courage to visit the woman and he'd been prepared to lay it all on the line. But now, as he studied Kat's determined expression, the set of her delicate jaw and the plea in her eyes, he was boxed into a corner. "I don't want to hurt Mattie Applegate."

"Then…don't."

"I want to know my son."

"You will. I promise." Her voice held conviction.

Justin stared at her. A promise from Katherine Grady? Could he trust her? The fool in him, who saw her as a beautiful, sexy, desirable woman, wanted so badly to believe her, but he couldn't chance it. The stakes were just too high. He had every right to know his son, to learn Connor tricks and comfort him when he was tired and grumpy. He wanted to bond with him and give him fatherly love.

Justin stepped closer to her. She smelled like gardenias, fresh and fragrant and distinct. Her light springtime scent contrasted sharply with the time of year, the chill in the air. "What are you suggesting?"

Kat's lashes fell to her cheeks, blond curls bouncing as she shook her head. "I don't know, Justin. We'll have to work it out secretly. I do know I won't stop you from seeing Connor. I'll make every effort to make it easy for you to be with him, as long as you don't tell Aunt Mattie the truth. Please."

Whether Matilda Applegate would truly die of a coronary or not upon learning the truth, no one would ever know, but Kat sure believed it as fact. And that's all he could go on right now. He couldn't chance it, but he damn well didn't have to like it.

He'd had a plan in mind for Mattie Applegate from the

start, to honor Brett and his late uncle Ralph, who had also been a war veteran. He wanted to help the Applegate family. Maybe now was the time to implement that plan.

He didn't want to deny his son's birth but what choice did he have? "All right. I won't tell her."

Gratitude filled her eyes as a broad smile graced her face. "Thank you, Justin. Thank you."

Swallowing hard, Justin couldn't look away. Her glowing appreciation and gleam in her pretty green eyes was a little too hard to take. He wondered if his good sense had taken a joy ride. Was he remembering too much about the leave he'd spent with Kat, or had he just been without a woman for too long?

He gathered the lapels of the bomber jacket in both hands and gently drew her onto her feet and close to him. "Oh."

He focused on her tempting pouty mouth. She didn't pull away and that was good enough for him. He reached behind her neck and tugged her mouth to his.

"What are you doing?" she whispered over the seam of his lips.

He brushed his mouth over hers, once, twice. Testing and tasting her.

From down deep in her throat, she purred.

What the hell *was* he doing? It was already too complicated between them, but that didn't stop him from delving deep into her mouth with strokes of his tongue. From bracing his hands inside the jacket and absorbing the heat of her skin burning through her clothes.

He held her hips, nestled her closer yet, and drew out sweet nectar from her inviting mouth. From the first touch of their lips, everything had come back to him. During those cold lonely nights overseas, how often he'd think of the time he'd spent with her like this. Holding her, tasting her and making love to her. She hadn't been the only woman he'd been with during his time in the military, but she'd definitely been the most memorable.

From under the warmth of the jacket, he lifted her blouse and splayed his fingers across her belly. His fingertips touched where she'd carried his baby. Her skin now was firm and flat and silky smooth.

A whimper rose from her throat and she leaned into him. She smelled like heaven. Strands of silky hair fell across his cheek. From his gut, a low moan climbed up his throat as he slid his hand to the warm flesh around her waist. Raw, powerful desire zipped through his body.

Flashing lights from an oncoming car brightened the square for a second and touched on where they stood in the gazebo. Kat startled and backed away, her hand going to her mouth and her eyes lifting to his. In them, he saw longing, surprise and condemnation all at once.

Her lipstick was smeared, her hair ruffled, but none of that mattered on Kat. She was gorgeous no matter what. Drop-dead gorgeous. She wrapped the jacket tight around her torso and hugged herself as if summoning courage to say something. Then, her eyes flickered and she blurted, "I dated your brother a couple of times."

Justin snapped to attention. "What?"

"I thought it'd be better if you found out from me. Luke and I…"

"What about you and Luke?"

"It was nothing…. I was lonely and worried sick about Mattie. We saw each other briefly. You might as well know now, I've met your whole family."

A shudder wracked his body. Justin couldn't tear his gaze away from the woman who'd just dropped a bombshell on him. Kat and Luke? Her confession ripped right through him. His pride suffered and he gnashed his teeth at the thought of Kat with his brother. What other bombs would she drop on him? It served to remind him that he didn't really know Kat Grady at all.

"Do you want to know about what happened between—?"

"I'll get my information from Luke. But I do want something else from you."

She blinked then, her lips trembling. "What would that be?"

"A paternity test."

Justin followed her home and waited until she was safely in the house before revving the engine and speeding off. Kat sighed quietly. She wasn't thrilled about Justin doubting her word about the baby's parenthood and demanding a paternity test, but if it was necessary to ease his mind in order to keep the secret a little while longer, she had to agree for Mattie's sake.

Kat moved through the house she thought of as home, realizing that all this could come crashing down around her. She'd made some boner mistakes in her day, but protecting Mattie Applegate from the truth wasn't one of them. She felt it deep down in her core, that she was doing the right thing by keeping the truth from her.

She peeked in on Connor first, and the gentle beam of love she carried inside brightened when she looked at him cozy and warm in his crib. There weren't any words strong enough to explain the unconditional love she had for her son. There were no borders, no boundaries or limits in her adoration. She'd only wished she hadn't tried so hard to make it work with Michael Golden in New York. He was all wrong for Connor. She realized that now and she chalked up her bad decision to survival.

Next, she moved to Mattie's room and tiptoed two steps inside to peer at the patchwork quilt nestled around Mattie's slender shoulders.

"I'm still breathing," the older woman said.

Kat laughed softly. "I would hope so."

"Keeping awake, just in case Connor needs me."

"He's sound asleep, Aunt Mattie."

"That's good, sweetheart. Not a peep out of him to-night."

"You can go to sleep now," Kat said, backing out of the room.

"I think I will."

"Good night, Aunt Mattie," Kat said from the door-way. "Thank you."

"Good night, sweetheart."

The glow inside Kat's heart got a shade brighter with Mattie's affection. Kat may be saving her life, but Matilda Applegate might just be saving hers, too.

Kat walked quietly into the spare bedroom Mattie had used to store all of Ralph's clothing and fishing gear. He'd been gone for years, but Mattie said she liked to have his things surrounding her to keep him close. Kat thought it sweet and romantic. She'd never had that kind of re-lationship with anyone. But she had Connor now and he was enough.

Mattie had cleared out half of the closet and four dresser drawers for Kat's business. Kat had found an old pine desk in the barn, then sanded and lathered it with walnut stain to make it useful for her purposes. Now it housed a printer and her laptop computer. Fishing rods held up one corner of the room and tackle boxes were stacked up three high in another, with Aunt Mattie's sewing machine in between. Luckily it wasn't a relic and Kat had been able to update some parts to make it run more efficiently. Kat saw it as her salvation, a way to put her talent to good use.

She sat down at the machine and picked up the dress pattern she'd designed last month. Then she started pok-ing pins into the yellow dotted Swiss material of the garment she'd started working on early this morning, before Justin Slade had turned her world upside down.

Her lips tasted of him and his rugged musky scent filled her nostrils still. A steady low hum like a gentle spring breeze whispered through her body, invading her good sense. She could easily fall into those sensations again. Pitiful female that she was, she missed the strength of a man's arms around her and a strong shoulder to rely on when the strife of the day got to be too much. So sue her for responding to that kiss, for letting herself fall prey to Justin Slade's advances tonight.

She may have been guilty of some things, but he'd lied to her in the first place, causing this whole mess. Justin Slade was no saint.

Except that he was. He'd received the Medal of Honor for saving five soldiers' lives. She'd looked him up on the internet after he left this morning. She faintly recalled Luke mentioning once that his brother was a decorated soldier. At the time, she hadn't made any connection, but then, why would she? She'd had no idea Luke was related to her son's father. The paternity test, a mere swabbing of the baby's and father's mouths, would prove Justin's paternity, she had no doubt.

She fed material into the Singer and guided the fabric through. Her shoulders relaxed with each perfect stitch, her heart warming with the steady automatic buzzing of the machine. Kat let nimble fingers work their magic on cloth that would soon become a sunny Easter dress for one lucky little girl. With her prototype designs shipped to fashion houses and orders coming in now from local towns, Kat ran her small-time business, Babylicious, from Mattie Applegate's spare bedroom. But for right now, tonight, sewing this dress, losing herself in work she loved, helped bank her rising fear that somehow Justin Slade could make life extremely difficult for her.

* * *

Justin thought his time hiding behind corners and being suspicious of everything around him was over. He was wrong. Keeping a paternity test under wraps in Douglas County wasn't possible. He couldn't trust anyone within earshot of his doctor's office to keep a secret this big. Not now, when every acquaintance he'd ever known was stopping him on the street to shake his hand and friends he hadn't seen since high school were coming to pay him a visit on the ranch.

Justin had called in a favor from a family friend, a doctor who'd gotten a pretty sweet deal on a thoroughbred stallion from the Slade horse farm. Dr. Barrington practiced two towns over in another county, and promised discretion.

The next morning, he arranged to meet Kat in a minimall parking lot in Silver Springs. Then, with Connor strapped into the car seat, he drove Kat's car to Dr. Barrington's office for the appointment. It actually took longer to boil water than to give the test, and afterward Justin wasted no time driving them back to where he'd parked his truck.

The boy had fallen asleep, his little head propped against one side of the car seat, his hair damp with sleep sweat, breathing quietly. Justin's heart lurched. He'd experienced anger and regret and bitterness from this situation, but right now, all he felt was a magnetic pull to the child he might have fathered. Already, he was thinking of the future and of all the things he wanted to teach his son.

"That didn't take long," Kat said with quiet relief.

"Connor didn't seem to mind." Justin already felt protective about the boy. He was glad the swab test was just as accurate as a blood test. No needles. DNA was DNA, no matter how they acquired it, Dr. Barrington had assured them.

"It was painless, thank goodness," Kat said, glancing in the rearview mirror to check on Connor as they drove on.

Justin's chest filled with pride. "He seems like a good baby."

Kat's smile was bright as sunshine. "He has his moments. I suppose all babies do, but he's wonderful. He loves to laugh. We play giggle games. And he loves to eat. I don't think I've ever seen him refuse food." The look in her eyes when she spoke of Connor was something to see.

They stared at each other for several seconds.

Justin wanted to spend the day together, to take them to lunch and watch Connor eat his meal. To walk the baby around town in his stroller, just like a real family, and to do all the things he'd missed out on. But Justin stood to lose too much in the off chance the paternity test came back negative.

He'd learned patience in the marines. Wait for the right moment. And this wasn't it.

Justin just couldn't trust Kat. She was aware of the Slade wealth. She knew Justin's background. She'd seen Sunset Ranch and had already tried to get her foot in the door by dating Luke. Was passing her son off as a Slade just another ploy? When he returned home from war, he thought he'd never experience the type of suspicion that crept up his spine now. But how could he believe anything she had to say?

Waiting for the paternity test and finding out whether that little cherub-faced boy with the inky curls and big dark eyes was truly his son would make for the longest three days of his life.

He wanted Connor to be his for the boy's sake, so he wouldn't go through life fatherless.

But if the baby was his son, the peace and solitude he'd craved since Brett's death wouldn't come. The situation with Aunt Mattie would complicate matters.

Justin drove into the parking lot in the minimall and parked Kat's car next to his. With his hands draped on the steering wheel, he turned to her. She glanced at her wristwatch and sighed. "I'd better get going. When he wakes up, he'll want to eat. He howls when he's hungry."

"That I'd like to see."

"You will," she said softly, assuring him. "He's yours, Justin. But you'll have your proof in a few days."

Justin got out of the car and waited until Kat drove away before he climbed into his truck. Then he pulled out of the parking lot, and headed toward Silver Haven Cemetery where Brett's body had been laid to rest. After driving for twenty minutes, he passed through a four-way stop and slowed his truck when the stately iron gates of the cemetery came into view. They were opened wide like welcoming arms to the mourners who were there to pay their respects. He stared at the ivy-covered brick columns at the entrance as his heart pumped hard inside his chest.

Turn the wheel. Go in. Make your peace.

His hands were frozen in the ten and two position on the steering wheel as he sat in his truck, numbly staring at those gates. Closing his eyes, he said a silent prayer for Brett. But a car approaching from behind helped him make his decision. He touched his foot to the gas pedal and the truck limped along the road as Silver Haven vanished in his rearview mirror.

He'd lost his nerve. He wasn't ready to travel through those gates. He didn't know when he'd ever be ready. With trepidation in his heart, he changed direction and made the necessary turns that would lead him home, to Sunset Ranch.

He'd tried.

It would have to be enough for now.

It was late in the afternoon by the time Justin parked in front of his house. He sat there for a long while, studying the dashboard with eyes that only saw the past: things he couldn't change and mistakes he'd made along the way.

Rap. Rap. Rap.

Justin jerked to attention, brought out of his deep thoughts. When he was an on-duty marine, daydreaming like that could get a man killed.

Luke's voice penetrated the front window of the truck. "You having a party in there all by yourself?"

Justin rolled his eyes. "Yeah, and you just crashed it."

"Didn't anyone tell you a party has to involve at least two people and one of them should be female?"

Despite his teasing grin, Luke's eyes shone with understanding. Luke was the sensitive type, under all that blond brawn and bulk. He was Justin's go-to man when he had a problem. Except that now Luke could conceivably *be* the problem.

As Luke stepped back, Justin exited the truck. "We need to talk."

"Sounds serious." Luke lost the grin.

Justin squinted against sunlight, gazing across acres of Slade land. "You have time for a ride?"

Luke gave him a nod. "If it's important, I'll make time."

Justin squared him a look. "It's important."

Luke tipped his hat brim farther down on his forehead and spoke with a Clint Eastwood rasp. "Okay, then, let's saddle up and leave this ole ranch in the dust."

Justin appreciated Luke's attempt to lighten the moment, but not even an exaggerated cowboy drawl was going to make him smile until he found out the truth about Kat and his brother.

Four

"It's nice of you to visit again so soon, Justin," Mattie said, sitting across from him on the recliner in her parlor. "Are you sure you don't want any peach pie?"

"Not right now, ma'am." He was seated in the same spot on the sofa as the other day. "I'll have some later."

"Pie will keep. Just about everything keeps when you get to be my age."

Justin smiled. Aunt Mattie wore a housecoat with bright red, turquoise and orange flowers. Her hair was up in a do—straight back, then curling at the nape—that reminded him of his mother. He could almost see through Aunt Mattie's years to the attractive, flamboyant young girl she must have been once. "My grandma used to say age is just a number in your head. It's how you feel inside that matters."

She leaned forward in her seat and the smile she gave him took two decades off her face. "Well, then if that's true, I'm sixteen."

Justin nodded. "That's what my grandma used to say, too."

"'Course when your body breaks down, you tend to forget that."

"Yes, ma'am."

"So, you came to tell me about Brett. How nice. Did you know him very well?"

"Yes, ma'am, I did. He enlisted a few years after I did.

He was deployed to my unit at Delaram about two years ago. We served together and got on as friends."

Matilda leaned back in the chair and a distant, almost tragic smile spread across her thin cheeks. "He was like a son to me. Ralph and I raised him, you know. Now, my Ralph and Brett are serving the Lord up above. Tell me about your time with Brett."

Justin launched into story after story about his friendship with Brett. He told her about the barracks, how they lived in close quarters, the blazing heat and the frigid cold, and about how much friendship came to mean to the soldiers serving over there. They had little contact with the outside world—no television, no internet access most of the time. Justin told her about the poker games they'd play and how they would swap rations and break out pictures and talk about home. Always home. It got to be that they knew each other's home lives just as well as they knew their own. He told Aunt Mattie how much Brett talked about his uncle Ralph and about how much he'd loved her. He told her how Brett felt bad, leaving her alone, but hoped to come home one day to build Applegate Farms back to its original glory. Brett had every intention of doing that very thing.

He told her how Brett was as fine a soldier as there was.

He told her everything there was to tell, except the one thing that she needed to hear the most. How Brett died. The words were on his lips, begging to come forth, but they failed, time and again, either because Justin had just made her smile, or she'd gotten a faraway nostalgic look on her face, or she'd gather her hands to her chest as if holding his words near to her heart with such hope that it tore Justin up inside.

He'd come ready to purge his guilt and lay down the heavy burden he'd been carrying around for months. His memories haunted him. His dreams had turned nightmarish. He thought that today he could finally own up to his part in Brett's death, knowing that Aunt Mattie deserved the truth, and then he'd be able to deal with all the rest.

But he couldn't do it.

The time was never right. He didn't want to blurt out something that would hurt the older woman. A battle raged in his head, and he was glad that Kat and Connor were out this morning shopping in town. Glad that he'd had this time to speak with Mattie alone.

At first, when Mattie had answered the door to his knock, he'd been disappointed. He'd wanted to see Connor. He'd gotten his expectations up and had been anxious to see the child again, anxious to look upon his chubby cheeks and glimpse the spark of intelligence in his eyes.

He'd wanted to see Kat, too.

She hadn't lied to him about Luke. They'd dated briefly and had shared nothing more than a kiss or two. Luke had sworn on his unborn baby's life that nothing had happened between him and Kat other than friendship, and that was more than good enough for Justin to hear. His relief was as powerful as anything he'd ever experienced.

Luke had been stunned when Justin then told him the entire story of his involvement with Kat. It wasn't the kind of thing that happened every day. Mostly, Justin hated admitting to his brother about making and following through on such a fool bet.

"Guess that makes you far from perfect," Luke had said. "Something I've always known."

Justin appreciated his brother's frank assessment. It was hard living up to war-hero status. Luke always knew the right thing to say.

Unlike Justin, who now couldn't summon the words he'd practiced saying a dozen times over: *Brett is dead because of me.*

And Aunt Mattie had the good grace not to ask about

Brett's death. The older woman was as wise as her years. He suspected she knew the pain it would cause both of them.

So Justin moved onto another subject. "Aunt Mattie," he said. "Is it all right if I call you that?"

The woman's eyes brightened. "I'd be honored."

"I have an idea and I need your okay first. I've been thinking on this for a few months. And I hope you don't mind me saying, the land around here has gone to ruin."

"I won't fault anyone the truth," she said, nodding. "The place is a weed trap, full of gopher holes and snakes, and out beyond the dilapidated barn, there's nothing but hard dirt and cactus. Ralph tried and tried, but when the doggone contracts dried up around here, he couldn't keep the place right as rain like he wanted. He was a good man, my Ralph."

"I know that, ma'am. Brett was always singing his praises. He said the hog farmers lost out to big companies and then the place sort of shriveled up along with those contracts. Brett wanted so much to bring this farm back to life when he got home."

Tears misted in her eyes. "I know it. Brett's heart was as big as this house and then some."

"Well, I'm hoping to honor both Brett and your Ralph along with other war veterans. Ralph served in Vietnam and Brett gave his…his life in the Middle East. There's a whole lot of men out there wounded on the inside and out who need help. I'm hoping you'll sell your outer land to me. There's got to be at least six hundred acres here that could be—"

"Six hundred and thirty-five," she added.

Justin nodded. "With that acreage, I hope to build a retreat for wounded soldiers. We'd have horses here, and we'd build a facility, away from your house, that could be used for temporary lodging for the men. Young and old could come to work with horses. Sunset Ranch can provide mares and geldings that need some tender loving care of their own. It'd be an equine horse retreat. If you're willing to sell, I'll make sure this house gets the repairs it needs, too. It was Brett's dream to restore this place, and I'd like to see that happen."

Mattie's teary eyes spilled over. "Why…I don't know… oh, my goodness. That's about the darnedest idea I've ever heard. My land…a retreat for soldiers?" Her voice broke to a frail whisper of awe. "Wouldn't my Ralph and Brett love a notion like that?"

"Don't cry, Aunt Mattie." Justin slid down the sofa and plucked a tissue from a table by her recliner. He offered it to her and she thanked him as she dabbed at her tears. "I'd make you a fair offer for the land," Justin assured her.

She waved him off with the hand holding the tissue. Sniffing, she spoke quietly. "I don't have a doubt about it."

Such blind faith. Justin took a hard swallow. Stabbed with guilt, a nagging voice in his head urged him on. This was the absolute right thing to do to honor Brett and Ralph and all soldiers who'd sacrificed their bodies as well as their souls for their country. They needed some TLC of their own. In a small way, he could make up for Mattie's loss.

"If you agree to it, we can call the place the Gateway Equine Retreat."

"Oh, my…" Joyful light beamed from her eyes, even though wet eyes. "I don't know what I did to deserve all this," she whispered, clearly astonished. "First Connor and Kat come into my life and now you, with an offer like this. I don't see how I can refuse such a wonderful thing."

"I think Brett would approve," Justin said softly.

She began nodding. "Yes, he would."

The front door swung open and Kat entered with a grocery bag on one hip and the baby flat up against her chest. Connor faced forward, his legs dangling from two openings in the sling that kept him plastered against her. Justin's heart tumbled, seeing the two of them again. He rose from his seat and looked the boy straight in the eye. Connor didn't turn away like he had before and his sweet inquisitive gaze nearly knocked Justin off his ass.

Baby mortar. More explosive and deadly than any IED he'd come across in Afghanistan.

He took hold of his emotions and walked over to help Kat with the bag, but before he could get close enough, she moved and let the grocery bag slip from her arm onto a maple end table.

Ignoring him, her gaze flew to Mattie's teary face and a quick gasp escaped her throat. She turned accusing eyes toward him. "Justin, why are you here?"

"Kat, dear, Justin's just told me something so—"

"What did you tell her?" Her face pinched tight with panic.

"Hold on," he said quietly.

"I won't hold on. You didn't tell me you were coming by today."

"I told Mattie I'd come by to talk about Brett."

"He doesn't need an invitation, dear. He told me the nicest stories, Kat. I'm sure you'd like to hear them, too."

Kat's shoulders slumped in relief, although Justin noted her annoyance, as well. She worked the latches on the baby sling and undid the contraption, wrapping her arms tight around Connor as she pulled him free. "Nice stories?" She raised her eyebrows. "Then why is Aunt Mattie crying?"

He pointed to the grocery bag. "You have any more of those in the car?"

She nodded.

"I'll get them while Aunt Mattie tells you why I'm here."

"Sit down with Connor, Kat," the older woman said

sweetly, dabbing at her eyes. "Justin's come up with such a wonderful idea."

Kat, in tight jeans and a soft pink sweater that revealed all her curves without revealing an inch of skin, did crazy things to him. The baby she held in her arms only added to the beautiful picture that stirred all of his emotions.

Baby mortar *and* blonde bombshell.

Pummeled by unexpected combative forces, he walked outside, climbed down the steps and leaned against the porch column to catch his breath.

Closing his eyes, he let go a few choice cuss words, then pushed off from the wall to unload the grocery bags from the car.

Coming home wasn't supposed to be this hard.

Kat made the gravy, scraping at the crusted drippings from the pot roast she'd just removed from the pan. The gravy popped with bubbles as she stirred the rich brown sauce with the wooden spoon. Justin worked directly beside her, slicing the roast.

"Don't need a knife for this," he said. "The meat's just falling away. I guess that's what they mean by fork tender."

Darn Aunt Mattie for inviting Justin to dinner.

He'd been hanging around all afternoon, helping her put groceries away, talking up his idea for the equine retreat to Aunt Mattie and now assisting in the dinner preparation while Connor and Aunt Mattie both napped.

"Didn't get anything fork tender at the base."

They bumped hips. It seized her breath, being so close to him. "I don't imagine so."

"The cooks wouldn't win the first round in the *Top Chef* competition, that's for sure."

"Was it awful being there?" she asked as she focused her attention on the gravy. She didn't want lumps to form in the sauce because she was distracted by the sexy man beside her. But he smelled so good. Woodsy and fresh.

It hurt to know he'd used her. She'd been running from abusive men all her life, but when Justin had pretended to be Brett, she'd poured her heart out to him. She'd told him things she hadn't shared with anyone else, about her young life, about her dreams. Maybe it was because she knew he'd be leaving and she'd never have to face him again or maybe she just felt she could trust him. Could've been a little of both.

"Awful? It was kinda hard being isolated from the world. Makes a man feel out of touch with himself, his life, everything he's ever known. All that's up ahead is the mission and seeing that it turns out successful." He put his head down, staring at the platter. "Losing Brett was the awful part."

She turned and looked into eyes that couldn't hide pain.

"You saved lives, Justin."

"You've done some homework."

She shrugged. "You're a hero. Douglas County is throwing a parade in your honor. It's been in the news."

"Not my idea."

"But you can't deny that you saved five men. They would have died if you hadn't been there."

"I didn't save Brett," he whispered, taking a swallow, staring at the kitchen wall, "and I could have."

Kat didn't know about that. Nothing she'd read about Justin Slade mentioned his connection to Brett Applegate. Justin had been honored with the Congressional Medal of Honor and that wasn't something to sneeze at. Five men were alive today because of his bravery.

"I'm sorry Brett died," Kat found herself saying. "The retreat is a good way to honor him."

Justin's lips twisted and he shook his head. "I wanted to do something."

"You are," she said, turning off the burner. She faced him with a direct look and lowered her voice. "You're keeping a secret that will protect his aunt's life."

"A few hours ago, you thought I'd gone back on that promise."

"Aunt Mattie was crying. I didn't know what to think."

"You really care about her?"

His question unnerved her. Didn't he think she was capable of caring for a woman who had shown her nothing but kindness? Didn't he think her capable of putting someone else's needs above her own? Not that Aunt Mattie could replace the mother she'd lost, but she felt a kinship with the older woman, a bond that was brought on by their mutual love of Connor. "Of course I care about her."

Justin braced his hand on the kitchen counter and leaned in close, until his handsome face was all she could see in her line of vision. He touched a wisp of her hair, so gently, so tenderly. Her body reacted with warmth and a tingle that went down to her toes. He traced the line of her jaw with his index finger and shifted his gaze to her mouth. "I don't go back on my promises, Kat."

She swallowed. Aware they were alone in the small kitchen for the time being, she couldn't muster the strength to back away. Tempted by his dark eyes and sensual memories, she spoke quietly. "But you lied to me over an entire weekend."

"I wanted you."

His hands came out to rest on her waist. Through her soft sweater, she felt the urgency of his touch, the potent pull as he gathered her closer. Their legs meshed together, her breasts crushed his chest. He groaned softly, letting her know what he intended. Their lips were inches apart.

"I still want you," he whispered, right before his mouth claimed hers.

Kat fell into the kiss, the power of his sensual words

and touch too much to fend off. She wanted him close. She wanted to feel his mouth on hers, to feel his body's urgency and know she was the cause of his desire. She kissed him back, throwing her arms around his neck and feeling immeasurable heat between them.

He plunged his tongue into her mouth and she welcomed him with a soft moan. His kiss deepened and awakened her lust for the opposite sex. She hadn't felt a need this powerful since before Connor was born. She needed Justin's lips on hers, needed his body close, and reveled in the sensations he stirred in her.

He trailed away from her mouth to drizzle tiny biting nibbles on her throat. She craned her neck, allowing his lips to drift down to the base of her shoulders. His hands inched their way up the material of her sweater. Caressing the soft cashmere, he found her breasts and rubbed them with his palms. Between her legs, she throbbed with sparks of delight. She pulled his mouth to hers once again. She wanted more from him, now. Right now.

It was impossible. Connor and Aunt Mattie slept in the next room.

It was dangerous, and normally, she enjoyed sexy games, but not now. Not with her son so close. It was madness. Justin tugged at her sweater, yanking the material away from her body. His hands found her skin and hot needy fingers pulled the underside of her bra down. He caressed her breasts, flesh to flesh, his firm rough palms teasing her soft nipples. Steam rose up, swamping her with heat.

"You feel just like I remember," he whispered. "Do you know how hard it was not sleeping with you that first night? Do you know how much I wanted you?"

Kat's mind filled with memories. She'd almost fallen for a hog farmer, a man with empty pockets, the kind of man Kat didn't want in her life ever again. Dirt-poor and earnest. But now, it was different. Justin wasn't Brett Applegate. And he was driving her crazy.

"We…can't, Justin."

His hands froze as he stared into her eyes. She could relate to the disappointment on his face. She felt it, too. With a reluctant nod and taking a deep breath, Justin removed his hands from her body. "You're right. We can't do this here."

Trembling, she wrapped her arms around her waist, still tingling from the places Justin had ignited on her body. "It's complicated enough."

"It's not that complicated between you and me. With us, everything's pretty clear."

They locked gazes for beats of a minute. "I know," she admitted quietly and then her mind drifted to Mattie and Connor and all the lies she'd told in the past for her own survival. And to insure a good life for her son. "I've got to check on Connor, would you mind putting out the—"

"I'll go with you. Then I'll help you with the meal."

Kat couldn't refuse him. He had a right to see Connor. While he wasn't sure of it, Kat was certain that Connor was his son. She'd conceived him that weekend before she took up with Michael Golden. She gave him a small smile. "All right."

He followed her into the bedroom. Connor was just rousing. When he saw her, he rolled to a sit-up position in his crib. His eyes still drugged from sleep, his hair curling at his nape, the baby just looked around as if trying to get his bearings. "Hi, sweet baby."

His little face contorted as he rubbed his eyes with the full force of his palms, up and down, stretching the skin. Kat gently removed his hands from his face before he poked himself in the eye. "Takes him a few minutes to fully wake up," she said to Justin.

"Okay by me. I could watch him all day long."

She glanced at this tough soldier, this hero standing beside her, his eyes full of pride and warmth. How quickly he'd fallen under Connor's spell. It wasn't hard. Kat would move heaven and earth for her child. She had a feeling that Justin would do the same. A shiver of dread rode down her spine, but this time, she wouldn't cave to those feelings. "Yeah, me, too."

She turned to Justin. "I have to change his diaper. You can leave if you'd like."

He gave her an are-you-kidding squint and shook his head. "I've seen worse in my day."

"Okay, but remember you asked for it. Smell that? It's gonna be a good one."

A resounding chuckle rose from Justin's throat and both she and Connor glanced at him. "You're not scaring me. Diaper away."

Later, with all of them seated at the kitchen table, Connor in his high chair, the pot roast and potatoes served, Justin began talking business about the sale of Aunt Mattie's outer land and how he wanted to get the ball rolling as quickly as possible with the equine retreat.

The change in his demeanor gave Kat some breathing room. Up until that point, he'd been watching her every move, darting quick glances at her mouth and sending sexy secretive smiles her way. Worse yet, the adoring, yet cautious look in his eyes when he studied Connor was hard to miss. Aunt Mattie wasn't born yesterday; Kat saw her watching them and wondered just what the older woman was thinking.

"I'm having the papers drawn up and will bring them by in a few days," he said to Aunt Mattie. "If you're sure about this?"

The money from the sale of the land would help pay Aunt Mattie's medical expenses and give her a nice cushion for her old age. Aunt Mattie had no use for the neglected land anyway, and no one could've come up with a better plan than Justin's to restore the land and do some good along the way.

Aunt Mattie glanced at Connor in his high chair, eating vegetable puffs that looked suspiciously like Cheetos, and her eyes narrowed to thin slits. Her face fell short of the contented expression she usually wore. "I don't think I realized up until this moment," she said, easing the words out slowly, "that I might be robbing the boy of his birthright."

Justin shot Kat a sharp look.

Kat's cheeks burned.

No one had thought of this before and of course, Aunt Mattie wouldn't be robbing Connor of anything, since he wasn't really her great-nephew. "Oh…but Aunt Mattie, we don't want anything from you. You've already done too much, putting a roof over our head."

"Nonsense, girl. You came here and immediately took over my care. You've brought joy to this old woman's life. You're doing more for me than I could ever do for you."

"But Aunt Mattie, I told you when we arrived here, we didn't expect anything."

"But the boy's my kin. He deserves—"

"Not run-down parched land that won't do anybody any good," Justin said gently. "Remember, I'm giving you a fair price for the land. It's like trading one thing for another. Connor's not losing out. And you'll still have this house, fully refurbished as I promised."

Aunt Mattie leaned back in the kitchen chair, her wrinkles bunching up as she nodded. "I suppose you're right. It's hard making these decisions at my age." She looked at Kat with such trust that Kat's heart swelled. "If you think it's a good idea, Kat. I'll take your advice."

Kat drew a deep breath. She had no right making decisions for Mattie, but the look on her face said otherwise. She was banking on her advice. "Connor won't know the difference. And the equine retreat would help heal a lot of good men."

"I suppose you're right. It's a good thing."

"It is a good thing." Kat rose from her seat and drew open the box of weekly pills she had sorted out for Mattie's care. She plucked two out, one to regulate her heart, the other a blood thinner. "Here you go," she said, placing the pills on the tablecloth, "time for your medicine."

"Thank you, dear."

Justin was back to watching her every move again.

"So then, it's settled?" Kat asked.

"Yes," Aunt Mattie said, swallowing her medicine. "I'll sell Justin the land."

After the dishes were cleaned, Justin bid Aunt Mattie good-night. Kat, with Connor in her arms, walked him outside. They stood on the porch, the moonlight and chilly air casting a momentary spell. Connor was warming up to Justin now. He no longer shied away and he'd begun to recognize the sound of his deep voice.

"This works out in your favor, doesn't it?" he asked Kat.

"What are you talking about?"

"You'd stand to win, no matter what. If that woman dies, you'd get everything she owned. A quarter of a million dollars for dried-up acreage would serve you well, wouldn't it?"

"That's not why I'm keeping the secret, Justin. I came here—"

"Yeah, I know the story. What I can't figure is what took you so long to decide to find Brett's family. Connor was what…nine months old when you came to Silver Springs? What were you doing for all that time?"

I lived with Michael Golden, who'd promised to raise my son in the lap of luxury.

Kat would lose all credibility if she confessed the truth.

She kept her lips buttoned tight. With the mood Justin was in, she wasn't going to win this argument.

"If he's my boy, he'd be worth eighty times the sale of the land, but you know that, as well, being that you dated Luke."

"I told you, Luke and I were...just friends."

Justin's lips pursed, but she noticed a hint of relief in his eyes. "He confirmed it. Wouldn't have kissed you in the kitchen the way I did if it turned out otherwise."

"You wouldn't believe me when I told you that very thing," Kat said, hoisting her chin up.

"Sugar, I don't know what to believe."

His eyes softened when he looked at the baby. Slowly, he put his hand out to touch Connor's ruddy little cheek. His fingers lingered there. "Better get him inside. It's cold out here."

Then he turned around and climbed down the steps, leaving Kat to wonder at the conflicting emotions stirred up inside her belly.

The next morning, Justin clicked off his cell phone and stared at the darn thing for a full minute, before striding behind the bar in the corner of the parlor. He pulled out a bottle of fifty-year-old whiskey and glanced at the label.

"The good stuff," he mumbled and then grabbed a tumbler. Placing it on the polished surface, he poured himself two inches of liquor and raised his glass. "To fatherhood."

The first sip he swallowed slid down his throat easily. Unfamiliar tears wet his lashes and he blinked them away. "And to Connor. My son."

Taking a steady breath, he absorbed the truth and grinned like a silly old fool. He was Connor's father. Man, it felt good to know for certain about the boy.

Images of his own father popped into his mind. He'd had a good relationship with Randall Slade. The man was stern in some ways, but Justin always knew where he stood with him. He always knew his father had his back. He wanted that for Connor, too. He wanted his boy to know that no matter what, Justin would be there for him.

Love—that had probably surfaced since the first day he'd met the little guy—filled his heart. The strong emotion stifled him a bit with its powerful intensity.

Connor had to be his son. He looked just like him. Had the same eyes, hair and skin coloring. But hearing it confirmed by Dr. Barrington sent a string of emotions barreling through his system. He was happy. No denying that. He wanted that beautiful boy to be his son. Through a twisted set of circumstances they'd been kept apart and there was no going back to make up for the time lost. It was a convoluted mess, more complicated than anything he could've imagined.

He couldn't do a darn thing about it now, what was done was done. But now that he knew about Connor, he'd damn well change the things he had the power to change.

"I want my son to know his family."

Kat had shuddered at the demand when Justin called this morning and told her to make it happen. He would come pick her and Connor up. She'd begged him not to, and made a compromise to drive to Sunset Ranch this afternoon. She'd wanted at least that much on her terms. If things got too weird and awkward or if Aunt Mattie needed her, she could leave anytime she wanted.

Justin had balked at that solution, but finally agreed. It wasn't as easy as Justin thought to come up with a viable excuse to leave Aunt Mattie at dinnertime and to make arrangements for one of the neighbors to drop in on her at a moment's notice.

Aunt Mattie always assured her she was fine when left alone, and Kat didn't argue, but she also didn't leave her for more than an hour or two at a time and rarely in the evening. She liked knowing Aunt Mattie and Connor were sleeping before she headed into the sewing room to work on her designs for Babylicious.

When she'd come to Silver Springs, she'd vowed her lying days were over. She'd done enough of that in her early years to last a lifetime. She hated that she'd broken her vow not to lie to Matilda Applegate about anything else. And to add to her problems, today Connor's paternity would come to light, at least among the Slades now that Justin knew the truth. His prideful tone and the proprietary way he spoke to her this morning still rang in her ears. She'd begged for secrecy and Justin promised that his family could be trusted with the truth.

But she'd learned the hard way that no one could be trusted.

It was five o'clock when she pulled up in front of the main house at Sunset Ranch. The sun dipped low, nearly hidden behind the rocky mountain wall surrounding the property. "Okay, sweet baby, let's get you out of the car."

She leaned into the back and unfastened the car seat straps. Connor flung his arms out, eager to be lifted from the contraption. He wrapped his arms around her neck and she nuzzled him as she straightened with him in her arms. His sweet baby smells filled her nostrils, blocking out the pungent sent of manure, earth and straw. She slung the loaded diaper bag down next.

The ranch was grand, with stately buildings, corrals, barns and a sprawling one-story main house. She'd been here once before, on Luke's arm. But that had never taken off and it was a good thing.

Connor caught sight of movement in the corrals. He loved horses and he began pointing and grunting and bouncing in her arms, urging her in his own little way of communicating. "Okay, sweetie. We'll go see the horses."

She set the diaper bag down beside the car and walked the distance to the corrals. She stopped at the fence post and turned Connor so he could see, bracing him against her chest. His eyes rounded, filled with fascination as he studied three mares.

She enunciated slowly, "Hor...ses."

"Oh...sees." Connor mimicked.

"Yes, that's good, baby," she said, squeezing him tight.

"Must be in his blood."

She turned to find Luke Slade coming up beside her. She froze. She'd dreaded facing him and the rest of the family. "Wh-what's that?"

"His love of horses."

She gave him a quick nod. "This is weird, Luke."

"I know, but don't feel strange around us. Me, in particular. I spoke with Justin and told him how it was between us."

"Thanks for that." Her nerves settled a little. Luke had always been fair to her. He was a nice man. "But the circumstances are pretty...extraordinary."

He smiled at Connor and ruffled his hair. "They're downright bizarre. But now, here you are and this little guy is my nephew."

"Crazy, isn't it?"

He shrugged. "I guess. But life's like that. It's not always neat and tidy."

"No, it's not. So, I hear you're marrying the fainter?"

Luke laughed. "I am. Pretty happy about it, too. And don't mention the fainting, okay? Audrey was embarrassed about that. She thought she'd never have to face you again. She's pregnant."

"It's a good reason to faint. I went through a light-headed phase when I was pregnant. Some people might say I never got over that."

Luke shook his head, amused. "You'll keep my brother

on his toes. Good thing, too. I was afraid he'd be bored when he got home. Nothing's further from the truth."

She smiled. "Congratulations, Luke. I'm truly happy for you."

Out of the corner of her eye, she saw Justin approach. She swiveled halfway around, adjusting Connor in her arms.

Justin stared into her eyes.

Her body reacted, zinging with memories of the kiss that would've taken them to wicked places if there were opportunity. He looked handsome as ever, his military crew cut having grown out enough to drop a lock of dark hair onto his forehead. Dressed in faded jeans, a black shirt and a black hat, he looked like the villain in a spaghetti western.

The baby craned his neck and pointed his finger toward the corral.

His gaze softened the second it landed on Connor. "Likes horses, does he?"

Luke walked over to him, grinned and gave him a slap on the back. "Congratulations, Papa. He's a beautiful boy."

Justin nodded as Luke walked away. "See you at the house."

Justin moved closer to her. "I'm glad you brought him."

"You didn't give me much choice."

Justin could always hold the truth over her head, maybe even reveal it to Aunt Mattie, and it was a vulnerable place to be.

"You said you'd make sure I knew my son."

"You. Not your family. It's risky."

"No, it's not. They know the situation. They'll keep quiet."

Kat allowed her gaze to flow to the horses in the corral. Connor, still captivated by them, bounced in her arms, kicking his legs.

"I want to hold him. Do you think he'll come to me?"

The look of longing in Justin's eyes nearly did her in.

"We can try. Just keep him facing the horses. He's fascinated."

"I can see that," Justin said softly. "Come here, son."

Justin put out his arms and Kat did the transfer.

Kat had never had to share Connor with anyone before. Not like this. Not with knowing that Justin had every bit as much right to Connor as she had. But their son barely noticed that he was being held by Justin. Instead, the little boy's eyes honed in on one gray mare in particular that had ventured closer.

Justin stood stiff, his grip on the baby awkward. He was treating Connor like a delicate gem that would break if he made a wrong move. It was another monumental moment in her life, watching father and son bond for the first time.

"That's Starlight," he said to Connor. There was awe in his voice, and a gentleness that Kat understood, as well. "She's about as old as you are, son."

Connor lifted his eyes to his father. "When you get older, I'll teach you to ride."

The baby looked a little confused, and turned to her, his lower lip quivering. His arms jutted out, reaching for her at the same time his body lurched in her direction. "He wants his mommy."

Justin slid Connor back into her arms and Connor squeezed her neck as tight as he ever had. Rocking him prevented his tears. She swayed back and forth. "He'll warm up to you. It's just been him and me for so long."

Justin's stare lingered on Connor for a few seconds more. Then he inhaled a sharp breath. "The family's waiting. Are you ready to come inside with me?"

Mustering her courage and burying her dread, she gave him a nod. "As ready as I'll ever be."

With a hand to her waist, he guided her toward the

house. She clung to the warmth of his touch, taking what little comfort she could grab.

This was going to be awkward with a capital *A*.

Five

Connor banged the keys on the LeapFrog piano, making dogs bark, ducks quack and the letters of the alphabet sing out in the middle of the parlor floor. He was surrounded by stacking cups, a plastic giraffe teething toy and a Baby Elmo, along with half a dozen other gifts. Sophia and Audrey, women Kat had already met before any of them had known the truth, made her feel comfortable right away. Logan was equally charming, offering her a hug when she'd walked into the house, and Luke gave her a friendly smile. Connor received unconditional love from the entire Slade clan immediately. He was a sweet little boy, so she wouldn't expect any less, but it was strange to say the least, knowing that these people were his family. For the longest time, she'd thought he would never have a family other than Aunt Mattie.

Despite the cordial reception by the Slades, Kat's stomach twisted and she felt out of place. She didn't have a clue where all of this was leading. Justin made her nervous, period. Seated next to him on the sofa, she was aware of his every move, his every breath, the scent of his lime aftershave wafting by her nose. The kiss they'd shared the other day was embedded in her mind so forcefully, she couldn't recall any other man's touch. It was bad. She wanted more kisses, his hands on her and all the things that went along with it, but she couldn't forget that they had to tread carefully. One wrong move, one bad decision and Connor could get hurt in the long run.

Seeing the look of adoration in Justin's eyes as he leaned forward on the sofa, his elbows braced on his knees, fully smitten with Connor's symphony of noise, should've made her feel better about things. Yet a string of nerves kept her on the edge of her seat. Her entire life had been turned upside down. She'd come to Silver Springs to make a fresh start. And look how well that had turned out! Now, the Slade family was entwined in a web of lies, too.

"He loves making music," Luke's pregnant fiancée said. Audrey's small baby bump was high and round. She stood behind the sofa, her hand on her belly, watching Connor poke at all the knobs and buttons on the toy.

"If you can call it that," Luke said, a glint in his eyes. "Sounds like a racket to me."

"Baby sounds," Kat offered. "I don't even hear it anymore. It all blends into the background."

Audrey nibbled on her lower lip. "Oh, boy. I have a lot to learn for when our baby arrives."

"It kind of comes at you in small doses. You don't have to know it all, right away. A lot of it is instinct," Kat reassured her.

Audrey glanced at Luke. "That's good to know. I can handle anything in small doses."

Luke gave her a quizzical look and Logan burst out laughing. "I'm sure you've had to deal with a lot of *small* things, with Luke."

Audrey rolled her eyes and pointed her finger at him. "Don't start with me, Logan. You know I didn't mean it like that."

"I didn't take offense," Luke said. "It's your pregnancy brain talking."

She whirled on him. "I do not have pregnancy brain!"

Luke's expression faltered and he glanced at the women in the room for help. "I thought that was a good thing."

Slowly, Kat and Sophia shook their heads. Luke sent Logan an I'll-get-back-at-you glare, but Logan continued grinning and switched his attention to Connor and the piano.

Kat watched the Slades in action with sweeping sadness. She'd never had a family surrounding her with love, teasing her mercilessly, offering her advice or giving support when she was pregnant. She'd had no one to rely on. It was pretty much how she'd lived her life after her mother died. Alone. Fending for herself.

Now Connor's every whim would be granted and Kat didn't know how she felt about that. Justin had mentioned giving him a filly for his first birthday, a thoroughbred he'd already handpicked for his son, so that child and horse could grow up together.

It was too early for such a gift. Connor was still a baby. Justin couldn't make up for lost time with lavish gifts, and she would have that discussion privately with him at some point. She had to be careful how she broached the subject, though.

Justin's fatherhood had been thrust upon him instantly, with no preparation, and now he wanted to give Connor the world, but some of that eagerness and enthusiasm had to be tempered. It was hard for Kat to share the decision-making regarding Connor. It was something she'd never had to do before.

Lately, she'd begun to really wonder if things might've turned out differently had she known the hog farmer she'd gotten involved with was really Justin Slade, wealthy rancher. Would she have wanted a long-distance relationship with Justin, even though he was a soldier? She wasn't going to delve into what that said about her. She'd heard it all and most of it had come from her own father when she was a child.

"You whorin' little bitch, you mind me now, or that stupid smile will be minus two front teeth."

From the age of five, she'd learned how to let the bad words slide off of her.

The Slades' housekeeper, Ellie, walked in. "Dinner's ready. The dining room's all set up with the good dishes and everything."

Logan raised his eyebrows. "We rated the good dishes?"

"I made Justin's favorite. It's a good way to celebrate his homecoming," Ellie said. The housekeeper's eyes filled with a warm glow as she looked at Connor.

"We're having macaroni and cheese?" Logan asked.

Ellie nodded. "Your mama's recipe. It's by Justin's request. But don't you worry, I've made a roasted pork and sweet potato pie, too."

"Hey, I love your mac and cheese, Ellie," Logan said.

"So do I," Luke added. "We haven't had it in a long time."

Justin looked Kat's way and explained, "It's gourmet mac and cheese. I can pretty much guarantee you've never tasted anything better. I think the boy will like it, too."

"He usually eats mac and cheese out of a box," Kat said softly, "but I'm sure he'll love it."

Kat wondered how much the housekeeper knew about Connor. Justin's expression didn't give anything away as he rose to his feet and offered her his hand. She took it, whispering, "Connor will make a mess in the dining room. Good dishes? I hope they're not heirlooms."

"There's a new high chair waiting for him in there. He'll be fine. And there's nothing in this house he can break that's worth more than me having him here with all of us."

She understood. The Slades were rich. Items could be replaced easily. Connor couldn't do anything wrong at this point. Kat held her thoughts close as she scooped Connor up and carried him into the dining room with Justin at her side.

"Of course, you and Connor are invited to our wedding," Sophia said, three minutes into the meal. "Logan and I would love to have you join us."

Kat looked up from her plate. Struggling to keep her composure, she had to think fast. Unfortunately, she'd lost some of her moxie when motherhood came along. "Oh…I, uh."

Seated next to her, Justin nodded. "Of course. I want Connor at the wedding."

"It's next week," Sophia said. "On Saturday in Reno. Justin is the best man."

"I don't think…it's…a good idea."

She sent Justin a pleading look. He had to know how it would look if she attended the wedding on his arm. "It's not because we don't want to, but, well, with the situation with Mattie and all, it'd be hard to explain our presence."

"Justin's explained it all to us," Audrey said quietly. "And personally, I think it's wonderful how loyal you are to her. It's a tough situation, but we all have agreed to keep the secret."

"Yes," Sophia added, "we know the woman's health might be jeopardized. We'll be careful."

Justin stiffened. On a heavy sigh, he reached for her hand under the table and gave it a gentle squeeze, letting her know he had more to say on the subject. "We'll talk about it later, after dinner."

As he let her go, he pushed the material of her skirt away to give her thigh a gentle, sensual stroke. Her eyes rounded in shock, as his hand skimmed over her sensitive skin and glided farther up her leg. She squirmed in her seat, praying that no one noticed. "O-kay."

She turned her attention toward Connor, who had been

a perfect angel sitting in his new high chair gnawing on the giraffe teether. "Want to try the mac and cheese, sweet boy?"

He let the giraffe fall from his mouth, his eyes trained on the food. "Oh, that means that you do, don't you?"

Kat lifted the spoon to his lips and he gobbled down the cut-up morsels of mac and cheese and mashed sweet potato. Justin's gaze never left him and Kat got a sinking feeling in the pit of her stomach.

For better or worse, through Connor, she would be tied to Justin Slade for the rest of her life.

With his belly full and after all the attention from the Slades, Connor conked out in Kat's arms right after the meal.

Justin walked her to a guest room in the spacious estate and busied himself making up a little bed for him on the floor with blankets and a paisley blue-and-gray quilt.

"That's fine," she whispered. "He'll be comfy here."

She kneeled and laid him down carefully. As he nestled in, he automatically rolled onto his side. Then she folded the quilt so that it covered him up to the waist and bent low to brush a kiss over his cheek.

"You sure he can't sleep on the bed?" Justin asked quietly.

"I'm sure. He might roll off it in his sleep."

Fear entered Justin's eyes. His Adam's apple bobbed up and down when he took a big swallow. "I guess I should know things like that."

He got down on his knees and cradled the back of Connor's head in his hand, ever so gently, wisps of the baby's hair filtering through Justin's fingertips. With obvious love shining in his eyes, Justin's gaze stayed on Connor a long time, and a pang of guilt wedged its way into Kay's mind, making her question her decisions.

Justin rose and walked over to the queen bed, leaving Kat to follow. His gaze flowed over the room, with its wooden shutters instead of curtains, hardwood flooring and dark walnut furniture. It spelled out masculine without going overboard. In a lowered voice, he said, "This will be Connor's room. I'll have the room decorated any way you like. You just tell me what he needs. The bed is yours, too, for those times that Connor stays overnight."

Immediately struck by Justin's assumptions, Kat put up a hand to stop him. "Whoa, Justin. You're getting way ahead of me here." She kept her voice low enough not to wake her sleeping baby.

"I'm not ahead of you. I'm behind. By about eleven months."

Wow, she'd walked right into that one. While Justin had deceived her, he wasn't about to let her forget what he'd missed in not knowing Connor. She could understand his impatience to create a bond with his son, yet she struggled with how to make all of this work. "I can't guarantee that Connor's going to spend a lot of time here. As for me…" Her traitorous eyes darted to the bed.

Justin must've seen something in her moment of hesitation. A glint entered his eyes.

"Never mind," she said.

"Can we leave him for a few minutes?" he whispered. "We need to talk and I don't want to risk waking him."

Kat glanced at her baby sleeping cozily on the bank of blankets. Then she picked up pillows from the bed and secured them around Connor's precious little body, creating a barrier of protection for him. "He should be fine now. He's a sound sleeper."

Justin clasped her hand. "My room's next door. If he cries, we'll hear him."

Kat let him lead her to the next room. She was immediately struck by the boyish theme of this former soldier's bedroom. Old computers, stacks of videos and sports trophies littered the room in a homey, lived-in way. She pictured what life was like for Justin Slade growing up here on Sunset Ranch. Envy stabbed at the hollow places in her heart. Justin could give Connor this. Justin could provide a better life for Connor than she could.

"Have a seat, Kat." His voice was soothing as he gestured toward his bed.

She took a seat and he settled down beside her in the middle of the bed. The subtle hint of lime cologne sweetened her senses and drew her to him. His nearness was a force she couldn't combat. Why did Justin Slade have this effect on her? She rebelled against the endorphins racing through her body.

Right now, Justin held all the cards. He had legal rights to her son. With one word, he could injure Mattie and make her whole world come crashing down around her.

Her thoughts scattered as soon as he spoke. "I want to know my son. That's a given. I won't tell anyone else about him, you have my word. And my family will do the same, but I do want a few things. Connor will have a place here on Sunset Ranch. Secondly, I really do want him at my brother's wedding. He's missed out on so much family time already."

Kat immediately saw the problems in that. "It won't be easy. What will I say to people?"

"I'll introduce you as a family friend. You don't have to explain yourself. And if some nosey person asks, you'll stick to the story you've been telling all along."

Kat took a sharp breath. "You may not believe this, but I don't like lying, and when I came to Silver Springs I believed all those things to be true."

"I know you did. We'll work through this, Kat. We have to for Aunt Mattie's sake, right?"

Kat nodded slowly. What choice did she have? She

struggled with the situation, wanting to do what was right by giving Justin the time he craved with his son. Going to the wedding was just the beginning of the concessions she'd have to make.

"Listen, I know nothing about this is easy," he said. "I'm asking you to come to Logan and Sophia's wedding with me. We'll stay overnight in Reno. You'll have your own room, don't worry."

"I sure will have my own room," she said, her voice curt to her own ears.

"So then you'll go?"

She shrugged. She didn't want to go. She didn't want to be placed in this position, but she saw no way out. "I'll go. I just have to figure out what to tell Aunt Mattie."

He gave her a nod and then his lips curled into a big warm smile. It was devastating—and so appealing—when he let down his guard like that. "Then it's settled. I'll get back to you with the details. But I do have one more request. I want to hire you to work with me."

"What?" Kat blinked several times. "Why? I don't know anything about developing a retreat for soldiers or horses."

"Ah, but you know about design and decorating. I promised Mattie to refurbish the house and I need help. That's where you come in. I don't know anything about style, color schemes, appliances and flooring. That's not my thing. But apparently it's yours. And there's no denying that you put yourself together pretty well. You've got style."

Heat bubbled up at the way his gaze softened and traveled over her body. He took in her clothes, but it felt more like he was remembering her naked. She thought back to when he'd touched her under the table tonight. She'd nearly melted. He had good hands and he knew what to do with them. If she wasn't careful she could get suckered in and fall for the guy in a big way. "Why hire me? You know I'd do it for free."

"I don't know that. There's very little I really know about you. Once the ball gets rolling, it's going to get very hectic and chaotic, very fast. I'll need a commitment and I'd rather hire someone that Mattie trusts than a complete stranger."

She began nodding. "Okay…I'll do it. For Aunt Mattie. And to prove to you that I'm not going anyplace anytime soon."

Justin blinked. "I never said that you were."

Kat raised her chin. "But that's part of the reason. You want me invested in a project as insurance that I won't pick up and leave town. Admit it."

Justin's lips thinned to a fine line and his gaze shifted away. He was battling with something, and more than a few seconds passed before he said, "Maybe I want to work with you for selfish reasons."

"Like what?"

"Like this." He wrapped his arms around her waist and drew her tight against his chest.

Heat flamed between their bodies. Her nipples pebbled and she willed the sensual sensation away. Justin drew a sharp breath and tugged her into his lap. Her skirt slid up her thighs, baring her legs to his gaze. The force between them pulled at her. It had been this way in New York, too. She'd been hopelessly drawn to him, even though he'd been all wrong for her. She still couldn't keep her distance, when it was more important than ever.

His hot palms caressed her thighs with sure and bold strokes. His gaze fastened on her mouth, and everything below her waist ignited. She bit back a curse at her own weakness, at the way Justin only had to look at her with desire before she caved to his caresses.

One hand left her thigh to move to the underside of her breast. His fingers teased and touched there, making her nipples pucker more and her belly squirm with desperate need. But he didn't stop there. He moved to the side of her throat, the tips of his fingers barely whispering over her. Goose bumps broke out on her neck and she shivered with anticipation of more touching, more temptation. Then he sank his hand into her hair and drew her head down to his lips. "No more teasing, sugar," he said right before his lips came over hers in a kiss that tasted like rich, heady wine.

Kat's breath caught. Heat flooded through her body and her skin tingled. Justin was giving her unbelievable pleasure. He smelled lime-fresh, but like the earth, too, his masculine scent bringing overwhelming memories to the front of her mind. "Straddle me, Kat," he whispered over her lips. "I'm gonna touch you."

Kat obeyed his command. She wrapped her legs around his waist and a groan came from deep in his throat. He plunged his tongue into her mouth, his teeth scraping with hers as he sought to go deeper and deeper. She was pliant, moving with him now, allowing him to pleasure her without question.

There were no thoughts beside the present—what was happening to her now and the growing need building up inside her. When his hand rode up her thigh this time, she welcomed him with a moan and an arch of her back. He shoved aside her panties and his thumb stroked over the sensitive folds of her womanhood. Her moan grew louder, still within the whispers of the night and darkness surrounding them.

She was vulnerable to him, in this position, allowing him to do what he would to her. But she trusted in him, trusted that he only sought to please her. He kissed her over and over as his fingers played a tune of their own on her body, slipping in and out of her womanhood, until she wanted to scream her joy. It was unbelievable. She rocked with him as he stroked her again and again, swaying with him and uttering low unintelligible things.

Justin's eyes widened with pleasure just as she closed her own. Her body pulsed, straining with release that was so needed, so necessary to her life, that she wanted to cry tears of joy and relief when it was all over.

Justin slipped his hand out from under her panties, straightened out her skirt then brought his lips to hers one more time, murmuring, "I've dreamed of doing this to you a thousand times in Afghanistan."

Sated, Kat swallowed the lump in her throat. She'd dreamed of him, too. But she never thought she'd ever be with him like this again. "Justin…"

She had no words and he seemed to understand.

He lowered her down on the bed and held her tightly in his arms. She saw his need, the strength of will he mustered to contain his lust.

Turning his body, he took her face into his hands. "This is how it is between us."

She searched his eyes for more, to find some hope. Something to show that he trusted her, something to show that she could trust him. There were lies between them, and a son and an old woman neither of them wanted to hurt.

"I'm not going to run out on Mattie…or on…you."

"Connor will be part of my life, Kat." Her heart tripped seeing such love in his eyes. She understood that love. The boy was the best thing about herself. "If I'm at all wary and cautious, it's because I'm not taking any chances when it comes to Connor."

Kat thought about that a few seconds. "I understand, and in a weird sort of way, I'm relieved that you feel protective about him. He deserves…"

"The best from both of us."

She stared at the deep emotions displayed in Justin's eyes and heard the little catch in his throat when he spoke Connor's name.

"Yes," she whispered. Then her gaze skimmed over Justin's taut, rigid body. He had yet to find any release or relief. With Connor sleeping in the room next door and the family still in the house, making love wasn't an option. Not that Kat was ready for that. The physical side of lovemaking wasn't the issue, but all the implications and complications that would follow would be too much for her right now. "Are you going to be okay?"

One corner of his mouth lifted in a smile as he gazed at the ceiling. "I learned a lot about self-discipline in the marines. They put us through mind-blowing tests of will. Lying here with you, on this bed, and not losing my head puts me at Level Four."

Kat couldn't keep her lips from curling up. "I take it that's bad?"

"It's no walk in the park."

"How far do the levels go?"

"Five."

"What would that be?"

"That would be if you stripped me naked and touched me in places that needed touching."

"And you couldn't respond?"

"Oh, I'd respond. There would be no stopping that, but I wouldn't be allowed to touch you back."

Kat thought that sounded intriguing. And sexy.

"You're a Level Five if I ever saw one," Justin whispered in a gentle caress.

He brought his hand to her hair and played with the tendrils, watching them slide through his fingers. Air filled his lungs and he gave her one last piercing look, then rose from the bed. Leaning close, he spoke in a tortured voice. "I've got to get out of here. Why don't you check in on the baby. The family will want to say good-night to both of you and then I'll follow you home."

She opened her mouth to protest. She didn't need a

chaperone, but Justin gave a firm shake of his head, declaring his intentions nonnegotiable.

She clamped off her words of refusal and nodded.

Some battles she was better off not fighting.

The next morning, Kat rose earlier than usual and checked on Connor, who was still sleeping in his crib. Then she peeked into Mattie's room. She was sitting up in her bed, reading her bible. "Morning, Kat."

"How are you feeling this morning?"

The older woman peered over her eyeglasses and gave a watery smile. "Excellent…I'm a new woman."

It was the same response she'd given Mattie for the past two months. "I'm glad you're feeling well. What would you like for breakfast?"

Mattie's lips twisted. "Well, since I can't have ham and eggs with biscuits and gravy, I guess I'll settle for one of those vegetarian sausage patties." She made a face. "Never heard of a hog farmer not being able to eat the hog."

"You don't have hogs anymore," Kat said with a smile. "And the doctor says those veggie sausages are good for you."

"I know, but my Ralph is turning over in his grave right about now."

Kat laughed. Dear old Aunt Mattie was no wilting flower. She had a lot of pep in her still.

"I'll get our breakfast…I'm feeling up to cooking this morning," Mattie continued. "I bet you've got some work to do today. You go on and do what you have to, I'll holler if I need help."

"Okay, thanks, Aunt Mattie. I'm working on a new design for a little boy's Christmas suit."

"Oh, that sounds lovely." Aunt Mattie closed her bible, removed her eyeglasses and folded herself out of bed.

Reaching for a terry-cloth robe lying across her bed, she put her arms through the sleeves and tied the belt.

"I've got some news," Kat said, lingering in the door-way.

"Did you get another rejection from those fool buyers?"

Kat had been receiving letters, almost weekly, reject-ing her line of affordable baby clothing from major de-partment stores. Those rejections were a big letdown. She believed in her work and knew it would be a hit judging by the success of her growing sales on the Babylicious web-site. She just needed a chance, yet her dream of becoming a professional fashion designer kept eluding her. "No, but I was offered a job from Justin Slade. He wants to pay me to refurbish the house."

"Oh?"

"He says he has to pay someone anyway and it would make your life easier if I did it. He wouldn't have to bring a designer into the house. We could work together, Aunt Mattie. We'll fix this place up and make it shine. What do you think? Want me to do it?"

"Well, sure...of course. Nobody knows me or this place better than you. You'll do a bang-up job." Aunt Mattie's expression grew serious. "But that's a lot to ask of you, isn't it? You're already so busy."

Kat shrugged. "Not really. I work on the designs, be-cause I love to do it and I'm selling a little here and there, but that only takes a few hours in the evenings. This we can do together, and we'll work around Connor's schedule."

Aunt Mattie tilted her head slightly to one side. "It's what they call multitasking, isn't it? Back in our day, it was simply called chores. Doing what needed to get done, and if that meant fourteen-hour days, we did it."

Kat laughed. "You're right. The label is different, but it's the same thing."

"Well, all right, then."

A loud ruckus from outside the yard filtered into the house and Kat walked over to the parlor window. "What on earth?"

"Oh, it's the bulldozer," Aunt Mattie said, approaching the window. "The sale hasn't gone through yet, but I figured it was okay to let Justin start up the work. That boy is in a hurry to get things done before the cold weather sets in. Tractors are going to clear the acres beyond the house and the bulldozer's going to knock down the rotted barns and feed shacks on the grounds." Mattie's eyes sparkled with curiosity. "I'm surprised Justin didn't tell you, being that you saw him last night."

Kat immediately balked. "It wasn't a date or anything. We talked and he offered me the job."

Aunt Mattie gave a quick nod of her head. "Nice boy, that Justin."

"The Slades also invited Connor and I to Logan Slade's wedding. It was a very generous offer and all, but I don't want to go."

"I bet Justin wants you to go. He did the asking, didn't he?"

"Actually, no. Logan's fiancée, Sophia, did. I think they were just being nice."

Aunt Mattie's eyes narrowed in on her. "You don't want to go, or you don't want to leave me alone?"

Kat focused on the banged-up canary-yellow bulldozer rolling past the house. Two tractors followed behind. "Both. I'd have to spend the night in a hotel."

"Well, shoot, Kat. If you're invited to a fancy shindig with a good-looking man and asked to stay in a nice hotel, you're gonna do it. You know I don't want to stop you from living your life."

"You're not, Aunt Mattie." She turned her attention away from the bulldozer to look into her eyes. "You're not stopping me from anything."

"You know Ralph's sister Maisey's been wanting to come for a visit. You just tell me the date and I'll have Maisey come by and stay with me. You'll have time all to yourself."

"But the wedding's this Saturday. That's not much notice to make arrangements."

"Why, that's almost a week away. Maisey's got nothing on her dance card. She's a widow, just like me. I'm sure she'll come. You go on now. Accept that invitation. You deserve a little break from tending to me."

The bulldozer crawled past the house. Justin moved fast when he wanted something. The way he was stepping up the time frame for the retreat was just another reminder that she had to be on her toes around him.

He'd boxed her into a corner with this wedding invitation. Justin wanted Connor there. With Connor, he also got Kat. And now Aunt Mattie wasn't giving her a way to refuse the invitation.

Kat had no choice. She would go to Sophia and Logan's wedding and Connor would get to know his relatives a little better. She shuddered at the thought. Justin's prank, switching places with Brett and deceiving her, was a constant reminder not to believe in anyone but herself. Now Justin was asking her to trust him and his family to keep their secret.

How could she trust in anything, when she'd been let down so many times in the past?

She gazed into Aunt Mattie's aged blue eyes. "Go ahead and call Maisey."

"So then, you'll go?"

Kat let a sigh escape her throat. "I'll go."

Aunt Mattie reached out and clasped her hand. Her thin fingers gave a little encouraging squeeze. "I'm glad. You'll have fun."

Aunt Mattie's generosity only made Kat feel guilty

about everything. She was the one person she didn't want to lie to and yet the lie about Connor's paternity was the biggest lie of all.

Six

It figured the wedding was at a Golden Hotel.

Kat couldn't catch a break. The knot inside her belly twisted another turn when Justin made that announcement on the drive up to Reno. Logan wanted the very best for Sophia, to make up for all the grief he'd caused her in the past. And Golden Hotels, renowned for impeccable service, elegantly decorated rooms and culinary excellence, were at the top of the hotel food chain. The family-run hotels were located in every major American city from New York to Los Angeles. Kat was a walking encyclopedia on the subject.

She took a swallow and trembled.

"Come here, little man," Justin said, removing Connor from the car seat and securing him in one arm.

The valet helped Kat out of the front seat and took care of their luggage.

She kept the diaper bag and hung it over her shoulder. Connor gazed up at Justin with curiosity, and Kat smiled, her heart pounding in her chest as they entered the hotel together.

Check-in was quick. Justin had reserved adjoining suites that required taking a special elevator up to the fourteenth floor. As they approached her suite, Justin slid the plastic key card over the brass door plate. A light flashed green, the lock clicked open and he pulled the handle down to let them in. "After you," he said to Kat. "I think you'll like your room."

She took a few steps inside. "It's...beautiful." And it was. She knew the decorator, Amando Guerrero. They'd had lunch several times in New York. He was a man with an eye for location. A Reno hotel would have all the same Golden amenities, but would also include subtle changes that emphasized the feel of the West. Remington statues of cowboys astride horses, artful rustic trim and patterns that depicted Nevada history gave the entire hotel tasteful ambience.

Justin scanned the suite with a satisfied glance and nodded. He was more interested in the little guy in his arms. But Connor began squirming and reaching for her and Justin didn't push it. He handed Connor over. "He wants his mommy."

Connor hugged her neck tight and then turned, giving Justin his stink face, which consisted of narrowing his eyes and pursing his rosy lips. Kat chuckled.

Justin made a similar face back at him. "Hey, buddy. You don't know it yet, but I'm your best friend."

Connor whipped back around in her arms. She'd assured Justin several times in the past that Connor needed time to warm up to him. It would happen in time, so she kept her lips clamped this time. She could tell Justin was impatient to have his son's affection. He wanted Connor's acceptance and love...*now*.

Kat walked to the rectangular bay window that overlooked the Reno landscape. It wasn't New York with its towering buildings and mere slices of sky above. It was Nevada, sparse and dry, with rambling blue clouds visible for miles—white puffs that you could almost reach out and touch.

"Your luggage and baby gear should arrive shortly."

"We'll be fine."

"Do you think he'll nap?"

She glanced at the parlor sofa and then beyond to two French doors opening to a large bedroom. "Maybe. I'll give him a snack and a bottle and see if I can get him down."

"Okay, good. If you'll be needing anything, I'm in the next suite. Just knock on the adjoining door. I've got to clean up and get ready for a quick walk-through rehearsal downstairs. I'll be back for you in two hours."

She kissed the top of the baby's head and nodded.

Justin focused on where her lips had just touched Connor's baby-fine brown hair and smiled. He strode over to them and took the baby's cheek in his palm, his eyes filled with longing as Connor looked at him. With the pad of his thumb he stroked the baby's cheek. "It's pretty amazing, isn't it?"

Kat knew what he meant. One glimpse at her big-eyed, dark-haired little son was enough to make her believe in miracles. He was the only thing beautiful about her world. "It is," she said quietly.

Justin dropped his hand before the baby had a chance to turn away and focused his attention on her now. He cast soft caring eyes her way. "I'm glad he's here today."

She was reduced to mush when he turned on the charm. And she almost forgot how uncomfortable she was being here. But there was too much at stake. Too much to lose. She'd known hardship in her life and she'd known powerful men. Justin could hand her a world of hurt if he wanted to make her life difficult. She felt compelled to cooperate and attend this wedding but she wasn't fooled into thinking Justin cared about her. He was trying to make up for lost time with his son. He blamed her for missing out on the first year of Connor's life.

But he wasn't blameless, either.

She found no need to rehash all that.

"We'll be ready."

* * *

It was trickier than she thought getting them both dressed and ready for a wedding. She didn't know how long the little guy would hold up at the reception, although she had managed to get him down for a thirty-minute nap in a crib that was set up by the hotel staff. She'd brought along his monkey sheets, just in case, and Connor felt right at home when she'd laid him down on his own bedding. Room service had arrived shortly after with an array of lunch entrees that Justin had ordered.

The penniless soldier she'd met had turned into a man of privilege.

Odd how life sometimes turned out.

She dipped the mascara wand into the tube and gave her eyelashes one final upward stroke. "There," she said to the baby. "A diaper change for you and we're all set."

He watched her from a standing position in the crib, his head barely peeking over the slats. Dressed in a navy-blue suit with a miniature bow tie and hat, her little man was ready to attend his first wedding.

A light tapping on the door came five minutes early. Not a slow learner, Justin was already discovering the intricacies of fatherhood by deliberately knocking quietly in case the baby was sleeping. "That's your daddy," she whispered to Connor, leaving him in his crib to walk over and open the door.

Justin stood at the threshold in a charcoal suit, brocade vest and black tie, hat in hand. He made her palms sweat when he gave her a low whistle of approval.

"You're a little early."

He didn't wait for an invitation, but strolled in and walked right past her. "Looks to me like you're ready. You sure couldn't get any more gorgeous."

Her face flushed with heat. She closed the door and stared at it, taking a steadying breath. When she turned around, she found his eyes fastened on her. "You look nice, too."

"Isn't every day I stand up for my brother."

"It is a special day."

Another flick of his eyes told her he approved of her dress. Pride swelled in her chest. She'd designed it herself, with her bust size and curves in mind. Too tight, and she looked trashy. Too loose, and it was frump city. Kat's one-of-a-kind dress was deep violet with a high rounded sheer neckline, a lacy overlay and a scalloped hemline. The dress dipped low enough in the back to be provocative but not too dangerous. Petite rhinestone chandelier earrings and four-inch open-toed satin pumps finished off the look.

Connor uttered his baby sounds and Justin's gaze strayed to the crib. *Thank goodness.*

"I'll get him," she said, scurrying past Justin to the crib set up just inside her bedroom. "He needs a diaper change."

"Gawd, he looks cute," Justin said, walking over. The awe in his voice was another source of pride for Kat.

"I know, doesn't he?"

"Where'd he get that outfit? He looks like—"

"A little prince?" Kat asked.

"I was gonna say, a little dude. He just needs a miniature Stetson."

Kat smiled. "I'll be sure to remember that next time."

Justin eyes lifted to her. "You made that suit?"

Kat nodded. "I did. It's part of my line of baby clothes, but I made this one a bit more special since Connor was wearing it to his…his uncle's wedding."

Justin's expression didn't change, only now his awe was directed at her. "Talented."

"Thank you."

She made quick work of changing the baby's diaper while Justin looked on. Kat's stomach began to ache when they left and took the elevator down to the lobby. They exited the building through automatic doors that led to a private outdoor garden where the wedding would take place.

Trees and greenery draped with twinkle lights created a natural perimeter for the garden. Stone steps separated by patches of groomed green grass led to the raised altar. Sweet William adorned the archway over the altar and dozens of small candelabra twinkled alongside the adjoining wooden beams. As they approached, she noticed rows upon rows of Chiavari chairs lined up. And a lot of people milling around. Before they fully entered the garden, Kat stopped and put a hand on Justin's arm. "How many people are invited?"

Justin pursed his lips. "Does it matter?"

"Two hundred?" she guessed.

Justin shrugged.

"More?"

"Two hundred and fifty, give or take. Are you nervous?"

"Only about lying. People are going to look at the three of us and assume…"

"The truth?"

Kat squeezed her eyes closed. "No one could ever possibly guess the full truth. It's too bizarre."

"If it were up to me, and Mattie wouldn't get hurt, I'd tell the entire world about my boy."

His proprietary tone didn't help matters.

"You promised," she reminded him.

"I know what I said. I won't break that promise," he said quietly to reassure her. "So don't you worry. We'll stick to our story for now. It's believable enough."

It was about all she could do. And it only took two minutes before she had to put his theory to the test when a hulk of a man walked over to greet them. He took Justin's hand and pumped hard, giving Justin a quick look before staring at Kat and Connor. She tamped down her initial panic. She used to be a better liar, but somewhere along the line,

Kat had grown to hate lies and liars. Circumstances being what they were, Kat had no choice right now.

"Katherine, this is Sheriff Robbie Dunphy. You get outta line in Douglas County and Robbie here knows all about it."

She smiled. "Well, then I'd better be careful."

"Pleased to meet you, ma'am." He removed his hat and took her hand, giving it a surprisingly gentle shake before glancing at Connor. "And who's this cute little tyke?"

"This is my son, Connor," Kat said. "It's his first wedding."

"He looks like a well-behaved boy."

Kat grinned. "Thanks, but tell me that *after* the ceremony. I might have to dash out if he fusses."

"Aw, I'm sure he'll do fine."

Awkward silence ensued and just as the sheriff was about to ask Kat a question, Justin distracted him with talk of Douglas County politics. Connor began squirming in her arms and Kat focused her attention on him, only hearing snippets of the sheriff urging Justin to enter into the fray. Justin in politics? Of course, he was viewed as a hero and would win hearts and minds, but Kat couldn't quite put that square peg into the round hole. The man she was beginning to know wasn't cut out for the political arena.

A few more men approached Justin and the sheriff. There was a good deal of hand shaking and backslapping. Curious eyes drifted her way and Justin smoothly introduced her as a good friend of the Slade family.

An older gentleman with a handlebar moustache and gentle eyes put his hand on Justin's shoulder. "The parade is set to go as scheduled. Three weeks from today."

Justin looked like he wanted to jump out of his own skin, but simply smiled and nodded. As the circle around Justin grew larger, Kat felt someone touch her arm. She swiveled her head and was relieved to see Audrey beside her. Luke's new fiancée stared straight into her eyes and spoke slowly. "There's a little fishpond over behind the altar I think Connor would like to see."

Kat wasn't slow on the uptake. She thanked heaven for astute women like Audrey Thomas. "Connor would *love* to see the fish."

Audrey's blue eyes lit, silently saying *save succeeded* with her grin. "I thought so. Follow me."

Kat excused herself and strolled away from Justin's entourage, arm in arm with Audrey.

"Thank you," Kat said a few seconds later. "I owe you. You look fabulous, by the way."

"You think so? Sophia asked me to be in the wedding a few days ago and we picked out this dress. I look a little lumpy in it, don't I?"

Kat chuckled. "I remember feeling that way when I was pregnant, too. But actually, the empire fit is perfect for a woman with a baby bump. I love the deep lavender on you." The one-shoulder style gave Audrey a sultry look. "No reason you can't be sexy just because you're pregnant. Remember *bump,* not *lump,* and you'll be fine."

"Okay, got it. Do you think your little man will give me a dance later?"

"I'm sure he will. He loves music."

As they approached the tropical fishpond, Kat made one mistake. She swung her head around at the last minute to find Justin still encircled by the group, his focus fastened right on her and Connor, his incredible dark eyes filled with wishful longing.

Something squeezed tight in her heart.

She wished Justin could join them.

And she felt a twinge of guilt in abandoning him.

How crazy was that?

In a wedding gown of ivory satin with a sweetheart neckline and subtle folds cascading to the floor, Sophia made a stunning bride standing beside Logan. His eyes beamed with adoration for his soon-to-be wife. Justin and Luke stood beside him a few feet away. Little Edward Branford, a sweet boy who lived on the ranch with his grandma Connie, Sunset Lodge's head chef, balanced a ring bearer's pillow on the steps of the altar. Audrey was standing at the altar next to Sophia, and Kat thought she looked great, like a budding flower ready to blossom.

With Connor on her lap, she sat in the second row near the far aisle, just in case. It wouldn't be hard to make a clean getaway if Connor got loud or fidgety. But luckily her son was still captivated by the fishpond from minutes ago and was on his best behavior.

Tears filled her eyes when Logan spoke his vows. His devotion to his soon-to-be bride touched the very core of her. Kat didn't know too many people who were so desperately in love like Logan and Sophia. Or like Luke and Audrey for that matter.

Audrey and Luke had invited her to their courthouse wedding next month. It would be more of the same on a less grand scale. She couldn't refuse Audrey. She'd been a friend and an understanding presence when Kat needed her.

The Slade family stuck together. They were devoted to each other. Even some of their employees, like Ward Halliday, Sunset Ranch's head wrangler, and Constance Branford, the lodge's executive chef, were close-knit with the Slades.

Kat wasn't used to being surrounded by loved ones like this. Instead of family dinners and gatherings, she and her mother had spent their days trying to elude her father and his unholy harsh hand.

Sometimes Kat felt phantom pain on her cheeks where her father had struck so often. Sometimes Kat would dream of standing up to him when he'd vented his rage on her mother. Sometimes Kat wished her father had died twenty years ago, instead of two, and she wondered if that made her a horrible person.

Connor wrapped his little arms around her neck and laid his head on her shoulder. "That's my sweet baby," she whispered into his ear as she began to gently rock him. He tightened his grip on her and it was the best feeling in the world.

She'd never once regretted her pregnancy. She'd never once wished anything but good things for her son. He was her glue. He kept things in perspective. There wasn't anything she wouldn't do for him.

Sometimes that devotion got her into trouble.

She lifted her lashes at that moment and found Justin's eyes on her, the hard lines of his mouth softening just a bit.

She tilted her head and regarded him. It wasn't difficult to react to Justin. He swept her in with a magnetic force that she couldn't quite explain. She sensed he was more than a military hero, a man everyone wanted a piece of, a man hell-bent on doing right by Brett Applegate. At times a haunted look took over his expression. At times, he seemed distant and wary and Kat wasn't naive enough to think he'd had it easy overseas. On the drive up here, Justin had retreated into himself. She'd see him shake off a thought as if it tortured him. She'd wondered what he was remembering. Or what he was trying to forget.

He was a complicated man, who could complicate her life.

And he wanted Connor.

She fought off a wave of panic and focused on the vows being spoken. Minutes later, with love shining in their eyes, Logan and Sophia said "I do" to each other and the marriage ceremony concluded with a flourish of applause and a few hoots and hollers. The newlyweds marched arm in arm down the steps, sweeping past her, their smiles beaming from ear to ear.

Kat joined in the applause as tears welled in her eyes. She always got a little sappy at weddings. Images flashed in her head of when she was in the throes of despair, sleeping under a rickety roof at a women's shelter, wearing threadbare clothes, her mother's arms firmly around her. Kat would dream of her wedding day. She'd think of the handsomest boy at her school and pretend he was her fiancé. She'd wear a Cinderella dress of frothy lace—the design stayed in her mind even to this day—and she would be smiling. It was all pretend, a fantasy she knew, by the light of day, would never come true.

She banked her sentimental urges, burying them away for now. She vowed to never forget the hard times, but to never dwell on them either if she could help it.

Clasping Connor's hands in hers, she encouraged him to clap. He took his cue and put his palms together at an angle, his chubby fingers spread wide, and began to clap along with the other guests. "That's it, sweetheart," she said.

He bounced happily in her lap, eager to show off his talent and turned to her with a big four-tooth smile.

Her heart exploded with pride. She snuggled him close, kissing the top of his head. "You're such a good clapper, baby boy."

Lost in the moment, she slowly lifted her lashes to find Justin standing in front of her, watching them. Fatherly pride filled his eyes, a dead giveaway to anyone paying attention, but luckily, the guests were filing out of the garden, one row at a time behind the wedding party, and no one noticed Justin's display. Or that Justin had taken a detour to come get them.

She understood his adoring look, as dangerous as it

might be, because her love for Connor was so intense, she couldn't imagine anyone not loving this sweet little boy.

Kat stared at Justin and for a second forgot all about the predicament she was in.

"Ready to go inside?" he asked, offering his hand.

The sun took its final bow on the horizon, casting the garden in a soft crimson glow. It was peaceful and quiet now. She could sit out here all evening and watch the candles flicker. "Sure. We'll go in now."

"That's good, because my brother will never let me live it down if I neglect my best man duties."

She smiled and took his hand. His touch brought immediate warmth. "I wouldn't want you to disappoint Logan."

"I was talking about Luke. You know, the old favorite-brother thing." His wide grin and the firm grasp on her hand, shot her blood pressure up. "He'd never let me live it down."

Joking about sibling rivalry seemed so normal to the Slades.

Justin put his arm around her waist and they walked back into the hotel where the elaborate reception was just beginning.

There was no doubt in Justin's mind that he was dancing with the most beautiful woman in the room. There was also no doubt that he was going to make love to Kat tonight.

"He's fine with Audrey," he whispered for her ears only. Kat's mothering instincts kicked in as soon as he'd taken her onto the dance floor. She kept looking over his shoulder, swiveling her head to find the little guy.

"I know he's fine. It's just that, I'm…"

"Paranoid?"

She gathered her brows. "Cautious…with him."

His brothers had danced with Kat already, so he figured one turn around the dance floor with her wasn't out of line. Hell, he'd watched her dance with a few other men and it had been hard to take. He would've thought the baby would be a deterrent instead of a magnet.

Yet baby or no baby, Kat was hot. She was unique. She had a curvy body that could destroy lesser men.

"My family wouldn't let anything happen to him," he assured her.

He drew Kat an inch closer. It was hard to keep a proper distance from her, when all he wanted to do was feel every soft morsel of her skin against his, to run his hands up and down her arms and bring her close enough to sniff her platinum hair and breathe in her female scent. But she'd set limits when he'd asked her to dance. Katherine Grady and Justin Slade were just supposed to be family friends.

God, he hated the lies. The pretense. He hated not being able to claim Connor as his son.

"I know your family is good with him, Justin. But it's been just me and him…and I'm…I'm overprotective."

Justin let that comment go. She was a good mother. He liked that about her. But he wanted more from Kat tonight than arguments or explanations.

"Are you having a good time?" he asked.

A hum purred from her throat. His groin tightened from the breathy sound. "I haven't danced in a long time."

"You're a pretty good dancer, keeping up with my two left feet."

Her eyes went dewy soft. "You're not so bad."

He wanted to tuck her in close and hold her to his chest. "This isn't easy."

She snapped her head back and looked injured. "Dancing with me?"

Gently tugging her half an inch closer, he spoke with a rasp in his voice. "Not being able to pull you into my arms and slow dance with you the way I want to."

Her body trembled and he was glad he wasn't the only one feeling tense. "Oh."

He took a step back and then twirled her around in a smooth exchange of places in rhythm to the music, thanking high heaven he'd learned some basic dance moves from Betsy Ann Stankowski. That girl had given him lessons in more than a few things.

When he took hold of Kat's hands again, he brought her another inch closer. To anyone watching, it was an innocent move and that's the way it had to be for now.

But it was hard. Erotic perfume tickled his nose and he couldn't hold back a quietly executed groan. "You smell so damn good."

"Thank you."

He lowered his arm to her waist and splayed his hand over her back, drawing her a little bit closer into the circle of his arms. His fingers found the exposed part of her back, her skin the softest there, the flesh supple and silky smooth. Her pretty green eyes blazed in question. He answered her with unspoken words in the way he held her, the way he returned her gaze. Everything uniquely female about her pounded into his skull. He wasn't going to be denied tonight, but he was grateful when the music stopped.

"I'd better go," she whispered softly.

He stood still and nodded, releasing his hold on her.

He wasn't a good actor, not even close. Anyone watching him now would guess his intentions from the way he was looking at her. At the moment he didn't give a damn.

She turned from him, hips swaying as she walked off the dance floor. She stopped when she reached Logan and Sophia's sweetheart table where Audrey was standing with the baby. The entire family gathered around Connor, taking turns holding him.

So much for being discreet. Babies attracted attention.

And Connor certainly was doing that, not only with the Slades, but with many of the guests in attendance.

Audrey handed the baby over to Kat and she braced him tight to her chest. Peeking over the baby's shoulder, Kat found Justin again and the sensual glint in her eyes told him what he wanted to know.

A rare kind of emotion poured into his heart.

He glanced at his watch. The best man's speech came next and then a few more wedding day rituals. Logan deserved the happiness he was getting and Justin had every intention of being here for him. Both the bride and groom had waited for him to return home so that he could be a part of the ceremony and celebration, but as soon as the reception was over, Justin wouldn't delay in taking his family back up to the hotel room.

Seven

Standing over the crib in Kat's suite, they watched their son sleep. Justin's warm breath drifted over her throat, sending her mind in a direction it shouldn't be taking. Kat had always imagined being a family like this. As a young girl, she'd clung to her dreams when life pounded her from all sides. When all she had was her mother's distracted love and no real place to call home.

If only the circumstances for the three of them weren't so darn messy.

The wedding had been wonderful, and she was greatly relieved she hadn't been put on the spot. No one had asked her probing questions and she hadn't had to tell any lies. Thank goodness.

"I want to be here when the baby wakes up," Justin said.

Justin's request was reasonable. He'd never been around when Connor awakened; the baby was usually in his best mood at the first light of day, cackling and smiling and affectionate. "Okay, I'll knock on the adjoining door when he—"

Justin grabbed her hand and tugged her out of the room. She let him lead her, though she was a little surprised by his abrupt behavior. He brought her to the parlor just outside the bedroom and pinned her against the wall. He wasn't rough, but he wasn't gentle, either, and her heartbeats sped with delicious anticipation. "I meant, I want to be in bed with you, when the baby wakes up."

Her throat clamped. "Oh," she squeaked. "Do...do I have a choice in this?"

Justin yanked off his tie and unfastened the buttons on his white dress shirt with one hand, while he grasped both of her wrists with the other. He held them high above her head, slamming them up against the wall. A thrill raced through her body as his mouth hovered close to hers. "You always have a choice, sugar."

But then his lips closed over hers and she was completely swept up a bruising kiss that took all choice away. "Yes, yes," she uttered, as he kissed her once more.

Her back arched away from the wall, her body responding to him naturally as she pressed against him. Beautiful desperate groans spilled from his lips and he continued to kiss her. She had an urge to touch him, to rip his clothes off.

He might've read her mind, because in that instant, he yanked his shirt free, shifting to keep her hands pinned above her head. Her body heated like a furnace kicking on full steam. With nearly unquenchable need driving her wild, she moved her hips and bucked toward him. He plunged his tongue into her mouth, leaving her chest heaving, her nipples aching and her legs wobbly.

He was muscled, ripped like a man who'd had to be strong, not for vanity but for survival. She ached to touch him, to weave her fingers through the light cropping of hairs on his chest. To feel his muscles under her fingertips and run her tongue along his belly.

"Easy, sugar, easy," he said, his breaths labored. "Don't rush this."

But Kat needed him. She needed to feel the connection from something deep and lonely inside her. Justin was perfect, probably too good for her, and that made her want him all the more. She was from the gutter. He was bred to be a hero. None of this made sense. Except that the two of them, making love, always made sense.

She didn't have to deal with appearances right now. She could have this one moment, this one ounce of unabashed pleasure. It wasn't as if she and Justin were strangers. They knew each other well, sexually. She wanted him inside her. She wanted the release that came when you placed one hundred percent of your trust in another person. "Touch me, baby. Touch me."

She'd nearly shouted her plea and it surprised her, how desperate she sounded.

Justin broke the kiss, and she whimpered from the loss.

His hand closed over her breast. "Like this?"

Through her clothes, she felt the scorching heat of his palm as he massaged her back and forth. Jolts of electricity traveled with lightning speed through her body. Her nipples puckered in response. "Yes, oh, yes."

He kept her pinned and it frustrated her not to touch him back. Every time she tried to loosen his grip, he tightened his hold on her.

His one hand did enough magic though, as he expertly rubbed the sensitive tips of her breasts. Heat puddled in her belly. Below that, she felt herself go suddenly taut. Tension built to extremes until Kat couldn't comprehend anything but the pleasure that was about to explode inside.

She felt her dress being hiked up, and Justin's fingers finding and caressing her oh-so-sensitive sweet spot.

It was enough to topple her.

Spasms wracked her body, everything went hot and tight. Quick, short gasps spurted from her mouth from the sudden, unexpected release.

It was crazy. It had only taken seconds for Justin to completely arouse her. Still fully clothed, and so surprised, she'd had one of the best orgasms of her life.

Thank you, Justin Slade.

Her eyes slowly opened as she came down to earth. Justin looked on in awe and spoke with reverence. "Amazing."

Somewhere along the line, he'd released her hands and she was now free to touch him, but before she could lay a hand on his chest, she found herself being lifted up and carried away.

She had the good sense to remember Connor. "The baby."

"We'll keep the door between the suites open. We'll hear him if he needs us and we'll check in on him later."

For the first time since she'd met Justin, she didn't mind hearing the "we" in Justin's command. "Okay," she said, leaning her head on his shoulder.

His bedroom was in shadow. Justin loosened his grip on her and she slid down his body, balancing on her high heels once her feet touched the carpeted floor. He took half a step back to look at her. Then she brought her fingertips to his toned, bronze chest.

He trembled from her touch and a fierce possessive gleam sparkled in his eyes. She stroked him more, laying the palm of her hands flat on his chest. He closed his eyes slowly with an expression of pure pleasure. Then she let her hands roam free, touching every cord, every ripple of muscle under his skin. It unnerved her how much she wanted to please him, to hear his soft groans, to see his arousal displayed in the veins popping in his neck and the breadth of his taut body tightening even more.

Then she rose up to run her tongue along the seam of his lips. He took her into his arms and kissed her thoroughly until her limbs went limp. A sexy thought entered her mind and Kat wasn't going to play shy. She whispered her desire over his tempting lips. "I want to touch you, Justin. But you can't touch me back yet."

His eyes narrowed on her cryptically. "You want to torture me?"

A throaty chuckle escaped her throat. She thought of all the reasons she might want to torture him, but that wasn't her intention at the moment. Tonight was about satisfying pleasure. The more she thought about it, the more she wanted Justin at her mercy. With a tilt of her head, she asked, "Would you consider it torture to have me touch you?"

He gave it one second of thought and the hot glint in his eyes told her he was ready for anything she might send his way. He pulled her close and kissed her again, whispering, "Hell yeah, if I couldn't touch you."

"You've already touched me plenty." She'd gone undone in his arms. "I want to reciprocate."

His brows arched. "I'm not gonna refuse an offer like that."

"Are you sure?"

He didn't hesitate to nod and smile. "Do your damage, Kat."

"Okay, then." With a keen sense of triumph, she spun around. "Will you unzip my dress?"

He stepped closer, his breath whispering over her shoulder. He planted tiny kisses there and up the back of her neck. Goose bumps erupted everywhere. "You're touching."

"We haven't started yet."

He eased the zipper down past her waist and his fingertips lingered on the curve of her spine just above her buttocks.

Kat's skin tingled in response. "I see I have a cheater on my hands."

"And they say cheaters never win." His fingers skimmed over the slope of her derriere.

She shuddered in response. "I'll get back at you for that," she said on a stifled breath.

"I'm hoping you do."

A gasp broke from her throat and she whirled around to face him. His eyes devoured her. She'd never seen hunger as strong or powerful before. If she wasn't careful, she'd lose her nerve. "Will you lie down on the bed?"

"What are you going to do?"

"Undress for you."

"I'm there," he said. And he was. In seconds, Justin was sprawled across the king-size bed, waiting for her. Memories rushed forth of making love with Justin before and she knew tonight would be equally satisfying.

She slipped her dress over her hips and gave a wiggle. Violet material pooled at her feet. She took a little step over it. Next came her bra and panties; as she hastily removed them, she suddenly felt less bold than a minute ago when she suggested this. She shot Justin a quick glance. He gave her an encouraging nod, his expression filled with patient, reverent awe.

Oh, how she wanted him.

There was no backing out now anyway. She stood naked in the shadows and came forth into a ray of light slicing through the window.

Justin rolled to his side, braced an elbow on the bed and watched Kat move toward him. If he wasn't so damn turned on, he'd be amused at her sudden shyness as she approached the bed. She was one hundred and fifteen pounds of creamy, smooth-skinned perfection. She had big breasts, a tiny waistline and curvy hips. Her hair was the color of rich French vanilla ice cream and her lips were as juicy as ripe apples.

When she put her knees on the bed, Justin rolled onto his back, giving her room to join him. He put his hands behind his head, lacing his fingers tight. The lady wanted to play this game and he wouldn't deny her.

"Close your eyes," she said as she lay down next to him.

"That's not part of the deal. I like watching you."

"You're going to like what I plan to do even more."

He shut his eyes. Immediately, the mattress dipped a little and he felt her presence. The aura that was Kat, along with her heady perfume, intoxicated him. For a minute, she said nothing. Did nothing. He was about to protest, until she moved a little closer and soft strands of her hair brushed over his face. He breathed in sunshine and freshness. Then her lips covered his.

Her kiss jerked his body to attention.

Instantly, he knew keeping his hands off would surely kill him.

Her slender delicate fingertips grazed over his skin, lightly, gently, and she removed her mouth from his to drizzle dozens of tiny kisses onto his throat. He took a deep swallow and maintained his position. Next she nipped at his earlobe, her teeth nibbling, her breath coming in short bursts as the fingers of one hand probed below his waist.

She worked at his belt buckle and then unzipped his dress pants.

What came next tempted him to reach for her and wind his hand in her hair, but he held firm, keeping both hands behind his head, his fingers entwined.

Kat worked magic on him, her mouth, her tongue making him crazy. He bucked and arched, feeling her hair caress his belly, her soft cheeks brush against his skin. He broke out in a sweat, beads of moisture pooling on his brow, his head thrashing back and forth on the pillow. She made mush of his resolve. He was ready to cave, ready to cry uncle, but he didn't want her brand of punishment to end. It was too good, too damn exciting even if it was killing him at the same time.

He loved the sexual being that she was. He loved that she was uninhibited. Every touch, every damn stroke of her tongue was meant to give them both pleasure. No wonder he hadn't forgotten that one night they'd had together in New York. While his memories of her appearance had begun to fade when he was stationed overseas, the memories of making love to Kat hadn't. They had kept him warm on many a cold night. Being Brett that weekend had had only one advantage...making love with Kat.

His groans filled the silence of the room. Every fiber of his being battled to claim her, to untie the imaginary bonds on his hands. His body was on high idle, ready to race toward the finish line. He wanted to take her...now.

He shook with uncontrollable force, trying to take his mind other places. But it wasn't working. All he could think about was fishing a condom out of his pants pocket and bringing them both to completion. "In my pants, get it," he managed to say, opening his eyes.

Kat didn't hesitate. She must've sensed he was on the brink. He watched her get the condom and rip the package open. When he was sheathed, she rose over him and straddled his legs. Lying on the bed, seeing Kat above him, blonde and beautiful and seductive, knocked him ten ways to Sunday. It was more than having great sex with her. It was more...so much more.

She went slow and easy, and he could tell it'd been a long time for her. She moved cautiously at first and Justin kept pace, aching to slam into her, to release the pressure that had built from a small tornado into a raging twister. But he wouldn't hurt Kat. He wouldn't do anything to ever harm her.

Her movements grew more frantic and she took him faster and faster until she breathed out, "Touch me, Justin. It's okay. Please...I need you to touch me."

Justin didn't need any more encouragement. He brought his hands to her hips and guided them both home.

Sated and drowsy-eyed, Kat lay on the bed nestled up to him. Justin ran a hand along her body, letting her warmth and softness sink in. He stroked the slope of her breast and brushed a kiss into her hairline.

"Do you think I should check on the baby again?" she asked.

"We just did ten minutes ago. He's out. Let's give it a few more minutes and we'll both go in again."

"Okay. Mmm, feels good."

"Me touching you? I'm trying to make up for lost time."

"That, too," she purred, snuggling closer under the covers. "But it feels good having someone else to rely on with Connor. I never thought I'd say that."

"You can always count on me."

"I know."

"You put me through hell, you know," he whispered, splaying his hand over her waist and giving it a squeeze.

"Really?"

"You've been killing me in small doses since I met you at Mattie's house. You're beautiful and talented and I've wanted to be like this with you since the second I caught sight of you bending over that old clunker when you were trying to fix that tire."

She chuckled. "That must've been a sight."

"You kidding?" He smoothed his hand over the curve of her hip and blew out a breath. "You don't see sights like that when you're overseas."

"But you're a civilian now."

"Yeah...feels weird in some ways. In other ways it's pretty much perfect." He gave her hip a little squeeze to prove his point.

"How is it weird for you?"

He didn't really want to talk about the weirdness of coming home. About people's perception of him, how everyone expected him to behave in a certain way because that's how they remembered him in the past. But because Kat had asked him in earnest and seemed to really want an answer, he offered, "Combat changes you. It puts life in a big ole glass bowl and makes you see what's really important. You bond with people you might never ordinarily associate with, and they become important to you on an everyday basis. Your life is contained in a small cylinder of space. Your focus, your mission, the friendships you develop are all a part of that cylinder. If that makes any sense?"

"Yeah, I think it does. And when you lose someone, the cylinder gets even smaller."

"Yeah," he said. "That's how it works."

"Justin, will you tell me a little bit about Brett? Not now, if you can't. But maybe in the future? I'm curious about him."

His chest constricted at her request. He cradled her closer in his arms as his thoughts turned somber.

"What do you want to know?"

She laid her palm on his cheek, her fingers soft against his beard stubble. "He was your good friend?"

"We were close. As close as two men could get in that kind of environment."

"Aunt Mattie says wonderful things about him. Was he a good guy?"

Justin tensed. He wasn't sure why the conversation had taken this turn. He had a sexy woman in bed with him and didn't know if they'd ever get the chance to have a repeat performance of tonight. Was he ruining the moment with talk of his soldiering days? Yet he found that talking to Kat came easy and maybe he needed to get some things off his chest.

He began in a quiet voice. "He was no saint by any means. Sometimes I thought the devil caught him by the tail. But he was real decent and a lotta fun to be around. He had this innocent charm about him and he'd…he'd do anything for the people he cared about."

"You've never grieved for him, have you?"

Her question came out of left field, shocking him. "I'm not sure I know how."

"Maybe talking about it will help, Justin."

"Maybe I don't want help. Maybe I need to suffer."

"You don't really mean that."

Justin drew a sharp breath. "I think I do. I'm responsible for Brett's death and I'll never forgive myself."

She stroked his face with a tenderness he didn't deserve. The comfort she offered almost brought him to tears. "You need to pour out your heart, Justin. You need to tell someone."

He grabbed her wrist and kissed her fingertips. "I don't want to let it go."

"Yes, you do. You want to tell me," she said gently. "And I want to listen."

He sat in silence for a few moments, fighting the emotion warring inside his head. Where were Connor's waking cries when he needed them? Why wasn't the phone ringing off the hook? Why wasn't room service knocking on their door by mistake?

One look at Kat's sweetly sympathetic face threw his world off kilter. Those reassuring eyes told him she would understand. That beautiful mouth would speak words of comfort. She was offering him a way out, a way to ease his conscience. She was cracking the fortress walls he'd built up. Maybe Kat was right. Maybe he did want to tell her. Maybe he needed to speak of it. Sure as anything, he had her rapt attention. Maybe he needed to let go of the part of him that caused all his nightmares.

He released a deep breath and started talking slowly. "I guess I was still reeling from the Qaisar mission in northern Afghanistan."

"That's when you saved five men from an ambush, right?"

"Right. I was just doing my job the way I was trained to do. The result was a good one and no one died that day. The praise started flowing from generals all the way down to privates and I appreciated it. I really did, but I didn't much like the label of hero. It's something I still don't embrace. Real soldiers don't think about being heroes, they think about staying alive and helping their buddies stay alive. It's grueling over there and there's no glory in it, just survival."

"But you have to feel good about saving so many," Kat said.

"Hell yeah, I do. I wouldn't change a thing about that day. But what happened with Brett came a few months later. I was thinking I had it all figured out. I was a little cocky, which is dangerous when you're over there. I was assigned to check out an abandoned schoolhouse in an Afghani village. We'd gotten tipped off that there was a cache of explosives and ammo hidden there.

"Brett had been battling pneumonia. He'd been laid up for two weeks and was eager to get his boots on the ground again. He'd been bored out of his mind in the infirmary and wanted in on this mission. Originally I told him no, it was too soon. But he'd gotten clearance for regular duty and he convinced me he was feeling up to it. 'I'm right as rain,' he'd said. 'C'mon, buddy. Let me in on this one.' He pulled the friendship card, and I caved. Against my better judgment, I changed my mind and allowed him on the mission.

"When we got to the village, we detached from our convoy and eight of us walked over some rugged terrain to get to the schoolhouse. On orders, our demolition guy would detonate the explosives if they were there. We took all the usual precautions and were careful going inside. The dust was heavy that day, blowing in from the west, and we were covered in it. Brett started coughing, loud, hard coughs that could split a gut. I knew then he wasn't fully recovered. Disgusted at my lack of judgment, I ordered him back to the convoy for his own safety. He was in no shape for the mission. Just as he stepped outside to obey my orders, shots were fired.

"Immediately I knew we'd been set up and ambushed by hostile forces. Three of the patrol guards I'd stationed around the school perimeter fired back and then dove for cover inside the schoolroom. But Brett never made it back inside. He'd been caught off guard from those damn coughing fits and shot to death. We called for backup from our convoy and the troops scared off our attackers. But it was too late for my friend."

Justin's lips quivered and he put his head in his hands. The memory fierce, his harsh words to Brett resounded in his head. "My last command to him was to get the hell back to the convoy and stay put.

"There wasn't anything I could do to save him. I held him, was covered in his blood when he took his last breaths. I made two mistakes that day. Letting him sweet-talk me into going on the mission was one. He wasn't fit for combat. But I should have left it alone once he was there. The truth was, I was pissed at myself for not standing firm."

Kat sat up on her knees. She touched his forearm and rubbed comforting circles on his skin. "No, Justin. No. It wasn't your fault he was shot."

He stared into her pretty green eyes, saw her adamant expression and turned away. "Don't give me a break on this. Don't tell me it wasn't my fault. I should've known better."

"You sent him back for his own good. You couldn't possibly have known about the ambush—"

"Ambushes are part of the deal over there. I needed my men to be one hundred percent healthy, for everyone's safety. Brett wasn't, not that day. And my bad judgment cost him his life, damn it."

"You did what you thought was best."

"Maybe I got too damn cocky, believing my own press. Maybe I wasn't careful enough with my men."

"You're punishing yourself for something that wasn't your fault. Maybe—and here's a revelation—it was Brett's fault. Did you ever think of that? That maybe Brett shouldn't have pushed so hard. That maybe the error in judgment was with him."

Justin refused to let Brett take the blame for his own death. "You don't know what you're talking about, Kat."

"Oh, I know. I've been there and I can tell you, blaming yourself for things out of your control doesn't work. The guilt you feel isn't going to bring Brett back. It isn't going to fix you, Justin. Just like it didn't fix me."

Justin turned partway toward her. "What do you mean, it didn't fix you?"

"I mean…I had a horrible childhood. About as horrible as you can imagine. My father was abusive. In the beginning, it was just to my mom. But then, he started in on me. He was a nasty drunk and he'd say awful things to me. I had very low self-esteem because of him. How could I be anything but insecure, when my own father told me a dozen times a day how stupid I was? How much he hated that I was born. How he wished I'd grow some brains. I'd go to bed at night and cry my eyes out, thinking I was to blame. If only I could do better, and not leave the milk cap off, or put away all my clothes, or get A's on all my tests, my father would love me more. Every time he took a hand to my mother because she defended me, I blamed myself. Over and over and over."

"Ah hell, Kat." Justin looked at the naked woman on his bed and saw more than her beautiful body—he saw into her soul. Into the heart of who Kat really was. He gently cupped her face in his hands and looked into her eyes. "That's rough for a kid."

"I'm not trying to outdo you in the sympathy department, Justin," she said softly. He let his hands drop away, completely captivated by the sincerity in her eyes. "I'm trying to help. Guilt isn't healthy. You have to come to terms with what happened to Brett."

"Did you? Did you finally come to terms with your father?"

"Yes. My mother ran away from my dad. She got a restraining order that didn't do much to stop him and we ended up living out of a suitcase, going from one women's shelter to another. We never had money, but we had each other. My mother...was amazing. She tried like crazy to make up for our sorry lives and to this day I think she was the best person I've ever known. I see my father for who he was now. I have no guilt about him."

"It's different with Brett," he whispered. "And someday I'm going to have to explain to Mattie Applegate my part in how he died."

Soft baby whimpers drew their attention. "It's Connor," Kat said. She rose from the bed and picked up Justin's shirt. She threw her arms through the sleeve, and the material fanned out like a cape, before gently settling against her body. That, and the wild, blond wisps around her head, made a beautiful disheveled picture as she waited for him to retrieve Connor. Something wonderful squeezed tight in his gut.

He got up and quickly put on his pants. Then he strode

toward her and offered his hand. With a sweet smile she clasped it.

"Let's go get our son," he said.

And together they walked hand in hand to ease the soft cries of their boy.

The Golden's luxurious columns blocked sunlight from beaming down on Connor as Kat held him in her arms outside the hotel. "Your daddy will be here soon," she whispered near his ear.

Connor played with the thin silver necklace around her neck. There was just something about shiny things and babies. His fascination with the tiny crystal beads on the links kept him occupied while they waited for Justin to say his goodbyes to his family. The baby's dark curly hair ruffled in the slight breeze and Kat rocked him gently, more out of habit than need.

A black Lincoln limousine pulled up and came to a stop ten feet away. Kat watched as a chauffeur got out and opened the door to the backseat. A handsome light-haired man climbed out, ducking his head and then standing to full height.

Kat froze. "Oh, no," she murmured. It was too late to make a hasty exit. Michael Golden's eyes were on her instantly. They locked gazes and Kat tightened her hold on Connor.

Up until four months ago, she'd been living in New York in a penthouse suite with him. They were engaged to be married until Kat had broken it off.

Memories flashed of her time with Michael. She'd begun dating him a few weeks after she'd been with Justin in New York. Michael was witty, charming and very attentive. When she discovered she was pregnant, she'd been honest with Michael, telling him up front that she would understand if he wanted to end their relationship. Michael couldn't have children, so they'd known the child wasn't his. He'd often thought of adopting, so news of Kat's pregnancy didn't throw him for a loop. Quite the opposite. He continued his healthy pursuit of her and had been overly kind during her pregnancy. She'd moved into his penthouse even as thoughts of Brett Applegate stayed in her mind.

"Kat?" he said, tilting his head as he approached. "Is that really you?"

The sound of his baritone voice made her nerves stand on end.

He strode toward them. His clear blue eyes sharpened on her before he directed his gaze to the baby. It lingered there and Kat nervously shifted Connor in her arms. "Yes, it's me. Hello, Michael."

The most eligible billionaire in New York City smiled a winning smile. "Hello, Kat. I never expected to see you in Reno. At one of my hotels, no less."

"There was a wedding." She didn't volunteer anything more. Michael looked like a zillion bucks. What else was new? He had a flare for fine clothes. He put himself together well, or rather his valet did. It was one of the first things she'd noticed about him when they'd met, his desire for fine fashion. She'd thought that his connections could get her foot in the fashion industry door. And he would have helped her after the big wedding he'd promised to give her.

He continued gazing at Connor but didn't reach out or try to touch him. Longing filled his eyes. For months, Michael had treated him as his own son. "He looks good. Healthy."

"He is. We're doing fine."

"I've spent a long time missing him."

Which said it all. Michael missed the idea of Connor as his son. He might have even loved him, but that was the problem. Michael didn't love her. She didn't love him.

They were using each other for what was missing in their lives. Michael wanted children, Kat wanted a career. New York society labeled Kat a gold digger, a woman who was after Michael for his money and the connections he had. In a sense, that had been true. She'd been alone after her mother died, and here was this man…an extremely rich man, who wanted a child and would provide an amazing life for both of them.

"It was a mutual agreement, Michael. We decided it was best to have a clean break."

"That's not how I remember it."

"No, I don't suppose you would." He'd been resistant to the idea of a breakup initially and it had gotten a little ugly before she finally left.

"I gave you everything." He ground the words out. "But it wasn't enough."

After Connor was born, Kat began seeing a different side to Michael Golden. He was a control freak and had to have a say in everything she did and everywhere she went with the baby. He questioned her every move. The walls began closing in on her. She was being suffocated, choking down Michael's manipulations until she couldn't take it anymore.

He'd been very much like her troublesome father, and it had taken Connor's birth to make her really see it. She shuddered as bad memories poured over her like hot oil. Michael Golden hadn't been abusive physically, but every day she'd borne the brunt of his caustic words. Every day she'd been slapped with his harsh demands. She'd vowed to never allow another man to control her or make her life hell like that.

"It's in the past, Michael. Let's leave it there."

He glanced at her son again and snarled with accusation. "You took Connor away from me."

She began shaking her head and glancing around, trying

to find a way to make a clean exit. "He was never yours, Michael. We've talked about this. I'm sorry it didn't work out between us."

He blinked. "Are you? Did you ever find the baby's real father?"

Kat wasn't going to answer that question. It was none of his business now. For months, he'd discouraged her from pursuing Connor's father and she'd allowed him to influence her. She certainly wasn't blameless, though. Her decision to initially not seek out Brett to tell him of her pregnancy rested fully on her shoulders. It was something she'd have to live with the rest of her life.

She did a quick inconspicuous scan of the surroundings, searching for Justin. The last thing she wanted was to see the two men face-to-face.

That wouldn't be good at all.

She was saved from answering his question as a leggy woman with platinum-blond waves and pouty red lips climbed out of Michael's limo behind him. Blood rushed to Kat's face. The woman was almost a mirror image of her...and Marilyn Monroe. The resemblance was uncanny. Kat recognized her as a soap opera star.

"Are you coming, Michael?" The woman's impatience cut through the warm Nevada air.

"I'll be right there, honey."

The smile he aimed at Kat was lopsided and cocky, as if to say *you're replaceable*. He began backing away. "Goodbye, Kat." Then his gaze roamed over Connor with genuine regret before he turned away and took hold of the starlet's hand.

Kat's body sagged. She'd dodged a bullet today. It wasn't too often that happened to her. Her luck wasn't always this good

Michael disappeared into the hotel lobby with his date and just seconds later, Justin walked up behind her wearing a big smile. He gave her a kiss on the cheek. "Sorry to keep you waiting."

"No problem."

He studied her face for a second and she hoped he hadn't noticed her distress. "Everything okay?"

Kat drew a breath and gave him a quick nod. "Everything's fine."

"You ready to head home to Silver Springs?"

"So ready." She smiled and squeezed Connor's little body tight. With Justin by her side and Connor in her arms, her life seemed perfect and…complete. She wasn't going to let running into Michael today ruin that. "You have no idea."

Eight

Kat leaned against her bedroom dresser and unfolded the letter she'd received yesterday from Lowery's Department Store. Her shoulders sagged with despair and she shook her head as she reread the words. Her future on the line, she stood there for a few seconds contemplating what she should do with the rest of her life before she refolded the paper and slipped it back into its envelope.

She pulled the dresser drawer open, lifted up her underpants and placed the letter on top of the pile of rejections she kept there. A nice neat stack had accumulated during the past weeks, and when she put her underwear back to cover the letters, it came to the very top of the drawer. She flattened the fabric with the palm of her hand and then used her hip to slide the drawer closed.

When Kat entered the kitchen, Aunt Mattie was at the table, feeding Connor breakfast in his high chair. The creamy concoction of oatmeal, bananas and blueberries warranted a fingertip taste test. "Yummy, Connor," Kat said, after taking a second taste. "Mommy likes it, too."

The baby smiled.

She kissed the top of his head and ruffled his dark hair.

Noise from the demolition crew working a short distance away drew her attention. Sheds, old feed shacks and outer buildings on the property were being torn down.

"Won't be long now before the sale will go through and

we'll see a building going up for the retreat," Aunt Mattie said matter-of-factly.

After the special night Kat had spent with Justin in Reno two days ago, she better understood his need and determination to get this project underway. Justin didn't waste time. He was used to acting and then reacting and she sensed that getting the Gateway Equine Retreat started quickly would help ease his tremendous guilt over Brett's death.

He'd let her inside, for a few stolen minutes, and allowed her to see his pain when he was most vulnerable. She'd like to think he'd trusted her—at least for that one night—with his innermost, deepest thoughts and secrets.

Sexually, they were compatible... Oh, boy, they were compatible. Justin was an amazing lover and Kat wasn't one to hold back with him. She gave and she took equally and they both enjoyed the consequences. But even she knew that great sex wasn't enough. And right now, that's about all that they had together.

Connor pointed to his oatmeal that was more blueberry and banana than oats.

"You want more?"

Aunt Mattie fed him another spoonful. "The boy certainly has an appetite this morning."

"He sure does."

"Brett loved breakfast the best. He'd eat a half a dozen eggs if I let him, then he'd start on pancakes and then of course about a pound of—"

"Bacon," they said in unison.

Aunt Mattie's eyes lit and they both chuckled. The laughter was loud enough and Kat's smile wide enough to conceal her own guilt over the lies she'd told and would continue to tell the older woman. It shook her resolve some, but not enough to open up to Mattie with the truth. That would have to come sometime in the future.

"Wouldn't expect anything less from a hog farmer, now would you?" the older woman asked.

"No, I wouldn't." But Kat refrained from adding to the lies by agreeing that Connor took after Brett.

Kat fixed Connor a bottle. When he'd finished his solid food, she lifted him out of his high chair and sat down next to Mattie to feed him the formula.

"Ah, I never do get over the sight of mama and baby like that."

"It's sweet," Kat said. "One of my favorite things to do."

She snuggled Connor a little tighter in her arms, loving him with every ounce of her being as he suckled on the bottle. In just a short time, he'd be drinking real milk in a sippy cup, but for now, she'd hold on to the small things, letting the baby be a baby for as long as possible.

An image flashed of Justin in the hotel suite, holding Connor and giving him a bottle in the wee hours of the morning. There'd been a sense of calm and peace and normalcy when the three of them had been together. Kat had tried to absorb that feeling…she'd never before felt such stability.

"I've got a few appointments with contractors lined up today, if you're up to it. We'll start on the kitchen first, since it's in the worst shape."

"Oh, dear," Aunt Mattie said, glancing at the chipped kitchen cabinets and the flooring with big hunks of vinyl missing. "Where do we begin?"

"Well, we could gut it all and start over."

Aunt Mattie shook her head. "I don't need newfangled everything. There's a lot of…of memories in this kitchen for me. I remember looking out that window and seeing the boys playing catch out there. And well, my Ralph built me that hutch over there with his own two hands. I don't want everything gone."

"Aunt Mattie, that's fine. I sort of figured you'd feel that way. We'll take on one project at a time. You can pick new cabinets and floors and we'll get you a few new appliances, ones that don't spark when you turn them on. We'll pick out new paint and counters and we can keep everything in the same place. It'll just be updated and sparkling new. Would that make you happy?"

"Yes, with your help, sweetheart…I think that would suit me just fine."

Kat reached over to squeeze her hand. Aunt Mattie wasn't her mother, but she was a dear woman whom Kat had come to love. "Well, then, why don't you rest up a little bit. The first appointment isn't until the afternoon. Then we'll get cracking."

"Cracking, yes." The older woman's face beamed just a little bit brighter. "I don't know what I've done to deserve you in my life, but I'm sure glad you're here, Kat. You and Connor make life worth living."

And it wasn't a big surprise to Kat that she felt exactly the same way about Mattie Applegate.

Justin appeared at the front door two hours later in a pair of black dress slacks, a white shirt rolled up at the sleeves and opened at the collar and black boots coated with a thin layer of construction dust. Startled and a little awestruck, Kat didn't particularly like the emotions clicking away at the immediate sight of him. "Justin, I didn't expect to see you today."

Kat opened the screen door to let him in.

"Where is everyone?" he asked, striding in, removing his hat and tossing it on the sofa. His ink-black hair shone almost blue-ish as sunlight trailed after him.

"Connor's napping and Aunt Mattie is reading in her room," she said, wiping her hands on a kitchen towel. "I was just tidying up the—"

Justin's expression stopped her cold. He had a devastating look on his face. Hunger burned in his eyes. Kat's throat constricted and she took a hard swallow.

He grabbed her hand and she didn't protest when he led her into the kitchen. With his back to the farthest wall, he tugged her to his chest and wound his arms around her waist, planting her firmly against his taut body.

"Oh," she breathed quietly. "This—this isn't a good idea." As she said the words, her body called her a liar and softened to him immediately. And her fool heart... her heart had leaped in her chest the second she'd found him at the door.

"Tell me about it," he said, right before his lips claimed hers. "I've been thinking about you for two days, Kat. Ever since the wedding." He gave her another kiss that she eagerly returned. "I've had meeting after meeting and I can't concentrate on anything but you." He cupped her head in his hands, using his thumbs to caress her cheeks, and stared deep into her eyes. "I've missed you. I came here thinking we could talk business, but the second I laid eyes on you..."

"Mattie could walk in any second," she was quick to point out.

"I know." He had a hopeless look on his face now.

"We shouldn't—"

"Be quiet, Kat." He coaxed her into silence with another passionate, intoxicating kiss. "Don't waste what time we have."

She couldn't argue with him. She'd craved him, craved seeing him again, and she hadn't known just how badly until he'd walked into the house today.

His mouth moved to her throat and her skin prickled when he pushed the material of her blouse aside to touch the sensitive skin there with his lips. "Oh, Justin."

He was aroused and determined and oh-so-hard to resist. "I need to see you again, Kat. I want to be alone with you."

He planted tiny kisses up and down her throat, sending her nerve endings soaring. If she wasn't careful, his sweetly spoken words could get to her. He could fill her head with all sorts of crazy ideas. He could make her believe in a man again, after so many failures, so many disappointments.

"Come to me tonight, Kat. Come and be with me."

This time his kiss was filled with persuasion, with dire unabashed want.

How easy it would be to fall for him in a big way. But Kat had more than herself to think about. She had a son. And a dear friend who needed her. She wasn't going to mess this up.

She found the strength to push him away slightly, mere inches, but enough to grab his full attention. "I want that, too, but it can't be just about sex, Justin. I can't be your horny soldier booty call. It can't be that."

Justin lowered his head. His gaze went to the floor and he stared at her bare feet. She was thankful her toenails were polished cotton-candy pink.

Then he slowly lifted his head and their gazes locked. His deep-set eyes were rich with sincerity. "That's not what this is about, Kat. Not at all. I'm no sex-starved kid and I'm assuming you aren't, either."

"Maybe just a little. With you." Kat was dreadfully honest.

A smile trembled at the corner of his mouth. "I think we both know how serious getting involved might be for us. We have a child together, a son that we both love. I'm not going to blow the one shot we might have at this. I think we have a chance at something here." He pushed a hand through his hair. "Or am I reading too much into what happened between us the other night?"

Kat squeezed her eyes closed. She was about to take a giant leap of faith. "No, you're not reading too much into it." She focused on him now and nodded. "It was... special for me."

She'd connected to Justin in a way she hadn't connected to another human being. She'd listened to him admit things that hadn't come easy for him. He'd given her that much trust and she wanted more from him. She wanted a solid chance, but up until this point, she hadn't believed it could happen.

There were major forces working against them right now.

"Is it possible?" she heard herself ask.

"I think so." The look he cast her wasn't lust now, but something else, something that touched deep within her heart.

"But how?"

He shrugged a shoulder casually, as if the answer were simple. "We'll start dating."

"Dating?" She heard surprise rise in her voice. "We can't."

He hoisted her chin with the pad of his thumb so they were eye to eye. "We can. It's a natural occurrence. Returning lonely soldier meets gorgeous young widow and child and is besotted."

"Besotted?" Kat laughed and Justin kissed away her amusement.

"Humor me, okay."

"I thought I heard voices in here," Aunt Mattie's called from the parlor. "Kat, are you talking to someone?"

Kat jumped three feet back, her eyes wide and focused on Justin's big silly grin.

He gathered himself up first and stepped out into the doorway to the parlor. "It's just me, Aunt Mattie."

Aunt Mattie ambled a little farther into the room, just

enough to spot both of them. "Oh, hello, Justin. It's good to see you. I didn't expect you to pay us a visit today. Did Kat tell you we've got several appointments this afternoon? We're going to start remodeling the kitchen."

Justin gave Kat an innocent look. "No, she didn't mention that. Actually, Kat and I were discussing something else entirely."

Aunt Mattie darted a look her way and then returned her attention to Justin. "Oh? Something I should know about?"

"No!" Kat shook her head.

"Yes, actually," Justin said.

Her blood pressure elevated when Justin contradicted her.

Voice laced with enough charm to convince a mob boss to go to confession, Justin spoke directly to Aunt Mattie. "It's something I think you should know. Something I hope you'll take kindly to." He bumped shoulders with Kat as he reached around her waist to draw her close. She instantly relaxed, the tension seeping out of her pores. For some reason, it felt right, even though there was potential for disaster. But Kat wasn't a coward. She would take the risk. Besides, judging from the stubborn look on Justin's face, there was no stopping this now.

"Kat and I are going to start dating."

Aunt Mattie stared at both of them. Seconds clicked by. Kat hoped the news wouldn't hurt Mattie. She hoped she wouldn't feel threatened in any way.

"Well, that's good news, but you don't need my permission. I've seen the looks you two give each other. I think I'll go back to my room so you two can resume fooling around."

"Aunt Mattie!" Kat's face flushed with heat.

"You saw that?" Justin's eyes beamed with admiration.

"I'm not blind as a bat. Just got a bad ticker."

After Justin had a good chuckle and Kat's embarrassment ebbed, he said, "Please don't leave because of me. Stay. I'd like to discuss our progress on the retreat."

"Yes, stay and talk to us," Kat said to Aunt Mattie. "I'll fix lunch right after I check on Connor. He should be waking up soon."

"Well, all right. That sounds nice."

Kat left the room and returned five minutes later with a diapered, dressed Connor in her arms. She found Justin and Mattie sitting at the kitchen table. Mattie was entertaining him with tales of life on a hog farm. His gaze followed Connor and her into the room and Kat's heart leaped again, this time seeing the love and pride Justin had for their son. "Justin, would you mind holding Connor while I get Aunt Mattie her pills and throw some lunch on the table?"

The big strong man lowered Connor down into his arms. "Not at all. Come here, little buddy."

And Connor went to his daddy.

Without complaint.

The screen door slapped closed behind Justin as he walked outside the Applegate house with Kat. "It's official," he said, taking her hand and dragging her down the porch steps. "We're dating."

Her gaze darted in three different directions, looking for errant workmen who might, heaven forbid, see them holding hands. But there wasn't a soul in sight at the moment.

"You sort of bamboozled me into it. Like I have time for dating."

He didn't try to hide the grin spreading across his face. "You'll find time."

"You're so sure of yourself."

"Sort of reminds me of the time when we first met. And you told me you didn't date soldiers."

"You charmed the pants off me."

He leaned against the hood of his car, folding his arms across his chest. "I did, didn't I?"

Kat's mouth turned down in a tempting pout. In a pair of light blue jeans and some kind of billowy blouse she'd probably designed, she looked sensational. She flattened her palms against his chest and shoved playfully. "You think you're so clever. Clever Mr. Slade."

"I think…I'm lucky."

She batted her eyelashes. "Yes, well, there's a difference between *getting* lucky and *being* lucky."

"I plan to do both."

She shook her head slowly. "Sure of yourself, aren't you?"

He leaned forward, away from the hood. His lips hovered near her beautiful mouth. "Admit you're glad about it."

She leaned back and scanned the grounds again. She nibbled nervously on her lower lip. "I'm not sure yet."

He clasped the back of her neck and brought her up close. Their noses touched. Hell, she smelled good. Her scent nearly killed his restraint. "You will be." And then his lips came down on hers. He kissed her long and hard and didn't give a damn who saw them playing house.

After they broke apart, Kat spoke in a breathless whisper. "Why are you so darn cocky?"

A chuckle emerged from his throat. There were things about Kat he found vastly entertaining. Her way with words, for one. And the way she'd filled out his shirt the other night, for another. "When I get you alone again, I'll tell you."

"What does that mean?"

Around Kat, his willpower wouldn't win awards, but he summoned every shred of it and set her away from him. On a sigh, he said, "You'll have to wait and see what I have cooked up. But believe it or not, I brought you out here for another reason. There's something I want to show you and I need your input."

He'd scouted locations on the property and found a hilly rise that overlooked the entire facility—the perfect area to build a monument in Ralph and Brett's honor. He wanted Kat's opinion before proposing it to Aunt Mattie. "Connor is in his playpen, right? Do you think Mattie can watch him for a few minutes?"

Kat blinked. "We have the guy from Kitchen Redo coming over in half an hour."

"I'll have you back here in plenty of time. We'll take my truck. It's important, Kat."

Her brow lifted curiously. "Okay. Let me tell Aunt Mattie what's going on. It'll just take me a sec."

"Tell her it's our first date. Then she'll be sure to allow us time to *fool around*."

"I *will not* tell her that." He caught an eyeful watching her hip action as she sauntered away. *Man, oh, man.* There wasn't a woman alive who filled out a pair of jeans as well as Katherine Grady.

Several minutes ticked by. Justin glanced at his watch, then at the front door. What was taking her? Gut instincts told him either Connor needed his mother's attention, which happened more times than not…or something was wrong. Justin reached the porch steps when the screen door flew open. He immediately saw the look of panic on Kat's face. "It's Aunt Mattie. She's having tightness in her chest and feeling weak. I have her resting on the sofa. Come inside…I can't leave her another second." She whipped around and went back into the house.

Justin followed her. "I'll call for an ambulance. Does she take nitroglycerin?"

"Yes, I've given her one already. It's almost time for the next one."

Connor sat in the play yard, holding his little beetle bug

toy. He was occupied right now. Justin made the phone call and was assured the paramedics would be here shortly. Kat had already done all the right things, according to the dispatcher on the phone.

He walked over to the sofa and knelt down beside Kat. She held Mattie's hand. "Aunt Mattie, it's Justin. You take it slow and easy now. Help is on the way."

"Okay." Her eyes were closed, her voice weak. "I don't know…what happened. I was feeling fine when I woke up this morning, just a little tired." Moisture pooled on her forehead and at her hairline, darkening her bright red roots.

"You just rest now and don't fret about a thing."

Kat slid a worried glance at Justin.

He could only return the look.

The ambulance arrived. Two paramedics and an EMT hooked Mattie up to oxygen, poked her with IVs and did a thorough assessment. Justin knew something about following medical protocol. He didn't doubt Mattie needed observation and treatment at the hospital.

They worked on getting her ready to leave, bracing her head and limbs with restraints. Bravely, she did what she was told. They transferred her onto a gurney and rolled her carefully out of the house.

He took Kat aside. "You go with her in the ambulance. She shouldn't be alone."

Troubled, Kat glanced at Connor. "But the baby—"

"He'll be fine with me. I know the routine. I'll get him ready, pack up his clothes and bottles and meet you at the hospital. Just leave me your keys so I can use the car seat."

Kat's eyes closed. Seconds ticked by. Finally, she nodded. "Okay, I know you'll take good care of him."

Thank goodness she was going to let him help. She didn't need to be alone right now. "I'd give my life for him, Kat. So don't worry. I can figure out the small stuff."

She lifted on tiptoes and brushed his cheek with a kiss "I know you can."

She picked up Connor and covered him with kisses before setting him back in the play yard. "You be a good little boy...."

Connor's sweet face crumbled with tears. Poor kid. Three strangers wearing white uniforms marching into the house must've confused the hell out of him. "Maybe I shouldn't go," Kat said. Her loyalties were clearly split in two.

"Go... Mattie needs you." Justin walked over to Connor. He lifted him out of the playpen and situated him in his arms. Then he rocked him like a melodic pendulum swing, to and fro. The baby's inquisitive eyes widened, his crying stopped. Connor's cooperation proved Justin's point. "There, you see, I can handle him. I promise I'll be a few minutes behind you. I'll meet you at the hospital."

Kat agreed with a nod and grabbed her purse. Digging her hand inside, she came up with her keys and handed them over. "Here you go. Thank you... I'd better run." She smothered the boy with another round of kisses. If Connor wasn't his kid, Justin would be jealous. "I don't want to delay the ambulance." Kat hurried out the door.

Justin hugged the baby tight to his chest. "Looks like it's me and you now, son."

Nine

When the doctor asked Kat to leave the room so that he could examine Mattie again, the older woman gave her a small brave smile that nearly broke her heart. Reluctant to go, Kat pushed through the emergency room doors on wobbly legs and ran her hand through her hair. It was hard leaving Mattie alone. She'd almost lost it in there seeing her tied to all those machines.

Poor Mattie. She didn't deserve this.

After a short walk, Kat reached the waiting room at Silver Springs General Hospital. Framed pastel landscapes decorated the beige walls, and the chairs were cushioned with durable mauve material. It was a whole lot more cheery than the room she'd just left. Not that any of it mattered—the most important thing was Mattie's diagnosis and aftercare.

She scanned the room and immediately honed in on Connor in the crowd. He was lying across Justin's broad chest, his head nuzzled under his father's chin, sleeping soundly. What a sight. The two of them were a matched set. So incredibly alike. They looked beautiful together.

Happy endings rushed into her mind.

Kat had never had things go her way before.

She'd never had smooth sailing in her life.

Because of her father's abuse, her young life had been filled with fear, mistrust and poverty. Her mother died years before her time and Kat had had to scrounge and fight her way to a decent existence. Under her wavy blond hair and flashy clothes was a scarred, frightened woman she concealed from the rest of the world. For Connor's sake, she'd been strong, and done things that wouldn't gain her sainthood. She'd thought them necessary at the time.

Looking at Justin and Connor now and picturing the three of them together as a unit...as a real family, could be a foolish move. Did she dare to hope for something she'd never really had before? Kat wouldn't risk it. The hurt she carried inside still smarted like a son-of-a-gun.

Don't go there, Kat. Don't start believing.

Justin lifted his head; there was a question in his eyes. She put a finger to her lips as she approached. He nodded and understood she didn't want to wake Connor right now. Phones rang, nurses' chatter filtered into the room and elevator bells pinged. More power to her baby if he could continue to sleep through the noise.

She eyed the seat next to Justin. Her weary body welcomed the rest and she plunked down into a chair and closed her eyes.

She had some serious praying to do anyway...for Mattie Applegate.

Kat had held her hand in the ambulance, reassuring her with soothing words. "I'm going to stay with you," Kat told her. "You're going to be just fine." She wasn't sure Aunt Mattie had bought her Pollyanna act, but she'd nodded and her tired eyes had lit briefly with gratitude. Kat couldn't stand the thought of losing the dear spirited woman.

When Connor woke up, she explained to Justin that they were running tests to see if Mattie had suffered a mild heart attack or if it was a case of her meds needing adjustments. Kat hoped it was the latter. At any rate, the doctor said that she wouldn't be coming home anytime soon.

Images popped into her head of another hospital, another time, holding hands with her mother, and reassuring her, too, that all would be right soon. But her mom's battered body hadn't been able to fight off the bacterial infection that led to the complications that finally took her life.

A tear dripped from Kat's eye and then another and another until her cheeks burned. She wiped at the droplets with the back of her hand. If only she could've protected her mother. If only she could've defended her from a man who wouldn't control his rage.

Kat would never be a victim again. She would never let anyone hurt those she loved. But Kat was helpless now. She couldn't do anything for Aunt Mattie.

She sobbed.

She felt a hand on her arm and knew it was Justin. His gentle touch seeped into her skin and released some of her pain. She absorbed his warmth and tenderness and drew strength from it. He slowly moved his hand along her arm to her hand. She opened her eyes as he entwined their fingers. Once their hands were joined, he tightened his hold. The connection brought her peace. His strength made all the bad things in her life disappear.

She gazed into his dark eyes—her son's eyes—and was hit with a jolt of awareness. A single moment elapsed, and in the very next instant, Kat knew. There'd be no talking herself out of this. She couldn't wish it away. No amount of mental hammering would pound this out of her brain.

She loved Justin Slade.

She was deeply in love with him.

And she'd never felt anything so potent, so wonderful and so incredibly scary in her life.

"Come back to the ranch with me tonight," Justin said to Kat in the parlor of Aunt Mattie's home. "Connor would love it and I'll make sure you have everything you need."

Kat sighed quietly. He already did have everything she

needed. She had to disguise her new feelings for him… they were just that…new, and she needed time to work it all out in her head. "It's tempting. But you know I can't."

Justin frowned.

It was terribly tempting. He'd asked her to stay at his ranch yesterday, too, and she hated refusing him a second time. So she clarified her reasons. "It's easier for us to be here, Justin. All of Connor's stuff is here. And this house is closer to the hospital in case Aunt Mattie needs me. I have to take care of the place for her."

It turned out that Mattie had had a mild heart attack after all. Luckily, there wasn't too much damage to her heart, but she was weak and they were still in the process of observing her and adjusting her medications. The doctor had informed Kat that it would be at least a week or two before Mattie was released to come home. She'd probably have to spend time in a rehab facility.

Justin approached her. He slanted a quick look over his shoulder at Connor banging away at the new baby keyboard piano he'd given him. "If I was still into betting, I'd bet that I could change your mind."

Musical notes and baby sounds zinged from the piano. Justin zeroed in on her.

She faced him head-on, holding her ground. Okay, mellowing a little. Gosh, he was hard to resist with those melt-your-heart dark eyes and sharp handsome features.

His hands snaked around her waist. He drew her up against his body and the fit was darn near perfect. Kat blinked as he leaned in, touched his lips to hers and kissed her tenderly.

When the kiss ended, Justin said, "I don't think you should be alone tonight. I'm going to stay here with you. I'll sleep on the sofa."

Last night, Justin had been a dream, taking her home from the hospital after visiting hours were over. He'd helped her settle the baby down and get Connor off to bed, then stayed until very late, comforting her about Mattie's medical condition.

"Justin, that's a sweet offer, but are you sure you want to do that?"

Justin was quick with a nod. "The sofa's a heck of a lot nicer than some of the places I've slept during the last nine years. I'm good with that. I want to be here for you and Connor."

There was no way she could refuse his generous offer. Having him stay over and lend support meant the world to her. "Thank you. I would like that very much."

Later that evening they fed Connor, gave him a bath and put him into his pajamas. Justin got down on the floor and played with him for a long time while Kat did the dishes and took care of some Babylicious business. As soon as she could, she joined them, and when nine o'clock rolled around and the baby rubbed his eyes, Justin rocked him to sleep in his arms. "Little guy is tuckered out," he said softly, brushing a kiss to his forehead.

"Wonder why?" She grinned.

Kat marveled at how close Justin was getting to Connor. Not too long ago, she'd forgiven Justin the lies and deceit of that New York weekend. If that weekend had never happened, she wouldn't have Connor, her precious little boy and the one really good thing she'd done in her life. How could she continue to hold a grudge against the father of her child, especially when she saw them together like this?

"Let's put him down," she said.

Justin transferred the baby into her arms and they walked to her room together. Kat laid the baby down gently on his back in the crib. He stirred for just a second before falling asleep.

It was sweet to see Justin stare at Connor and watch him sleep. "Still can't believe it."

"I know," she said on a sigh. "He's a miracle."

"He is." Justin took her hand and led her away from the crib. They stood just outside the doorway. "I know how concerned you are about Mattie."

"I'm worried sick about her," she said.

"From what I can tell, she's a strong woman. She'll pull through." He ran his hands up and down her arms with reassuring strokes. It felt like heaven having him touch her with such warmth and caring.

"You should get some rest while Connor is sleeping," he whispered.

"That's a good idea. I'm beat."

"I'll be here if you need me," he said.

She was grateful that he'd sacrifice his comfortable king-size bed for a bunch of pillows and blankets on a lumpy sofa to stay over tonight.

He reached out and tipped her chin up with his thumb. Then he lowered his mouth to hers and she squeezed her eyes shut, absorbing the taste and feel of his tenderness as he kissed her. "Good night, Kat."

"Good night," she said and before she opened her eyes, he was gone.

Justin thrashed back and forth on the sofa. His breathing was rapid and sweat pooled on his forehead and ran down his brows. He struggled to wipe away the drops.

It had happened again. He'd dreamed of the firefight and the day Brett died. The dream was mixed up, a concoction of his brain, where saving five men in that village coincided with Brett's death. It had all run together somehow and he'd been a part of it. This time, Brett was one of the men he'd rushed in and saved that day. Brett was alive in his dream. Justin's heart pounded. The rest of the dream jogged his memory and he trembled.

In real life, Brett had been taken out by a sniper's bullet.

He sat up and opened his eyes. Darkness surrounded him, but in that instant he remembered he wasn't with his platoon. He wasn't in Afghanistan. He was in Brett Applegate's home. He planted both feet on the ground, his head in his hands as he leaned forward.

"Justin, are you okay?" Kat rushed into the parlor, her concerned expression illuminated by a sliver of moonlight streaming through the curtains. She sat down beside him.

He sighed. "I didn't mean to wake you." Keeping his voice calm, he told her, "It's just a bad dream."

She leaned over to stroke his arm. He was amazed at how much comfort she packed into that touch. "You've had a lot of those lately."

"Some. It's getting better."

"I'm sorry," she said.

"I didn't mean to disturb you."

"It's okay. I want to help."

She bent to kiss his cheek. The sweet peck calmed him like nothing else could.

"Would you like me to stay with you for a little while?" Kat asked gently.

He took a swallow and nodded. There wasn't anything he wanted more at the moment. He didn't have the strength to refuse her or deny himself the comfort.

She nestled close to him and he wrapped his arms around her shoulders. In her light flowery scent and the warmth of her skin, he found a keen sense of peace.

"I'm here for you, too, if you need me," Kat whispered. The woman was good for his soul.

His eyes drifted closed.

Hell, he was quickly coming to the conclusion that he did need Katherine Grady.

In his life.

Always.

* * *

Justin checked in on Connor taking quiet sweet breaths in his crib for the third time in a span of thirty minutes. His little boy was tuckered out. A smile emerged on Justin's face and his boots hit the floor quietly as he walked out of the room.

Kat was visiting Aunt Mattie again at the hospital tonight and babysitting duties fell to him in her absence. The boy was responding to Justin more and more each day, giving him smiles and allowing him to hold him without instantly reaching out for his mama. Yep, he had mad fathering skills now. Pride tipped his heart off kilter. The love he felt for Connor was immeasurable. It kinda blew him away, these powerful feelings he held inside.

He glanced at the broken cuckoo clock on the wall that told time without the usual fanfare. No cuckoos, just clock. It was almost nine. Kat should be home within the hour.

He missed her.

Strolling over to Aunt Mattie's thirty-two-inch television set, he picked up the remote, making a mental note. Her wall was big enough for a flat-screen television almost double the size of the old TV she had now. He'd make sure it was part of her remodel.

He lowered himself down on the sofa and clicked on the TV. He had ten solid minutes until another bunk check on Connor.

Leaning back, he stretched out his legs and surfed through a limited choice of stations, searching for any kind of sports. Baseball, golf or basketball highlights? Nothing looked appealing and he was about to shut the darn thing off when he came across an entertainment news show where ace Arizona Diamondback pitcher, Doug Broadmeyer, was being interviewed about a possible move to the Los Angeles Dodgers. Broadmeyer was big news to Douglas County sports fans. He was a local high school boy who'd made his way up the ranks from the minors to the major leagues. Justin leaned back settling in for a few minutes of tube.

It wasn't long before the show's host steered the conversation to the pitcher's love life. "Is there truth to the rumor that you and Mia are talking wedding?"

"Oh, man." He should've known the host wouldn't stick to sports news. *Leisure and Luxury Lifestyles,* or *LLL* for short, was pure tabloid TV. He put his finger on the remote's off button.

"And in luxury news," the English-accented male host announced as he moved on to the next segment, "owner and CEO of *the* Golden Hotels, Michael Golden, is dating another Marilyn look-alike. Yes, that's right, this time it's Belinda Brubaker. We all know her as Charity McGrath on the nighttime soap opera, *Avenue M.*"

"What's up with *that,* Michael?" the TV host asked rhetorically.

A split screen flashed two photos, side by side…on the left, one of Belinda, the woman the hotel mogul was presently dating, a dead ringer for Marilyn Monroe, and on the right…a picture of Kat?

Justin blinked rapidly. His brain scrambled for some sense. He slid forward onto the edge of his seat and focused on the photograph again. Yeah, there was no mistaking it. It sure as hell was Kat. She was holding Connor and gazing happily into the camera with Golden by her side.

What the hell?

"This rare photo of Golden with his ex-fiancée, Katherine Grady, is proof positive that Mike certainly doesn't stray too far in his taste of women," the *LLL* host was saying. "Too bad this happy little trio never made it to the altar after a year-long engagement. Rumor has it Golden was heartbroken that his instant family didn't work out. Maybe actress Belinda Brubaker will have better luck snaring the insanely wealthy bachelor. We're sure *Avenue M* fans want her to have a happy ending."

The host's words banged like a drum in his head. He tuned out the rest of his dribble about Golden's preference for blondes and punched the off button on the remote.

He'd seen enough.

Kat had been engaged to Michael Golden? For a whole damn year?

True, Justin had been overseas for the past nine years, but hell, he knew the Golden name. His own brother had been married in one of the hotels, for heaven's sake. The Golden Hotels were everywhere in the United States. Even an out-of-touch soldier knew the power and influence that name wielded.

He ground his teeth together, hating that his heart ached so badly. Hating that his soul was seared with the truth Kat didn't tell him. The truth he'd had to hear on a gossip television show.

His initial instincts about Kat were correct. She was a social climber, a woman out to snare a rich man. When she'd thought he was Brett, she'd made it clear she wanted nothing more to do with him. One fling, one weekend, and that was that.

Her lies and bone-sharp betrayal made bitter acid churn in his stomach.

He bounded off the sofa and paced the floor. Everything made sense now. She'd dumped the man she'd thought was a hog farmer, refusing him knowledge of his baby, and didn't waste time getting engaged to the hotel giant. Was that it? Was it all about money? If it wasn't, then why hadn't she told him about Golden? Hell, he'd poured his heart out to her, telling her things he'd never told another human being. He'd given her a piece of himself with his confessions about Brett.

He heard the rattle of the screen door and a key turning

in the lock. The scent of gardenias preceded Kat into the room. He breathed her in, for a second remembering only the past few days of their lives together. He'd been a fool to believe in her in the first place. His instincts had been dead on. If only he'd listened.

"Justin." Her soft voice floated over him as she smiled and walked inside the house.

He braced his nerves. This wasn't going to be pretty. He stood facing her by the front door.

"How did it go? Did you get the baby to sleep?"

"He's napping," he said curtly. He was glad he didn't have time to stew about this. He wanted this out in the open, pronto.

"Everything okay?" she asked, her smile slowly fading.

"He's fine. Go check on him. We need to talk when you get back."

"Oh, okay." She swallowed and narrowed her eyes, watching him curiously as she brushed past him. Justin stayed rooted to the spot, hands on hips, breathing hard.

By the time she walked back into the room he'd calmed his nerves a little bit.

"He's so beautiful when he sleeps. I could stand there and watch him forever." There was a sweetly whimsical quality to her voice when she spoke of Connor that seeped into Justin's soul.

He glanced away.

"What is it, Justin?" She walked over to face him by the sofa, her eyes troubled. "What's wrong?"

"Were you engaged to Michael Golden in New York?"

She jerked back as if he'd hit her. A gasp sprung from her mouth. "How did you…?"

"Does it matter how I found out? *You* didn't tell me. Is it true? You lived with him for a year?"

She shook her head. "Not a year."

Justin rolled his eyes. "So *LLL* got it wrong. How long were you with him?"

"*LLL?* The television show? Are you telling me that you saw it on television?"

Justin pursed his lips before saying, "The host was happy to share a rare photo of the three of you together."

"They showed a picture of Connor? How? Why? I don't understand."

"He's a famous man. He's in the gossip news, that's how. Apparently, he has a thing for beautiful platinum blondes. No one in the public eye can avoid scrutiny, Kat. If you lived with him, you should've known that."

"But he promised me Connor would never be exploited. He promised me he'd protect us from the media."

"Well, something's changed, hasn't it?"

Kat opened her mouth to say something. But no denial came forth and slowly her lips came together again as a glimmer of knowledge flickered in her eyes.

She was holding something back. Her expression closed up tight. "Aside from the obvious, what aren't you telling me?"

Kat lowered herself down onto the sofa. It was as if she couldn't hold herself upright any longer than her need to sit. "I saw him the day after Logan's wedding."

"You saw him? As in, spoke to him in person?" Now Justin needed to sit. Did he know this woman at all? Who was the real Katherine Grady? He wished to hell he had the answer.

He lowered himself onto Mattie's chair and uttered a curse.

Kat's gaze found the floor. "I'm sorry, Justin. It wasn't planned. I bumped into him outside while I was…I was waiting for you. I guess I didn't realize how much I'd hurt him. He'd gotten attached to Connor."

Her eyes lifted to him. At the mention of his son's name,

Justin's mind clicked back in gear. "Why'd you do it, Kat? Was it just about the money?"

She shook her head vehemently, causing all that gorgeous blond hair to fly around. "No."

"Why don't I believe you?"

The light in her green eyes dimmed. "It's not that simple."

"Lies never are."

Her pretty face crumbled. "I know."

She should just spit it all out and lay the truth at his feet. It might even be liberating for her.

"Explain it to me."

"I, uh, well, I've already told you about my childhood. About the abuse and the way my mother and I lived in fear for years. Keeping one step away from my father messed up our lives. We never had anything of value. My mother's car was twenty years old. We were lucky it ran and if it didn't, we were at the mercy of some kind soul who would fix it for us. Those things most people take for granted. We never had that luxury. We were fortunate to have a roof over our heads. Thanks to the women's shelters and the generosity of friends, we had clothes on our back. Mom and I loved each other. We were very close. We never let my father's abuse come between us.

"As I got older, I saw the toll it had taken on her. She was worn out and sickly before she reached forty. It was hard to watch, you know? As a kid, I thought she was invincible. She was my strong, solid, rock.

"When I was a teen, I started playing around with fabric, using material from donated clothing that didn't fit. I used kitchen shears to redesign our clothes. I had a real talent for sewing and I loved every aspect of design. I was determined to make something of myself. Mom and I moved to New York and I promised her we'd live better. It was time for me to take care of her. I got a job at an upscale store and later started working behind the scenes with designers. I had talent, but no connections and no money. It's a competitive field, hard to break in. I was struggling."

"That's where Golden came in. He had money and connections."

"Fast forward a few years. I met Michael for the very first time a few weeks after you and I were together. If you recall, I had a blind date that never showed."

"And I was the fill-in."

She sighed. "I didn't look at it that way. Michael had been called out of town on business. I was lonely and grieving my mother's death. That's when I met you." Despite the situation, she gave him a warm smile. "You... you were amazing."

He frowned. "So amazing you slept with Golden a few weeks later?"

Her chin lowered and she shook her head. "It wasn't like that. We started dating and he was charming. I was flattered. When I found out I was pregnant, I did really try to find Brett. I wrote him and I never heard back. I was with Michael at that time, and we were becoming serious about each other. But I decided to tell Michael about the baby right away. Michael can't have children, so he knew he wasn't the father. I offered to end our relationship. I told him I'd understand if he didn't want to see me anymore. Instead, he was overjoyed at the news of my pregnancy. He wanted us to be a family. As the weeks went on and I didn't hear back from Brett, no news at all, I continued to see Michael.

"I was frightened, Justin. I didn't have a dime to my name. I didn't have a way to support my son. I didn't want Connor to have the same life I'd had growing up. I know you won't believe this, but my thoughts back then were only for my baby. I saw a way for Connor to have a good life. I was enamored with Michael."

"With Michael or his money?"

Her cheeks flamed red against her creamy complexion. "You think you've got it all figured out. But you have no right to judge me. You grew up wealthy, having everything at your disposal. You had money, friends, influence. I had none of those things…and it didn't look as if I was going anywhere in my career. My dreams had to be put aside… for the baby's sake. What I did wasn't right, I know that. But in my heart and at that time, it was my only option."

"The truth is always an option."

Tears rolled down her cheeks. "I'm telling you the truth now."

"Would've been nice if I didn't have to hear it on TV first. Would've been nice if you'd come clean when we'd first met in Silver Springs. You passed my son off to another man. He had the time with Connor I missed out on."

Her eyes squeezed shut. "I'm sorry about that. So sorry, and if I could go back and change things, I would. If I'd known who you were…but you lied to me, Justin. You can't forget your part in this."

"I know," he said, quietly agreeing. "I can't deny that. But you've had all this time to tell me about your past. Here I thought you were all alone, struggling to survive with a baby in New York. Wasn't that the impression you wanted me to have?"

"No, it's not." She opened her eyes; they were beautifully green and brilliantly clear as she focused directly on him. There was clarity in her voice, as well. "You're a good man, Justin. A good father to Connor. I know I messed up. I know that you probably h-hate me."

Justin rose from his seat. Hell, he didn't hate her. He hated her lies. He was halfway in love with her before all of this happened. His fingers dug into his scalp. "I don't know how I feel about you right now, but that's not important. What's important is to get all the facts out. If you had everything you wanted with Golden, then why'd you leave your perfect little setup? Why did you come here? And don't tell me you had a stroke of conscience."

Her hand lifted to wipe away her tears and she drew in a deep breath. "Michael started getting very controlling."

"What?"

She nodded. "When things didn't go his way, he got nasty. He's a man who expects his demands to be met. He'd been 'yessed' all of his life. While we were dating, he was the most attentive man I'd ever met. I thought I was falling for him. He thought he loved me. After Connor was born, things changed. He was smitten with Connor. He wanted a child very badly, but things started going downhill between us. He started ordering me around. He wanted things for Connor I didn't approve of. He tried to completely take over my life. I started feeling…suffocated. Like I was being choked with his orders. I won't go into details, but at one point it got so bad, I trembled with fear whenever he walked into the room. I never knew what he'd find to pick on, what he'd find wrong.

"It was as if I was reliving my past with my father. Michael got verbally abusive with me. That's how it starts. I'm not saying that Michael would've physically abused me, but his harsh words were enough. I knew it was a matter of time, before Connor…Connor… Oh, my sweet baby… I couldn't subject him to a life like that."

The veins in Justin's neck popped. His nerves jumped, picturing that big man verbally slashing Kat, trying to undermine her self-esteem and confidence. And Connor? Anyone who called himself a man wouldn't bully a woman and child.

"We fought like crazy and I hated subjecting the baby to all that arguing. Finally, Michael agreed to let me go. I was afraid he would follow me because of Connor. I never told him where I was going and I'm grateful he never tried to find me."

The blood pumping in his veins simmered. "I'm trying to wrap my head around all of this."

"Justin?"

"Is this all the truth, Kat?"

"Yes, I had to leave him. I couldn't go back to that kind of life."

"Leaving that jerk was the right move."

"It was the only move I could make."

He looked deep into her eyes. "Answer me this one question, Kat. Were you deceiving Matilda Applegate with your intentions? Were you using her to put a roof over your head hoping to ingratiate yourself into her life?"

Her face crumpled, and her voice fell to barely a whisper. "You know the answer to that, Justin. I love Aunt Mattie. Connor loves her. And when we came here, we believed her to be Connor's great-aunt. Remember, it wasn't until you showed up and revealed *your* lies that I found out Brett Applegate wasn't Connor's father. So no, I wasn't using Aunt Mattie in any way."

All of this was hard to digest. There were so many lies, so many omissions. "Then if that's the case, why didn't you tell me about your engagement to Golden?"

"Because I knew you'd think what you're thinking now. That you'd look at me the way you're looking at me now."

Justin clamped his jaw tight. Her suspicions were justified…he didn't trust her.

"If I'd told you right away…wouldn't you have thought that I was only after Michael's money? That I was desperate and wanted a secure life for my son at any cost?"

"Maybe. Maybe not. Your explanation makes sense to me. But you didn't trust me enough to tell me the truth. I had a right to know another man was raising my son."

"I thought I was doing the right thing, Justin. What's happening between us is new and special and—"

"You didn't want to muck it up with the truth."

"I planned on telling you…one day."

He stared at her and sighed. Shaking his head, he spoke quietly. "Kiss Connor for me when he wakes up. I'd better go."

Kat rose and braced her hands on the back of the sofa. Unmasked fear entered her eyes. "I hope you understand, Justin. I didn't mean for anyone to get hurt. Especially you."

"I guess you paid me back for the lie I told you in New York."

Kat's eyes closed. "It wasn't like that."

"Look, I get it. I really do." He was dizzy from the different directions his mind was going. "I don't know when I'll be back."

Harsh words.

Twin tears rolled down her cheeks. "I hope it's soon."

His shoulder lifted in a shrug. He'd never abandon his son. Connor would always be in his life.

Kat, on the other hand, was a different matter.

Ten

Connor's chunky feet hit the floor and he pushed off, springing up and down in the seat of his baby bouncer. His smiles seared her heart and the sweet sound of his cackling echoed against the parlor walls. "He's loving this," Kat said.

The new bouncer, decorated with giraffes, lions and monkeys, was a hit. "I think our son likes his new toy."

"He's a natural. Maybe there's some bronc busting in his future." Justin stood a distance away watching him. "I'm glad he likes it."

"It's generous of you."

Justin's eyes remained glued to his boy. He didn't look at her much these days. His shut-out was a cool blast of reality. How long could he continue to freeze her out? "It's only the beginning. I'm making up for lost time."

His comment grated on her jumpy nerves. At least he was still speaking to her. That was something, wasn't it? "Thanks again for coming by and watching Connor every day, while I visit Aunt Mattie."

Five days and counting.

"He's my son. I'm not going to abandon him, because things didn't work out between us."

Wow. Point taken and heart crushed in one single blow. Justin must've been a good soldier—he had killer instincts.

Connor went even higher in his bouncer and his giggles rang out.

A smile broke the barrier of Justin's tight lips. At least Connor could do what Kat hadn't been able to accomplish… make Justin happy.

"How do you like the new kitchen floor?" she asked hopefully. She'd had a crew in here yesterday and they'd worked into the night to get the floor finished. Tomorrow, the cabinets would be replaced and the new granite counters came after that.

He slid a glance from the baby to the kitchen tiles poking out from the doorway. "Whatever Mattie wants is fine with me. The floor looks good."

That wasn't exactly a glowing endorsement. But what did she expect? Justin wasn't giving her an inch.

"I hope she's happy with everything. I've been gradually getting her to make decisions about the remodel. The good news is if all goes as expected, she should be home from rehab in two weeks."

His eyes lifted to hers. She soaked in the impact of his gaze. "Two weeks? So she's better?"

"Apparently…if they're sending her home."

"That's good."

"She asked about you."

His gaze shifted to Connor. "Give her my best."

"You should go see her. Talk to her. She'd like that." Kat knew the reason Justin didn't visit her. Guilt about Brett's death still managed to dictate the terms of his life. But she loved him enough to want to see him unburden himself from the pain eating him alive.

"I will. Soon."

Kat kept her lips sealed. It was difficult keeping her thoughts to herself these days. She wanted things back to where they were before. No, that wasn't true. She wanted to go back in time, and tell Justin the truth from the very beginning. If only she'd been less of a coward.

"It's difficult, you know."

So much for biting her tongue.

A frown creased his forehead but didn't say anything. Kat pressed on, summoning her inner diva. "Having this distance from you is worse torture than not being able to touch you. Or have you touch me."

Hot sparks flashed in his eyes. Good. She'd hit a nerve. Finally. "Sheesh, Kat. Don't you think this is killing me, too? It's eating me alive. It's just too much, all at once. There's too many lies between us. Torture goes both ways."

"But that's a good thing, isn't it?" she asked. "It means we still care about each other?"

Their gazes locked and held for a few beats. She was teetering on the edge here, hoping he wouldn't push her over.

Then his jaw clamped tight and he shook his head. "Leave it alone for now, Kat. If you're going to visit Mattie today, you should go. I'll take care of Connor while you're gone. When does he get his next bottle?"

Her hope vanished. It was hard keeping her voice light and breezy. The only thing that helped was looking at Connor's smiling face as he played in the baby bouncer. "In an hour. It's ready in the fridge. Just take it out ten minutes before, like you always do, to take the chill off."

He nodded with more enthusiasm now. He couldn't wait to be rid of her. "Got it."

"Okay," she offered softly. "I'll be going now."

She moved toward Connor, bent to kiss his cheek and whispered, "Be good for your daddy."

Feet planted, knees bent, Connor sprang up again. His baby laughter filled all the holes in her heart but one. That one only Justin could repair.

* * *

The house was lonely in the mornings. She missed being with Justin. She missed cooking him breakfast, and having him make French roast coffee for her. They'd lived that way for only a few days, but those days had been magical.

"That's what love does to you, sweet baby," she said to Connor in his crib. He tried a few times to stand up and then plopped back down. She smiled. "Makes you believe in magic."

She tied her pink cotton terry bathrobe around her waist and put her cold feet in her slippers. Even though it was still only late fall, there was a winter chill in the air and she shivered. If it were up to her, she'd have eighty-degree days every day. "Let's go get the newspaper," she said.

She wrapped Connor up in his blanket, plucked him off the crib mattress and marched the short steps down the porch to a patch of dirt where today's copy of the *Douglas County Sentinel* lay. Rural living meant no newspapers delivered on the penthouse doormat but she didn't miss the high life as much as she thought she would.

A crisp, cool wind followed her inside the house and she closed the door. "Wow, that's cold. Brrr," she said to Connor. "Momma's gonna put you in thermals today right after we eat."

The thermostat cranked up the heat in the house as she made Connor breakfast. His breakfast today was creamed oatmeal mixed with pureed pears. Mixing a little sweet with the healthy went a long way.

Her cell phone rang as she spooned the last bite into his mouth.

She wiped his oatmeal mustache away with a napkin and answered on the third ring.

"Hi, Kat. This is Audrey."

Kat glanced at the clock. Seven in the morning was kind of early for a social call. Audrey Thomas was usually tending the animals at this hour of the day. "Hi, Audrey. It's great to hear from you. How are you feeling? Everything good with the baby?"

"I'm feeling fine. Baby's doing yoga inside my belly."

"It's a wonderful feeling. I remember those flutters and waves of movement. Just wait until he does karate in there."

"Uh…Kat, I'm sorry to have to tell you this." Suddenly, Audrey's voice turned somber. "Last night one of the reporters from *Insider Buzz* flew into town and sort of ambushed Justin for an interview. He was caught off guard outside the ranch gates. Apparently, the reporter recognized you from that *LLL* show and asked Justin about his relationship with you. The guy was a real sleaze. He'd dug into your past and all Justin would tell us was that the questions were not flattering to you."

She took a sharp breath. "Oh, no."

"Justin was furious with the guy. There was a shouting match and Justin threatened to toss the guy back to New York on his ass. Oh, Kat, I'm sorry to say, there's a story on the *Insider Buzz* website and an article about the altercation between Justin and the reporter in the *Sentinel* this morning."

"The *Sentinel?*" She slid a glance at the newspaper on the table. "Is it…horrible?"

"No, I wouldn't say horrible, but there's speculation about Justin being Connor's real father. It lays out some fine points that aren't disputable, putting Justin in New York at the time of Connor's conception and mentioning rumors that the baby looks just like him. There's a bit about your relationship with Michael Golden, too."

"Oh, Audrey…I'm sorry I didn't tell you about Michael. It was a time in my life I didn't want to dredge up. I've made…mistakes."

"It's okay, Kat. You don't owe me an explanation. But

how do you think a reporter from New York found out about you and Justin?"

"Logan's wedding was at the Golden Hotel. We were together there and well...the next day I saw Michael. It was rotten timing—he was coming as I was going and we talked briefly."

"That six degrees of separation thing?"

"Maybe. Either the reporter really did his homework or Michael was behind leaking some information. I can only guess what terrible things were written."

"The Slades' phone has been ringing off the hook. Justin asked me to call you to explain."

"Oh, wow. He's doing my damage control." Tears stung her eyes. Her life had just gotten messier and now she was dragging Justin's good name down.

"I haven't lived here long, but I do know gossip travels fast," Audrey said.

Her heart dipped down to her stomach. "Aunt Mattie?"

"If she's got friends in Silver Springs, the grapevine will reach her."

"Oh, no. I've got to talk to her. I've got to explain everything."

"I think that's a good idea. Good luck and give little Connor a hug for me."

Kat pushed the button to end the call and her phone clicked off. Hesitating, she stared at the copy of the *Sentinel* on the table and scolded herself for not being braver. *Take a look. See what was written about you.* The chicken in her didn't want to pick up the newspaper. The chicken in her wanted to pretend this never happened.

Putting her phone down, she turned to the high chair. "Uppie arms," she said to her son. He waved his hands high in the air and she was quick about sliding the high chair tray off. Then she lifted Connor out of the seat, poured him a bottle of formula and set him down in his play yard.

"Drink your bottle, sweet boy. While Mommy…" She gulped. "While Mommy sees what all the fuss is about."

Picking up the newspaper, she plopped onto the sofa and opened it, turning the pages until she found the headline: War Hero Doing Battle at Home. She scanned the article quickly; it was just as Audrey had described.

She went into her sewing room, steeling her jumpy nerves as she opened her laptop and went to the *Insider Buzz* website.

The first thing she saw when she clicked on the article were two photos that took up about a quarter of the screen. The first had been taken at a charity gala when she was seven months pregnant. Her belly protruded from the silver satin gown she was wearing. She remembered how Michael had proudly told her she looked elegantly pregnant that night.

Then she scanned down to the second picture. It was a shot of Justin in full dress uniform—white gloves, white cap and all. Photo credit was given to the web archives of Medal of Honor recipients.

She did a quick read of the article. "Bleached-blonde social climber" stuck to her like Scotch tape, while Justin was described as a decorated war hero and Michael Golden as the injured party in their broken engagement.

Mortified, she bit back tears as she realized her entire pitiful life, minus anything that would paint her in a good light, was out there for all the world to see now.

She was only glad that no one had figured out the whole truth about Connor yet, and Matilda Applegate's name had not been mentioned in the article. But that didn't mean Aunt Mattie wouldn't hear about this or worse yet, read it herself. She'd find out from a gossipy neighbor or a well-meaning friend that Kat hadn't been entirely truthful with her. She'd find out about her engagement to Michael Golden and hear speculation regarding Justin's role in her life.

She tried to rein in the tears dripping down her cheeks as best she could. Connor shouldn't see her sobbing. He didn't need to see his mommy's grief over how she'd made a mess of things and the people she loved were being hurt.

One thing she knew for sure: she had to tell Aunt Mattie the truth. And she prayed it wouldn't send her back into cardiac arrest.

Or worse.

Justin kept a watchful eye on the rearview mirror, making sure he wasn't being followed. He had something to do. Something he should have done months ago. It was time for all of the truths to come out. Today, he was going to set his life to rights. No more secrets, no more lies.

He steered his truck through the gates of Silver Haven Cemetery and parked by the Tombstones of Soldiers monument. Climbing down from the cab of his truck, he didn't hesitate. His boots hit gravel as he moved to the grassy area, reading one tombstone after another. He should've guessed Brett's headstone would be the shiny new one, the one that wasn't ravaged by inclement weather and time. It felt odd, being here, about to talk to his friend this way. But he needed to wipe the slate clean. It would take a few swipes and today he was determined to see it through.

Removing his hat, he knelt on both knees. He no longer held back the tears. Unexpected relief came as they ran down his cheeks. He opened his mouth and the words he'd rehearsed over and over in his head flowed freely.

"Hello, buddy...I've got a few things to tell you. Now, it'd be too darn weird if you had something to tell me back, so don't spook me. Let me get this off my chest. First off, I miss you. The world isn't a better place without you. I'm sorry you're not here. For months I've beat myself up about my decision that day. I wish I could go back in time and piss you off royally. I should've kept you in the infirmary, out of action. You weren't fit for duty and I should've second-guessed myself. If I had, you'd be back on your farm again with your aunt Mattie. She's a kick in the pants, by the way. I've come to know her and she's as great as you said. I'm doing my best to protect her. In fact, I'm going to see her today, pay her a little visit. Oh, and there's one more thing I wanted to tell you. I've got a son. A sweet little boy named Connor. Man, I'm so thankful I lost that bet to you, you have no idea…."

Pungent scents of alcohol, medicine and sickness filled Kat's nostrils as she sat on the edge of Aunt Mattie's bed. The older woman's hands were small and fragile in her grasp. Mattie's skin was soft as butter though.

The Silver Springs rehab center was a halfway house for the infirm, but it was no royal palace. Aunt Mattie needed to get out of this place—the sooner, the better.

"I'm sorry about all of this, Aunt Mattie. Really, I am."

The *Sentinel* lay across the bedspread, open wide to Kat's personal living obituary. At least it felt that way to her, when she'd carefully explained the circumstances of Connor's birth and read the entire article to Aunt Mattie.

"I'm sorry, too."

"Everything in that article about me is t-true." Heavens, this was hard. A biting chill raced up and down her spine. Mattie's welfare was at stake. Kat wouldn't protect herself by easing up on her confession. Mattie needed to hear the truth from her lips. "I didn't try very hard to find Brett, I'll admit that to you. I didn't want to be tied to a hog farmer from a small town. In my mind, I'd come too far and I didn't want to backtrack. Michael doesn't know about Brett's bet with Justin so that part wasn't printed in the article. Thank God. Could you imagine if Connor

found out how I met his father—how he was conceived—
in a newspaper article when he grew up? But the rest is
true about me, Aunt Mattie. I did do all those things. I
wanted to provide a good life for Connor but I went about
it the wrong way."

"Oh, dear girl, it's a lot for me to take in," Aunt Mattie said.

"I know. I'm sorry, Aunt Mattie. Please don't be upset.
We, Justin and I, were afraid of your reaction when you
found out. We didn't want you to get hurt. I was terribly
afraid that if you knew the truth about Connor, you would
have another health scare."

Mattie smiled for the first time today. "You thought I'd
have another heart attack."

Slumping on the bed, Kat whispered, "Yes. I'm still
terrified of that."

"Don't be scared. I'm not as fragile as I appear." Mattie
squeezed Kat's hand hard to prove her point.

"I was stunned, angry and frustrated when I found out
that Justin was Connor's real father. For almost two years
of my life, I'd lived one lie, only to find out I'd really been
living another. I can only imagine how hurt you are, learning that Connor isn't, isn't…"

"I love that boy. Nothing will change that, Kat."

"I know you do. You have to b-believe me…." Her voice
cracked with a sob. "When I came to Silver Springs, I really
did believe Brett was Connor's father. I didn't know anything about his bet with Justin Slade until he showed
up that day." Kat sighed. "We've really made a mess of
things."

"Not so much of a mess," Aunt Mattie said. Hinging
forward on the bed, she released Kat's hand. "You see, I
have a confession to make too." She paused and rubbed
her temple. "I've always sort of known that Connor wasn't

Brett's boy. In my head, that is. In my heart, Connor will always be mine."

Air puffed out of her lungs. What was she saying? Kat wasn't sure she heard right. "What do you mean?"

"My Brett was built like his uncle, solid and wide. He had reddish-brown hair and freckles across his nose. His eyes were bluer than mine. Connor looks nothing like him. So I had my suspicions. Then I went into my pack of old letters from Brett and found one where he spoke about a bet he'd won with his commanding officer. They'd switched identities for one weekend in New York. Brett had a great time going to movies and eating in expensive restaurants by himself. He never mentioned a woman. When Justin came knocking on my door and introduced himself, I got a chance to see him up close next to Connor. That boy is the spitting image of his daddy."

Kat's mouth dropped open. She hadn't expected this. "Why didn't you say something to me?"

Aunt Mattie pulled the material of her bed robe tighter. "If my suspicions were correct, I figured you'd tell me when the time was right."

"But you invited me to stay with you. To live at your house even when you weren't sure I was telling the truth."

A warm beam of light brightened her eyes. "Honey, I took one look at you and that little angel standing on my doorstep, and knew you needed my help. My goodness, I've lived a long, long time. I know despair when I see it. You needed me. And I wasn't about to turn you away." Aunt Mattie leaned back against the pillows on her bed. Immediately, Kat rose to straighten them out and fluff them to make her more comfortable.

"There, you see," she said. "You've come into my life and only made it better. You're always helping me."

"I lied to you."

"To protect me."

"I'm not a good person."

Her eyes lifted to the ceiling. "Dear Ralph. Are you hearing this? You've seen her goodness. You've seen Kat help me with the cooking and cleaning. You've seen her make sure I take my medications on time. You've seen her work into the night to earn her keep. And Ralph, I swear to you, if there's a better mother in the entire world, I've not met her."

Aunt Mattie's gaze lowered to meet Kat's eyes. "Not only do I love Connor," she said, her gravelly voice smooth and silky now, "but I love you, too, Kat. You're like a daughter to me."

Warmth and joy ran laps inside Kat's body and she couldn't get the words out fast enough. "Oh, Aunt Mattie. I love you, too."

Kat put her arms around Brett's aunt and hugged her carefully. Moments ticked by as Kat counted her blessings and good fortune in meeting Mattie Applegate.

"I'm so glad everything is out in the open," Kat said softly into Mattie's ear. "But I want you to know Connor will always be your great-nephew. You will always have a place with us. You are part of our family."

"That makes an old woman very happy. No heart attacks today for me."

Kat squeezed her tighter. "You promise?"

"I can surely promise you that."

Justin stood behind the partition in Mattie's rehab room listening to her to talking to Kat. He didn't mean to eavesdrop but he also didn't want to barge in on their private conversation, so he stood quietly waiting for the right moment. He'd heard every word Kat had spoken and now his boots propelled him forward and he stepped past the hospital curtain. "Hello."

His eyes reached Mattie first. She smiled back. "Hello."

"Am I interrupting?" he asked her.

"Not at all. We're just chillin'."

He couldn't hide a grin. Mattie was as feisty as ever. She must be feeling better. She knew the truth and was okay with it. That said something wonderful about her character.

"Chillin' is a good thing."

His gaze slid to Kat. Her eyes softened on him. Her lips parted and she did that innocent little gesture with her hand in her hair that rocketed through his nerve endings. His breathing quickened and something powerful clicked inside his head, pounding sense into it.

His heart squeezed tight.

He'd been wrong about Kat. He'd come to that conclusion after his sorely bruised ego had healed up. He'd seen her side of things for the first time. She did have a rough life, and despite her hardships, she'd always done what she believed best for their son. He had to give her credit where it was due.

What he'd just witnessed now told him in a thousand different ways that she was a good woman. He didn't care about her past. She was strong, a survivor. Just the kind of girl a tough-minded former marine should pair up with.

"Come join us, Justin," Mattie was saying.

Kat rose quickly from the hospital bed. "Actually," she said to her, "I've got to get back to the house. Audrey was nice enough to babysit Connor. I told her I wouldn't be gone too long."

Slipping her purse over her shoulder, she leaned down and kissed Mattie's cheek. "You and Justin should talk. I'll be back tomorrow."

She spared him a glance as she strode toward the door.

"Kat? We need to talk, too," he said.

She stopped and focused her gaze on the floor, refusing to look at him. "I can't tell you how sorry I am about all of this." Then without another word, she brushed by him and slipped out the door.

Justin turned his head and peered down the hallway, but Kat was already out of sight. Sighing, he swiveled back to Mattie. Grabbing the only chair in the room, he swung it around to her bedside and straddled it backward so he was facing her.

"You know about Connor now?"

"Kat explained everything to me." She gestured toward the newspaper. "I imagine this isn't easy for you, either."

"I couldn't care less about myself. It's you I'm worried about. You know, Kat and I didn't want to see you hurt."

"Yes, I know. Kat made sure I understood. I don't blame either of you for keeping the truth from me. You were both trying to protect me."

"Kat more than me," he said. He had to be honest. "I wanted to claim Connor as my son, but Kat insisted and I finally agreed it would be best to hold back the truth until you were fully recovered."

"It doesn't matter, Justin. I already love that boy like my own. I always will. Kat assured me that I'd always be a part of her family. That's all I want."

"You got it. You're Connor's great-aunt, as far as I'm concerned."

"Thank you. It means everything to me. My Ralph always would say, the truth shall set you free."

Justin took a big swallow. It was time to shed light on one more truth. It was time to unburden himself of the heavy weight he carried. He faced his fears and forced the words out. "There's one more truth, Aunt Mattie. It's about Brett and how he died that day. I'm afraid it's my fault."

"Oh, dear boy. I doubt that very much."

Justin set out to change her mind. He spoke to her now, leaving nothing out about the events leading up to Brett's death. He held Mattie's hand and confessed, pouring out his guilt, baring his soul and crying tears of enormous grief. "H-he was a good man and a fine soldier. Maybe too good a soldier. He was so damn eager to get back to active duty. He loved being a marine," he finally concluded.

"He did love it." Tears filled Mattie's eyes. She tried not to show it, but she was in a lot of pain.

"I'm sorry. I'm sorry. This is too much for you all at once," he said.

"I'm going to be just fine, Justin. Lordy, you've held this grief inside for so long, boy."

She rose from her bed and came around his chair. He wanted to tell her to stay in bed, to take care with her fragile body, but she set her jaw firm and filled her eyes with determination. She cradled his head and gently ran a hand down his cheek. Her fingers were touches of peace to his tortured spirit. "Please don't feel responsible. Brett was a stubborn one. He wanted what he wanted, when he wanted it. He told you he was ready. He made that decision. He did. Not you," she whispered. "Not you, Justin."

"But when we got to the schoolhouse, I ordered him to go back. That's when he got shot."

"You saw that he was sick. You sent him to safety." She lowered her weary body down on the edge of her bed. The warmth in her eyes spoke of forgiveness. "You were being a friend and a good commander. Brett would always say the unit was only as strong as the weakest link. I miss that boy something fierce, Justin, but I won't see you torture yourself with regrets. If Brett wasn't up to the task, it was your duty to send him back. You didn't know what would happen to him."

"I, uh, don't know what to say. I've dreaded having to tell you about Brett for a long time. I thought you'd hate me."

A kind smile parted her lips. "Now, how could I hate Connor's real daddy?"

He lowered his head and stared down at her bed slippers. "You're a good woman, Matilda Applegate."

"Too bad I'm too old for you."

His chuckle rose up from his mending heart.

"But if you're looking for a really fine woman, I've got me a roommate I think you'd like."

He searched her knowing eyes. "I like her just fine."

"You love her. Don't know if you realize it or not."

Oxygen whooshed into his lungs and he blinked.

"She's kicking herself in the behind about the mess she's made. I think a fine upstanding man like yourself could undo that mess with three magical words."

He gave a shake of his head. "I don't know."

She frowned. "Those aren't the three words." She took his hand in hers. The pressure she applied was forceful, much stronger than he gave her credit for. Then she looked him dead in the eyes. "If you have any doubts about Kat's intentions or her character, ask her about Lowery's."

His brow furrowed in confusion. "What's that supposed to mean?"

"Ah, it's not for me to say." She gave him a final squeeze of the hand and a quick nod of the head. "You go see her first thing tomorrow morning and ask her. You won't be sorry."

Tomorrow morning worked for him. He had some unsettled business that he needed to tend to tonight before he spoke with her. "Okay, I'll do that."

"Good. Now, if you'll excuse me, I think I need my beauty sleep."

She climbed into bed and he helped her get settled in the sheets. Then he gave her a little kiss on the cheek. "You couldn't get any more beautiful, Aunt Mattie."

"Hush now. Talk like that will surely get my heart pumping too hard."

He smiled. How could he ever repay her generosity? Not only had she helped him rid himself of his guilt about Brett's death, but she'd given Kat and his baby son a roof over their heads and unconditional love when they'd needed it the most.

Matilda Applegate was turning out to be his savior, his conscience and his couples counselor all rolled up into one.

Justin left the construction site at the Gateway Equine Retreat and headed east on foot. A walk would do him good. He had things to say to Kat. And he wanted a clear head to say them. Pulling the brim of his hat down, he shaded his eyes from the morning sunshine peeking out through scattered gray clouds.

He glanced at his watch. Seven-thirty. Was it too early to show up unannounced at Mattie's house? Suddenly, he was a teenager again, full of nerves and anxious as all get-out to see his high school crush.

The Applegate house came into view from fifty yards away. Movement on the porch caught his eye. He stopped abruptly and shoved his hat off his forehead to get a better look. Straining his eyes, he narrowed in on a brown-haired woman entering the house with his son. Who was she? He didn't recognize her. Was she someone else from Kat's past that he didn't know about?

"Damn it." His gut told him something was wrong.

It was too early for a social call from one of the neighbors.

His boots ate grass and gravel getting to the house. Heart hammering, he pushed his way through the unlocked front door. He'd have to caution Kat about keeping the door locked later. "Kat? Connor?"

"We're in here," Kat called out, her voice sounding as sultry as the day they'd first met.

Relief swooped down to replace his fear. He crossed the parlor and strode down the hallway. Once he reached Kat's bedroom, he blinked and refocused his eyes.

The woman who'd just finished diapering Connor

turned to face him and his mouth fell open. It wasn't the rosy-lipped, wavy-haired, platinum-blonde seductress, Katherine Grady, staring back at him. It was a clean-faced, green-eyed natural beauty with straight ordinary brown hair.

As the seconds ticked by, his heart bludgeoned his chest. He couldn't take his eyes off her. "Kat?"

Her lips trembled and turned down. "This is the real me."

A slow nod moved his head up and down. "O-kay."

"I'm a fraud, Justin."

Man, oh, man. She looked so different. Equally beautiful, but different. "No, you're not."

Her gaze landed on Connor in the crib. She handed him his bottle.

Justin walked over to stroke his head and watch him take the first few gulps. His little mouth sucked hard, drawing the formula out. There was nothing more precious in the world than his son. Justin stole a glance at Kat—they were his family.

Kat took a step back, away from the crib. "Yes, I'm the worst kind of fraud. Anyone who knows anything about Michael Golden knows he likes platinum blondes. He had this thing for Marilyn, you know. My blind date had been set up a month in advance. I invented my look. I designed clothes for myself that would give off a certain impression. I transformed myself into someone else just to gain the attention of a certain rich man."

Justin didn't care about any of that. It was never clearer than right now. "So what?"

"So what? Aren't you afraid that I'm only here for your money? Aren't you—?"

"No."

"You're not?" Her eyes opened wide.

"No, I'm not."

"Why not?"

A smile spread across his face. "Because I know you."

"You don't know the real me."

"I know you're a scrapper. I know you truly care about that old woman. I know you've worried about her, taken care of her, protected her even when it was probably in your best interest to tell the world Connor was a Slade. I know you'd do anything for our son. I admire that about you, Kat."

She gulped. "You admire me?"

"Yes, I do." He took her hand and tugged. She landed up against his chest. He wrapped his arms around her waist and then moved them lower. As he flattened his hands against her buttocks, a tiny gasp escaped her throat. "I like you as a brunette, sugar. You're still gorgeous."

"I'm not flashy anymore."

"Flashy is so twenty minutes ago."

Her eyes beamed and a chuckle burst from her lips.

He brought his mouth to her hair and kissed her there. "Mattie knows the truth about everything now."

She pulled away from him. "You spoke to her about Brett?"

"I did. Yesterday. It was one of the hardest things I've had to do. But I made my peace with it all. Thanks to you."

"Me?"

He spoke from deep in his heart. "You helped me through a tough time, Kat. You were just what I needed. Your encouragement guided me in the right direction. You didn't condemn me, not even when I had the worst suspicions about you."

"I'm glad I was able to help," she whispered. "Very glad."

He brought her hand to his lips and kissed it. "I have a confession to make."

"What's that?"

"After what you told me about Michael Golden, I suspected him of having leaked the story to that reporter at *Insider Buzz*. There was something about that guy that didn't ring true. He flew in from New York to get a story about you and me? Then he deliberately provoked me? None of that added up. I'm sure it was a setup. Since then, Logan's been helping me dig into Golden's past. My brother found out some things about Michael Golden that wouldn't go over well in the public eye. Let's just say there's a few women from his past who'd also been harassed and abused."

"Really? I guess that shouldn't surprise me. Michael is very good at hiding his true colors. And it's only recently that he's become a focus of the media. When we were together, he promised to keep Connor and I out of the limelight."

"Golden is out of your life now. He won't be causing you any trouble."

"How do you know?"

"To a man who deals with the public, bad press is worse than a bad economy. It's the kiss of death. He's not the only one who can leak a story. His PR people must be going crazy right now, worried their stock will drop if some of those women come forward and Golden Hotels' squeaky clean name gets tarnished."

"I guess the moral of the story is, no one should mess with a Slade."

"Got that right."

"Me included?"

"*You* should always mess with this Slade."

His hand moved through her silky straight hair, cupping her head as he brought her mouth close to his. Her flowery scent tickled his nose. He pressed his lips to hers and touched softness. He poured everything he had into that kiss, his heart, his mind, his soul. He could go on kissing her for hours, but he wasn't through with all the truths yet. Summoning his willpower, he stepped back, breaking their connection. "Tell me about Lowery's."

Her pretty green eyes rounded and her voice turned breathless. "H-how do you know about that?"

"I don't know much. I'm asking you to tell me."

Her shoulders fell. "Aunt Mattie must've flapped her gums to you yesterday."

"I wouldn't blame her if I were you. She was singing your praises to me. Not that I needed to hear any of it. I'm already crazy in love with you. I don't think I could possibly love you any more than I already do."

"Justin," she whispered through pale pink lips. Her head tilted upward and she ran her hand through the strands of her hair again. The gesture didn't need blond roots to turn him on. "You really love me?"

Unable to resist, he kissed her again. "With all my heart."

Her eyes softened and her hand came to rest on his cheek. "I love you, too."

A wide grin spread across his face. He reached for her waist with both hands and in one swift move, lifted her in the air. Her hands came to his chest as he twirled her around and around. Her laughter filled the room and he joined in, bellowing his happiness. When he lowered her down and her feet hit the floor, tears spilled from her eyes.

"Why are you crying, sugar?"

"Because I love you so much, Justin, and I never thought you'd love me back. It means so much to me that you told me before you found out about Lowery's."

He took her hands in his. "You'll never have to doubt my love, but I'm dying to know what's up with Lowery's."

"Wait one more second." She stepped out of his arms and went to her dresser. Pulling open the top drawer, she lifted out a handful of letters. "I've kept this secret for two weeks. Even before Aunt Mattie took ill. Even before I thought there was any hope for us."

Her gaze fastened on one letter in particular. "You know how hard I've worked to make a success of myself. I've told you about my designs and my dreams. I've been rejected by every major department chain." She took the envelope out of the drawer. "But one. Lowery's Department Store offered to buy my line of baby clothes for their stores. It's a lucrative contract. More money than I've earned in over ten years of struggling. More than I ever imagined. I'd be financially independent."

Walking over to her, he gave her shoulders a squeeze. "That's your dream, Kat. Congratulations."

"But it's not my dream anymore, Justin. That's just it. I thought I wanted it and sure, I needed some security for Connor's future, but I couldn't bring myself to accept the offer."

"Why?"

"Because it meant leaving Silver Springs. It meant leaving you and Aunt Mattie. I just couldn't do it. I couldn't bring myself to leave the people I love. I'm happy here, Justin. I've finally figured it out. I'd transformed myself on the outside, but inside, I never really changed. All I've wanted in life was a shred of happiness, a family to love and a way to earn a living. I have the start of a great online business with Babylicious. I can develop that right here. I thought I needed wealth to make me happy because of the way I grew up. But all I really want is a simple life."

He peered deeply into her eyes. "I hope that simple life includes me."

A smile radiated from her face. "Of course it does."

"Well, then, let me introduce myself properly," he said. He entwined his fingers with hers. "I'm Justin Slade, filthy rich war hero and a man who loves you beyond reason." He brought her fingertips to his lips and kissed each one.

"Nice to meet you, Justin," she said, her voice barely above a whisper. "I'm Katherine Grady, a scrappy survivor who has finally found her true self."

Justin didn't need another second to think about this. He loved Kat and Connor and wanted them with him for the rest of his life.

His knee hit the floor right there in Kat's bedroom, beside the crib where his young son lay. His sweet baby breaths were the music that soothed Justin's soul. Lifting his face to Kat, he saw love enter her eyes. He knew this was right. They had come down a very jagged path to find each other, but now he'd do everything in his power to keep them together.

"Beautiful Katherine, will you marry me? Will you become my wife? Will you and Connor be my family?"

"Oh, Justin. Yes. Yes. I'll marry you. We already *are* your family."

He rose to his feet and smiled. How lucky could he get? He kissed her deeply, soundly, and let his lips linger on hers for long moments after.

"I can't wait to make it official," he said, gazing into her eyes. "The sooner the better for me. Do you think you'd like a double wedding? Luke and Audrey wouldn't mind if we tagged along. I've already hinted at it and Audrey was all over the idea."

Her voice broke tenderly. "Really? You've discussed this with Audrey and your brother?"

"Yeah, late last night."

"But their wedding is coming up fast."

He gulped air. Was he pressing her? "Too soon?"

She braced both hands on his chest and nestled closer to him, laying her head on his shoulder. "Not at all. I'm a simple girl, remember? I don't need a fancy wedding. I just need you and Connor."

Soft whimpers rose up from the crib. His son had good timing. "He's agreeing."

Kat moved away and bent over the crib to lift the baby up. Cradling him in her arms, she whispered, "He's smart as a whip."

"Takes after his mommy."

"I won't argue with that." Her lips pressed against Connor's eyebrow and Justin kissed him on the other one. Then he wrapped his arms around the two people he loved most in the world, huddling them into his embrace.

"Family hug," Kat said, laughing.

Connor's lips formed a big smile and Justin's heart zinged. "I don't think I could be any happier."

Connor shifted from Kat's steady hold and leaned toward Justin with arms outstretched, waving for his attention. "Oh, look. He wants his daddy."

Justin reached for him and Kat made the easy transfer. His son nestled into his chest, spreading warmth.

Standing back, a warm loving beam entered Kat's eyes. "That just looks right. I don't think I could be any happier, either."

Justin grinned.

All the secrets were out.

The three of them were where they belonged.

And finally a family.

Epilogue

Kat's engagement ring caught sunlight and sparkled, dazzling her almost as much as the man standing at the podium on the front steps of the Douglas County office. Dressed in a fitted dark suit and tie, his Congressional Medal of Honor pinned to his lapel, Justin addressed the thousands of townspeople who'd honored him with a parade through the main street of town. All five of the servicemen whose lives he'd saved stood behind him, a living, breathing testament to his bravery. Aunt Mattie, holding Connor in her arms, sat beside Kat in the front row. Luke and Audrey, Logan and Sophia were seated directly next to them.

"Thank you. Thank you." Justin's voice was filled with gratitude. "For all of you who have come here today, it's an honor to serve you and my country. I have to say I'm humbled by the turnout. Your generosity and support mean a lot to me. Though I didn't want all the hoopla—and certainly when I commanded my unit in Afghanistan, a parade in my honor wasn't something I'd ever dreamed of—I do appreciate what you've done for me today."

He sent Kat a nod. She rose from her seat and he waited while she picked up Connor. As soon as they reached the podium to take their place beside Justin, the baby, dressed in his little blue suit, opened and closed his hand, waving to the onlookers. Sighs and giggles rang out.

Justin's prideful chuckle boomed over the loudspeaker. "And before I go on, I want to introduce you to a very special woman…someone who's made a big difference in my life, someone who, by this time tomorrow, will be my wife. Katherine Grady."

Justin set his hand on her waist and drew her close. Their hips bumped, and she smiled at the crowd. She didn't want the attention—this was Justin's time to shine—but he'd insisted she stand up here with him. He wanted to put to rest once and for all the rumors and innuendo from those scandalous articles. He wanted a fresh start and to show the world he was behind her one hundred percent. He wanted to introduce his family. "And this little tyke, who's got his wave down pretty darn good, is our son, Connor Brett Slade."

Applause broke out. "I know," Justin said over the noise, "he is pretty darn cute, isn't he?"

Justin waited for the noise to settle down, his big smile warming her heart. Oh, how she loved him. She could hardly believe tomorrow she'd be Mrs. Justin Slade, wife, mother and Babylicious clothes designer.

Justin went on. "We gave our boy the middle name of Brett, because it means something real important to all of us." Justin's gaze flowed over to Mattie. "Brett Applegate was a buddy of mine, a damn good marine and a great person. Brett lost his life in a firefight in Afghanistan. To honor him and his uncle Ralph Applegate, who was also a veteran, along with all of the great men and women who've served our country in the military, I'm happy to announce that come next spring, a project I'm very proud of will be opening its doors in Silver Springs. On the spot of Brett's family farm, we're building an equine retreat for veterans called the Gateway Equine Retreat. Soldiers helping horses, horses helping soldiers. Can't think of anything better. The construction is already in the works thanks to the cooperation and help of Brett's aunt, Matilda Apple-gate. It's going to be something remarkable and I hope you'll join us at the grand opening."

After concluding his speech, Justin pulled Kat aside, grabbing her hand and taking her back behind the county building. He trapped her against a wall, his hands braced on the building bricks behind her. "Thanks for standing by my side." His lips tenderly touched hers.

"Always."

He smiled. "You're beautiful."

She lifted a hand to a wayward lock of his hair and set it in place. "So are you."

"I can't wait to get you alone tonight."

"Mmm, sounds good. But you're not getting me alone."

His eyes opened a little wider. "I'm not?"

"Nope. Sophia has invited me and Audrey over for a good old-fashioned night-before-the-double-wedding girls' party. After tomorrow, we'll all be Slades. That's some-thing to celebrate. I'll be staying at Sophia's cottage to-night."

"And what will I be doing?"

"Well, you, Connor, Logan and Luke can have a boys' night."

"You mean I'm babysitting?"

She tilted her head to one side. "I thought you'd like that."

A smile broadened his lips. "I love it. But I'll miss you."

"I'll miss you, too." Her fingers walked up his chest to his collarbone and she massaged the hollow spot there. "What if I make it up to you?"

"Keep talking."

"I think I'll leave it to your very vivid imagination."

His eyes burned hot and hungry. "Man, oh, man, I love you, Kat."

She'd never imagined this much happiness could fill her

life. It beamed inside of her. She'd never forget her past, but now she had the promise of a wonderful future ahead with no detours or roadblocks in her path.

It was smooth sailing from here on out.

Kat smiled.

"I love you, too, Justin."

He covered her hand with his and led her toward a life as brilliant and beautiful as a Nevada sunset.

* * * * *

"Do you really think people are going to believe we went from professional adversaries to lovers in a heartbeat?"

"Lovers, huh? I like the sound of that."

"This isn't a plan." Mariama pulled free, inching her chair back. "It's insanity."

"It's a plan that will work. Everyone will want to hear more about the aloof princess finding romance and playing Good Samaritan at Christmastime."

Her eyes went wide with panic, but she stayed in her seat. She wasn't running. Yet.

Rowan shoved to his feet. "Time for bed."

"Bed?" she squeaked, standing, as well.

He could see in her eyes that she'd envisioned them sharing a bed before this moment. And it gave him a surge of victory.

* * *

Yuletide Baby Surprise
is a Billionaires and Babies novel:

Powerful men...wrapped around
their babies' little fingers

YULETIDE
BABY SURPRISE

BY
CATHERINE MANN

MILLS
BOON

Published in Great Britain 2013
by Mills & Boon, an imprint of Harlequin (UK) Limited,
Eton House, 18-24 Paradise Road, Richmond, Surrey TW9 1SR

© Catherine Mann 2013

ISBN: 978 0 263 90491 8

51-1113

Harlequin (UK) policy is to use papers that are natural, renewable and recyclable products and made from wood grown in sustainable forests. The logging and manufacturing processes conform to the legal environmental regulations of the country of origin.

Printed and bound in Spain
by Blackprint CPI, Barcelona

USA TODAY bestselling author **Catherine Mann** lives on a sunny Florida beach with her flyboy husband and their four children. With more than forty books in print in over twenty countries, she has also celebrated wins for both a RITA® Award and a Booksellers' Best Award. Catherine enjoys chatting with readers online—thanks to the wonders of the internet, which allows her to network with her laptop by the water! Contact Catherine through her website, www.catherinemann.com, find her on Facebook and Twitter (@CatherineMann1) or reach her by snail mail at PO Box 6065, Navarre, FL 32566, USA.

To Savannah

One

Dr. Mariama Mandara had always been the last picked for a team in gym class. With good reason. Athletics? Not her thing. But when it came to spelling bees, debate squads and math competitions, she'd racked up requests by the dozens.

Too bad her academic skills couldn't help her sprint faster down the posh hotel corridor.

More than ever, she needed speed to escape the royal watchers tracking her at the Cape Verde beachside resort off the coast of West Africa, which was like a North Atlantic Hawaii, a horseshoe grouping of ten islands. They were staying on the largest island, Santiago.

No matter where she hid, determined legions were all too eager for a photo with a princess. Why couldn't they accept she was here for a business conference, not socializing?

Panting, Mari braced a hand against the wall as she

stumbled past a potted areca silk palm strung with
twinkling Christmas lights. Evading relentless pursu-
ers wasn't as easy as it appeared in the movies, especially if you weren't inclined to blow things up or leap
from windows. The nearest stairwell door was blocked
by two tourists poring over some sightseeing pamphlet.
A cleaning cart blocked another escape route. She could
only keep moving forward.

Regaining her balance, she power-walked, since
running would draw even more attention or send her
tripping over her own feet. Her low-heeled pumps thud-
thud-thudded along the plush carpet in time with a poly-
rhythmic version of "Hark! The Herald Angels Sing"
wafting from the sound system. She just wanted to finish this medical conference and return to her research
lab, where she could ride out the holiday madness in
peace, crunching data rather than candy canes.

For most people, Christmas meant love, joy and family. But for her, the "season to be jolly" brought epic
family battles even twenty years after her parents' divorce. If her mom and dad had lived next door to each
other—or even on the same continent—the holidays
would not have been so painful. But they'd played trans-
continental tug-of-war over their only child for decades.
Growing up, she'd spent more time in the Atlanta air-
port and on planes with her nanny than actually celebrating by a fireside with cocoa. She'd even spent one
Christmas in a hotel, her connecting flight canceled
for snow.

The occasional cart in the hall now reminded her
of that year's room-service Christmas meal. Call her
crazy, but once she had gained more control over her
world, she preferred a simpler Christmas.

Although simple wasn't always possible for someone

born into royalty. Her mother had crumbled under the pressure of the constant spotlight, divorced her Prince Charming in Western Africa and returned to her Atlanta, Georgia, home. Mari, however, couldn't divorce herself from her heritage.

If only her father and his subjects understood she could best serve their small region through her research at the university lab using her clinical brain, rather than smiling endlessly through the status quo of ribbon-cutting ceremonies. She craved her comfy, shapeless clothes, instead of worrying about keeping herself neat as a pin for photo ops.

Finally, she spotted an unguarded stairwell. Peering inside, she found it empty but for the echo of "Hark! The Herald Angels Sing" segueing into "Away in a Manger." She just needed to make it from the ground level to her fifth-floor room, where she could hole up for the night before facing the rest of the week's symposiums. Exhausted from a fourteen-hour day of presentations about her research on antiviral medications, she was a rumpled mess and just didn't have it in her to smile pretty for the camera or field questions that would be captured on video phone. Especially since anything she said could gain a life of its own on the internet in seconds these days.

She grasped the rail and all but hauled herself up step after step. Urgency pumped her pulse in her ears. Gasping, she paused for a second at the third floor to catch her breath before trudging up the last flights. Shoving through the fifth-floor door, she almost slammed into a mother and teenage daughter leaving their room. The teen did a double take and Mari turned away quickly, adrenaline surging through her exhaustion and power-

ing her down the hall. Except now she was going in the
opposite direction, damn it.

Simply strolling back into the hall wasn't an option until she could be sure the path was clear. But she
couldn't simply stand here indefinitely, either. If only
she had a disguise, something to throw people off the
scent. Head tucked down, she searched the hall through
her eyelashes, taking in a brass luggage rack and mon-
strously big pots of African feather grass.

Her gaze landed on the perfect answer—a room-
service cart. Apparently abandoned. She scanned for
anyone in a hotel uniform, but saw only the retreating
back of a woman walking away quickly, a cell phone
pressed to her ear. Mari chewed her lip for half a second then sprinted forward and stopped just short of the
cloth-draped trolley.

She peeked under the silver tray. The mouth-watering
scent of saffron-braised karoo lamb made her stomach
rumble. And the tiramisu particularly tempted her to
find the nearest closet and feast after a long day of talking without a break for more than coffee and water. She
shook off indulgent thoughts. The sooner she worked
her way back to her room, the sooner she could end
this crazy day with a hot shower, her own tray of food
and a soft bed.

Delivering the room-service cart now offered her
best means of disguise. A hotel jacket was even draped
over the handle and a slip of paper clearly listed Suite
5A as the recipient.

The sound of the elevator doors opening spurred
her into action.

Mari shrugged the voluminous forest-green jacket
over her rumpled black suit. A red Father Christmas
hat slipped from underneath the hotel uniform. All the

better for extra camouflaging. She yanked on the hat over her upswept hair and started pushing the heavily laden cart toward the suite at the end of the hall, just as voices swelled behind her.

"Do you see her?" a female teen asked in Portuguese, her squeaky tones drifting down the corridor. "I thought you said she ran up the stairs to the fifth floor."

"Are you sure it wasn't the fourth?" another high-pitched girl answered.

"I'm certain," a third voice snapped. "Get your phone ready. We can sell these for a fortune."

Not a chance.

Mari shoved the cart. China rattled and the wheels creaked. Damn, this thing was heavier than it looked. She dug her heels in deeper and pushed harder. Step by step, past carved masks and a pottery elephant planter, she walked closer to suite 5A.

The conspiring trio drew closer. "Maybe we can ask that lady with the cart if she's seen her...."

Apprehension lifted the hair on the back of Mari's neck. The photos would be all the more mortifying if they caught her in this disguise. She needed to get inside suite 5A. Now. The numbered brass plaque told her she was at the right place.

Mari jabbed the buzzer, twice, fast.

"Room service," she called, keeping her head low.

Seconds ticked by. The risk of stepping inside and hiding her identity from one person seemed far less daunting than hanging out here with the determined group and heaven only knew who else.

Just when she started to panic that time would run out, the door opened, thank God. She rushed past, her arms straining at the weight of the cart and her nose catching a whiff of manly soap. Her favorite scent—

clean and crisp rather than cloying and obvious. Her feet tangled for a second.

Tripping over her own feet as she shoved the cart was far from dignified. But she'd always been too gangly to be a glamour girl. She was more of a cerebral type, a proud nerd, much to the frustration of her family's press secretary, who expected her to present herself in a more dignified manner.

Still, even in her rush to get inside, curiosity nipped at her. What type of man would choose such a simple smell while staying in such opulence? But she didn't dare risk a peek at him.

She eyed the suite for other occupants, even though the room-service cart only held one meal. One very weighty meal. She shoved the rattling cart past a teak lion. The room appeared empty, the lighting low. Fat leather sofas and a thick wooden table filled the main space. Floor-to-ceiling shutters had been slid aside to reveal the moonlit beach outside a panoramic window. Lights from stars and yachts dotted the horizon. Palms and fruit trees with lanterns illuminated the shore. On a distant islet, a stone church perched on a hill.

She cleared her throat and started toward the table by the window. "I'll set everything up on the table for you."

"Thanks," rumbled a hauntingly familiar voice that froze her in her tracks. "But you can just leave it there by the fireplace."

Her brain needed less than a second to identify those deep bass tones. Ice trickled down her spine as if snow had hit her African Christmas after all.

She didn't have to turn around to confirm that fate was having a big laugh at her expense. She'd run from an irritation straight into a major frustration. Out of all the hotel suites she could have entered, somehow she'd landed in the room of Dr. Rowan Boothe.

Her professional nemesis.

A physician whose inventions she'd all but ridiculed in public.

What the hell was he doing here? She'd reviewed the entire program of speakers and she could have sworn he wasn't listed on the docket until the end of the week.

The door clicked shut behind her. The tread of his footsteps closed in, steady, deliberate, bringing the scent of him drifting her way. She kept her face down, studying his loafers and the well-washed hem of his faded jeans.

She held on to the hope that he wouldn't recognize her. "I'll leave your meal right here then," she said softly. "Have a nice evening."

His tall, solid body blocked her path. God, she was caught between a rock and a hard place. Her eyes skated to his chest.

A very hard, muscle-bound place encased in a white button-down with the sleeves rolled up and the tail untucked. She remembered well every muscular—annoying—inch of him.

She just prayed he wouldn't recognize her from their last encounter five months ago at a conference in London. Already the heat of embarrassment flamed over her.

Even with her face averted, she didn't need to look further to refresh her memory of that too handsome face of his. Weathered by the sun, his Brad Pitt–level good looks only increased. His sandy blond hair would have been too shaggy for any other medical professional to carry off. But somehow he simply appeared too immersed in philanthropic deeds to be bothered with anything as mundane as a trip to the barber.

The world thought he was Dr. Hot Perfection but she simply couldn't condone the way he circumvented rules.

"Ma'am," he said, ducking his head as if to catch her attention, "is there a problem?"

Just keep calm. There was no way for him to identify her from the back. She would rather brave a few pictures in the press than face this man while she wore a flipping Santa Claus hat.

A broad hand slid into view with cash folded over into a tip. "Merry Christmas."

If she didn't take the money, that would appear suspicious. She pinched the edge of the folded bills, doing her best to avoid touching him. She plucked the cash free and made a mental note to donate the tip to charity. "Thank you for your generosity."

"You're very welcome." His smooth bass was too appealing coming from such an obnoxiously perfect man.

Exhaling hard, she angled past him. Almost home free. Her hand closed around the cool brass door handle.

"Dr. Mandara, are you really going so soon?" he asked with unmistakable sarcasm. He'd recognized her. Damn. He was probably smirking, too, the bastard.

He took a step closer, the heat of his breath caressing her cheek. "And here I thought you'd gone to all this trouble to sneak into my room so you could seduce me."

Dr. Rowan Boothe waited for his words to sink in, the possibility of sparring with the sexy princess/research scientist already pumping excitement through his veins. He didn't know what it was about Mariama Mandara that turned him inside out, but he'd given up analyzing the why of it long ago. His attraction to Mari was simply a fact of life now.

Her disdain for him was an equally undeniable fact, and to be honest, it was quite possibly part of her allure.

He grew weary with the whole notion of the world painting him as some kind of saint just because he'd rejected the offer of a lucrative practice in North Carolina and opened a clinic in Africa. These days, he had money to burn after his invention of a computerized medical diagnostics program—a program Mari missed no opportunity to dismiss as faux, shortcut medicine. Funding the clinic hadn't even put a dent in his portfolio so he didn't see it as worthy of hoopla. Real philanthropy involved sacrifice. And he wasn't particularly adept at denying himself things he wanted.

Right now, he wanted Mari.

Although from the look of horror on her face, his half-joking come-on line hadn't struck gold.

She opened and closed her mouth twice, for once at a loss for words. Fine by him. He was cool with just soaking up the sight of her. He leaned back against the wet bar, taking in her long, elegant lines. Others might miss the fine-boned grace beneath the bulky clothes she wore, but he'd studied her often enough to catch the brush of every subtle curve. He could almost feel her, ached to peel her clothes away and taste every inch of her café-au-lait skin.

Some of the heat must have shown on his face because she snapped out of her shock. "You have got to be joking. You can't honestly believe I would ever make a move on you, much less one so incredibly blatant."

Damn, but her indignation was so sexy and yeah, even cute with the incongruity of that Santa hat perched on her head. He couldn't stop himself from grinning.

She stomped her foot. "Don't you dare laugh at me."

He tapped his head lightly. "Nice hat."

Growling, she flung aside the hat and shrugged out of the hotel jacket. "Believe me, if I'd known you were in here, I wouldn't have chosen this room to hide out."

"Hide out?" he said absently, half following her words.

As she pulled her arms free of the jacket to review a rumpled black suit, the tug of her white business shirt against her breasts sent an unwelcome surge of arousal through him. He'd been fighting a damned inconvenient arousal around this woman for more than two years, ever since she'd stepped behind a podium in front of an auditorium full of people and proceeded to shoot holes in his work. She thought his computerized diagnostics tool was too simplistic. She'd accused him of taking the human element out of medicine. His jaw flexed, any urge to smile fading.

If anyone was too impersonal, it was her. And, God, how he ached to rattle her composure, to see her tawny eyes go sleepy with all-consuming passion.

Crap.

He was five seconds away from an obvious erection. He reined himself in and faced the problem at hand— the woman—as a more likely reason for her arrival smoked through his brain. "Is this some sort of professional espionage?"

"What in the hell are you talking about?" She fidgeted with the loose waistband on her tweedy skirt.

Who would have thought tweed would turn him inside out? Yet he found himself fantasizing about pulling those practical clunky shoes off her feet. He would kiss his way up under her skirt, discover the silken inside of her calf...

He cleared his throat and brought his focus up to her heart-shaped face. "Playing dumb does not suit you." He knew full well she had a genius IQ. "But if that's the way you want this to roll, then okay. Were you hoping to obtain insider information on the latest upgrade to my computerized diagnostics tool?"

"Not likely." She smoothed a hand over her swept-back hair. "I never would have pegged you as the conspiracy theorist sort since you're a man of science. Sort of."

He cocked an eyebrow. "So you're not here for information, Mari." If he'd wanted distance he should have called her Dr. Mandara, but too late to go back. "Then why are you sneaking into my suite?"

Sighing, she crossed her arms over her chest. "Fine. I'll tell you, but you have to promise not to laugh."

"Scout's honor." He crossed his heart.

"You were a Boy Scout? Figures."

Before he'd been sent to a military reform school, but he didn't like to talk about those days and the things he'd done. Things he could never atone for even if he opened free clinics on every continent, every year for the rest of his life. But he kept trying, by saving one life at a time, to make up for the past.

"You were going to tell me how you ended up in my suite."

She glanced at the door, then sat gingerly on the arm of the leather sofa. "Royal watchers have been trailing me with their phones to take photos and videos for their five seconds of fame. A group of them followed me out the back exit after my last seminar."

Protective instincts flamed to life inside him. "Doesn't your father provide you with bodyguards?"

"I choose not to use them," she said without explanation, her chin tipping regally in a way that shouted the subject wasn't open for discussion. "My attempt to slip away wasn't going well. The lady pushing this room-service cart was distracted by a phone call. I saw my chance to go incognito and I took it."

The thought of her alone out there had him biting back the urge to chew out someone—namely her father. So what if she rejected guards? Her dad should have insisted.

Mari continued, "I know I should probably just grin for the camera and move on, but the images they capture aren't...professional. I have serious work to do, a reputation to maintain." She tipped her head back, her mouth pursed tight in frustration for a telling moment before she rambled on with a weary shake of her head. "I didn't sign on for this."

Her exhaustion pulled at him, made him want to rest his hands on her drooping shoulders and ease those tense muscles. Except she would likely clobber him with the silver chafing dish on the serving cart. He opted for the surefire way to take her mind off the stress.

Shoving away from the bar, he strode past the cart toward her again. "Poor little rich princess."

Mari's cat eyes narrowed. "You're not very nice."

"You're the only one who seems to think so." He stopped twelve inches shy of touching her.

Slowly, she stood, facing him. "Well, pardon me for not being a member of *your* fan club."

"You genuinely didn't know this was my room?" he asked again, even though he could see the truth in her eyes.

"No. I didn't." She shook her head, the heartbeat throbbing faster in her elegant neck. "The cart only had your room number. Not your name."

"If you'd realized ahead of time that this was my room, my meal—" he scooped up the hotel jacket and Santa hat "—would you have surrendered yourself to the camera-toting brigade out there rather than ask me for help?"

Her lips quivered with the first hint of a smile. "I guess we'll never know the answer to that, will we?" She tugged at the jacket. "Enjoy your supper."

He didn't let go. "There's plenty of food here. You could join me, hide out for a while longer."

"Did you just invite me to dinner?" The light of humor in her eyes animated her face until the air damn near crackled between them. "Or are you secretly trying to poison me?"

She nibbled her bottom lip and he could have sworn she swayed toward him. If he hooked a finger in the vee of her shirt and pulled, she would be in his arms.

Instead, he simply reached out and skimmed back the stray lock of sleek black hair curving just under her chin. "Mari, there are a lot of things I would like to do to you, but I can assure you that poisoning you is nowhere on that list."

Confusion chased across her face, but she wasn't running from the room or laughing. In fact, he could swear he saw reluctant interest. Enough to make him wonder what might happen if...

A whimper snapped him out of his passion fog.

The sound wasn't coming from Mari. She looked over his shoulder and he turned toward the sound. The cry swelled louder, into a full-out wail, swelling from across the room.

From under the room-service cart?

He glanced at Mari. "What the hell?"

She shook her head, her hands up. "Don't look at me."

He charged across the room, sweeping aside the linen cloth covering the service cart to reveal a squalling infant.

TWO

The infant's wail echoed in the hotel suite. Shock resounded just as loudly inside of Mari as she stared at the screaming baby in a plastic carrier wedged inside the room-service trolley. No wonder the cart had felt heavier than normal. If only she'd investigated she might have found the baby right away. Her brain had been tapping her with the logic that something was off, and she'd been too caught up in her own selfish fears about a few photos to notice.

To think that poor little one had been under there all this time. So tiny. So defenseless. The child, maybe two or three months old, wore a diaper and a plain white T-shirt, a green blanket tangled around its tiny, kicking feet.

Mari swallowed hard, her brain not making connections as she was too dumbstruck to think. "Oh, my God, is that a baby?"

"It's not a puppy." Rowan washed his hands at the wet-bar sink then knelt beside the lower rack holding the infant seat. He visibly went into doctor mode as he checked the squalling tyke over, sliding his hands under and scooping the child up in his large, confident hands. Chubby little mocha-brown arms and legs flailed before the baby settled against Rowan's chest with a hiccupping sigh.

"What in the world is it doing under there?" She stepped away, clearing a path for him to walk over to the sofa.

"I'm not the one who brought the room service in," he countered offhandedly, sliding a finger into the baby's tiny bow mouth. Checking for a cleft palate perhaps?

"Well, I didn't put the baby there."

A boy or girl? She couldn't tell. The wriggling bundle wore no distinguishing pink or blue. There wasn't even a hair bow in the cap of black curls.

Rowan elbowed aside an animal-print throw pillow and sat on the leather couch, resting the baby on his knees while he continued assessing.

She tucked her hands behind her back. "Is it okay? He or she?"

"Her," he said, closing the cloth diaper. "She's a girl, approximately three months old, but that's just a guess."

"We should call the authorities. What if whoever abandoned her is still in the building?" Unlikely given how long she'd hung out in here flirting with Rowan. "There was a woman walking away from the cart earlier. I assumed she was just taking a cell phone call, but maybe that was the baby's mother?"

"Definitely something to investigate. Hopefully there will be security footage of her. You need to think through what you're going to tell the authorities, review every detail in your mind while it's fresh." He sounded more like a detective than a doctor. "Did you see anyone else around the cart before you took it?"

"Are you blaming this on me?"

"Of course not."

Still, she couldn't help but feel guilty. "What if this is my fault for taking that cart? Maybe the baby wasn't abandoned at all. What if some mother was just trying to bring her child to work? She must be frantic looking for her daughter."

"Or frantic she's going to be in trouble," he replied dryly.

"Or he. The parent could be a father." She reached for the phone on the marble bar. "I really need to ring the front desk now."

"Before you call, could you pass over her seat? It may hold some clues to her family. Or at least some supplies to take care of her while we settle this."

"Sure, hold on."

She eased the battered plastic seat from under the cart, winging a quick prayer of thankfulness that the child hadn't come to some harm out there alone in the hall. The thought that someone would so recklessly care for a precious life made her grind her teeth in frustration. She set the gray carrier beside Rowan on the sofa, the green blanket trailing off the side.

Finally, she could call for help. Without taking her eyes off Rowan and the baby, she dialed the front desk.

The phone rang four times before someone picked up. "Could you hold, please? Thank you," a harried-sounding hotel operator said without giving Mari a chance to shout "No!" The line went straight to Christmas carols, "O Holy Night" lulling in her ear.

Sighing, she sagged a hip against the garland-draped wet bar. "They put me on hold."

Rowan glanced up, his pure blue eyes darkened with an answering frustration. "Whoever decided to schedule a conference at this time of year needs to have his head examined. The hotel was already jam-packed with holiday tourists, now conventioneers, too. Insane."

"For once, you and I agree on something one hundred percent." The music on the phone transitioned to "The Little Drummer Boy" as she watched Rowan cradle the infant in a way that made him even more handsome. Unwilling to get distracted by traveling down that mental path again, she shifted to look out the window at the scenic view. Multicolored lights blinked from the sailboats and ferries.

The Christmas spirit was definitely in full swing on the resort island. Back on the mainland, her father's country included more of a blend of religions than many realized. Christmas wasn't as elaborate as in the States, but still celebrated. Cape Verde had an especially deep-rooted Christmas tradition, having been originally settled by the Portuguese.

Since moving out on her own, she'd been more than happy to downplay the holiday mayhem personally, but she couldn't ignore the importance, the message of hope that should come this time of year. That a parent could abandon a child at the holidays seemed somehow especially tragic.

Her arms suddenly ached to scoop up the baby, but she had no experience and heaven forbid she did something wrong. The little girl was clearly in better hands with Rowan.

He cursed softly and she turned back to face him. He

held the baby in the crook of his arm while he searched the infant seat with the other.

"What?" she asked, covering the phone's mouthpiece. "Is something the matter with the baby?"

"No, something's the matter with the parents. You can stop worrying that some mom or dad brought their baby to work." He held up a slip of paper, baby cradled in the other arm. "I found this note tucked under the liner in the carrier."

He held up a piece of hotel stationary.

Mari rushed to sit beside him on the sofa, phone still in hand. "What does it say?"

"The baby's mother intended for her to be in this cart, in *my* room." He passed the note. "Read this."

Dr. Boothe, you are known for your charity and generosity. Please look over my baby girl, Issa. My husband died in a border battle and I cannot give Issa what she needs. Tell her I love her and will think of her always.

Mari reread the note in disbelief, barely able to process that someone could give away their child so easily, with no guarantees that she would be safe. "Do people dump babies on your doorstep on a regular basis?"

"It's happened a couple of times at my clinic, but never anything remotely like this." He held out the baby toward her. "Take Issa. I have some contacts I can reach out to with extra resources. They can look into this while we're waiting for the damn hotel operator to take you off hold."

Mari stepped back sharply. "I don't have much experience with babies. No experience actually, other than kissing them on the forehead in crowds during photo ops."

"Didn't you ever babysit in high school?" He cradled the infant in one arm while fishing out his cell phone with his other hand. "Or do princesses not babysit?"

"I skipped secondary education and went straight to college." As a result, her social skills sucked as much as her fashion sense, but that had never mattered much. Until now. Mari smoothed a hand down her wrinkled, baggy skirt. "Looks to me like you have Issa and your phone well in hand."

Competently—enticingly so. No wonder he'd been featured in magazines around the globe as one of the world's most eligible bachelors. Intellectually, she'd understood he was an attractive—albeit irritating—man. But until this moment, she hadn't comprehended the full impact of his appeal.

Her body flamed to life, her senses homing in on this moment, on *him*. Rowan. The last man on the planet she should be swept away by or attracted to.

This must be some sort of primal, hormonal thing. Her ticking biological clock was playing tricks on her mind because he held a baby. She could have felt this way about any man.

Right?

God, she hoped so. Because she couldn't wrap her brain around the notion that she could be this drawn to a man so totally wrong for her.

The music ended on the phone a second before the operator returned. "May I help you?"

Heaven yes, she wanted to shout. She needed Issa safe and settled. She also needed to put space between herself and the increasingly intriguing man in front of her.

She couldn't get out of this suite soon enough.

"Yes, you can help. There's been a baby abandoned just outside Suite 5A, the room of Dr. Rowan Boothe."

Rowan didn't foresee a speedy conclusion to the baby mystery. Not tonight, anyway. The kind of person who threw away their child and trusted her to a man based solely on his professional reputation was probably long gone by now.

Walking the floor with the infant, he patted her back for a burp after the bottle she'd downed. Mari was reading a formula can, her forehead furrowed, her shirt half-untucked. Fresh baby supplies had been sent up by the hotel's concierge since Rowan didn't trust anything in the diaper bag.

There were no reports from hotel security or authorities of a missing child that matched this baby's description. So far security hadn't found any helpful footage, just images of a woman's back as she walked away from the cart as Mari stepped up to take it. Mari had called the police next, but they hadn't seemed to be in any hurry since no one's life was in danger and even the fact that a princess was involved didn't have them moving faster. Delays like this only made it more probable the press would grab hold of information about the situation. He needed to keep this under control. His connections could help him with that, but they couldn't fix the entire system here.

Eventually, the police would make their way over with someone from child services. Thoughts of this baby getting lost in an overburdened, underfunded network tore at him. On a realistic level, he understood he couldn't save everyone who crossed his path, but something about this vulnerable child abandoned at Christmas tore at his heart all the more.

Had to be because the kid was a baby, his weak spot.

He shrugged off distracting thoughts of how badly he'd screwed up as a teenager and focused on the present. Issa burped, then cooed. But Rowan wasn't fooled into thinking she was full. As fast as the kid had downed that first small bottle, he suspected she still needed more. "Issa's ready for the extra couple of ounces if you're ready."

Mari shook the measured powder and distilled water together, her pretty face still stressed. "I think I have it right. But maybe you should double-check."

"Seriously, I'm certain you can handle a two-to-one mixture." He grinned at seeing her flustered for the first time ever. Did she have any idea how cute she looked? Not that she would be happy with the "cute" label. "Just think of it as a lab experiment."

She swiped a wrist over the beads of sweat on her forehead, a simple watch sliding down her slim arm. "If I got the proportions wrong—"

"You didn't." He held out a hand for the fresh bottle. "Trust me."

Reluctantly, she passed it over. "She just looks so fragile."

"Actually, she appears healthy, well fed and clean." Her mother may have dumped her off, but someone had taken good care of the baby before that. Was the woman already regretting her decision? God, he hoped so. There were already far too few homes for orphans here. "There are no signs she's been mistreated."

"She seems cuddly," Mari said with a wistful smile.

"Are you sure you wouldn't like to hold her while I make a call?"

She shook her head quickly, tucking a stray strand of hair back into the loose knot at her neck. "Your special contacts?"

He almost smiled at her weak attempt to distract him from passing over the baby. And he definitely wasn't in a position to share much of anything about his unorthodox contacts with her. "It would be easier if I didn't have to juggle the kid and the bottle while I talk."

"Okay, if you're sure I won't break her." She chewed her bottom lip. "But let me sit down first."

Seeing Mari unsure of herself was strange, to say the least. She always commanded the room with her confidence and knowledge, even when he didn't agree with her conclusions. There was something vulnerable, approachable even, about her now.

He set the baby into her arms, catching a whiff of Mari's perfume, something flowery and surprisingly whimsical for such a practical woman. "Just be careful to support her head and hold the bottle up enough that she isn't drinking air."

Mari eyed the bottle skeptically before popping it into Issa's mouth. "Someone really should invent a more precise way to do this. There's too much room for human error."

"But babies like the human touch. Notice how she's pressing her ear against your heart?" Still leaning in, he could see Mari's pulse throbbing in her neck. The steady throb made him burn to kiss her right there, to taste her, inhale her scent. "That heartbeat is a constant in a baby's life in utero. They find comfort in it after birth, as well."

Her deep golden gaze held his and he could swear something, an awareness, flashed in her eyes as they played out this little family tableau.

"Um, Rowan—" her voice came out a hint breathier than normal "—make your call, please."

Yeah, probably a good idea to retreat and regroup while he figured out what to do about the baby—and about having Mari show up unexpectedly in his suite.

He stepped into his bedroom and opened the French door onto the balcony. The night air was that perfect temperature—not too hot or cold. Decembers in Cape Verde usually maxed out at between seventy-five and eighty degrees Fahrenheit. A hint of salt clung to the air and on a normal night he would find sitting out here with a drink the closest thing to a vacation he'd had in... He'd lost count of the years.

But tonight he had other things on his mind.

Fishing out his phone, he leaned on the balcony rail so he could still see Mari through the picture window in the sitting area. His gaze roved over her lithe body, which was almost completely hidden under her ill-fitting suit. At least she wouldn't be able to hear him. His contacts were out of the normal scale and the fewer people who knew about them, the better. Those ties traced back far, all the way to high school.

After he'd derailed his life in a drunk-driving accident as a teen, he'd landed in a military reform school with a bunch of screwups like himself. He'd formed life-time friendships there with the group that had dubbed themselves the Alpha Brotherhood. Years later after college graduation, they'd all been stunned to learn their headmaster had connections with Interpol. He'd recruited a handful of them as freelance agents. Their troubled pasts—and large bank accounts—gave them a cover story to move freely in powerful and sometimes seedy circles.

Rowan was only tapped for missions maybe once

a year, but it felt damn good to help clean up underworld crime. He saw the fallout too often in the battles between warlords that erupted in regions neighboring his clinic.

The phone stopped ringing and a familiar voice said, "Speak to me, Boothe."

"Colonel, I need your help."

The Colonel laughed softly. "Tell me something new. Which one of your patients is in trouble? Or is it another cause you've taken on? Or—"

"Sir, it's a baby."

The sound of a chair squeaking echoed over the phone lines and Rowan could envision his old headmaster sitting up straighter, his full attention on the moment. "You have a baby?"

"Not *my* baby. *A* baby." He didn't expect to ever have children. His life was too consumed with his work, his mission. It wouldn't be fair to a child to have to compete with third-world problems for his father's attention. Still, Rowan's eyes locked in on Mari holding Issa so fiercely, as if still afraid she might drop her. "Someone abandoned an infant in my suite along with a note asking me to care for her."

"A little girl. I always wanted a little girl." The nostalgia in the Colonel's voice was at odds with the stern exterior he presented to the world. Even his clothes said stark long after he'd stopped wearing a uniform. These days, in his Interpol life, Salvatore wore nothing but gray suits with a red tie. "But back to your problem at hand. What do the authorities say?"

"No one has reported a child missing to the hotel security or to local authorities. Surveillance footage hasn't shown anything, but there are reports of a woman walking away from the cart where the baby was abandoned. The police are dragging their feet on showing up here to investigate further. So I need to get ahead of the curve here."

"In what way?"

"You and I both know the child welfare system here is overburdened to the crumbling point." Rowan found a plan forming in his mind, a crazy plan, but one that felt somehow right. Hell, there wasn't any option that sat completely right with his conscience. "I want to have temporary custody of the child while the authorities look into finding the mother or placing her in a home."

He might not be the best parental candidate for the baby, but he was a helluva lot better than an overflowing orphanage. If he had help…

His gaze zeroed in on the endearing tableau in his hotel sitting room. The plan came into sharper focus as he thought of spending more time with Mari.

Yet as soon as he considered the idea, obstacles piled in his path. How would he sell her on such an unconventional solution? She freaked out over feeding the kid a bottle.

"Excuse me for asking the obvious, Boothe, but how in the hell do you intend to play papa and save the world at the same time?"

"It's only temporary." He definitely couldn't see himself doing the family gig long-term. Even thinking of growing up with his own family sent his stomach roiling. Mari made it clear her work consumed her, as well. So a temporary arrangement could suit them both well. "And I'll have help…from someone."

"Ah, now I understand."

"How do you understand from a continent away?" Rowan hated to think he was that transparent.

"After my wife wised up and left me, when I had our

son for the weekend, I always had trouble matching up outfits for him to wear. So she would send everything paired up for me." He paused, the sound of clinking ice carrying over the phone line.

Where was Salvatore going with this story? Rowan wasn't sure, but he'd learned long ago that the man had more wisdom in one thumb that most people had in their entire brain. God knows, he'd saved and redirected dozens of misfit teenagers at the military high school.

Salvatore continued, "This one time, my son flipped his suitcase and mixed his clothes up. I did the best I could, but apparently, green plaid shorts, an orange striped shirt and cowboy boots don't match."

"You don't say." The image of Salvatore in his uniform or one of those generic suits of his, walking beside a mismatched kid, made Rowan grin. Salvatore didn't offer personal insights often. This was a golden moment and Rowan just let him keep talking.

"Sure, I knew the outfit didn't match, although I didn't know how to fix it. In the end, I learned a valuable lesson. When you're in the grocery store with the kid, that outfit shouts 'single dad' to a bevy of interested women."

"You used your son to pick up women?"

"Not intentionally. But that's what happened. Sounds to me like you may be partaking of the same strategy with this 'someone' who's helping you."

Busted. Although he felt compelled to defend himself. "I would be asking for help with the kid even if Mari wasn't here."

"Mariama Mandara?" Salvatore's stunned voice reverberated. "You have a thing for a local princess?"

Funny how Rowan sometimes forgot about the princess part. He thought of her as a research scientist. A professional colleague—and sometimes adversary. But most of all, he thought of her as a desirable woman, someone he suddenly didn't feel comfortable discussing with Salvatore. "Could we get back on topic here? Can you help me investigate the baby's parents or not?"

"Of course I can handle that." The Colonel's tone returned to all business, story time over.

"Thank you, sir. I can't tell you how much I appreciate this." Regardless of his attraction to Mari, Rowan couldn't lose sight of the fact that a defenseless child's future hung in the balance here.

"Just send me photos, fingerprints, footprints and any other data you've picked up."

"Roger. I know the drill."

"And good luck with the princess," Salvatore said, chuckling softly before he hung up.

Rowan drew in a deep breath of salty sea air before returning to the suite. He hated being confined. He missed his clinic, the wide-open spaces around it and the people he helped in a tangible way rather than by giving speeches.

Except once he returned home in a week to prepare for Christmas, his window of time with Mari would be done. Back to business.

He walked across the balcony and entered the door by the picture window, stepping into the sitting room. Mari didn't look up, her focus totally on the baby.

Seeing Mari in an unguarded moment was rare. The woman kept major walls up, giving off a prickly air. Right now, she sat on the sofa with her arms cradling the baby—even her body seemed to wrap inward protectively around this child. Mari might think she knew nothing about children, but her instincts were good. He'd watched enough new moms in his career to identify the ones who would have trouble versus the ones who sensed the kid's needs.

The tableau had a Madonna-and-child air. Maybe it was just the holidays messing with his head. If he wanted his half-baked plan to work, he needed to keep his head on straight and figure out how to get her on board with helping him.

"How's Issa doing?"

Mari looked up quickly, as if startled. She held up the empty bottle. "All done with her feeding."

"I'm surprised you're still sticking around. Your fans must have given up by now. The coast will be clear back to your room."

Saying that, he realized he should have mentioned those overzealous royal watchers to Salvatore. Perhaps some private security might be in order. There was a time he didn't have the funds for things like that, back in the days when he was buried in the debt of school loans, before he'd gone into partnership with a computer-whiz classmate of his.

"Mari? Are you going back to your room?" he repeated.

"I still feel responsible for her." Mari smoothed a finger along the baby's chubby cheek. "And the police will want to speak to me. If I'm here, it will move things along faster."

"You do realize the odds are low that her parents will be found tonight," he said, laying the groundwork for getting her to stick around.

"Of course, I understand." She thumbed aside a hint of milk in the corner of the infant's mouth. "That doesn't stop me from hoping she'll have good news soon."

"You sure seem like a natural with her. Earlier, you said you never babysat."

She shrugged self-consciously. "I was always busy studying."

"There were no children in your world at all?" He sat beside her, drawing in the scent of her flowery perfume. Curiosity consumed him, a desperate need to know exactly what flower she smelled like, what she preferred.

"My mother and father don't have siblings. I'm the only child of only children."

This was the closest to a real conversation they'd ever exchanged, talk that didn't involve work or bickering. He couldn't make a move on her, not with the baby right here in the room. But he could feel her relaxing around him. He wanted more of that, more of her, this exciting woman who kept him on his toes.

What would she do if he casually stretched his arm along the back of the sofa? Her eyes held his and instead of moving, he stayed stock-still, looking back at her, unwilling to risk breaking the connection—

The phone jangled harshly across the room.

Mari jolted. The baby squawked.

And Rowan smiled. This particular moment to get closer to Mari may have ended. But make no mistake, he wasn't giving up. He finally had a chance to explore the tenacious desire that had been dogging him since he'd first seen her.

Anticipation ramped through him at the thought of persuading her to see this connection through to its natural—and satisfying—conclusion.

Three

Pacing in front of the sitting room window, Mari cradled the baby against her shoulder as Rowan talked with the local police. Sure, the infant had seemed three months old when she'd looked at her, but holding her? Little Issa felt younger, more fragile.

Helpless.

So much about this evening didn't add up. The child had been abandoned yet she seemed well cared for. Beyond her chubby arms and legs, she had neatly trimmed fingernails and toenails. Her clothes were simple, but clean. She smelled freshly bathed. Could she have been kidnapped as revenge on someone? Growing up, Mari had been constantly warned of the dangers of people who would try to hurt her to get back at her father, as well as people would use her to get *close* to her father. Trusting anyone had been all but impossible.

She shook off the paranoid thoughts and focused on

the little life in her arms. Mari stroked the baby's impossibly soft cheeks, tapped the dimple in her chin. Did she
look like her mother or father? Was she missed? Round
chocolate-brown eyes blinked up at her trustingly.

Her heart squeezed tight in her chest in a totally il-
logical way. She'd only just met the child, for heaven's
sake, and she ached to press a kiss to her forehead.

Mari glanced to the side to see if Rowan had ob-
served her weak moment, but he was in the middle of
finishing up his phone conversation with the police.

Did he practice looking so hot? Even in jeans, he
owned the room. Her eyes were drawn to the breadth
of his shoulders, the flex of muscles in his legs as he
shuffled from foot to foot, his loafers expensive but
well worn. He exuded power and wealth without waste
or conspicuous consumption. How could he be such a
good man and so annoying at the same time?

Rowan hung up the phone and turned, catching her
studying him. He cocked an eyebrow. She forced herself to stare back innocently, her chin tipping even as
her body tingled with awareness.

"What did the police say?" she asked casually, swaying from side to side in a way she'd found the baby
liked.

"They're just arriving outside the hotel." He closed
the three feet between them. "They're on their way up
to take her."

"That's it?" Her arms tightened around Issa. "She'll
be gone minutes from now? Did they say where they
will be sending her? I have connections of my own.
Maybe I can help."

His blue eyes were compassionate, weary. "You and
I both already know what will happen to her. She will
be sent to a local orphanage while the police use their

limited resources to look into her past, along with all the other cases and other abandoned kids they have in their stacks of files to investigate. Tough to hear, I realize. But that's how it is. We do what we can, when we can."

"I understand." That didn't stop the frustration or the need to change things for this innocent child in her arms and all the children living in poverty in her country.

He scooped the baby from her before she could protest. "But that's not how it has to be today. We *can* do something this time."

"What do you mean?" She crossed her empty arms over her chest, hope niggling at her that Rowan had a reasonable solution.

"We only have a few more minutes before they arrive so I need to make this quick." He hefted the baby onto his shoulder and rubbed her back in small, hypnotic circles. "I think we should offer to watch Issa."

Thank heaven he was holding the child because he'd stunned Mari numb. She watched his hand smoothing along the baby's back and tried to gather her thoughts. "Um, what did you say?"

"We're both clearly qualified and capable adults." His voice reverberated in soothing waves. "It would be in the best interest of the child, a great Christmas message of goodwill, for us to keep her."

Keep her?

Mari's legs folded out from under her and she sank to the edge of the leather sofa. She couldn't have heard him right. She'd let her attraction to him distract her. "What did you say?"

He sat beside her, his thigh pressing warm and solid against hers. "We can have temporary custody of her, just for a couple of weeks to give the police a chance to find out if she has biological relatives able to care for her."

"Have you lost your mind?" Or maybe she had lost hers because she was actually tempted by his crazy plan.

"Not that I know of."

She pressed the back of her wrist to her forehead, stunned that he was serious. Concerns cycled through her head about work and the hoopla of a media circus. "This is a big decision for both of us, something that should be thought over carefully."

"In medicine I have to think fast. I don't always have the luxury of a slow and steady scientific exam," he said, with a wry twist to his lips. "Years of going with my gut have honed my instincts, and my instincts say this is the right thing to do."

Her mind settled on his words and while she never would have gotten to that point on her own, the thought of this baby staying with him rather than in some institution was appealing. "So you'll be her temporary guardian?"

"Our case is more powerful if we offer to do this as a partnership. Both of us." His deep bass and logic drew her in. "Think of the positive PR you'll receive. Your father's press corps will be all over this philanthropic act of yours, which should take some pressure off you at the holidays," he offered, so logically she could almost believe him.

"It isn't as simple as that. The press can twist things, rumors will start about both of us." What if they thought it was *her* baby? She squeezed her eyes closed and bolted off the sofa. "I need more time."

The buzzer rang at the door. Her heart went into her throat.

She heard Rowan follow her. Felt the heat of him at her back. Felt the urgency.

"Issa doesn't have time, Mari. You need to decide if you'll do this. Decide to commit now."

She turned sharply to find him standing so close the three of them made a little family circle. "But you could take her on your own—"

"Maybe the authorities would accept that. But maybe not. We should lead with our strongest case. For her." He cradled the baby's head. "We didn't ask for this, but we're here." Fine lines fanned from the corners of his eyes, attesting to years of worry and long hours in the sun. "We may disagree on a lot of things, but we're people who help."

"You're guilt-tripping me," she accused in the small space between them, her words crackling like small snaps of electricity. And the guilt was working. Her concerns about gossip felt absolutely pathetic in light of the plight of this baby.

As much as she gave Rowan hell about his computer inventions, she knew all about his humanitarian work at the charity clinic. He devoted his life to helping others. He had good qualities underneath that arrogant charm.

"Well, people like us who help in high-stakes situations learn to use whatever means are at our disposal." He half smiled, creasing the lines deeper. "Is it working?"

Those lines from worry and work were real. She might disapprove of his methods, but she couldn't question his motivations, his altruistic spirit. Seeing him deftly rock the baby to sleep ended any argument. For this one time at least, she was on his team.

For Issa.

"Open the door and you'll find out."

* * *

Three hours later, Mari watched Rowan close the hotel door after the police. Stacks of paperwork rested on the table, making it official. She and Rowan had temporary custody of the baby while the police investigated further and tried to track down the employee who'd walked away from the cart.

Issa slept in her infant seat, secure for now.

Mari sighed in relief, slumping in exhaustion back onto the sofa. She'd done it. She'd played the princess card and all but demanded the police obey her "request" to care for the baby until Christmas—less than two weeks away—or until more information could be found about Issa's parents. She'd agreed to care for the child with Rowan Boothe, a doctor who'd saved countless young lives. The police had seemed relieved to have the problem resolved so easily. They'd taken photos of the baby and prints. They would look into the matter, but their faces said they didn't hold out much hope of finding answers.

Maybe she should hire a private detective to look deeper than the police. Except it was almost midnight now. Any other plans would have to wait until morning.

Rowan rested a hand on Mari's shoulder. "Would you get my medical bag so I can do a more thorough checkup? It's in the bedroom by my shaving kit. I'd like to listen to her heart."

He squeezed her shoulder once, deliciously so, until her mouth dried right up from that simple touch.

"Medical bag." She shot to her feet. "Right, of course."

She was too tired and too unsettled to fight off the sensual allure of him right now. She stepped into Rowan's bedroom, her eyes drawn to the hints of him everywhere. A suit was draped over the back of a rattan rocker by sliding doors that led out to a balcony. She didn't consider herself a romantic by any stretch but the thought of sitting out there under the stars with someone...

God, what was the matter with her? This man had driven her bat crazy for years. Now she was daydreaming about an under-the-stars make-out session that would lead back into the bedroom. His bedroom.

Her eyes skated to the sprawling four-poster draped with gauzy netting, a dangerous place to look with his provocative glances still steaming up her memories. An e-reader rested on the bedside table, his computer laptop tucked underneath. Her mind filled with images of him sprawled in that massive bed—working, reading—details about a man she'd done her best to avoid. She pulled her eyes away.

The bathroom was only a few feet away. She charged across the plush carpet, pushing the door wide. The scent of him was stronger in here, and she couldn't resist breathing in the soapy aroma clinging to the air—patchouli, perhaps. She swallowed hard as goose bumps of awareness rose on her skin, her senses on overload.

A whimpering baby cry from the main room reminded her of her mission here. She shook off frivolous thoughts and snagged the medical bag from the marble vanity. She wrapped her hands around the well-worn leather with his name on a scratched brass plate. The dichotomy of a man this wealthy carrying such a battered bag added layers to her previously clear-cut image of him.

Clutching the bag to her stomach, she returned to the sitting room. Rowan set aside a bottle and settled the baby girl against his shoulder, his broad palm patting her back.

How exactly were they going to work this baby bargain? She had absolutely no idea.

For the first time in her life, she'd done something completely irrational. The notion that Rowan Boothe had that much power over her behavior rattled her to her toes.

She really was losing it. She needed to finish this day, get some sleep and find some clarity.

From this point forward, she would keep a firmer grip on herself. And that meant no more drooling over the sexy doc, and definitely no more sniffing his tempting aftershave.

Rowan tapped through the images on his laptop, reviewing the file on the baby, including the note he'd scanned in before passing it over to the police. He'd sent a copy of everything to Colonel Salvatore. Even though it was too early to expect results, he still hoped for some news, for the child's sake.

Meanwhile, though, he'd accomplished a freaking miracle in buying himself time with Mari. A week or so at the most, likely more, but possibly less since her staying rested solely on the child. If relatives were found quickly, she'd be headed home. He didn't doubt his decision, even if part of his motivation was selfish. This baby provided the perfect opportunity to spend more time with Mari, to learn more about her and figure out what made her tick. Then, hopefully, she would no longer be a thorn in his side—or a pain in his libido.

He tapped the screen back to the scanned image of the note that had been left with the baby.

Dr. Boothe, you are known for your charity and generosity. Please look over my baby girl, Issa.

My husband died in a border battle and I cannot give Issa what she needs. Tell her I love her and will think of her always.

His ears tuned in to the sound of Mari walking toward him, then the floral scent of her wrapped around him. She stood behind him without speaking and he realized she was reading over his shoulder, taking in the note.

"Loves her?" Mari sighed heavily. "The woman abandoned her to a stranger based on that person's reputation in the press."

"I take it your heart isn't tugged." He closed the laptop and turned to face her.

"My heart is broken for this child—" she waved toward the sleeping infant in the baby seat "—and what's in store for her if we don't find answers, along with a truly loving and responsible family."

"I'm hopeful that my contacts will have some information sooner than the police." A reminder that he needed to make the most of his time with Mari. What if Salvatore called with concrete news tomorrow? He looked over at Mari, imagining being with her, drawing her into his bedroom, so close to where they were now. "Let's talk about how we'll look after the baby here during the conference."

"Now?" She jolted in surprise. "It's past midnight."

"There are things to take care of, like ordering more baby gear, meeting with the hotel's babysitting service." He ticked off each point on his fingers. "Just trying to fill in the details on our plan."

"You actually want to plan?" Her kissable lips twitched with a smile.

"No need to be insulting," he bantered right back, enjoying the way she never treated him like some freaking saint just because of where he chose to work. He wasn't the good guy the press painted him to be just because he'd reformed. The past didn't simply go away. He still had debts that could never be made right.

"I'm being careful—finally. Like I should have been earlier." Mari fidgeted with the hem of her untucked shirt, weariness straining her face, dark circles under her eyes. "She's a child. A human being. We can't just fly by the seat of our pants."

He wanted to haul Mari into his arms and let her sleep against his chest, tell her she didn't have to be so serious, she didn't have to take the weight of the world on her shoulders. She could share the load with him.

Instead, he dragged a chair from the tiny teak table by the window and gestured for her to sit, to rest. "I'm not exactly without the means or ability to care for a child. It's only for a short time until we figure out more about her past so we don't have to fly by the seat of our pants." He dragged over a chair for himself as well and sat across from her.

"How is it so easy for you to disregard the rules?" She slumped back.

"You're free to go if you wish."

She shook her head. "I brought her in here. She's my responsibility."

Ah, so she wasn't in a rush to run out the door. "Do you intend to personally watch over her while details are sorted out?"

"I can hire someone."

"Ah, that's right. You're a princess with endless resources," he teased, taking her hands in his.

She pulled back. "Are you calling me spoiled?"

He squeezed her fingers, holding on, liking the feel

of her hands in his. "I would never dare insult you, Princess. You should know that well enough from the provocative things I said to you five minutes ago."

"Oh. Okay." She nibbled on her bottom lip, surprise flickering through her eyes.

"First things first." He thumbed the inside of her wrists.

"Your plan?" Her breathing seemed to hitch.

"We pretend to be dating and since we're dating, and we'd be spending this holiday time together anyway, we decided to help with the child. How does that work for a plan?"

"What?" She gasped in surprise. "Do you really think people are going to believe we went from professional adversaries to lovers in a heartbeat?"

He saw her pulse throb faster, ramping up his in response.

"Lovers, huh? I like the sound of that."

"You said—"

"I said dating." He squeezed her hands again. "But I like your plan better."

"This isn't a plan." She pulled free, inching her chair back. "It's insanity."

"A plan that will work. People will believe it. More than that, they will eat it up. Everyone will want to hear more about the aloof princess finding romance and playing Good Samaritan at Christmastime. If they have an actual human interest piece to write about you it will distract them from digging around to create a story."

Her eyes went wide with panic, but she stayed in her seat. She wasn't running. Yet. He'd pushed as far as he could for tonight. Tomorrow would offer up a whole new day for making his case.

He shoved to his feet. "Time for bed."

"Oh, um," she squeaked, standing, as well. "Bed?"

He could see in her eyes that she'd envisioned them sharing a bed before this moment. He didn't doubt for a second what he saw and it gave him a surge of victory. Definitely best to bide his time and wait for a moment when she wasn't skittish. A time when she would be all in, as fully committed as he was to exploring this crazy attraction.

"Yes, Mari, bed. I'll watch the baby tonight and if you're comfortable, we can alternate the night shift."

She blinked in surprise. "Right. The night schedule. Are you sure you can handle a baby at night and still participate in the conference?"

"I'm a doctor. I've pulled far longer shifts with no sleep in the hospital. I'll be fine."

"Of course. Then I'll call the front desk to move me to a larger suite so I'll have enough space for the baby and the daytime sitter."

"No need to do that. This suite is plenty large enough for all of us."

Her jaw dropped. "Excuse me?"

"All of us," he said calmly, holding her with his eyes as fully as he'd held her hand, gauging her every blink. Needing to win her over. "It makes sense if we're going to watch the baby, we should do it together for efficiency. The concierge already sent someone to pack your things."

Her chest rose faster and faster, the gentle curves of her breasts pressing against the wrinkled silk of her blouse. "You've actually made quite a few plans."

"Sometimes flying by the seat of your pants works quite well." Otherwise he never would have had this chance to win her over. "A bellhop will be delivering your luggage shortly along with more baby gear that I ordered."

"Here? The two—three—of us? In one suite?" she asked, although he noticed she didn't say no.

Victory was so close.

"There's plenty of space for the baby. You can have your own room. Unless you want to sleep in mine." He grinned. "You have to know I wouldn't object."

Four

Buttoning up her navy blue power suit the next morning, Mari couldn't believe she'd actually spent the night in Rowan Boothe's hotel suite. Not his room, but a mere wall away. He'd cared for the baby until morning as he'd promised. A good thing, since she needed to learn a lot more before she trusted herself to care for Issa.

She tucked pins into her swept-back hair, but the mirror showed her to be the same slightly rumpled academic she'd always been. While she wasn't a total innocent when it came to men, she wasn't the wild and reckless type who agreed to spend the night in the same suite as a guy she'd never actually dated. She'd expected to toss and turn all night after the confusing turn of events. She couldn't believe she'd agreed.

Yet in spite of all her doubts, she'd slept better than anytime she could remember. Perhaps because the odds of anyone finding her here were next to nil. Her longtime professional feud with him was well-known, and they hadn't yet gone public with this strange idea of joint custody of an abandoned baby. The hotel staff or someone on the police force would likely leak juicy tidbits about the royal family to the press, but it would all be gossip and conjecture until she and Rowan made their official statement verifying the situation.

Soon enough the world would know. Eventually the cameras would start snapping. Her gut clenched at the thought of all those stalkers and the press feeding on the tiniest of details, the least scrap of her life. What if they fed on the innocence of the baby?

Or what if they picked up on the attraction between her and Rowan?

There was still time to back out, write it all off as simple gossip. The urge was strong to put back on that Christmas hat and slip away, to hide in her lab, far, far from the stress of being on show and always falling short. She craved the peace of her laboratory and cubbyhole office, where she truly reigned supreme. Here, in Rowan's suite, she felt so off-kilter, so out of control.

A coo from the other room reminded her she needed to hurry. She stepped away from the mirror and slid her feet into her low, blue pumps. She pulled open her bedroom door, then sagged to rest against the doorjamb. The sight of the little one in a ruffled pink sleeper, resting against Rowan's shoulder, looked like something straight off a greeting card. So perfect.

Except that perfection was an illusion.

Even though Rowan had the baby well in hand, the child was helpless outside their protection. Issa had no one to fight for her, not really, not if Mari and Rowan gave up on her. Even if Mari left and Rowan stayed, he couldn't offer the baby everything Mari could. Her fame—that fame she so resented—could be Issa's salvation.

The baby would get an exposure the police never could have provided. In these days of DNA testing, it wasn't as if fake relatives could step forward to claim a precious infant. So Mari wasn't going anywhere, except to give her presentation at the medical conference, then she'd take the baby for a walk with Rowan.

Looking around the suite strewn with baby paraphernalia, anyone would believe they were truly guardians of the child. Rowan had ordered a veritable nursery set up with top-of-the-line gear. A portable bassinet rested in the corner of the main room, a monitor perched beside it. He'd ordered a swing, a car seat, plus enough clothes, food and diapers for three babies for a month.

He knew what an infant needed, or at least he knew who to call.

Hopefully that call had included a sitter since he was dressed for work as well, in a black Savile Row suit with a Christmas-red tie. God, he was handsome, with his blond hair damp and combed back, his broad hand patting the baby's back. His face wore a perpetual five-o'clock shadow, just enough to be nighttime sexy without sliding over into scruffy.

He filled out the expensive suit with ease. Was there any realm that made this man uncomfortable? He'd taken care of the baby through the night and still looked totally put together.

His eyes searched hers and she shivered, wondering what he saw as he stood there holding Issa so easily. The man was a multitasker. He was also someone with an uncanny knack for getting into a person's mind. He'd found her vulnerable spot in one evening. After all of her tense and bicontinental Christmases, she simply couldn't bear for this child to spend the holidays confused and scared while the system figured out what to do with her—and the other thousands of orphans in their care.

She couldn't replace the child's mother, but she could make sure the child was held, cared for, secure. To do that, she needed to keep her mind off the charismatic man a few feet away.

He looked over at her as if he'd known she was there the whole time. "Good morning. Coffee's ready along with a tray of pastries."

And some sweet, sticky *bouili* dipping sauce.

Her mouth watered for the food almost as much as for the man. She walked to the granite countertop and poured herself a mug of coffee from the silver carafe. She inhaled the rich java fragrance steaming up from the dark roast with hints of fruity overtones. "Did she sleep well?"

"Well enough, just as I would expect from a baby who's experienced so much change," he said, tucking the baby into a swing with expert hands. "The hotel's sending up a sitter for the day. I verified her references and qualifications. They seem solid, so we should be covered through our lecture presentations. Tonight we can take Issa out for dinner and a stroll incognito, kill time while we let the cops finish their initial investigation. If they haven't found out anything by tomorrow, we can go public."

Dinner out? Revealing their plan to the world? Her heart pounded with nerves, but it was too late to go back now. The world would already be buzzing with leaked news. Best to make things official on their own terms.

If Issa's family wasn't found by tomorrow, she would have to call her parents and let them know about her strange partnership with Rowan. First, she had to decide how she wanted to spin it so her parents didn't jump to the wrong conclusions—or try to interfere. This needed to be a good thing for the baby, not just about positive press. She would play it by ear today and call them tonight once she had a firmer idea of what she'd gotten herself into.

Maybe Issa would be back with relatives before supper. A good thing, right?

Rowan started the baby swing in motion. The click-click-click mingled with a low nursery tune.

Mari cleared her throat. "I'll check on Issa during lunch and make sure all's going well with the sitter."

"That's a good idea. Thank you." He cradled a cup in strong hands that could so easily crush the fine china.

She shrugged dismissively. It was no hardship to skip the luncheon. She disliked the idle table chitchat at these sorts of functions anyway. "No big sacrifice. Nobody likes conference lunch food."

Laughing softly, he eyed her over his cup of coffee. "I appreciate your working with me on this."

"You didn't leave me much choice, Dr. Guilt Trip."

His smile creased dimples into his face. "Who'd have thought you'd have a sense of humor?"

"That's not nice." She traced the rim of her cup.

"Neither is saying I coerced you." He tapped the tip of her scrunched nose. "People always have a choice."

Of course he was right. She could always walk, but thinking overlong about her compulsion to stay made her edgy. She sat at the table, the morning sun glistening off the ocean waters outside. "Of course I'm doing this of my own free will, for Issa's sake. It has absolutely nothing to do with you."

"Hello? I thought we weren't going to play games."

She avoided his eyes and sipped her steaming java. "What do you mean, games?"

"Fine. I'll spell it out." He set down his cup on the table and sat beside her, their knees almost touching. "You have made it your life's mission to tear down my research and to keep me at arm's length. Yet you chose to stay here, for the baby, but you and I both know there's more to it than that. There's a chemistry between us, sparks."

"Those sparks—" she proceeded warily "—are just a part of our disagreements."

"Disagreements? You've publically denounced my work. That's a little more than a disagreement."

Of course he wouldn't forget that. "See, sparks. Just like I said."

His eyes narrowed. If only he could understand her point. She only wanted to get past his impulsive, pigheaded mindset and improve his programs.

"Mari, you're damn good at diverting from the topic."

"I'm right on point," she said primly. "This is about our work and you refused to consider that I see things from another angle. You've made it your life's mission to ignore any pertinent input I might have for your technological inventions. I am a scientist."

He scraped a hand over his drying hair. "Then why are you so against my computer program?"

"I thought we were talking about what's best for Issa." She glanced at the baby girl still snoozing in the swing with the lullaby playing.

"Princess, you are making my head spin." He sagged back. "We're here for Issa, but that doesn't mean we can't talk about other things, so quit changing the subject every three seconds. In the interest of getting along better during these next couple of weeks, let's discuss your public disdain for my life's work."

Was he serious? Did he really want to hash that out now? He certainly looked serious, drinking his coffee and downing bites of breakfast. Maybe he was one of those people who wanted to make peace at the holidays in spite of bickering all year round. She knew plenty about that. Which should have taught her well. Problems couldn't be avoided or the resolutions delayed. Best to confront them when given the opening.

"Your program is just too much of a snapshot of a diagnosis, too much of a quick fix. It's like fast-food medicine. It doesn't take into account enough variables." Now she waited for the explosion.

He inhaled a deep breath and tipped back in his chair before answering. "I can see your point. To a degree, I agree. I would welcome the chance to give every patient the hands-on medical treatment of the best clinic in the world. But I'm treating the masses with a skeleton team of medical professionals. That computer program helps us triage in half the time."

"What about people who use your program to cut corners?"

Rowan frowned. "What do you mean?"

"You can't truly believe the world is as altruistic as you? What about the clinics using that program to funnel more patients through just to make more money?"

His chair legs hit the floor, his jaw tightening. "I can't be the conscience for the world," he said in an even tone although a tic had started in the corner of his azure-blue eye. "I can only deal with the problems in front of me. I'm working my tail off to come up with help. Would I prefer more doctors and nurses, PAs and midwives, human hands? Hell, yes. But I make do with what I have and I do what I can so those of us who are here can be as efficient as possible under conditions they didn't come close to teaching us about during my residency."

"So you admit the program isn't optimal?" She couldn't believe he'd admitted to the program's shortcomings.

"Really?" He threw up his hands. "That's your takeaway from my whole rambling speech? I'm being practical, and you're being idealistic in your ivory tower of research. I'm sorry if that makes you angry to hear."

"I'm not the volatile sort." She pursed her lips tightly to resist the temptation to snap at him for devaluing her work.

Slowly, he grinned, leaning closer. "That's too bad."

"Pardon me?" she asked, not following his logic at all.

"Because when you get all flustered, you're really hot."

Her eyes shot open wide, surprise skittering through her, followed by skepticism. "Does that line really work for you?"

"I've never tried it before." He angled closer until his mouth almost brushed hers. "You'll have to let me know."

Before she could gasp in half a breath of air, he brushed his mouth over hers. Shock quickly turned to something else entirely as delicious tingles shimmered through her. Her body warmed to the feel of him, the newness of his kiss, their first kiss, a moment already burning itself into her memory, searing through her with liquid heat.

Her hand fluttered to his chest, flattening, feeling the steady, strong beat of his heart under her palm matching the thrumming heartbeat in her ears. His kiss was nothing like she would have imagined. She'd expected him to be out of control, wild. Instead, he held her like spun glass. He touched her with deft, sensitive hands, surgeon's hands that knew just the right places to graze, stroke, tease for maximum payoff. Her body thrilled at the caress down her spine that cupped her bottom, bringing her closer.

Already she could feel herself sinking into a spiral of lush sensation. Her limbs went languid with desire. She wanted more of this, more of him, but they were a heartbeat away from tossing away their clothes and inhibitions. Too risky for a multitude of reasons, not the least of which was the possibility of someone discovering them.

Those sorts of exposé photos she absolutely did not want circulating on the internet or anywhere else.

Then, too soon he pulled away. How embarrassing that he was the one to stop since she already knew the kiss had to end. Never had she lost control this quickly.

Cool air and embarrassment washed over her as she sat stunned in her chair. He'd completely knocked the world out from under her with one simple kiss. Had he even been half as affected as she was by the moment? She looked quickly at him, but his back was to her already and she realized he was walking toward the door.

"Rowan?"

He glanced over his shoulder. "The buzzer—" Was that a hint of hoarseness in his voice? "The baby sitter has arrived."

Mari pressed her fingers to her still tingling lips, wondering if a day apart would be enough time to shore up her defenses again before their evening out.

* * *

That evening, Rowan pushed the baby stroller along the marketplace road. Vendors lined the street, and he eyed the place for potential trouble spots. Even with bodyguards trailing them, he kept watch. The baby in the stroller depended on him.

And so did the woman beside him. Mari wore her business suit, without the jacket, just the skirt and blouse, a scarf wrapped over her head and large sunglasses on for disguise, looking like a leggy 1940s movie star.

She strolled beside him, her hand trailing along stalls that overflowed with handwoven cloths and colorful beads. Bins of fresh fruits and vegetables sat out, the scent of roasting turkey and goat carrying on the salty beach breeze. Waves crashed in the distance, adding to the rhythmic percussion of a local band playing Christmas tunes while children danced. Locals and tourists angled past in a crush, multiple languages coming at him in stereo—Cape Verdean Creole, Portuguese, French, English…and heaven knew how many others.

Tonight, he finally had Mari out of the work world and alone with him. Okay, alone with him, a baby, bodyguards and a crush of shoppers.

The last rays of the day bathed Mari in a crimson glow. She hadn't referenced their kiss earlier, so he'd followed her lead on that, counting it a victory that she wasn't running. Clearly, she'd been as turned on as he was. But still, she hadn't run.

With the taste of her etched in his memory, there was not a chance in hell he was going anywhere. More than ever, he was determined to get closer to her, to sample a hell of a lot more than her lips.

But he was smart enough to take his time. This

woman was smart—and skittish. He made his living off reading subtle signs, deciphering puzzles, but this woman? She was the most complex individual he'd ever met.

Could that be a part of her appeal? The mysterious element? The puzzle?

The "why" of it didn't matter so much to him right now. He just wanted to make the most of this evening out and hopefully gain some traction in identifying Issa's family. While they'd gotten a few curious looks from people and a few surreptitiously snapped photos, so far, no one had openly approached them.

He checked left and right again, reconfirming their unobtrusive security detail, ensuring the men were close enough to intervene if needed. Colonel Salvatore had been very accommodating about rounding up the best in the business ASAP, although he still had no answers on the baby's identity. Issa's footprints hadn't come up in any databases, but then the child could have been a home birth, unregistered. Salvatore had insisted he hadn't come close to exhausting all their investigative options yet.

For now, their best lead would come from controlled press exposure, getting the child seen and praying some legit relative stepped up to claim her.

Meanwhile, Rowan finally had his chance to be with Mari, to romance her, and what better place than in this country he loved, with holiday festivities lightening the air. He would have cared for the baby even if Mari had opted out, so he didn't feel guilty about using the child to persuade Mari to stay. He was just surprised she'd agreed so easily.

That gave him pause—and encouragement.

She hesitated at a stall of clay bowls painted with

scenes of everyday life. She trailed her fingers along a piece before moving on to the jewelry, where she stopped for the longest time yet. He'd found her weakness. He wouldn't have pegged her as the type to enjoy those sorts of baubles, but her face lit up as she sifted through beads, necklaces. She seemed to lean more toward practical clothes and loose-fitting suits or dresses. Tonight she wore a long jean jumper and thick leather sandals.

Her hand lingered on the bracelets before she stepped back, the wistfulness disappearing from her golden eyes. "We should find somewhere to eat dinner. The conference food has left me starving for something substantial."

"Point the way. Ladies choice tonight," he said, curious to know what she would choose, what she liked, the way he'd just learned her preferences on the bracelets. Shoppers bustled past, cloth sacks bulging with purchases, everything from souvenirs to groceries.

Instinctively, she moved between the baby stroller and the hurrying masses. "How about we eat at a streetside café while we watch the performances?"

"Sounds good to me." He could keep watch better that way, but then he always kept his guard up. His work with Interpol showed him too well that crime didn't always lurk in the expected places.

He glanced down the street, taking in the carolers playing drums and pipes. Farther down, a group of children acted out the nativity in simple costumes. The sun hadn't gone down yet, so there was less worry about crime.

Rowan pointed to the nearby café with blue tables and fresh fish. "What about there?"

"Perfect, I'll be able to see royal watchers coming."

"Although your fan club seems to have taken a break." He wheeled the stroller toward the restaurant where the waitress instructed them to seat themselves. Issa still slept hard, sucking on a fist and looking too cute for words in a red Christmas sleeper.

Mari laughed, the scarf sliding down off her head, hanging loosely around her neck. "Funny how I couldn't escape photo-happy sorts at the hotel—" she tugged at either end of the silky scarf "—and yet now no one seems to notice me when some notoriety could serve some good."

"Issa's photo has already been released to law enforcement. If nothing comes of it by tomorrow morning, the story will break about our involvement and add an extra push. For now, anyway, the baby and I make good camouflage for you to savor your dinner."

"Mama-flage," she said as he held out her chair for her.

"Nice! I'm enjoying your sense of humor more and more." And he was enjoying a lot more about her as well this evening. He caught the sweet floral scent on her neck as he eased her chair into place.

His mind filled with images of her wearing only perfume and an assortment of the colorful beads from the marketplace. Damn, and now he would be awake all night thinking about the lithe figure she hid under her shapeless suits.

Mari glanced back at him, peering over her sunglasses, her amber eyes reflecting the setting sun. "Is something the matter?"

"Of course not." He took his seat across from her, his foot firmly on the stroller even knowing there were a half-dozen highly trained bodyguards stationed anonymously around them. She might not use them, but he'd made sure to hire a crew for the safety of both Mari and Issa.

The waitress brought glasses and a pitcher of fruit juice—guava and mango—not showing the least sign of recognizing the royal customer she served. This was a good dry run for when they would announce their joint custody publicly.

"What a cute baby," the waitress cooed without even looking at them. "I just love her little red Christmas outfit. She looks like an adorable elf." She toyed with toes in tiny green booties.

"Thank you," Mari said, then mouthed at Rowan, "Mama-flage."

After they'd placed their order for swordfish with *cachupa*—a mixture of corn and beans—Mari leaned back in her chair, appearing far more relaxed than the woman who'd taken refuge in his suite the night before. She eased the sunglasses up to rest on top of her head.

"You look like you've had a couple of servings of grogue." Grogue was a sugar cane liquor drunk with honey that flowed freely here.

"No alcohol for me tonight, thank you." She lifted a hand. "My turn to watch the baby."

"I don't mind taking the night shift if you're not comfortable."

She raised a delicately arched dark eyebrow. "Somewhere in the world, a couple dozen new moms just swooned and they don't know why."

"I'm just trying to be helpful. You have the heavier presentation load."

She stirred sugar into her coffee. "Are you trying to coerce me into kissing you again?"

"As I recall, I kissed you and you didn't object."

She set her spoon down with a decisive clink. "Well, you shouldn't count on doing it again."

"Request duly noted," he replied, not daunted in the least. He saw the speeding of her pulse, the flush of awareness along her dusky skin.

He started to reach for her, just to brush his knuckles along that pulse under the pretense of brushing something aside—except a movement just out of the corner of his eye snagged his attention. Alert, he turned to see an older touristy-looking couple moving toward them.

Mari sat back abruptly, her hand fluttering to her throat. Rowan assessed the pair. Trouble could come in any form, at any age. The bodyguards' attention ramped up as they stalked along the perimeter, closing the circle of protection. Mari reached for her sunglasses. Rowan didn't see any signs of concealed weapons, but he slid his hand inside his jacket, resting his palm on his 9 mm, just in case.

The elderly husband, wearing a camera and a man-purse over his shoulder, stopped beside Mari.

"Excuse us, but would you mind answering a question?" he asked with a thick New Jersey accent.

Was their cover busted? If so, did it really matter that they went public a few hours early? Not for him or the baby, but because he didn't want Mari upset, bolting away from the press, terrified, like the night before.

She tipped her head regally, her shoulders braced as she placed the sunglasses on the table. "Go ahead."

The wife angled in eagerly. "Are the two of you from around here?"

Rowan's mouth twitched. Not busted at all. "Not from the island, ma'am. We both live on the mainland."

"Oh, all right, I see." She furrowed her brow. "Maybe

you can still help me. Where's the Kwanzaa celebration?"

Mari's eyes went wide with surprise, then a hint of humor glinted before her face went politely neutral. "Ma'am, that's an American tradition."

"Oh, I didn't realize." Her forehead furrowed as she adjusted her fanny pack. "I just didn't expect so much Christmas celebration."

Mari glanced at the children finishing up their nativity play and accepting donations for their church. "Africa has a varied cultural and religious heritage. How much of each you find depends on which portion of the continent you're visiting. This area was settled by the Portuguese," she explained patiently, "which accounts for the larger influence of Christian traditions than you might find in other regions."

"Thank you for being so patient in explaining." The wife pulled out a travel guide and passed it to her husband, her eyes staying on Mari. "You look very familiar, dear. Have I seen you somewhere before?"

Pausing for a second, Mari eyed them, then said, "People say I look like the Princess Mariama Mandara. Sometimes I even let folks believe that."

She winked, grinning mischievously.

The older woman laughed. "What a wicked thing to do, young lady. But then I imagine people deserve what they get if they like to sneak photos for the internet."

"Would you like a photo of me with the baby on your phone?" Mari leaned closer to the stroller, sweeping back the cover so baby Issa's face was in clear view. "I'll put on my best princess smile."

"Oh, I wouldn't even know how to work the camera on that new phone our kids gave us for our fiftieth anniversary." She elbowed her husband. "We just use our old Polaroid, isn't that right, Nils?"

"I'm getting it out, Meg, hold on a minute." He fished around inside his man-purse.

Mari extended her arm. "Meg, why don't you get in the photo, too?"

"Oh, yes, thank you. The grandkids will love it." She fluffed her bobbed gray hair with her fingers then leaned in to smile while her husband's old Polaroid spit out picture after picture. "Now you and your husband lean in to pose for one with your daughter."

Daughter? Rowan jolted, the fun of the moment suddenly taking on a different spin. He liked kids and he sure as hell wanted Mari, but the notion of a pretend marriage? That threatened to give him hives. He swallowed down the bite of bile over the family he'd wrecked so many years ago and pretended for the moment life could be normal for him. He kneeled beside Mari and the baby, forcing his face into the requisite smile. He was a good actor.

He'd had lots of practice.

The couple finished their photo shoot, doling out thanks and leaving an extra Polaroid shot behind for them. The image developed in front of him, blurry shapes coming into focus, much like his thoughts, his need to have Mari.

Rowan sank back into his chair as the waitress brought their food. Once she left, he asked Mari, "Why didn't you tell that couple the truth about us, about yourself? It was the perfect opening."

"There were so many people around. If I had, they would have been mobbed out of the photo. When the official story about us fostering the baby hits the news in the morning, they'll realize their photo of a princess is real and they'll have a great story to tell their grand-children. We still get what we want and they get their cool story."

"That was nice of you to do for them." He draped a napkin over his knee. "I know how much you hate the notoriety of being royalty."

She twisted her napkin between her fingers before dropping it on her lap. "I'm not an awful person."

Had he hurt her feelings? He'd never imagined this boldly confident woman might be insecure. "I never said you were. I think your research is admirable."

"Really? I seem to recall a particular magazine in-terview where you accused me of trying to sabotage your work. In fact, when I came into your suite with the room-service cart, you accused me of espionage."

"My word choices may have been a bit harsh. The stakes were high." And yeah, he liked seeing her riled up with fire in her eyes. "My work world just doesn't give me the luxury of the time you have in yours."

"I simply prefer life to be on my terms when possi-ble. So much in this world is beyond anyone's control."

Her eyes took on a faraway look that made him burn to reel her back into the moment, to finish the thought out loud so he could keep learning more about what made this woman tick. But she'd already distanced her-self from him, deep in thought, looking off down the road at the musicians.

He needed those insights if he expected to get a sec-ond kiss—and more from her. But he was beginning to realize that if he wanted more, he was going to have to pony up some confidences of his own. An uncom-fortable prospect.

As he looked at Mari swaying absently in time with the music, her lithe body at ease and graceful, he knew having her would be well worth any cost.

Five

Mari soaked in the sound of street music mellowing the warm evening air. The steady beat of the *bougarabou* drum with the players' jangling bracelets enriching the percussion reminded her of childhood days. Back when her parents were still together and she lived in Africa full-time, other than visits to the States to see her maternal grandparents.

Those first seven years of her life had been idyllic—or so she'd thought. She hadn't known anything about the painful undercurrents already rippling through her parents' marriage. She hadn't sensed the tension in their voices over royal pressures and her mother's homesickness.

For a genius, she'd missed all the obvious signs. But then, she'd never had the same skill reading people that she had for reading data. She'd barely registered that her mother was traveling to Atlanta more and more frequently. Her first clue had come near the end when she'd overheard her mom talking about buying a home in the States during their Christmas vacation. They wouldn't be staying with her grandparents any longer during U.S. visits. They would have their own place, not a room with family. Her parents had officially split up and filed for divorce over the holidays.

Christmas music never sounded quite the same to her again, on either continent.

The sway melted away from her shoulders and Mari stilled in her wrought-iron seat. The wind still wound around her as they sat at the patio dining area, but her senses moved on from the music to the air of roasting meat from the kitchen and the sound of laughing children. All of it was almost strong enough to distract her from the weight of Rowan's gaze.

Almost.

She glanced over at him self-consciously. "Why are you staring at me? I must be a mess." She touched her hair, tucking a stray strand back into the twist, then smoothed her rumpled suit shirt and adjusted the silver scarf draped around her neck. "It's been a long day and the breeze is strong tonight."

Since when had she cared about her appearance for more than the sake of photos? She forced her hands back to her lap.

Rowan's tanned face creased with his confident grin. "Your smile is radiant." He waved a broad hand to encompass the festivities playing out around them. "The way you're taking in everything, appreciating the joy of the smallest details, your pleasure in it all is... mesmerizing."

His blue eyes downright twinkled like the stars in the night sky.

Was he flirting with her? She studied him suspiciously. The restaurant window behind him filled with the movement of diners and waiters, the edges blurred by the spray of fake snow. She'd always been entranced by those pretend snowy displays in the middle of a warm island Christmas.

"Joy? It's December, Rowan. The Christmas season of *joy*. Of course I'm happy." She thought fast, desperate to defer conversation about her. Talking about Rowan's past felt a lot more comfortable than worrying about tucking in her shirt, for God's sake. "What kind of traditions did you enjoy with your family growing up?"

He leaned back in his chair, his gaze still homed in solely on Mari in spite of the festivities going on around them. "We did the regular holiday stuff like a tree, carols, lots of food."

"What kind of food?" she asked just as Issa squirmed in the stroller.

He shrugged, adjusting the baby's pacifier until the infant settled back to sleep. "Regular Christmas stuff."

His ease with the baby was admirable—and heart-tugging. "Come on," Mari persisted, "fill in the blanks for me. There are lots of ways to celebrate Christmas and regular food here isn't the same as regular food somewhere else. Besides, I grew up with chefs. Cooking is still a fascinating mystery to me."

He forked up a bite of swordfish. "It's just like following the steps in a chemistry experiment."

"Maybe in theory." She sipped her fruit juice, the blend bursting along her taste buds with a hint of coconut, her senses hyperaware since Rowan kissed her. "Suffice it to say I'm a better scientist than a cook. But back to you. What was your favorite Christmas treat?"

He set his fork aside, his foot gently tapping the

stroller back and forth. "My mom liked to decorate sugar cookies, but my brother, Dylan, and I weren't all that into it. We ate more of the frosting than went on the cookies."

The image wrapped around her like a comfortable blanket. "That sounds perfect. I always wanted a sibling to share moments like that with. Tell me more. Details… Trains or dump trucks? Bikes or ugly sweaters?"

"We didn't have a lot of money, so my folks saved and tucked away gifts all year long. They always seemed a bit embarrassed that they couldn't give us more, but we were happy. And God knows, it's more than most of the kids I work with will ever have."

"You sound like you had a close family. That's a priceless gift."

Something flickered through his eyes that she couldn't quite identify, like gray clouds over a blue sky, but then they cleared so fast she figured she must have been mistaken. She focused on his words, more curious about this man than any she'd ever known.

"At around three-thirty on Christmas morning, Dylan and I would slip out of our bunk beds and sneak downstairs to see what Santa brought." He shared the memory, but the gray had slipped into his tone of voice now, darkening the lightness of his story. "We would play with everything for about an hour, then put it back like we found it, even if the toy was in a box. We would tiptoe back into our room and wait for our parents to wake us up. We always pretended like we were completely surprised by the gifts."

What was she missing here? Setting aside her napkin, she leaned closer. "Sounds like you and your brother share a special bond."

"Shared," he said flatly. "Dylan's dead."

She couldn't hold back the gasp of shock or the empathetic stab of pain for his loss. For an awkward moment, the chorus of "Silver Bells" seemed to blare louder, the happy music at odds with this sudden revelation. "I'm so sorry, Rowan. I didn't know that."

"You had no reason to know. He died in a car accident when he was twenty."

She searched for something appropriate to say. Her lack of social skills had never bothered her before now. "How old were you when he died?"

"Eighteen." He fidgeted with her sunglasses on the table.

"That had to be so horrible for you and for your parents."

"It was," he said simply, still toying with her wide-rimmed shades.

An awkward silence fell, the echoes of Christmas ringing hollow now. She chewed her lip and pulled the first question from her brain that she could scavenge. "Were you still at the military reform school?"

"It was graduation week."

Her heart squeezed tightly at the thought of him losing so much, especially at a time when he should have been celebrating completing his sentence in that school.

Without thinking or hesitating, she pushed aside her sunglasses and covered Rowan's hand. "Rowan, I don't even know what to say."

"There's nothing to say." He flipped his hand, skimming his thumb along the inside of her wrist. "I just wanted you to know I'm trusting you with a part of my past here."

Heat seeped through her veins at each stroke of his thumb across her pulse. "You're telling me about yourself to...?"

His eyes were completely readable now, sensual and steaming over her. "To get closer to you. To let you know that kiss wasn't just an accident. I'm nowhere near the saint the press likes to paint me."

Heat warmed to full-out sparks of electricity arcing along her every nerve ending. She wasn't imagining or exaggerating anything. Rowan Boothe *wanted* her.

And she wanted to sleep with him.

The inescapable truth of that rocked the ground underneath her.

The noise of a backfiring truck snapped Rowan back into the moment. Mari jolted, blinking quickly before making a huge deal out of attacking her plate of swordfish and *cachupa,* gulping coffee between bites.

The sputtering engine still ringing in his ears, Rowan scanned the marketplace, checking the position of their bodyguards. He took in the honeymooners settling in at the next table. The elderly couple that had photographed them earlier was paying their bill. A family of vacationers filled a long stretch of table.

The place was as safe as anywhere out in public.

He knew he couldn't keep Mari and the baby under lock and key. He had the security detail and he hoped Mari would find peace in being out in public with the proper protection. The thought of her being chased down hallways for the rest of her life made him grind his teeth in frustration. She deserved better than to live in the shadows.

He owed little Issa a lot for how she'd brought them together. He was moved by the sensitive side of Mari he'd never known she had, the sweetly awkward humanity beneath the brilliant scientific brain and regal royal heritage.

Leaning toward the stroller, Rowan adjusted the baby's bib, reassured by the steady beat of her little heart. He'd given her a thorough physical and thank God she was healthy, but she was still a helpless, fragile infant. He needed to take care of her future. And he would. He felt confident he could, with the help of Salvatore either finding the baby's family or lining up a solid adoption.

The outcome of his situation with Mari, however, was less certain. There was no mistaking the desire in her golden eyes. Desire mixed with wariness.

A tactical retreat was in order while he waited for the appropriate moment to resume his advances. He hadn't meant to reveal Dylan's death to her, but their talk about the past had lulled him into old memories. He wouldn't let that happen again.

He poured coffee from the earthen pot into his mug and hers. "You must have seen some lavish Christmas celebrations with your father."

Her eyes were shielded, but her hand trembled slightly as she reached for her mug. "My father keeps things fairly scaled back. The country's economy is stabilizing thanks to an increase in cocoa export, but the national treasury isn't flush with cash, by any means. I was brought up to appreciate my responsibilities to my people."

"You don't have a sibling to share the responsibility."

The words fell out of his mouth before he thought them through, probably because of all those memories of his brother knocking around in his gut. All the ways he'd failed to save Dylan's life. If only he'd made different decisions... He forced his attention back into the present, on Mari.

"Both of my parents remarried other people, divorced again, no more kids, though." She spread her hands, sunglasses dangling from her fingers. "So I'm it. The future of my country."

"You don't sound enthusiastic."

"I just think there has to be someone better equipped." She tossed aside the glasses again and picked up her coffee. "What? Why the surprised look? You can't think I'm the best bet for my people. I would rather lock myself in a research lab with the coffeemaker maxed out than deal with the day-to-day events of leading people."

"I think you will succeed at anything life puts in your path." Who had torn down this woman's confidence? If only she saw—believed in—her magnificence. "When you walk in a room, you damn near light up the place. You own the space with your presence, lady."

She blew into her mug of coffee, eyeing him. "Thanks for the vote of confidence. But people and all their intangibles like 'magnificence' are beyond me. I like concrete facts."

"I would say some people would appreciate logic in a leader."

She looked away quickly, busying herself with adjusting the netting around the baby's stroller. "I wasn't always this way."

"What do you mean?"

"So precise." She darted a quick glance at him out of the corner of her eye. "I was actually a very scatter-brained child. I lost my hair ribbons in hotels, left my doll or book on the airplane. I was always oversleeping or sluggish in the morning, running late for important events. The staff was given instructions to wake me up a half hour ahead of time."

His mom had woken him and Dylan up through elementary school, then bought them an alarm clock—a really obnoxious clock that clanged like a cowbell. No one overslept. "Did this happen in your mother's or your father's home?"

"Both places. My internal clock just wasn't impressed by alarms or schedules."

She was a kid juggling a bicontinental lifestyle, the pressures of royal scrutiny along with the social awkwardness of being at least five grades ahead of her peers.

When did she ever get to relax? "Sounds to me like you traveled quite a bit in your life. I'm sure you know that losing things during travel is as common as jet lag, even for adults."

"You're kind to make excuses." She brushed aside his explanation. "I just learned to make lists and structure my world more carefully."

"Such as?" he asked, suddenly finding the need to learn more about what shaped her life every bit as important as tasting her lips again.

"Always sitting in the same seat on an airplane. Creating a routine for the transatlantic trips, traveling at the same time." She shrugged her elegant shoulders. "The world seemed less confusing that way."

"Confusing?" he repeated.

She chewed her bottom lip, which was still glistening from a sip of coffee. "Forget I said anything."

"Too late. I remember everything you say." And what a time to realize how true that was.

"Ah, you're one of those photographic-memory sorts. I imagine that helps with your work."

"Hmm…" Not a photographic memory, except when it came to her. But she didn't need to know that.

"I'm sure my routines sound a bit overboard to you. But my life feels crazy most of the time. I'm a princess.

There's no escaping that fact." She set her mug down carefully. "I have to accept that no matter how many lists I make, my world will never be predictable."

"Sometimes unpredictable has its advantages, as well." He ached to trace the lines of her heart-shaped face and finish with a tap to her chin.

Her throat moved in a long swallow. "Is this where you surprise me with another kiss?"

He leaned in, a breath away, and said, "I was thinking this time you could surprise me."

She stared back at him so long he was sure she would laugh at him for suggesting such a thing, especially out in public. Not that the public problem bothered the honeymooners at the next table. Just when Rowan was certain she would tell him to go to hell—

Mari kissed him. She closed those last two inches between them and pressed her lips to his. Closemouthed but steady. He felt drunk even though he hadn't had anything but coffee and fruit juice all evening. The same drinks he tasted on Mari's lips. Her hands, soft and smooth, covered his on the table. Need, hard and insistent, coursed through his body over an essentially simple kiss with a table between them.

And just that fast, she let go, pushing on his chest and dropping back into her chair.

A flush spread from her face down the vee of her blouse. "That was not... I didn't mean..."

"Shhh." He pressed a finger to her lips, confidence singing through him along with the hammering pulse of desire. "Some things don't need to be analyzed. Some things simply are. Let's finish supper so we can turn in early."

"Are you propositioning me?" Her lips moved under his finger.

Deliberately seductive? Either way, an extra jolt of want shot through him, a want he saw echoed in her eyes.

He spread his arms wide. "Why would you think that?" he asked with a hint of the devil in his voice. "I want to turn in early. It's your night with the baby."

The tension eased from her shoulders and she smiled back, an ease settling between them as they bantered. God, she was incredible, smart and lithe, earnest and exotic all at once. He covered her hand with his—

A squeal from the next table split the air. "Oh, my God, it's her." The honeymooner at the next table tapped her husband's arm insistently. "That princess... Mariama! I want a picture with her. Get me a photo, pretty please, pookie."

Apparently the mama-flage had stopped working. They didn't have until the morning for Mari to become comfortable with the renewed public attention. The story about them taking care of a baby—*together*—was about to leak.

Big-time.

Two hours later, Mari patted Issa's back in the bassinet to be sure she was deeply asleep then flopped onto the bed in the hotel suite she shared with Rowan.

Alone in her bedroom.

Once that woman shouted to the whole restaurant that a princess sat at the next table, the camera phones started snapping before her head could stop reeling from that impulsive kiss. A kiss that still tingled all the way to the roots of her hair.

Rowan had handled the curious masses with a simple explanation that they were watching a baby in foster care. More information would be forthcoming at a morning press conference. Easy as pie.

Although she was still curious as to where all the bodyguards had come from. She intended to confront her father about that later and find out why he'd decided to disregard her wishes now of all times.

Granted, she could see the wisdom in a bit more protection for Issa's sake and she liked to think she would have arranged for something tomorrow...on a smaller scale. The guards had discreetly escorted her from the restaurant, along with Rowan and the baby, and all the way back to the hotel. No ducking into bathrooms or racing down hallways. Just a wall of protection around her as Rowan continued to repeat with a smile and a firm tone, "No further comment tonight."

Without question, the papers would be buzzing by morning. That press conference would be packed. Her father's promo guru couldn't have planned it better.... Had Rowan known that when they kissed? Did he have an agenda? She couldn't help but wonder since most people in her life had their own agendas—with extras to spare.

This was not the first time the thought had come to her. By the time she'd exited the elevator, she was already second-guessing the kiss, the flirting, the whole crazy plan. She knew that Rowan wanted her. She just couldn't figure out why.

Until she had more answers, she couldn't even consider taking things further.

She sat up again, swinging her legs off the side of the bed. Besides, she had a baby to take care of and a phone call to make. Since Issa still slept blissfully in the lacy bassinet after her bottle, Mari could get to that other pressing concern.

Her father.

She swiped her cell phone off the teak end table and thumbed auto-dial…two rings later, a familiar voice answered and Mari blurted out, "Papa, we need to talk…."

Her father's booming laugh filled the earpiece. "About the boyfriend and the baby you've been hiding from me?"

Mari squeezed her eyes shut, envisioning her lanky father sprawled in his favorite leather chair on the lanai, where he preferred to work. He vowed he felt closer to nature out there, closer to his country, even though three barriers of walls and guards protected him.

Sighing, she pressed two fingers to her head and massaged her temples. "How did you hear about Rowan and Issa? Have you had spies watching me? And why did you assign bodyguards without consulting me?"

"One question at a time, daughter dear. First, I heard about your affiliation with Dr. Boothe and the baby on the internet. Second, I do not spy on my family—not often, anyway. And third, whatever bodyguards you're referring to, they're not mine. I assume they're on your boyfriend's payroll."

Her head throbbed over Rowan hiring bodyguards without consulting her. Her life was snowballing out of control.

"He's not my boyfriend—" even though they'd kissed and she'd enjoyed the hell out of it "—and Issa is not our baby. She's a foster child, just like Rowan said at the restaurant."

Even though her heart was already moved beyond measure by the chubby bundle sleeping in the frilly bassinet next to her bed.

"I know the baby's not yours, Mariama."

"The internet strikes again?" She flopped back, rolling to her side and holding a pillow to her stomach as she monitored the steady rise and fall of Issa's chest as she slept.

"I keep tabs on you, daughter dear. You haven't been pregnant and you've never been a fan of Rowan Boothe."

An image flashed in her mind of Rowan pacing the sitting room with Issa in his arms. "The baby was abandoned in Dr. Boothe's hotel room and we are both watching over her while the authorities try to find her relatives. You know how overburdened Africa is with orphans. We just couldn't let her go into the system when we had the power to help her."

"Hmm…" The sound of him clicking computer keys filtered through the phone line—her father never rested, always worked. He took his position as leader seriously, no puppet leadership role for him. "And why are you working with a man you can't stand to help a child you've never met? He could have taken care of this on his own."

"I'm a philanthropist?"

"True," her dad conceded. "But you're also a poor liar. How did the child become your responsibility?"

She'd never been able to get anything past her wily father. "I was trying to get away from a group of tourists trying to steal a photo of me at the end of a very long day. I grabbed a room-service tray and delivered it." The whole crazy night rolled through her mind again and she wondered what had possessed her to act so rashly. Never, though, could she have foreseen how it would end. "Turns out it was for Rowan Boothe and there was an abandoned baby inside. There's nothing going on between us."

A squawk from Issa sent her jolting upright again to

pat the baby's back. An instant later, a tap sounded on the door from the suite beyond. She covered the mouthpiece on the phone. "We're okay."

Still, the bedroom door opened, a quizzical look on Rowan's face. "Everything all right?"

"I've got it." She uncovered the phone. "Dad, I need to go."

Rowan lounged against the doorjamb, his eyes questioning. Pressing the phone against her shoulder to hold it to her ear, she tugged her skirt over her knees, curling her bare toes.

"Mari, dear," her father said, "I do believe you have gotten better at lying after all. Seems like there's a lot going on in your life I don't know about."

Her pulse sped up, affirming her father was indeed right. This wasn't just about Issa. She was lying to herself in thinking there was nothing more going on with Rowan. His eyes enticed her from across the room, like a blue-hot flame drawing a moth.

But her father waited on the other end of the line. Best to deflect the conversation, especially while the object of her current hormonal turmoil stood a few feet away. "You should be thrilled about this whole setup. It will make for great publicity, a wonderful story for your press people to spin over the holidays. Papa, for once I'm not a disappointment."

Rowan scowled and Mari wished she could call back the words that had somehow slipped free. But she felt the weight of the knowledge all the same. The frustration of never measuring up to her parents' expectations.

"Mari, dear," her father said, his voice hoarse, "you have never been a disappointment."

A bittersweet smile welled from the inside out.

"You're worse at lying than I am. But I love you anyway. Good night, Papa."

She thumped the off button and swung her bare feet to the floor. Her nerves were a jangled mess from the emotions stirred up by talking to her dad…not to mention the smoldering embers from kissing Rowan. The stroke of his eyes over her told her they were a simple step, a simple word away from far more than a kiss.

But those tangled nerves and mixed-up feelings also told her this was not the time to make such a momentous decision. Too much was at stake, the well-being of the infant in their care…

And Mari's peace of mind. Because it would be far too easy to lose complete control when it came to this man.

Six

Refusing to back down from Rowan's heated gaze, Mari stiffened her spine and her resolve, closing the last three feet between them. "Why did you order body-guards without consulting me?"

He frowned. "Where did you think they'd come from?"

"My father."

"I just did what he should have. I made sure to look after your safety," he said smoothly, arrogantly.

Her chin tipped defiantly. He might have been right about them needing bodyguards—for Issa's sake—but she wasn't backing down on everything. "Just because I kissed you at the restaurant does *not* mean I intend to invite you into my bed."

Grinning wickedly, he clamped a hand over his heart. "Damn. My spirit is crushed."

"You're joking, of course." She stopped just shy of

touching him, the banter sparkling through her like champagne bubbles.

"Possibly. But make no mistake, I do want to sleep with you and every day I wait is…torture." The barely restrained passion in his voice sent those intoxicating bubbles straight to her head. "I'm just reasonable enough to accept it isn't going to happen tonight."

"And if it never happens?" she asked, unwilling to let him know how deeply he affected her.

"Ah, you said 'if.'" He flicked a loose strand of hair over her shoulder, just barely skimming his knuckles across her skin. "Princess, that means we're already halfway to naked."

Before she could find air to breathe, he backed away, slowly, deliberately closing the door after him.

And she'd thought her nerves were a tangled, jangled mess before. Her legs folded under her as she dropped to sit on the edge of the bed.

A suddenly very cold and empty bed.

Rowan walked through the hotel sliding doors that led out to the sprawling shoreline. The cool night breeze did little to ease the heat pumping through his body. Leaving Mari alone in her hotel room had been one of the toughest things he'd ever done, but he'd had no choice for two reasons.

First, it was too soon to make his move. He didn't want to risk Mari changing her mind about staying with him. She had to be sure—very sure—when they made love.

Second reason he'd needed to put some distance between himself and her right now? He had an important meeting scheduled with an Interpol contact outside the hotel. An old school friend of his and the person responsible for their security detail tonight.

Rowan jogged down the long steps from the pool area to the beach. Late-night vacationers splashed under the fake waterfall, others floated, some sprawled in deck loungers with drinks, the party running deep into the night.

His appointment would take place in cabana number two, away from prying eyes and with the sound of the roaring surf to cover conversation. His loafers sank into the gritty sand, the teak shelter a dozen yards away, with a grassy roof and canvas walls flapping lightly in the wind. Ships bobbed on the horizon, lights echoing the stars overhead.

Rowan swept aside the fabric and stepped inside. "Sorry I'm late, my friend."

His old school pal Elliot Starc lounged in a recliner under the cabana in their designated meeting spot as planned, both loungers overlooking the endless stretch of ocean. "Nothing better to do."

Strictly speaking that couldn't be true. The freelance Interpol agent used his job as a world-renowned Formula One race-car driver to slip in and out of countries without question. He ran in high-powered circles. But then that very lifestyle was the sort their handler, Colonel Salvatore, capitalized on—using the tarnished reputations of his old students to gain access to underworld types.

Of course, Salvatore gave Rowan hell periodically for being a do-gooder. Rowan winced. The label pinched, a poor fit at best. "Well, thanks all the same for dropping everything to come to Cape Verde."

Elliot scratched his hand over his buzzed short hair. "I'm made of time since my fiancée dumped me."

"Sorry about that." Talk about headline news. Elliot's past—his vast past—with women, filled headlines across multiple continents. The world thought that's what had broken up the engagement, but Rowan suspected the truth. Elliot's fiancée had been freaked out by the Interpol work. The job had risked more than one relationship for the Brotherhood.

What would Mari think if she knew?

"Crap happens." Elliot tipped back a drink, draining half of the amber liquid before setting the cut crystal glass on the table between them. "I'd cleared my schedule for the honeymoon. When we split I gave her the tickets since the whole thing was my fault anyway. She and her 'BFF' are skiing in the Alps as we speak. I might as well be doing something productive with my time off."

Clearly, Elliot wouldn't want sympathy. Another drink maybe. He looked like hell, dark circles under his eyes. From lack of sleep most likely. But that didn't explain the nearly shaved head.

"Dude, what happened to you?" Rowan asked, pointing to the short cut.

Elliot's curly mop had become a signature with his fans who collected magazine covers. There were even billboards and posters.... All their pals from the military academy—the ones who'd dubbed themselves the Alpha Brotherhood—never passed up an opportunity to rib Elliot about the underwear ad.

Elliot scratched a hand over his shorn hair. "I had a wreck during a training run. Bit of a fire involved. Singed my hair."

Holy hell. "You caught on fire?"

Elliot grinned. "Just my hair."

"How did I miss hearing about that?"

"No need. It's not a big deal."

Rowan shook his head. "You are one seriously messed-up dude."

But then all his former classmates were messed up in some form. Came with the territory. The things that had landed them in that reform school left them with baggage long after graduation.

"You're the one who hangs out in war-torn villages passing out vaccinations and blankets for fun."

"I'm not trailed by groupies." He shuddered.

"They're harmless most of the time."

Except when they weren't. The very reason he'd consulted with Elliot about the best way to protect Mari and Issa. "I can't thank you enough, brother, for overseeing the security detail. They earned their pay tonight."

"Child's play. So to speak." Elliot lifted his glass again, draining the rest with a wince. "What's up with your papa-and-the-princess deal?"

"The kid needed my help. So I helped."

"You've always been the saint. But that doesn't explain the princess."

Rowan ignored the last part of Elliot's question. "What's so saintly about helping out a kid when I have unlimited funds and Interpol agents at my disposal? Saintly is when something's difficult to do."

"And the woman—the princess?" his half-drunk buddy persisted. "She had a reputation for being very difficult on the subject of Dr. Rowan Boothe."

Like the time she'd written an entire journal piece pointing out potential flaws in his diagnostics program. Sure, he'd made adjustments after reading the piece, but holy hell, it would have been nice—and more expedient—if she'd come to him first. "Mari needs my help, too. That's all it is."

Elliot laughed. "You are so damn delusional."

A truth. And an uncomfortable one.

Beyond their cabana tent, a couple strolled arm-in-arm along the shoreline, sidestepping as a jogger sprinted past with a loping dog.

"If you were a good friend you would let me continue with my denial."

"Maybe I'm wrong." Elliot lifted the decanter and refilled his glass. "It's not denial if you acknowledge said problem."

"I am aware of that fact." His unrelenting desire for Mari was a longtime, ongoing issue he was doing his damnedest to address.

"What do you intend to do about your crush on the princess?"

"Crush? Good God, man. I'm not in junior high."

"Glad you know that. What's your plan?"

"I'm figuring that out as I go." And even if he had one, he wasn't comfortable discussing details of his—feelings?—his attraction.

"What happens if this relationship goes south? Her father has a lot of influence. Even though you're not in his country, his region still neighbors your backyard. That could be...uncomfortable."

Rowan hadn't considered that angle and he should have. Which said a lot for how much Mari messed with his mind. "Let me get this straight, Starc. *You* are doling out relationship advice?"

"I'm a top-notch source when it comes to all the wrong things to do in a long-term relationship." He lifted his glass in toast. "Here's to three broken engagements and counting."

"Who said I'm looking for long-term?"

Elliot leveled an entirely sober stare his way, holding for three crashes of the waves before he said, "You truly are delusional, dude."

"That's not advice."

"It is if you really think about it."

He'd had enough of this discussion about Mari and the possibility of a train wreck of epic proportions. Rowan shoved off the lounger, his shoes sinking in the sand. "Good night."

"Hit a sore spot, did I?" Still, Starc pushed.

"I appreciate your...concern. And your help." He clapped Elliot on the shoulder before sweeping aside the canvas curtain. "I need to return to the hotel."

He'd been gone long enough. As much as he trusted Elliot's choice of guards, he still preferred to keep close.

Wind rolled in off the water, tearing at his open shirt collar as he made his way back up the beach toward the resort. Lights winked from trees. Fake snow speckled windows. Less than two weeks left until Christmas. He would spend the day at his house by the clinic, working any emergency-room walk-ins as he did every year. What plans did Mari have? Would she go to her family?

His parents holed up on Christmas, and frankly, he preferred it that way. Too many painful memories for all of them.

He shut off those thoughts as he entered the resort again. Better to focus on the present. One day at a time. That's the way he'd learned to deal with the crap that had gone down. And right now, his present was filled with Mari and Issa.

Potted palms, carved masks and mounted animal heads passed in a blur as he made his way back to his suite. He nodded to the pair of guards outside the door before stepping inside.

Dimmed lights from the wet bar bathed the sitting

area in an amber glow. Silence echoed as he padded his way to Mari's room. No sounds came from her room this time, no conversation with her royal dad.

The door to Mari's room was ajar and he nudged it open slowly, pushing back thoughts of invading her privacy. This was about safety and checking on the baby.

Not an insane desire to see what Mari looked like sleeping.

To appease his conscience, he checked the baby first and found the chubby infant sleeping, sucking on her tiny fist as she dreamed. Whatever came of his situation with Mari, they'd done right by this baby. They'd kept at least one child safe.

One day at a time. One life saved at a time. It's how he lived. How he atoned for the unforgivable in his past.

Did Issa's mother regret abandoning her child? The note said she wanted her baby in the care of someone like him. But there was no way she could have known the full extent of the resources he had at his disposal with Interpol. If so, she wouldn't have been as quick to abandon her child to him because he could and would find the mother. It wasn't a matter of if. Only a matter of when.

He wouldn't give up. This child's future depended on finding answers.

All the more reason to tread carefully with Mari. He knew what he wanted, but he'd failed to take into consideration how much of a help she would be. How much it would touch his soul seeing her care for the baby. From her initial reaction to the baby, he'd expected her to be awkward with the child, all technical and analytical. But she had an instinct for children, a tenderness in her heart that overcame any awkwardness. A softness that crept over her features.

Watching her sleep now, he could almost forget the way Mari had cut him down to size on more than one occasion in the past. Her hair was down and loose on her pillow, black satin against the white Egyptian cotton pillowcase. Moonlight kissed the curve of her neck, her chest rising and falling slowly.

He could see a strap of creamy satin along her shoulder. Her nightgown? His body tightened and he considered scooping her up and carrying her to his room. To hell with waiting. He could persuade her.

But just as he started to reach for her, his mind snagged on the memory of her talking about how she felt like she'd been a disappointment to her family. The notion that anyone would think this woman less than amazing floored him. He might not agree with her on everything, but he sure as hell saw her value.

Her brilliance of mind and spirit.

He definitely needed to stick to his original plan. He would wait. He couldn't stop thinking about that snippet of her phone conversation with her father. He understood that feeling of inadequacy all too well. She deserved better.

Rather than some half-assed seduction, he needed a plan. A magnificent plan to romance a magnificent woman. The work would be well worth the payoff for both of them.

He backed away from her bed and reached for his cell phone to check in with Salvatore. Pausing at the door, he took in the sight of her, imprinting on his brain the image of Mari sleeping even though that vision ensured *he* wouldn't be sleeping tonight.

Mari's dreams filled with Rowan, filled with his blue eyes stroking her. With his hands caressing her as they floated together in the surf, away from work and responsibilities. She'd never felt so free, so languid, his kisses and touches melting her bones. Her mind filled with his husky whispers of how much he wanted her. Even the sound of his voice stoked her passion higher, hotter, until she ached to wrap her legs around his waist and be filled with his strength.

She couldn't get enough of him. Years of sparring over their work, and even the weather if the subject came up... Now all those frustrating encounters exploded into a deep need, an explosive passion for a man she could have vowed she didn't even like.

Although like had nothing to do with this raw arousal—she felt a need that left her hot and moist between the legs until she squirmed in her bed.

Her bed.

Slowly, her dream world faded as reality interjected itself with tiny details, like the slither of sheets against her skin. The give of the pillow as her head thrashed back and forth. The sound of the ocean outside the window—and the faint rumble of Rowan's voice beyond her door.

She sat upright quickly.

Rowan.

No wonder she'd been dreaming of him. His voice had been filtering into her dream until he took it over. She clutched the puffy comforter to her chest and listened, although the words were indistinguishable. From the periodic silences, he must be talking to someone on the phone.

Mari eased from the bed, careful not to wake the baby. She pulled her robe from over a cane rocking chair and slipped her arms into the cool satin. Her one decadent pleasure—sexy peignoir sets. They made her feel like a silver-screen star from the forties, complete with furry kitten-heel slippers, not so high as to trip her up, but still ultrafeminine.

Would Rowan think them sexy or silly if he noticed them? God, he was filling up her mind and making her care about things—superficial things—that shouldn't matter. Even more distressing, he made her want to climb back into that dream world and forget about everything else.

Her entire focus should be on securing Issa's future. Mari leaned over the lace bassinet to check the infant's breathing. She pressed a kiss to two fingers and skimmed them over Issa's brow, affection clutching her heart. How could one little scrap of humanity become so precious so fast?

Rowan's voice filtered through the door again and piqued her curiosity. Who could he be talking with so late at night? Common sense said it had to be important, maybe even about the baby.

Her throat tightened at the thought of news about Issa's family, and she wasn't sure if the prospect made her happy or sad. She grasped the baby monitor receiver in her hand.

Quietly, she opened the door, careful not to disturb his phone conversation. And yes, she welcomed the opportunity to look at Rowan for a moment, a double-edged pleasure with the heat of her dream still so fresh in her mind. He stood with his back to her, phone pressed to his ear as he faced the picture window, shutters open to reveal the moonlit shoreline.

She couldn't have stopped herself if she tried. And she didn't try. Her gaze skated straight down to his butt. A fine butt, the kind that filled out jeans just right and begged a woman to tuck her hand into his back pocket.

Why hadn't she noticed that about him before? Perhaps because he usually wore his doctor's coat or a suit.

The rest of him, though, was wonderfully familiar. What a time to realize she'd stored so much more about him in her memory than just the sexy glide of his blond hair swept back from his face, his piercing blue eyes, his strong body.

Her fingers itched to scale the expanse of his chest, hard muscled in a way that spoke of real work more than gym time with a personal trainer. Her body responded with a will of its own, her breasts beading in response to just the sight of him, the promise of pleasure in that strong, big body of his.

Were the calluses on his hand imagined in her dream or real? Right now it seemed the most important thing in the world to know, to find out from the ultimate test— his hands on her bare flesh.

His back still to her, he nodded and hmmed at something in the conversation, the broad column of his neck exposed, then he disconnected his call.

Anticipation coursed through her, but she schooled her face to show nothing as he turned.

He showed no surprise at seeing her, his moves smooth and confident. He placed his phone on the wet bar, his eyes sweeping over all of her. His gaze lingered on her shoes and he smiled, then his gaze stroked back up to her face again. "Mari, how long have you been awake?"

"Only a few minutes. Just long enough to hear you 'hmm' and 'uh-huh' a couple of times." She wrapped her arms around her waist, hugging the robe closed and making sure her tingling breasts didn't advertise her arousal. "If I may ask, who were you talking to so late?"

"Checking on our security and following up a lead on the baby."

She stood up straighter and joined him by the window, her heart hammering in her ears. "Did you find her family?"

"Sorry." He cupped her shoulder in a warm grasp, squeezing comfortingly. "Not yet. But we're working on it."

She forced herself to swallow and moisten her suddenly dry mouth. "Who is this 'we' you keep mentioning?"

"I'm a wealthy man now. Wealthy people have connections. I'm using them." His hand slid away, calluses snagging on her satin robe.

Calluses.

The thought of those fingers rasping along her skin made her shiver with want. God, she wasn't used to being this controlled by her body. She was a cerebral person, a thinker, a scientist. She needed to find level ground again, although it was a struggle.

Reining herself in, she eyed Rowan, assessing him. Her instincts told her he was holding something back about his conversation, but she couldn't decipher what that might be. She searched his face, really searched, and what a time to realize she'd never looked deeper than the surface of Rowan before. She'd known his history—a reformed bad boy, the saintly doctor saving the world and soaking up glory like a halo, while she was a person who preferred the shadows.

She'd only stepped into the spotlight now for the baby. And that made her wonder if his halo time had another purpose for him—using that notoriety for his causes. The possibility that she could have been mistaken about his ego, his swagger, gave her pause.

Of course she could just be seeking justification for how his kisses turned her inside out.

Then his hand slid down her arm until he linked fingers with her and tugged her toward the sofa. Her stomach leaped into her throat, but she didn't stop him, curious to see where this would lead. And reluctant to let go of his hand.

He sat, drawing her to sit beside him. Silently. Just staring back at her, his thumb stroking across the inside of her wrist.

Did he expect her to jump him? She'd already told him she wouldn't make the leap into bed with him. Had a part of her secretly hoped he would argue?

Still, he didn't speak or move.

She searched for something to say, anything to fill the empty space between them—and take her mind off the tantalizing feel of his callused thumb rubbing along her speeding pulse. "Do you really think Issa's family will be found?"

"I believe that every possible resource is being devoted to finding out who she is and where she came from."

The clean fresh scent of his aftershave rode every breath she took. She needed to focus on Issa first and foremost.

"Tomorrow—or rather, later this morning—we need to get serious about going public with the press. No more playing at dinner, pretend photos and controlled press releases. I need to use my notoriety to help her."

He squeezed her wrist lightly. "You don't have to put yourself in the line of fire so aggressively."

"Isn't that why you asked me to help you? To add oomph to the search?" His answer became too important to her.

"I could have handled the baby alone." He held her gaze, with undeniable truthfulness in his eyes. "If we're honest here, I wanted to spend more time with you."

Her tummy flipped and another of those tempting Rowan-scented breaths filled her. "You used the baby for selfish reasons? To get closer to me?"

"When you put it like that, it sounds so harsh."

"What *did* you mean then?"

He linked their fingers again, lifting their twined grasp and resting it against his chest. "Having you here does help with the baby's care and with finding the baby's family. But it also helps me get to know you better."

"Do you want to know me better or kiss me?"

His heart thudded against her hand as he leaned even closer, just shy of their lips touching. "Is there a problem with my wanting both?"

"You do understand that nothing is simple with me." Her breath mingled with his.

"Because of who you are? Yes, I realize exactly who you are."

And just that fast, reality iced over her. She could never forget who she was…her father's daughter. A princess. The next in the royal line since she had no siblings, no aunts or uncles. As much as she wanted to believe Rowan's interest in her was genuine, she'd been used and misunderstood too many times in the past.

She angled away from him. "I know you think I'm a spoiled princess."

"Sometimes we say things in anger that we don't mean. I apologize for that." He stretched his arm along the back of the sofa without touching her this time.

"What *do* you think of me?" The opinion of others hadn't mattered to her before…. Okay, that was a lie.

Her parents' opinion mattered. She'd cared what her first lover thought of her only to find he'd used her to get into her father's inner circle.

"Mari, I think you're smart and beautiful."

She grinned. "Organized and uptight."

He smiled back. "Productive, with restrained passions."

"I *am* a spoiled princess," she admitted, unable to resist the draw of his smile, wanting to believe what she saw in his eyes. "I've had every luxury, security, opportunity imaginable. I've had all the things this baby needs, things her mother is so desperate to give her she would give her away to a stranger. I feel awful and guilty for just wanting to be normal."

"Normal life?" He shook his head, the leather sofa creaking as he leaned back and away. "I had that so-called normal life and I still screwed up."

She'd read the press about him, the way he'd turned his life around after a drunk-driving accident as a teen. He was the poster boy for second chances, devoting his life to making amends.

Her negative reports on his program weren't always popular. Some cynics in the medical community had even suggested she had an ax to grind, insinuating he might have spurned her at some point. That assumption stung her pride more than a little.

Still, she couldn't deny the good he'd done with his clinic. The world needed more people like Dr. Rowan Boothe.

"You screwed up as a teenager, but you set yourself on the right path again once you went to that military high school."

"That doesn't erase my mistake. Nothing can." He plowed a hand through his hair. "It frustrates the hell out of me that the press wants to spin it into some kind of feel-good story. So yeah, I get your irritation with the whole media spin."

"But your story gives people hope that they can turn their lives around."

He mumbled a curse.

"What? Don't just go Grinchy on me." She tapped his elbow. "Talk. Like you did at dinner."

"Go Grinchy?" He cocked an eyebrow. "Is that really a word?"

"Of course it is. I loved that movie as a child. I watched a lot of Christmas movies flying across the ocean to spend Christmas with one parent or the other. So, back to the whole Grinchy face. What gives?"

"If you want to change my mood, then let's talk about something else." His arm slid from the back of the sofa until his hand cupped her shoulder. "What else did you enjoy about Christmas when you were a kid?"

"You're not going to distract me." With his words or his touch.

"Says who?" Subtly but deliberately, he pulled her closer.

And angled his mouth over hers.

Seven

Stunned still, Mari froze for an instant. Then all the simmering passion from her dream earlier came roaring to the surface. She looped her arms around Rowan's neck and inched closer to him on the sofa. The satin of her peignoir set made her glide across the leather smoother, easier, until she melted against him, opened her mouth and took him as boldly as he took her.

The sweep of his tongue carried the minty taste of toothpaste, the intoxicating warmth of pure him. His hands roved along her back, up and down her spine in a hypnotizing seduction. He teased his fingers up into her hair, massaging her scalp until her body relaxed, muscle by tense muscle, releasing tensions she hadn't even realized existed. Then he stirred a different sort of tension, a coiling of desire in her belly that pulled tighter and tighter until she arched against him.

Her breasts pressed to his chest, the hard wall of him

putting delicious pressure against her tender, oversensitized flesh.

He reclined with her onto the couch, tucking her beneath him with a possessive growl. She nipped his bottom lip and purred right back. The contrast of cool butter-soft leather beneath her and hot, hard male over her sent her senses on overload.

The feel of his muscled body stretching out over her, blanketing her, made her blood pulse faster, thicker, through her veins. She plucked at the leather string holding back his hair, pulled it loose and glory, glory, his hair slipped free around her fingers. She combed her hands through the coarse strands, just long enough to tickle her face as he kissed.

And this man sure did know how to kiss.

Not just with his mouth and his bold tongue, but he used his hands to stroke her, his body molding to hers. His knee slid between her legs. The thick pressure of his thigh against the core of her sent delicious shivers sparkling upward. All those sensations circled and tightened in her belly with a new intensity.

Her hands learned the planes and lines of him, along his broad shoulders, down his back to the firm butt she'd been checking out not too long ago. Every nerve ending tingled to life, urging her to take more—more of him and more of the moment.

She wanted all of him. Now.

Hooking a leg around his calf, she linked them, bringing him closer still. Her hips rocked against his, the thick length of his arousal pressing against her stomach with delicious promise of what they could have together. Soon. Although not soon enough. Urgency throbbed through her, pulsing into a delicious ache between her legs.

He swept aside her hair and kissed along the sensitive curve of her neck, nipping ever so lightly against her pulse. She hummed her approval and scratched gently over his back, along his shoulders, then down again to yank at his shirt. She couldn't get rid of their clothes fast enough. If she gave herself too long to think, too many practical reasons to stop would start marching through her mind—

A cool whoosh of air swept over her. She opened her eyes to see Rowan standing beside the sofa. Well, not standing exactly, but halfway bent over, his hands on his legs as he hauled in ragged breath after breath. His arousal was unmistakable, so why was he pulling away?

"What? Where?" She tried again to form a coherent sentence. "Where are you going?"

He stared at her in the moonlight, his chest rising and falling hard, like he'd run for miles. His expression was closed. His eyes inscrutable.

"Good night, Mariama."

Her brain couldn't make his words match up with what she was feeling. Something didn't add up. "Good night? That's it?"

"I need to stop now." He tucked his shirt in as he backed away. "Things are getting too intense."

She refused to acknowledge the twinge of hurt she felt at his words. She wasn't opening her emotions to this man.

"Yeah, I noticed." She brazened it out, still committed to re-creating the amazing feelings from her dream. "That intensity we were experiencing about twenty seconds ago was a good thing."

"It will be good, Mari. When you're ready."

Damn, but he confused her. She hated feeling like

the student in need of remedial help. The one who didn't "get" it.

"Um, hello, Rowan. I'm ready now."

"I just need for you to be sure." He backed away another step, his hair tousled from her hungry fingers. "See if you feel the same in the morning. Good night, Mariama."

He pivoted into his room and closed the door behind him.

Mari sagged back on the sofa, befuddled as hell. What was his game here? He bound her to him by enlisting her help with the baby. He clearly wanted her. Yet, he'd walked away.

She wasn't innocent. She'd been with men—two. The first was a one-night stand that had her clamping her legs shut for years to come after she'd learned he'd only wanted access to her family. Then one long-term deal with a man who'd been as introverted as her. Their relationship had dissolved for lack of attention, fading into nothing more than convenient sex. And then not so convenient. Still, the breakup had been messy, her former lover not taking well to having his ego stung over being dumped. He'd been a real jerk.

Whereas Rowan was being a total gentleman. Not pushing. Not taking advantage.

And he was driving her absolutely batty.

Holding back had threatened to drive Rowan over the edge all night long.

At least now he could move forward with the day. The salty morning breeze drifted through the open shutters as he tucked his polo shirt into his jeans, already anticipating seeing Mari. Soon. He'd never wanted a woman this much. Walking away from her last night had been almost impossible. But he was making progress. She wanted him and he needed this to be very, very reciprocal.

So he needed to move on with his plan to romance her. Neither of them had a presentation at the conference today. He suspected it wouldn't take much persuasion to convince her to skip out on sitting through boring slide presentations and rubber chicken.

During his sleepless night, he'd racked his brain for the best way to sweep her off her feet. She wasn't the most conventional of women. He'd decided to hedge his bets by going all out. He'd started off with the traditional stuff, a flower left on her pillow while she'd been in the shower. He'd also ordered her favorite breakfast delivered to her room. He planned to end the day with a beachside dinner and concert.

All traditional "dating" fare.

The afternoon's agenda, however, was a bit of a long shot. But then he figured it was best to hedge his bets with her. She'd seemed surprised by the breakfast, and he could have sworn she was at least a little charmed by his invitation to spend the day together. Although he still detected a hint of wariness.

But reminding her of how they could appease the press into leaving her alone by feeding them a story persuaded her. For now, at least. He just prayed the press conference went smoothly.

Rowan opened his bedroom door and found Mari already waiting for him in the sitting area with Issa cradled in her arms. She stood by the stroller, cooing to the baby and adjusting a pink bootie, her face softening with affection.

Mari wore a long silky sheath dress that glided across subtle curves as she swayed back and forth. And the pink tropical flower he'd left on her pillow was now tucked behind her ear. He stood captivated by her grace as she soothed the infant to sleep. Minutes—or maybe more—later, she leaned to place the baby in the stroller.

She glanced to the side, meeting his gaze with a smile. "Where are we going?"

Had she known he was there the whole time? Did she also know how damn difficult it had been to walk away from her last night? "It's a surprise."

"That makes me a little nervous." She straightened, gripping the stroller. "I'm not good at pulling off anything impetuous."

"We have a baby with us." He rested a hand on top of hers. "How dangerous could my plan be?"

Her pupils widened in response before her gaze skittered away. "Okay, fair enough." She pulled her hand from his and touched the exotic bloom tucked in her hair. "And thank you for the flower."

Ducking his head, he kissed her ear, right beside the flower, breathing in the heady perfume of her, even more tantalizing than the petals. "I'll be thinking of how you taste all day long."

He sketched a quick kiss along her regally high cheekbone before pulling back. Gesturing toward the private elevator, he followed her, taking in the swish of her curls spiraling just past her shoulders. What a time to realize how rarely he saw her with her hair down. She usually kept it pulled back in a reserved bun.

Except for last night when she'd gone to bed. And now.

It was all he could do to keep himself from walking up behind her, sliding his arms around her and pulling her flush against him. The thought of her bottom nestled

against him, his face in the sweet curve of her neck…
damn. He swallowed hard. Just damn.

He followed her into the elevator and thankfully the
glide down went quickly, before he had too much time
in the cubicle breathing in the scent of her. The elevator doors opened with a whoosh as hefty as his exhale.

His relief was short-lived. A pack of reporters waited
just outside the resort entrance, ready for them to give
their first official press conference. He'd expected it, of
course. He'd even set this particular one up. But having
Mari and the baby here put him on edge. Even knowing Elliot Starc's detail of bodyguards were strategically placed didn't give him total peace. He wondered
what would.

Mari pushed the stroller while he palmed her back,
guiding her through the lobby. Camera phones snap-
snap-snapped as he ushered Mari and Issa across the
marble floor. Gawkers whispered as they watched from
beside towering columns and sprawling potted ferns.

The doorman waved them through the electric doors
and out into chaos. Rowan felt Mari's spine stiffen. Pro-
tectiveness pumped through him anew.

He ducked his head toward her. "Are you sure you're
okay with this? We can go back to the suite, dine on the
balcony, spend our day off in a decadent haze of food
and sunshine."

She shook her head tightly. "We proceed as planned.
For Issa, I will do anything to get the word out about her
story, whatever it takes to be sure she has a real family who loves her and appreciates what a gift she is."

Her ferocity couldn't be denied—and it stirred the
hell out of him. Before he did something crazy like kiss
her until they both couldn't think, he turned to the reporters gathered on the resort's stone steps.

"No questions today, just a statement," he said firmly with a smile. "Dr. Mandara and I have had our disagreements in the past, but we share a common goal in our desire…to help people in need. This is the holiday season and a defenseless child landed in our radar, this little girl. How could we look away? We're working together to care for this baby until her family can be found. If even Mari and I can work together, then maybe there's hope.…"

He winked wryly and laughter rippled through the crowd.

Once they quieted, he continued, "That's all for now. We have a baby, a conference agenda and holiday shopping to juggle. Thank you and Merry Christmas, everyone."

Their bodyguards emerged from the crowd on cue and created a circular wall around them as they walked from the resort to the shopping strip.

Mari glanced up at him, her sandals slapping the wooden boardwalk leading to the stores and stalls of the shoreline marketplace. "Are we truly going shopping? I thought men hated shopping."

"It's better than hanging out inside eating conference food. I hope you don't mind. If you'd rather go back…"

"Bite your tongue." She hip-bumped him as he strode beside her.

"Onward then." He slipped his arm around her shoulders, tucking her to him as they walked.

She glanced up at him. "Thank you."

If he dipped his head, he could kiss her, but even though he'd set up this press coverage, he balked at that much exposure. "Thanks for what?"

"For the press conference, and taking the weight of that worry off me. You handled the media so perfectly.

I'm envious of your ease, though." She scrunched her elegant nose. "I wish I had that skill. Running from them hasn't worked out that well for me."

"I just hope the statement and all of those photos will help Issa."

"Why wouldn't it?"

Helping Interpol gain access to crooks around the world had given him insights into just how selfish, how Machiavellian, people could be. "Think of all the crackpots who will call claiming to know something just to attach themselves to a high-profile happening or hoping to gain access to you even for a short while knowing that DNA tests will later prove them to be frauds."

"God, I never thought of that," she gasped, her eyes wide and horrified.

He squeezed her shoulder reassuringly, all too aware of how perfectly she fit to his side. "The police are going to be busy sifting through the false leads that come through."

"That's why you wanted to wait a day to officially announce we're fostering her...." she whispered softly to herself as they passed a cluster of street carolers.

"Why did you think I waited?" He saw a whisper of chagrin shimmer in her golden eyes. "Did you think I was buying time to hit on you?"

She lifted a dark eyebrow. "Were you?"

"Maybe." Definitely.

She looked away, sighing. "Honestly, I'm not sure what I thought. Since I stumbled into your suite with that room-service cart, things have been...crazy. I've barely had time to think, things are happening so fast. I just hate to believe anyone would take advantage of this precious baby's situation for attention or reward money."

The reality of just how far people would go made his

jaw flex. "We'll wade through them. No one gains access to this child or you until they've been completely vetted. We will weed through the false claims and selfish agendas. Meanwhile, she's safe with us. She turns toward your voice already."

"You're nice to say that, but she's probably just in search of her next bottle."

"Believe what you want. I know differently." He'd seen scores of mothers and children file through his clinic—biological and adoptive. Bonds formed with or without a blood connection.

"Are you arguing with me? I thought we were supposed to be getting along now. Isn't that what you said at the press conference?"

"I'm teasing you. Flirting. There's a difference." Unable to resist, he pressed a kiss to her forehead.

"Oh."

"Relax. I'm not going to hit on you here." There were far too many cameras for him to be too overt. "Although a longer kiss would certainly give the press something to go wild about. Feed them tidbits and they'll quit digging for other items."

Furrows dug into her forehead. "But it feels too much like letting them win."

"I consider it controlling the PR rather than letting it control me." He guided her by her shoulders, turning toward a reporter with a smile before walking on. "Think about all the positive publicity you're racking up for your father."

"This may have started out to be about keeping the press off my back, but now it's more about the baby."

He agreed with her on that account. But the worry on her face reminded him to stay on track with his plan.

"This conversation is getting entirely too serious for a day of fun and relaxation."

"Of course…" She swiped her hand over her forehead, squeezing her eyes closed for an instant before opening them again and smiling. "Who are you shopping for today? For your family?"

"In a sense."

He stopped in front of a toy store.

Her grin widened, her kissable lips glistening with a hint of gloss. "Are we shopping for Issa?"

"For the kids at my clinic."

Toy shopping with Rowan and Issa, like they were a family, tore at Mari's heart throughout the day. The man who'd left a flower on her pillow and chosen her favorite breakfast was charming. But the man who went shopping for the little patients at his free clinic?

That man was damn near irresistible.

Riding the elevator back up to their suite, she grabbed the brass bar for balance. Her unsteady feet had nothing to do with exhaustion or the jerk of the elevator—and everything to do with the man standing beside her.

Her mind swirled with memories of their utterly carefree day. The outing had been everything she could have hoped for and more. Sure, the paparazzi had followed them, lurking, but Rowan had controlled them, fielding their questions while feeding them enough tidbits to keep them from working themselves into a frenzy. Best of all, Issa had gotten her press coverage. Hopefully the right people would see it.

As much as Mari's stomach clenched at the thought of saying goodbye to the baby, she wanted what was best for the child. She wanted Issa to feel—and be—loved unreservedly. Every child deserved that. And

Rowan was doing everything possible to help this child he'd never met, just like he did the patients at his clinic, even down to the smallest detail.

Such as their shopping spree.

It would have been easier to write it off as a show for the press or a trick to win her over. But he had a list of children's names with notes beside them. Not that she could read his stereotypically wretched doctor's scrawl. But from the way he consulted the list and made choices, he'd clearly made a list of kids' names and preferences. The bodyguards had been kept busy stowing packages in the back of a limo trailing them from store to store.

And he hadn't left Issa off his list. The baby now had a new toy in her stroller, a plush zebra, the black-and-white stripes captivating the infant. The vendor had stitched the baby's name in pink on the toy.

Issa.

The one part of her prior life the little one carried with her—a name. Used for both boys and girls, meaning savior. Appropriate this time of year... Her feet kicked. Could the name be too coincidental? Could whoever left the baby have made up the name to go with the season—while leading authorities astray?

She leaned in to stroke the baby's impossibly soft cheek. Issa's lashes swept open and she stared up at Mari for a frozen moment, wide dark eyes looking up with such complete trust Mari melted. What happened if family came forward and they didn't love her as she deserved?

Those thoughts threatened to steal Mari's joy and she shoved them aside as the elevator doors whooshed open. She refused to let anything rob her of this perfect day and the promise of more. More time with Issa. More time with Rowan.

More kisses?

More of everything?

He'd walked away last night because he thought she wasn't ready. Maybe he was right. Although the fact that he cared about her needs, her well-being, made it all the more difficult to keep him at arm's length. And she couldn't even begin to imagine how his plans for seducing her fit into this whole charade with the baby.

Questions churned in her mind, threatening to steal the joy from the day. In a rare impulsive move, she decided to simply go with the flow. She would quit worrying about when or if they would sleep together and just enjoy being with Rowan. Enjoy the flirting.

Revel in the chemistry they shared rather than wearing herself out denying its existence.

Butterflies stirred in her stomach. She pushed the stroller into their suite just as Rowan's arm shot out to stop her.

"Someone's here," he warned a second before a woman shot up from the sofa.

A woman?

The butterflies slowed and something cold settled in her stomach. Dread?

A redhead with a freckled nose and chic clothes squealed, "Rowan!"

The farm-fresh bombshell sprinted across the room and wrapped her arms around Rowan's neck.

Dread quickly shifted to something darker.

Jealousy.

Eight

Rowan braced his feet as the auburn-haired whirl-wind hit him full force. He'd spoken with his business partner and the partner's wife, Hillary, about the current situation. But he'd assured them Elliot Starc had things under control. Apparently his friends weren't taking him at his word.

Who else was waiting in the suite to blindside him? So much for romance tonight.

"Hillary." Rowan hugged his friend fast before pulling away. "Not that I'm unhappy to see you, but what are you doing here tonight?"

She patted his face. "You should know that word spreads fast among the Brotherhood and everyone available is eager to help." She glanced over her shoulder at Mari and the baby. "And of course, we're insanely curious about your new situation."

Mari looked back and forth between them, a look of confusion on her face. "The Brotherhood?"

"A nickname for some of my high school class-mates," Rowan explained. "We used to call ourselves the Alpha Brotherhood."

They still did, actually, after a few drinks over a game of cards. The name had started as a joke between them, a way of thumbing their noses at the frat-boy types, and after a while, the label stuck.

Hillary thrust a hand toward Mari. "Hi, I'm Hillary Donavan. I'm married to Rowan's former classmate and present business partner, Troy."

Mari's eyebrows arched upward. "Oh, your husband is the computer mogul."

Hillary took over pushing the stroller and preceded them into the suite as if it was her hotel penthouse. "You can go ahead and say it. My husband is the Robin Hood Hacker."

"I wasn't…" Mari stuttered, following the baby buggy deeper into the room. "I wouldn't…uh…"

"It's okay," Hillary said with a calm smile that had smoothed awkward moments in her days as an event planner for high-powered D.C. gatherings. "You can relax. Everyone knows my husband's history."

Mari smiled apologetically, leaning into the stroller to pull the sleeping baby out and cradle her protectively in her arms. "I'm not particularly good with chitchat."

"That's all right. I talk plenty for two people." She cupped the back of the infant's head. "What an ador-able baby. Issa, right?"

"Yes." Rowan pushed the stroller to a corner, light-weight gauzy pink blanket trailing out the side. "Did you see the gossip rags or did the Brotherhood tell you that, too?"

Hillary made herself at home on the leather sofa. "Actually, I'm here to help. Troy and Rowan are more than just business partners on that computer diagnostics project you so disapprove of—" Hillary winked to take the sting out the dig "—they're also longtime friends. I have some last-minute Christmas shopping to do for those tough-to-buy-for people in my life, and voilà. Coming here seemed the perfect thing to do."

The pieces came together in Rowan's mind, Hillary's appearance now making perfect sense. While the Brotherhood kept their Interpol work under wraps, Hillary knew about her husband's freelance agent work and Salvatore had even taken her into the fold for occasional missions. Now she was here. He should have thought of it himself, if his brain hadn't been scrambled by a certain sexy research scientist.

Hillary would make the perfect bodyguard for Mari and Issa. No one would question her presence and she added a layer of protection to this high-profile situation.

Although sometimes the whole Interpol connection also came with dangers. God, he was in the middle of an impossible juggling act.

The baby started fussing and Rowan extended his arms to take her. Mari hesitated, tucking the baby closer. Rowan lifted an eyebrow in surprise.

"Mari? I can take her." He lifted the baby from Mari's arms. "You two keep talking."

"Wow." Hillary laughed. "You sure handle that tiny tyke well. No wonder you're dubbed one of the world's hottest bachelors. Snap a photo of you now and you'll need your own bodyguard."

Mari's smile went tight and Rowan wondered... Holy hell, she couldn't be jealous. Could she? Was that the same look he'd seen drifting through her eyes when Hillary had hugged him earlier? He wanted her to desire him, but he also wanted—needed—for her to trust him.

"Enough, Hillary. You were talking about Troy's computer search...."

"Right—" she turned back to Mari "—and you're taking care of the baby, Rowan. So vamoose. Go fill out your list for Santa. I've got this."

Rowan cocked an eyebrow over being so summarily dismissed. And putting Issa in the bassinet in another room would give him the perfect excuse to slip away and call Troy.

Not to mention time to regroup for the next phase of winning over Mari. He'd made progress with her today.

Now he just had to figure out how to persuade his friends to give him enough space to take that romancing to the next level.

Mari sank to the edge of the sofa. Her head was spinning at how fast things were changing around her. Not to mention how fast this woman was talking.

"Hold on a moment, please." Mari raised a hand. "What were you saying about computer searches into Issa's past?"

Hillary dropped into the wide rattan chair beside her. "No worries. It's all totally legal computer work. I promise. Troy walks on the right side of the law these days. And yes, it's okay to talk about it. I know about my husband's past, and I assume you know about Rowan's. But they've both changed. They're genuinely trying to make amends in more ways than most could imagine."

Mari blinked in the wake of Hurricane Hillary, confused. Why would Rowan have needed to make amends for anything? Sure, he'd led a troubled life as a teen, but his entire adult life had been a walking advertisement for charity work. Even if she disputed some of his methods, she couldn't deny his philanthropic spirit. "I've read the stories of his good deeds."

"There's so much more to Rowan than those stories."

She knew that already. The press adored him and his work, and she had to admit his clinic had helped many. She just wished they could come to an agreement on how to make his work—the computerized side and even the personal side—more effective. If she could solve that problem, who knew how many more small clinics in stretched-thin outposts of the world would benefit from Rowan's model of aid?

"Hillary, why are you telling me this?"

"The competitive animosity between the two of you is not a secret." She tipped her head to the side, twirling a strand of red hair contemplatively. "So I find it strange that you're here."

"I'm here for the baby."

"Really?" Hillary crossed her legs, her eyes glimmering with humor and skepticism. No getting anything past this woman. "There are a million ways the two of you could care for this child other than sharing a suite."

Mari bristled, already feeling overwhelmed by this confident whirlwind who looked like a Ralph Lauren model in skinny jeans and a poet's shirt.

Smoothing her hands over her sack dress, Mari sat up stiffly, channeling every regal cell in her body. "This is quite a personal conversation to be having with someone I only just met."

"You're right. I apologize if I've overstepped." She held up a hand, diamond wedding band set winking in the sunlight. "I've become much more extroverted since marrying Troy. I just wanted you to know Rowan's a better man than people think. A better man than he knows."

Great. Someone else pointing out the perfection of Dr. Rowan Boothe. As if Mari didn't already know. God, how she resented the feelings of insecurity pumping through her. She wanted to be the siren in the peignoir, the confident woman certain that Rowan wanted her with every fiber of his soul. And yes, she knew that was melodramatic and totally unscientific.

Forcing her thoughts to slow and line up logically, she realized that Rowan's eyes had followed her all day long—no skinny jeans needed. And Hillary was right. He and Mari both could have figured out a dozen different ways to care for this baby and stir publicity without sharing a suite. She was here because she wanted to be and Rowan wanted her here, as well.

No more flirting. No more games. No more holding back. She burned to sleep with Rowan.

The next time she had him alone, she intended to see the seduction through to its full, satisfying conclusion.

Finally, Rowan closed his suite door after dinner with Hillary, Troy and Elliot. He plowed his hands through his hair as Mari settled the baby for the night in his room.

He appreciated the help of his friends—but by the end of supper he had never been happier to see them all head to their own suites. Troy and Hillary were staying in the suite across the hall. Elliot Starc was a floor below, monitoring the surveillance vans outside the resort.

Rowan was more than a little surprised that his friends felt such a need to rally around him just because another orphan had landed on his doorstep. Issa wasn't the first—and she certainly wouldn't be the last—child in need of his patronage.

He suspected his friends' increased interest had something to do with Mari's involvement. No doubt he hadn't been as successful as he would have liked at hiding his attraction to her all these years. They were here out of curiosity as well as genuine caring, stepping up on a personal level, even if Mari didn't know the full weight of what they brought to the table for security and he wasn't in a position to tell her.

Now that a story had broken about an orphan at Christmastime, the attention was swelling by the second. Holiday mayhem made it tougher than ever to record all the comings and goings at the resort. Bogus leads were also coming in by the hundreds. So far no sign of a valid tip. Hillary and Troy were rechecking the police work through computer traces, using Interpol databases.

Intellectually, he understood these things took time and persistence, but thinking about the kid's future, worrying about her, made this more personal than analytical.

Somewhere out there, the baby's family had to be seeing the news reports. Even if they didn't want to claim her, surely someone would step forward with information. Even if the answer came in the form of official surrender of parental rights, at least they would know.

He understood full well how family ties didn't always turn out to be as ideal as one would hope. Memories of his brother's death, of his parents' grief and denial burned through him. He charged across the sitting area to the bar. He started to reach for the scotch and stopped himself. After the way his brother died…

Hell, no.

He opted for a mug of fresh local ginger tea and

one of the Christmas sugar cookies instead and leaned against the bar, staring out over the water as he bit the frosted tree cookie in half. Tomorrow, he and Mari both had conference presentations, then this weekend, the closing dinner and ball. Time was ticking away for all of them. He had to make the most of every moment. Tomorrow, he'd arranged for a spa appointment for Mari after her last presentation. Surely she would appreciate some privacy after all the scrutiny....

The door from Rowan's room opened. Mari slid through and closed it quietly after her. "Baby's sleeping soundly. I would have taken her tonight, you know."

"Fair is fair," he said. "We struck a bargain."

"You're a stubborn man. But then I understand that trait well."

Walking toward him, her silvery-gray sheath dress gliding over her sleek figure, she set the nursery monitor on the edge of the bar. Christmas tunes played softly over the airwaves—jazz versions, soft and soothing. Mari had fallen into the habit of setting her iPhone beside the monitor and using the music to reassure herself the listening device was still on.

She poured herself a mug of steaming ginger tea as well, adding milk and honey. Cupping the thick pottery in both hands, she drank half then cradled the mug to her with a sigh.

He skimmed his knuckles along her patrician cheekbones. "Are you okay?"

Nodding, she set aside her glass. "I just didn't expect the press coverage to be so...comprehensive."

Was it his imagination or did she lean into his touch.

"You're a princess. What you do makes the news." Although even he was surprised at just how intense the media attention had become.

The hotel staff had closed off access to their floor aside from them and the Donavans, a measure taken after a reporter was injured on a window-washing unit trying to get a bonus photo. Rowan rubbed at a kink in the back of his neck, stress-induced from worrying his tail off about all the possible holes in the security. He wasn't sure he felt comfortable taking Mari and Issa out of the hotel again, even with guards.

"But I wanted to bring positive coverage for Issa. Not all of these cranks..."

And she didn't know the half of it. Troy had informed him about a handful of the more colorful leads the police hadn't bothered mentioning. A woman claiming to be Mari's illegitimate half sister had called to say the baby belonged to her. Another call had come from an area prison with someone saying their infant daughter resembled Issa and she thought it was her twin, whom they'd thought died at birth.

All of which turned out to be false, but there was no need to make Mari more upset by sharing the details. "My contacts will sift through them."

"Who are these contacts you keep talking about? Like Hillary and her husband?" She picked up the glass again and sipped carefully.

His glass.

His body tightened as her lips pressed to the edge.

He cleared his throat. "I went to a military high school. Makes sense that some of them would end up in law enforcement positions."

"It was a military *reform* school." She eyed him over the rim of the tumbler through long lashes.

"Actually, about half were there because they wanted a future in the military or law enforcement." He rattled off the details, anything to keep from thinking about how badly he wanted to take that glass from her and kiss her until they both forgot about talking and press conferences. "The rest of us were there because we got into trouble."

"Your Alpha Brotherhood group—you trust these friends with Issa's future?"

"Implicitly."

Shaking her head, she looked away. "I wish I could be as sure about whom to trust."

"You're worried."

"Of course."

"Because you care." Visions of her caring for the baby, insisting Issa stay in her room tonight even though it was his turn, taunted him with how attached she was becoming to the little one already. There was so much more to this woman than he'd known or guessed. She was more emotional than she'd ever let on. Which brought him back to the strange notion that she'd been jealous of Hillary.

A notion he needed to dispel. "What did you think of Hillary?"

"She's outspoken and she's a huge fan of yours." She folded her arms over her chest.

"You can't be jealous."

"At first, when she hugged you…I wondered if she was a girlfriend," she admitted. "Then I realized it might not be my right to ask."

"I kissed you. You have a right to question." He met her gaze full-on, no games or hidden agendas. Just pure honesty. "For the record, I'm the monogamous type. When I'm with a woman, I'm sure as hell not kissing other women."

Her eyes flashed with quick relief before she tipped

her head to the side and touched his chest lightly. "What happened last night—"

"What almost happened—"

"Okay, almost happened, along with the parts that did—"

"I understand." He pressed a hand over hers, wanting to reassure her before she had a chance to start second-guessing things and bolting away. "You want to say it can't happen. Not again."

"Hmm…" She frowned, toying with the simple watch on her wrist. "Have you added mind reader to your list of accomplishments now? If so, please do tell me why I would insist on pushing you away."

"Because we have to take care of the baby." He folded her hand in his and kissed her knuckles, then her wrist. "Your devotion to her is a beautiful thing."

"That's a lovely compliment. Thank you. I would say the same about you."

"A compliment?" he bantered back. "I did *not* expect that."

"Why ever not?" She stepped closer until her breasts almost brushed his chest.

The unmistakably seductive move wasn't lost on him. His pulse kicked up a notch as he wondered just how far she would take this.

And how far he should let it go.

"There is the fact that you haven't missed an opportunity to make it clear how much you don't like me or my work."

"That could be a compelling reason to keep my distance from you." She placed her other hand on his chest, tipping her face up to him until their lips were a whisper apart.

"Be on notice…" He took in the deep amber of her

eyes, the flush spreading across her latte-colored, creamy skin. "I plan to romance you, sweep you off your feet even."

"You are—" she paused, leaning into him, returning his intense gaze "—a confusing man. I thought I knew you but now I'm finding I don't understand you at all. But you need to realize that after last night's kiss…"

"It was more than a kiss," he said hoarsely.

"You're absolutely right on that." Her fingers crawled up his chest until she tapped his bottom lip.

He captured her wrist again just over the thin watch. He thought of the bracelets he'd surreptitiously picked up for her at the marketplace, looking forward to the right moment to give them to her. "But I will not make love to you until you ask me. You have to know that."

"You're mighty confident." Her breath carried heat and a hint of the ginger tea.

Who knew tea could be far more intoxicating than any liquor? "Hopeful."

"Good." Her lips moved against his. "Because I'm asking."

And damn straight he didn't intend to walk away from her again.

Nine

Mari arched up onto her toes to meet Rowan's mouth sealing over hers. Pure want flooded through her. Each minute had felt like an hour from the moment she'd decided to act on her desire tonight until the second he'd kissed her.

Finally, she would be with him, see this crazy attraction through. Whether they were arguing or working together, the tension crackled between them. She recognized that now. They'd been moving toward this moment for years.

She nipped his bottom lip. "We have to be quiet so we don't wake the baby."

"Hmm…" His growl rumbled his chest against her. "Sounds challenging."

"Just how challenging can we make it?" She grazed her nails down his back, the fabric of his shirt carrying the warmth and scent of him.

"Is that a dare?"

She tucked her hands into the back pockets of his jeans as she'd dreamed of doing more than once. "Most definitely."

Angling his head to the side, he stared into her eyes. "And you're sure you're ready for this?"

She dug her fingers into his amazing tush. "Could you quit being so damn admirable? I'm very clearly propositioning you. I am an adult, a very smart adult, totally sober, and completely turned on by you. If that's not clear enough for you, then how about this? Take me to bed or to the couch, but take me now."

A slow and sexy smile creased dimples into his sun-bronzed face. "How convenient you feel that way since you absolutely mesmerize me."

Her stomach fluttered at the obvious appreciation in his eyes, his voice. His *touch*. He made her feel like the sensuous woman who wore peignoirs. He made her feel sexy. Sexier than any man ever had, and yes, that was a part of his appeal.

But she couldn't deny she'd always found him attractive. Who wouldn't? He took handsome to a whole new level, in a totally unselfconscious way. The blond streaks in his hair came from the sun—his muscles from hard work.

And those magnificent callused hands… She could lose herself in the pure sensation of his caress.

He inched aside the strap of her silvery-gray dress. She'd chosen the silky fabric for the decadent glide along her skin—yes, she usually preferred shapeless clothes, but the appreciation in Rowan's eyes relayed loud and clear he'd never judged her by what she wore. He saw her. The woman. And he wanted her.

That knowledge sent a fresh thrill up her spine.

He kissed along her bared neck, to her shoulder, his teeth lightly snapping her champagne-colored satin bra strap—another of her hidden decadences, beautiful underwear. Her head fell back, giving him fuller access. But she didn't intend to be passive in this encounter. Not by a long shot. Her hands soaked up the play of his muscles flexing in his arms as she stroked down, down, farther still to his waistband.

She tugged his polo shirt free and her fingers crawled up under the warm cotton to find even hotter skin. She palmed his back, scaled the hard planes of his shoulder blades as a jazz rendering of "The First Noel" piped through the satellite radio. He was her latest fantasies come to life.

Unable to wait a second longer, she yanked the shirt over his head even if that meant he had to draw his mouth away from her neck. She flung aside his polo, the red shirt floating to rest on the leather sofa. Fire heated his eyes to the hottest blue flame. He skimmed off the other strap of her dress until the silk slithered down her body, hooking briefly on her hips before she shimmied it the rest of the way off to pool at her feet. She kicked aside her sandals as she stepped out of the dress.

His gaze swept over her as fully as she took in the bared expanse of his broad chest, the swirls of hair, the sun-bronzed skin. He traced down the strap of her bra, along the lace edging the cups of her bra, slowly, deliberately outlining each breast. Her nipples beaded against the satin, tight and needy. She burned to be closer to him, as close as possible.

Her breath hitched in her throat and she stepped into his arms. The heat of his skin seared her as if he'd stored up the African sun inside him and shared it with her now.

"Here," she insisted, "on the sofa or the floor. I don't care. Just hurry."

"Princess, I have waited too damn long to rush this. I intend to have you completely and fully, in a real bed. I would prefer it was my bed, but there's a baby snoozing in the bassinet in my room. So let's go to yours."

"Fine," she agreed frantically. "Anywhere, the sooner the better." She slipped a finger into the waistband of his jeans and tugged.

"I like a lady who knows what she wants. Hell, I just like you."

His hands went to the front clasp of her bra and plucked it open and away with deft hands. She gasped as the overhead fan swooshed air over her bared flesh. Then he palmed both curves, warming her with a heat that spread into a tingling fire.

Through the haze of passion she realized her hand was still on his buckle. She fumbled with his belt, then the snap of his jeans, his zipper, until she found his arousal hard and straining against her hand. A growl rumbled low in his throat and she reveled in the sound. Drew in the scent of his soap and his sweat, perspiration already beading his brow from his restraint as she learned the feel of him. She stroked the steely length down, up and again.

"We have to be quiet," she reminded him.

"Both of us," he said with a promise in his voice and in his narrowed eyes.

One of his hands slid from her breast down to her panties, dipping inside, gliding between her legs. She was moist and ready for him. If she'd had her way they would be naked and together on the sofa. He was the one who'd insisted on drawing this out, but then they'd always been competitive.

Although right now that competition was delivering a tense and delicious result rather than the frustration of the past. She bit her bottom lip to hold back a whimper of pleasure. He slipped two fingers inside, deeper, stroking and coaxing her into a moist readiness. She gripped his shoulders, her fingernails digging half-moons into his tanned skin. Each glide took her higher until her legs went weak and he locked an arm around her back.

She gasped against his neck, so close to fulfillment. Aching for completion. "Let's take this to the bed."

"Soon, I promise." His late-day beard rasped against her cheek and he whispered in her ear, "But first, I need to protect you."

She gritted her teeth in frustration over the delay. "Rowan, there are guards stationed inside and outside of the hotel. Can we talk about security forces later?"

Cupping her face in his broad palms, he kissed the tip of her nose. "I mean I need to get birth control."

"Oh…" She gasped, surprised that she hadn't thought of it herself. She'd come in here with the intention of seducing him and she hadn't given a thought to the most important element of that union. So much for her genius IQ in the heat of the moment.

"I'll take care of it." He stepped away and disappeared from her room, his jeans slung low on his hips. Lean muscles rippled with every step.

She was an intelligent, modern woman. A scientist. A woman of logic. She liked to believe she would have realized before it was too late.… Before she could complete the thought, Rowan returned. He tossed a box of condoms on the bed.

"My goodness," she said, smiling, "you're an ambitious man."

"I'll take that as another challenge."

"Sounds like one where we're both winners. Now how about getting rid of those jeans."

"Your wish is my command, Princess." He toed off his shoes, no socks on, and peeled down his jeans without once taking his eyes off her.

His erection strained against his boxers and she opened her arms for him to join her. Then he was kissing her again and, oh, my, but that man knew how to kiss. The intensity of him, the way he was so completely focused on her and the moment fulfilled a long-ignored need to be first with a man. How amazing that the man who would view her this way—see only her—would be Rowan.

He reclined with her on the bed, into the thick comforter and stack of tapestry pillows, the crash and recede of the waves outside echoing the throb of her pulse. The sound of the shore, the luxurious suite, the hard-bodied man stretched over her was like a fantasy come true.

Only one thing kept it from being complete—something easily taken care of. She hooked her thumbs into the band of his boxers and inched them down. He smiled against her mouth as his underwear landed on the floor. Finally—thank heavens—finally, they met bare body to bare body, flesh-to-flesh. The rigid length of him pressed against her stomach, heating her with the promise of pleasure to come.

She dragged her foot up the back of his calf, hooking her leg around him, rocking her hips against him. He shifted his attention from her lips to her neck, licking along her collarbone before reaching her breasts—his mouth on one, his hand on the other. He touched and tasted her with an intuition for what she craved and more, finding nuances of sensitive patches of skin she hadn't realized were favored spots.

And she wanted to give him the same bliss.

Her fingers slid between them until her hand found his erection, exploring the length and feel of him. His forehead fell to rest against her collarbone. His husky growl puffed along oversensitized skin as she continued to stroke. Her thumb glided along the tip, smoothing a damp pearl, slickening her caress. Her mind filled with images of all the ways she wanted to love him through the night, with her hands and her mouth, here and in the shower. She whispered those fantasies in his ear and he throbbed in response in her hand.

Groaning, he reached out to snatch up the box of condoms. Rolling to his side, he clasped her wrist and moved her hand away, then sheathed himself. She watched, vowing next time she would do that for him.

Next time? Definitely a next time. And a next night.

Already she was thinking into the future and that was a scary proposition. Better to live in the now and savor this incredible moment. She clasped Rowan's shoulders as he shifted back over her again.

He balanced on his elbows, holding his weight off her. The thick pressure of him between her legs had her wriggling to get closer, draw him in deeper. She swept her other leg up until her ankles hooked around his waist. Her world filled with the sight of his handsome face and broad shoulders blocking out the rest of the world.

He hooked a hand behind her knee. "Your legs drive me crazy. Do you know that?"

"I do now. I also know you're driving me crazy waiting. I want all of you. Now." She dug her heels into his buttocks and urged him to...

Fill her.

Stretch her.

Thrill her.

Her back bowed up to meet him thrust for thrust, hushed sigh for sigh. Perspiration sealed them together, cool sheets slipping and bunching under them. In a smooth sweep, he kicked the comforter and tapestry pillows to the floor.

Tension gathered inside her, tightening in her belly. Her head dug back into the mattress, the scent of them mingling and filling every gasping breath. He touched her with reverence and perception, but she didn't want gentle or reverent. She needed edgy; she needed completion.

She pushed at his shoulder and flipped him to his back, straddling him, taking him faster and harder, his heated gaze and smile of approval all the encouragement she needed. His hands sketched up her stomach to her breasts, circling and plucking at her nipples as she came, intensifying waves of pleasure, harder, straight to the core of her. She rode the sensations, rode him, taking them both to the edge…and into a climax. Mutual. She bit her bottom lip to hold back the sounds swelling inside her as she stayed true to their vow to keep quiet. Rowan's jaw flexed, his groans mingling with her sighs.

Each rolling wave of bliss drew her, pulling her into a whirlpool of total muscle-melting satisfaction. Her arms gave way and she floated to rest on top of him. Rowan's chest pumped beneath her with labored breaths. His arms locked around her, anchoring her to him and to the moment.

Her body trembled in the wake of each aftershock rippling through her.

Exhaustion pulled at her but she knew if she slept, morning would come too fast with too many questions and possibilities that could take this away. So she blinked back sleep, focusing on multicolored lights beyond the window. Yachts, a sailboat, a ferry. She took in the details to stay awake so once her languid body regained strength, she could play out all those fantasies with Rowan.

She wanted everything she could wring from this stolen moment in case this night was all they could have before she retreated to the safety and order of her cold, clinical world.

"Are you asleep?" Mari's soft voice whispered through Rowan's haze as he sprawled beside her.

He'd wanted Mari for years. He'd known they would be good together. But no way in hell could he have predicted just how mind-blowingly incredible making love to this woman would be.

Sleep wasn't even an option with every fiber of him saturated with the satiny feel of her, the floral scent of her, the driving need to have her again and again until...

His mind stopped short of thoughts of the end. "I'm awake. Do you need something?"

Was she about to boot him out of her bed? Out of her life? He knew too well how fast the loyalties of even good people could shift. He grabbed the rumpled sheet free from around his feet and whipped it out until it fanned to rest over them.

She rolled toward him, her fingers toying with the hair on his chest. "I'm good. *This* is good, staying right here, like this. The past couple of days have been so frenzied, it's a relief to be in the moment."

"I hear ya." He kissed the top of her head, thinking of the bracelets he'd bought for her from the market and planning the right time to place them on her elegant arm.

Her fingers slowed and she looked up at him through long sweeping eyelashes. "You're very good with Issa. Have you ever thought about having kids of your own?"

His voice froze in his throat for a second. He'd given up on perfect family life a long time ago when he'd woken in the hospital to learn he and his brother were responsible for a woman losing her baby. Any hope of resurrecting those dreams died the day his brother crashed his truck into the side of a house.

Rowan sketched his fingers along Mari's stomach. He'd built a new kind of family with the Brotherhood and his patients. "I have my kids at the clinic, children that need me and depend on me."

"So you know that it's possible to love children that aren't your blood relation."

Where was she going with this? And then holy hell, it became all too clear. She was thinking about the possibility of keeping Issa beyond this week. "Are you saying that you're becoming attached to the little rug rat?"

"How could I not?" She leaned over him, resting her chin on her folded hands as she looked into his eyes. "I wonder if Issa landed with me for a reason. I've always planned not to get married. I thought that meant no kids for me—I never considered myself very good with them. But with Issa, I know what to do. She even responds to my voice already."

She was right about that. They shared a special bond that had to be reassuring to an infant whose world had been turned upside down by abandonment. But questions about the baby's past *would* be answered soon. He thought of Hillary and Troy working their tails off to find the baby's family. He hated to think of Mari setting herself up for heartache.

She shook her head before he could think of how

to remind her. "I know it's only been a couple of days and she could well have family out there who wants her. Or her mother might change her mind. I just hate the limbo."

He swept her hair from her face and kissed her, hard. "You won't be in limbo for long, I can promise you that." Guilt pinched over how he'd brought her into this, all but forced her to stay with him. "My friends and I won't rest until we find the truth about Issa's past. That's a good thing, you know."

"Of course I do. Let's change the subject." She pulled a wobbly smile. "I think it's amazing the way your friends all came to help you at the drop of a hat."

"It's what we do for each other." Just as he'd done his best to help his buddy Conrad reconcile with his wife earlier this year. He owed Conrad for helping him start the clinic, but he would have helped regardless.

"In spite of your rocky teenage years, you and your friends have all turned into incredible success stories. I may not always agree with some of your projects, but your philanthropic work is undeniable. It's no secret that your other friend, the casino owner—Conrad Hughes—has poured a lot of money into your clinic, as well."

He tensed at her mention of one of his Alpha Brotherhood buddies, wishing he could share more about the other side of his life. Needing to warn her, to ensure she didn't get too close. There weren't many women who could live with the double life he and his friends led with their Interpol work. Mari had enough complicating her life with her heritage. Better to keep the conversation on well-known facts and off anything that could lead to speculation.

"Conrad invested the start-up cash for my clinic. He

deserves the credit. My financial good fortune came later."

"No need to be so modest. Even before your invention of the diagnostics program, you could have had a lucrative practice anywhere and you chose to be here in Africa, earning a fraction of the salary."

He grunted, tunneling his hand under the sheet to cup her butt and hopefully distract her. "I got by then and I get by even better now."

She smiled against his chest. "Right, the billions you made off that diagnostics program we keep arguing about. I could help you make it better."

He smacked her bottom lightly. "Is that really what you want to talk about and risk a heated debate?"

"Why are you so quick to deflect accolades? The press is totally in love with you. You could really spin that, if you wanted."

He grimaced. "No, thanks."

She elbowed up on his chest. "I do understand your reticence. But think about it. You could inspire other kids. Sure you went to a military reform school, but you studied your butt off for scholarships to become a doctor, made a fortune and seem to be doing your level best to give it all away."

"I'm not giving it *all* away," he said gruffly, a sick feeling churning in his gut at the detour this conversation was taking. He avoided that damn press corps for just this reason. He didn't want anyone digging too deeply and he sure as hell didn't want credit for some noble character he didn't possess. "If I donate everything, I'll be broke and no good to anyone. I'm investing wisely."

"While donating heavily of your money and time."

Throwing all his resources into the black hole of guilt

that he'd never fill. Ever. He took a deep breath to keep that dark cavern at bay.

"Stop, okay?" He kissed her to halt her words. "I do what I do because it's the right thing. I have to give back, to make up for my mistakes."

Her forehead furrowed. "For your drunk-driving accident in high school? I would say you've more than made restitution. You could hire other doctors to help you carry the load."

"How can a person ever make restitution for lives lost?" he barked out, more sharply than he'd intended. But now that he'd started, there was no going back. "Do you know why I was sentenced to the military reform school for my last two years of high school?"

"Because you got in a drunk-driving accident and a woman was injured. You made a horrible, horrible mistake, Rowan. No one's denying that. But it's clear to anyone looking that you've turned your life around."

"You've done your homework where my diagnostics model is concerned, but you've obviously never researched the man behind the medicine." He eased Mari off him and sat up, his elbows on his knees as he hung his head, the weight of the memories too damn much. "The woman driving the other car was pregnant. She lost the baby."

"Oh, no, Rowan how tragic for her." Mari's voice filled with sadness and a hint of horror, but her hand fluttered to rest on his back. "And what a heavy burden for you to carry as the driver of the car."

She didn't know the half of it. No one did. To let the full extent of his guilt out would stain his brother's memory. Yet, for some reason he couldn't pinpoint, he found himself confessing all for the first time. To Mari. "But I wasn't driving."

Her hand slid up to rub the back of his neck and she sat up beside him, sheet clasped to her chest. "The news reports all say you were."

"That's what we told the police." He glanced over at her. "My brother and I both filled out formal statements saying I was the driver."

She stared back at him for two crashes of the waves before her eyes went wide with realization. "Your brother was actually the one behind the wheel that night? And he was drunk?"

Rowan nodded tightly. "We were both injured in the car accident, knocked out and rushed to the nearest hospital. When I woke up from surgery for a punctured lung, my mother was with me. My dad was with my brother, who'd broken his nose and fractured his jaw. They wanted us to get our stories straight before we talked to the police."

That night came roaring back to him, the confusion, the pain. The guilt that never went away no matter how many lives he saved at the clinic.

"Did your parents actually tell you to lie for your brother?" Her eyes went wider with horror. Clearly her parents would have never considered such a thing.

Most never would. He understood that, not that it made him feel one bit better about his own role in what had happened. She needed to understand the position they'd all been in, how he'd tried to salvage his brother's life only to make an even bigger mistake. One that cost him...too much.

"We were both drunk that night, but my brother was eighteen years old. I was only sixteen, a minor. The penalty would be less for me, but Dylan could serve hard time in jail. If I confessed to driving the car, Dylan could still have a future, a chance to turn his life around while he was still young."

"So you took the blame for your brother. You allowed yourself to be sentenced to a military reform school because your family pressured you, oh, Rowan..." She swept back his hair, her hands cool against his skin. "I am so sorry."

But he didn't want or deserve her comfort or sympathy. Rather than reject it outright, he linked fingers with her and lowered her arms.

"There was plenty of blame to go around that night. I could have made so many different choices. I could have called a cab at the party or asked someone else to drive us home." The flashing lights outside reminded him of the flash of headlights before the wreck, the blurred cop cars before he'd blacked out, then finally the arrival of the police to arrest him. "I wasn't behind the wheel, but I was guilty of letting my brother have those keys."

His brother had been a charismatic character, everyone believed him when he said he would change, and Rowan had gotten used to following his lead. When Dylan told him he was doing great in rehab, making his meetings, laying off the bottle, Rowan had believed him.

"What about your brother's guilt for what happened that night? Didn't Dylan deserve to pay for what happened to that woman, for you giving up your high school years?"

Trust Mari to see this analytically, to analyze it in clear-cut terms of rights and wrongs. Life didn't work that way. The world was too full of blurred gray territory.

"My brother paid plenty for that night and the decisions I made." If Rowan had made the right choices in the beginning, his brother would still be alive today. "Two years later, Dylan was in another drunk-driving accident. He drove his truck into the side of a house. He died." Rowan drew in a ragged breath, struggling like hell not to shrug off her touch that left him feeling too raw right now. "So you see, my decisions that night cost two lives."

Mari scooted to kneel in front of him, the sheet still clasped to her chest. Her dark hair spiraled around her shoulders in a wild sexy mess, but her amber eyes were no-nonsense. "You were sixteen years old and your parents pressured you to make the wrong decision. They sacrificed you to save your brother. They were wrong to do that."

Memories grated his insides, every word pouring acid on freshly opened wounds. He left the bed, left her, needing to put distance between himself and Mari's insistence.

He stepped over the tapestry pillows and yanked on his boxers. "You're not hearing me, Mari." He snagged his jeans from the floor and jerked them on one leg at a time. "I accept responsibility for my own actions. I wasn't a little kid. Blaming other people for our mistakes is a cop-out."

And the irony of it all, the more he tried to make amends, the more people painted him as some kind of freaking saint. He needed air. Now.

A ringing phone pierced the silence between them.

Not her ringtone. His, piping through the nursery monitor. Damn it. He'd left his cell phone in his room. "I should get that before it wakes the baby."

He hotfooted it out of her room, grateful for the excuse to escape more of her questions. Why the hell couldn't they just make love until the rest of the world faded away?

With each step out the door, he felt the weight of her gaze following him. He would have to give her some kind of closure to her questions, and he would. Once he had himself under control again.

He opened the door leading into his bedroom. His phone rang on the bamboo dresser near the bassinet. He grabbed the cell and took it back into the sitting area, reading the name scrolling across the screen.

Troy Donavan?

Premonition burned over him. His computer pal had to have found something big in order to warrant a call in the middle of the night.

Mari filled the doorway, tan satin sheet wrapped around her, toga-style. "Is something wrong?"

"I don't know yet." He thumbed the talk button on the cell phone. "Yes?"

"Hi, Rowan." Hillary's voice filled his ear. "It's me. Troy's found a trail connecting a worker at the hotel to a hospital record on one of the outlying islands— he's still working the data. But he's certain he's found Issa's mother."

Ten

Mari cradled sleeping Issa in her arms, rocking her for what would be the last time. She stared past the garland-draped minibar to the midday sun marking the passage of the day, sweeping away precious final minutes with this sweet child she'd already grown to love.

Her heart was breaking in two.

She couldn't believe her time with Issa was coming to an end. Before she'd even been able to fully process the fact that she'd actually followed through on the decision to sleep with Rowan, her world had been tossed into utter chaos with one phone call that swept Issa from them forever.

Troy Donavan had tracked various reflections of reflections in surveillance videos, piecing them together with some maze of other cameras in everything from banks to cops' radar to follow a path to a hint of a clue. They'd found the woman who'd walked away from the room-service trolley where Issa had been hidden. They'd gone a step further in the process to be sure. At some point, Mari had lost the thread of how he'd traced the trail back to a midwife on the mainland who'd delivered Issa. She'd been able to identify the mother, proving the baby's identity with footprint records.

The young mother had made her plan meticulously and worked to cover her tracks. She'd uncovered Rowan's schedule to speak at this conference then managed to get hired as a temp in the extra staff brought on for the holiday crowd. That's why she hadn't been on the employee manifest.

It appeared she'd had a mental breakdown shortly after leaving her child and was currently in a hospital. Issa had no grandparents, but she had a great aunt and uncle who wanted her. Deeply. In their fifties, their four sons were all grown but they hadn't hesitated in stepping up to care for their great niece. They owned a small coastal art gallery on the mainland and had plenty of parenting knowledge. They weren't wealthy, but their business and lives were stable.

All signs indicated they could give Issa a wonderful life full of love. Mari should be turning cartwheels over the news. So many orphans in Africa had no one to call their own and here Issa had a great family ready and eager to care for her.

Still, Mari could barely breathe at the prospect of handing over the baby, even though she knew this was the best thing for Issa.

The main door opened and Mari flinched, clutching the tiny girl closer. Rowan entered, lines fanning from his eyes attesting to the sleepless night they'd both endured after the fateful phone call about Issa's identity.

Rowan had scraped his hair back with a thin leather tie, his jeans and button-down shirt still sporting the wrinkles from when she'd tossed them aside in an effort to get him naked. That seemed eons ago now. Those moments after the call when they'd hastily gotten dressed again had passed in a frenzied haze.

"Any news?" she asked, feeling like a wretched person for hoping somehow she could keep Issa. She wasn't in any position to care for a baby. She'd never even given much thought to being a mother. But right now, it was the only thing she could think about. Who knew that a baby could fill a void in her life that she would have never guessed needed filling?

He shook his head and sat on the arm of the sofa near her, his blue eyes locked on the two of them. "Just more verification of what we learned last night. The mother's note was honest. Her husband was a soldier killed in a border dispute. And just more confirmation to what we already knew—she picked up a job doing temp work here, which is why she didn't show up on the initial employee search. The woman you saw that night running from the cart was, in fact, Issa's mother. She has family support back on the mainland. But it appears her husband's death hit her especially hard when she was already suffering from postpartum depression."

That last part hadn't been in the early reports. The whole issue became muddier now that the baby hadn't been left out of selfishness, but rather out of a deep mental illness. "Issa ended up in a room-service cart because of postpartum depression?"

"Approximately one in eight new mothers suffer from it in the States." He pinched the bridge of his nose as if battling a headache. "Even more so here with the rampant poverty and lack of medical care."

Mari's arms twitched protectively around the bundled infant. Would it have made a difference for Issa's mother if the family had been more supportive? Or had they been shut out? So many questions piled on top of each other until she realized she was simply looking for someone to blame, a reason why it would be okay to keep Issa. The scent of baby detergent—specially bought so she could wash the tiny clothes herself—mingled with sweet baby breath. Such a tender, dear bundle...

When Issa squirmed, Mari forced herself to relax—at least outwardly. "I guess I should be grateful she didn't harm her child. What happens now?"

Mari's eyes dropped to the child as Issa fought off sleep, her tiny fingers clenching and unclenching.

"She goes to her family," he said flatly.

"Where were they when Issa's mother felt so desperate?" The question fell from Mari's heart as much as her mouth, the objective scientist part of her nowhere to be found. She had to be certain before she could let go.

Rowan's hand fell to a tiny baby foot encased in a Christmas plaid sleeper. "The aunt and uncle insist they offered help, and that they didn't know how badly their niece was coping."

"Do you believe them?"

"They don't live nearby so it's entirely possible they missed the signs. Issa's only three months old." He patted the baby's chest once before shoving to his feet again, pacing restlessly. "They came for the funeral six weeks ago, left some money, followed up with calls, but she told them she was managing all right."

"And they believed her." How awful did it make her that she was still desperately searching for something to fault them for, some reason why they couldn't be the right people to raise the little angel in her arms.

"From everything our sources can tell, they're good people. Solid income from their tourist shop." He stopped at the window, palming the glass and leaning forward with a weary sigh. "They want custody of Issa and there's no legal or moral reason I can see why they shouldn't have her."

"What about what we want?" she asked quickly, in case she might have second thoughts and hold back the words.

"We don't have any rights to her." He glanced back over his shoulder. "This is the best scenario we could have hoped would play out. That first night when we spoke to the cops, we both never really dreamed this good of a solution could be found for her."

"I realize that… It's just…"

He turned to face her, leaning back and crossing his arms over his chest. "You already love her."

"Of course I care about her."

A sad half smile tipped his mouth. "That's not what I said."

"I've only known her a few days." Mari rolled out the logic as if somehow she could convince herself.

"I've watched enough new mothers in my line of work to know how fast the heart engages."

What did he hope to achieve by this? By stabbing her with his words? "I'm not her mother."

"You have been, though. You've done everything a mother would do to protect her child. It's not surprising you want to keep her."

Mari's throat clogged with emotion. "I'm in no position to take care of a baby. She has relatives who want her and can care for her. I know what I have to do."

"You're giving her the best chance, like a good mother." He cupped the back of her head, comfort in his gaze and in his touch.

She soaked up his supporting strength. "Are you trying to soften me up again?"

"I'm wounded you would think I'm that manipulative." He winked.

"Ha," she choked on a half laugh. "Now you're trying to make me smile so I won't cry."

He massaged her scalp lightly. "It's okay to cry if you need to."

She shook her head. "I think I'll just keep rocking her, maybe sing some Christmas carols until her family arrives. I know she won't remember me, but..."

A buzzer sounded at their suite door a second before Hillary walked in, followed by Troy. Mari sighed in relief over the brief reprieve. The aunt and uncle weren't here yet.

Hillary smiled gently. "The family is on their way up. I thought you would want the warning."

"Thank you for your help tracking them down." Mari could hardly believe she managed to keep her voice flat and unemotional in light of the caldron churning inside her.

Troy sat on the sofa beside his wife, the wiry computer mogul sliding an arm around Hillary's shoulders. "I'm glad we were able to resolve the issue so quickly."

Yet it felt like she'd spent a lifetime with Rowan and the baby.

Hillary settled into her husband's arm. "Mari, did Rowan tell you the tip that helped us put the pieces together came from the press coverage you brought in?"

"No, not that I remember." Although he might have

said something and she missed it. Since she'd heard Issa was leaving, Mari had been in a fog.

"Thanks to the huge interest your name inspired, we were contacted by a nurse whose story sounded legit. We showed her the composite sketch we'd pieced together from the different camera angles." Hillary rambled on, filling the tense silence. "She identified the woman as a patient she'd helped through delivery. From there, the rest of the pieces came together. She never would have heard about this if not for you and Rowan. You orchestrated this perfectly, Mari."

"With your help. Rowan is lucky to have such great friends."

And with those words she realized she didn't have people to reach out to in a crisis. She had work acquaintances, and she had family members she kept at arm's length. She spent her life focused on her lab. She'd sealed herself off from the world, running from meaningful relationships as surely as she ran from the press. Shutting herself away from her parents' disapproval—her father wanting her to assume her role of princess, her mother encouraging her to be a rebellious child embracing a universe beyond. Ultimately she'd disappointed them both. Rowan and this baby were her first deep connections in so long....

And it was tearing her apart to say goodbye to them.

She didn't want this pain. She wanted her safe world back. The quiet and order of her research lab, where she could quantify results and predict outcomes.

The buzzer sounded again and Mari bit her lip to keep from shouting in denial. Damn it, she would stay in control. She would see this through in a calm manner, do nothing to upset Issa.

Even though every cell in her cried out in denial.

* * *

Rowan watched helplessly as Mari passed the baby over to her relatives—a couple he'd made damn sure to investigate to the fullest. He'd relocated orphans countless times in his life and he'd always been careful, felt the weight of responsibility.

Never had that weight felt this heavy on his shoulders.

He studied the couple, in their fifties, the husband in a crisp linen suit, the wife in a colorful dress with a matching headscarf. The aunt took Issa from Mari's arms while the uncle held a diaper bag.

Mari twisted her hands in front of her, clearly resisting the temptation to yank the baby back. "She likes to be held close, but facing outward so she can see what's going on. And you have to burp her after every ounce of formula or she spits up. She likes music—"

Her voice cracked.

The aunt placed a hand on her arm. "Thank you for taking such good care of little Issa, Princess. If we had known about our niece's intentions, we would have volunteered to take Issa immediately. But when a young mother assures you she is fine, who would ever think to step in and offer to take her child? Trust us though, we will shower her with love. We will make sure she always knows you have been her guardian angel...."

With teary eyes, Mari nodded, but said nothing.

Troy stepped into the awkward silence. "My wife and I will escort you to your car through a back entrance to be sure the press doesn't overrun you."

Thank God, Troy quickly ushered them out before this hellish farewell tore them all in half. Rowan stole one last look at the baby's sweet chubby-cheeked face, swallowed hard and turned to Mari. No doubt she needed him more now.

The second the door closed behind the Donavans, Mari's legs folded.

She sank into the rocking chair again, nearly doubled over as she gulped in air. Her lovely face tensed with pain as she bit her lower lip. "Rowan, I don't think," she gasped, "I can't...I can't give my presentation this afternoon."

He understood the feeling. Rowan hooked his arm around her shoulders. "I'll call the conference coordinator. I'll tell them you're sick."

"But I'm never sick." She looked up at him with bemused eyes, bright with unshed tears. "I never bow out at work. What's wrong with me?"

"You're grieving." So was he. Something about this child was different, maybe because of the role she'd played in bringing Mari to him. Maybe because of the Christmas season. Or perhaps simply because the little tyke had slipped past the defenses he worked so hard to keep in place as he faced year after year of treating bone-crushing poverty and sickness. "You're human."

"I only knew her a few days. She's not my child...." Mari pressed a hand to her chest, rubbing a wound no less deep for not being visible. "I shouldn't be this upset."

"You loved her—you still do." He shifted around to kneel in front of her, stroking her face, giving Mari comfort—a welcome distraction when he needed it most. "That's clear to anyone who saw you with her."

"I know, damn it." She blinked back tears. "I don't want to think about it. I don't want to feel any of this. I just need...this."

Mari grabbed his shirt front, twisted her fist in the

fabric and yanked him toward her as she fell into him. Rowan absorbed their fall with his body, his shoulders meeting the thick carpet. Mari blanketed him, her mouth meeting his with a frenzy and intensity there was no denying. She'd found an outlet for her grief and he was damn well ready to help her with that. They both needed this.

Needed an outlet for all the frustrated emotions roaring through the room.

She wriggled her hips erotically against his ready arousal. A moan of pleasure slipped from her lips as she nipped his ear. There was no need to be silent any longer. Their suite was empty. Too empty. Their first encounter had been focused on staying quiet, in control as they discovered each other for the first time.

Tonight, control didn't exist.

He pushed those thoughts away and focused on Mari, on making sure she was every bit as turned on as he was. He gathered the hem of her dress and bunched it until he found the sweet curve of her bottom. He guided her against him, met her with a rolling rhythm of his own, a synchronicity they'd discovered together last night.

Sitting up, increasing the pressure against his erection, she yanked his shirt open, buttons popping free and flying onto the carpet. Her ragged breathing mingled with his. He swept her dress off and away until she wore only a pale green satin bra and underwear. He was quickly realizing her preference for soft, feminine lingerie and he enjoyed peeling it from her. He flung the bra to rest on the bar. Then twisted his fist in her panties until the thin strap along her hip snapped. The last scrap of fabric fell away.

She clasped his head in her hands and drew his face

to her breasts. Her guidance, her demands, made him even harder. He took her in his mouth, enjoying the giving as much as the taking. Her moans and sighs were driving him wild. And yes, he had his own pent-up frustrations to work out, his own regret over seeing Issa leave… He shut down those thoughts, grounding himself in the now.

Arching onto her heels, Mari fumbled with the fly of his pants.

"Condom," he groaned. "In my pocket."

He lifted his butt off the floor and she stroked behind him to pluck the packet free. Thank heaven he'd thought to keep one on him even in a crisis. Because he couldn't stomach the thought of stopping, not even for an instant.

Then he felt her hands on him, soft, stroking. He throbbed at her touch as she sheathed him in the condom, then took him inside her. His head dug back as he linked fingers with her, following the ride where she took him, hard and fast, noisy and needy. The fallout would have to take care of itself, because right now, they were both locked in a desperate drive to block out the pain of loss.

Already, he could feel the building power of his release rolling through him. He gritted his teeth, grinding back the need to come. Reaching between them to ease her over the edge with him. One look at her face, the crescendo of her sweet cries, told him she was meeting him there now. He thrust, again and again until his orgasm throbbed free while hers pulsed around him.

He caught her as she collapsed into his arms. He soaked in the warmth of her skin, the pounding of her heart—hell, everything about her.

The cooling air brought hints of reality slithering

back, the world expanding around them. The roaring in his ears grew louder, threatening this pocket of peace. It was too soon for him to take her again, but that didn't rule out other pleasurable possibilities.

Rowan eased Mari from him and onto her back. He kissed her mouth, her jaw, along her neck, inhaling the floral essence of her. Her hands skimmed up and down his spine as she reclined languidly. Smiling against her skin, he nipped his way lower, nuzzling and stroking one breast then the other.

"Rowan?"

"Shhh…" He blew across her damp nipple. The damp brown tip pebbled even tighter for him and he took her in his mouth, flicking with his tongue.

He sprinkled kisses along the soft underside, then traveled lower, lower still until he parted her legs and stroked between her thighs, drawing a deep sigh from her. He dipped his head and breathed in the essence of her, tasted her. Teased at the tight bundle of nerves until she rambled a litany of need for more. He was more than happy to comply.

A primitive rush of possession surged through him. She was his. He cupped the soft globes of her bottom and brought her closer to him, circled and laved, worked her until her fingers knotted restlessly in his hair. He took her to the edge of completion again, then held back, taking her to the precipice again and again, knowing her orgasm would be all the more powerful with the build.

Her head thrashed against the carpet and she cried out his name as her release gripped her. Her hands flung out, knocking over an end table, sending a lamp crashing to the floor.

He watched the flush of completion spread over her

as he slid back up to lay beside her. The evening breeze drifted over them, threatening to bring reality with it.

There was only one way to make it through the rest of this night. Make love to Mari until they both collapsed with exhaustion. Rolling to his knees, he slid his arms under her, lifting as he stood. He secured her against his chest, the soft give of her body against his stirring him.

Her arm draped around his neck, her head lolling against him as she still breathed heavily in the aftermath of her release. He strode across the suite toward his bedroom, his jeans open and riding low on his hips. Hell, he'd never even gotten his pants off.

He lowered Mari to his bed, the sight of her naked body, long legs and subtle curves stirring him impossibly hard again. Shadows played along her dusky skin, inviting him to explore. To lose himself in the oblivion of her body. To forget for a few hours that the emptiness of their suite was so damn tangible... No baby sighs. No iPhone of Christmas lullabies. Gone.

Just like Issa. Their reason for staying together.

Eleven

Mari had spent a restless night in Rowan's arms. As the morning light pierced through the shutters, he'd suggested they get away from the resort and all the memories of Issa that lurked in their suite. She hadn't even hesitated at jumping on board with his plan.

Literally.

Mari stretched out on the bow of the sailboat and stared up at the cloudless sky, frigate birds gliding overhead with their wide wings extended full-out. Waves slapped against the hull, and lines pinged against the mast. Rowan had leased the thirty-three-foot luxury sailboat for the two of them to escape for the day to a deserted shore. No worries about the press spying on them and no reminders of the baby. Nothing to do but to stare into the azure waters, watching fish and loggerhead turtles.

God, how she needed to get away from the reminders. Her time with the baby had touched her heart and made her realize so many things were missing in her life. Love. Family. She'd buried herself in work, retreating into a world that made sense to her after a lifetime of feeling awkward in her own skin. But holding that sweet little girl had made Mari accept she'd turned her back on far too much.

That didn't mean she had any idea how to fix it. Or herself. She watched Rowan guiding the sailboat, open shirt flapping behind him, sun burnishing his blond hair.

Rowan had made love to her—and she to him—until they'd both fallen into an exhausted sleep. They'd slept, woken only long enough to order room service and made love again. She had the feeling Rowan was as confused and empty as she, but she couldn't quite put her finger on why.

For that matter, maybe she was just too lost in her own hurt to understand his.

In the morning, he'd told her to dress for a day on a boat. She hadn't questioned him, grateful for the distraction. Mari had tossed on a sarong, adding dark glasses and an old-school Greta Garbo scarf to make her escape. He'd surprised her with a gift, bracelets she'd admired at the marketplace their first night out with Issa. She stretched her arm out, watching the sun refract off the silver bangles and colorful beads.

Rowan sailed the boat, handling the lines with ease as the hull chopped through the water toward an empty cove, lush mountains jutting in the distance. They'd followed the coast all morning toward a neighboring island with a private harbor. If only the ache in her heart was as easy to leave behind.

She rolled to her tummy and stretched out along her

towel, her well-loved body languid and a bit stiff. Chin on her hands, she gazed out at the rocks jutting from the water along the secluded coastline. She watched the gannets and petrels swoop and dive for fish. Palm trees clustered along the empty shoreline, creating a thick wall of foliage just beyond the white sandy beaches. Peaceful perfection, all familiar and full of childhood memories of vacationing along similar shores with her parents.

A shadow stretched across her, a broad-shouldered shadow. She flipped to her back again, shading her eyes to look up at Rowan. "Shouldn't you be at the helm?"

"We've dropped anchor." He crouched beside her, too handsome for his own good in swim trunks and an open shirt, ocean breeze pulling at his loose hair. "Come with me and have something to drink?"

She clasped his outstretched hand and stood, walking with him, careful to duck and weave past the boom and riggings. The warm hardwood deck heated her bare feet. "You didn't have to be so secretive about our destination."

"I wanted to surprise you." He jumped down to the deck level, grasping her waist and lowering her to join him. He gestured to where he'd poured them two glasses of mango juice secured in the molded surface between the seat cushions, the pitcher tucked securely in an open cooler at his bare feet.

"That's your only reason?"

"I wasn't sure you would agree, and we both needed to get away from the resort." He passed her a glass, nudging her toward the captain's chair behind the wheel. "Besides, my gorgeous, uptight scientist, you need to have fun."

"I have fun." Sitting, she sipped her drink. The sweet

natural sugars sent a jolt of energy through her, his words putting her on the defensive. "My work is fun."

He cocked an eyebrow, shooting just above his sunglasses.

"Okay, my work is rewarding. And I don't recall being all that uptight when I was sitting on the bar last night." She eyed him over the glass.

"Fair enough. I'm taking you out because I want you mellow and softened up so when I try to seduce you later you completely succumb to my charm." He thudded the heel of his palm to his forehead, clearly doing his best to take her mind off things. "Oh, wait, I already seduced you."

"Maybe I seduced you." She tossed aside her sunglasses and pulled off his aviator shades, her bracelets chiming with each movement. She leaned in to kiss him, more than willing to be distracted from the questions piling up in her mind.

Like where they would go from here once the conference was over. Since she didn't have any suggestions in mind, she sure wasn't going to ask for his opinion.

"Whose turn is it, then, to take the initiative?" He pulled her drink from her and stepped closer.

"I've lost count." She let her eyes sweep over him seductively, immersing herself in this game they both played, delaying the inevitable.

"Princess, you do pay the nicest compliments." He stroked her face, along the scarf holding back her hair, tugging it free.

"You say the strangest things." She traced his mouth, the lips that had brought her such pleasure last night.

"We're here to play, not psychoanalyze."

Her own lips twitched with a self-deprecating smile. "Glad to know it, because I stink at reading people."

"Why do you assume that?" His question mingled with the call of birds in the trees and the plop of fish.

"Call it a geek thing."

"You make geek sexy." He nipped her tracing finger, then sucked lightly.

She rolled her eyes. "You are such a…"

"A what?"

"I don't even have words for you."

His eyes went serious for the first time this morning. "Glad to know I mystify you as much as you bemuse me."

"I've always thought of myself as a straightforward person. Some call that boring." She flinched, hating the feeling that word brought, knowing she couldn't—wouldn't—change. "For me, there's comfort in routine."

Those magnificently blue eyes narrowed and darkened. "Tell me who called you boring and I'll—"

She clapped a hand over his mouth, bracelets dangling. "It's okay. But thanks." She pulled her hand away, a rogue wave bobbing the boat beneath her. "I had trouble making friends in school. I didn't fit in for so many reasons—everything from my ridiculous IQ to the whole princess thing. I was either much younger than my classmates or they were sucking up because of my family. There was no sisterhood for me. It was tough for people to see the real me behind all that clutter."

"I wasn't an instant fit at school, either." He shifted to stand beside her, looping an arm around her shoulders bared by the sarong.

She leaned against him, looking out over the azure blue waters. The continent of her birth was such a mixture of lush magnificence and stark poverty. "You don't need to change your history to make me feel better. I'm okay with myself."

"God's honest truth here." He rested his chin on top of her head. "My academy brothers and I were all misfits. The headmaster there did a good job at redirecting us, channeling us, helping us figure out ways to put our lives on the right path again."

"All of you? That's quite a track record."

He went still against her. "Not all of us. Some of us were too far gone to be rehabilitated." His sigh whispered over her, warmer than the sun. "You may have read in the news about Malcolm Douglas's business manager—he was a schoolmate of ours. He lost his way, forgot about rules and integrity. He did some shady stuff to try and wrangle publicity for his client."

"Your friend. Malcolm. Another of your Brotherhood?"

"Malcolm and I aren't as close as I am to the others. But yes, he's a friend." He turned her by her shoulders and stared into her eyes. "We're not perfect, any of us, but the core group of us, we can call on each other for anything, anytime."

"Like how the casino owner friend provided the start-up money for your clinic..."

Rowan had built an incredible support system for himself after his parents failed him. While she'd cut herself off from the world.

"That he did. You wouldn't recognize Conrad from the high school photos. He was gangly and wore glasses back then, but he was a brilliant guy and he knew it. Folks called him Mr. Wall Street, because of his dad and how Conrad used his trust fund to manipulate the stock market to punish sweatshop businesses."

"You all may have been misfits, but it appears you share a need for justice."

"We didn't all get along at first. I was different

from them, though, or so I liked to tell myself. I didn't come from money like most of the guys there—or like you—and I wasn't inordinately talented like Douglas. I thought I was better than those overprivileged brats."

"Yet, Conrad must respect you to have invested so much money to start the clinic."

"If we're going to be honest—" he laughed softly "—I'm where I am today because of a cookie."

"A cookie?" She tipped her head back to the warm sunshine, soaking in the heat of the day and the strength of the man beside her.

"My mom used to send me these care packages full of peanut-butter cookies with M&M's baked into them." His eyes took on a faraway look and a fond smile.

Mari could only think that same mother had sent him to that school in his brother's place. Those cookies must have tasted like dust in light of such a betrayal from the woman who should have protected him. She bit back the urge to call his mother an unflattering name and just listened, ocean wind rustling her hair.

"One day, I was in my bunk, knocking back a couple of those cookies while doing my macro biology homework." He toyed with the end of her scarf. "I looked up to find Conrad staring at those cookies like they were caviar. I knew better than to offer him one. His pride would have made him toss it back in my face."

She linked fingers with him and squeezed as he continued, her cheek against the warm cotton of his shirt, her ear taking in the steady thrum of his heart.

"We were all pretty angry at life in those days. But I had my cookies and letters from Mom to get me through the days when I didn't think I could live with the guilt of what I'd done."

What his family had done. His mother, father and his brother. Why couldn't he see how they'd sacrificed him?

"But back to Conrad. About a week later, I was on my way to the cafeteria and I saw him in the visitation area with his dad. I was jealous as hell since my folks couldn't afford to fly out to visit me—and then I realized he and his dad were fighting."

"About what?" She couldn't help but ask, desperate for this unfiltered look into the teenage Rowan, hungry for insights about what had shaped him into the man he'd become.

"From what Conrad shouted, it was clear his father wanted him to run a scam on Troy's parents and convince them to invest in some bogus company or another. Conrad decked his dad. It took two security guards to pull him off."

Hearing the things that Rowan and his friends had been through as teens, she felt petty for her anger over her own childhood. The grief Rowan and his friends had faced, the storms in their worlds, felt so massive in comparison to her own. She had two parents that loved her, two homes, and yes, she was shuttled back and forth, but in complete luxury.

"And the cookie?"

"I'm getting there." He sketched his fingers up and down her bare arm. "Conrad spent a couple of days in the infirmary—his dad hit him back and dislocated Conrad's shoulder. The cops didn't press charges on the old man because the son threw the first punch. Anyhow, Conrad's first day out of the infirmary, I felt bad for him so I wrapped a cookie in a napkin and put it on his bunk. He didn't say anything, but he didn't toss it back in my face, either." He threw his hands wide. "And here I am today."

Her heart hurt so badly she could barely push words out. "Why are you telling me this?"

"I don't know. I just want you to understand why my work is so important to me, so much so that I couldn't have kept Issa even if her family didn't come through. Because if I start keeping every orphan that tugs at my emotions, I won't be able to sustain all I've fought so hard to build. The clinic…it's everything to me. It helps me fill the hole left by Dylan's death, helps me make up for the lives lost."

She heard him, heard an isolation in his words in spite of all those friends. He'd committed himself to a life of service that left him on a constant, lonely quest. And right then and there, her soul ached for him.

She slid her hand up into his hair, guiding his mouth to hers. He stepped between her knees, and she locked her arms around his neck. Tight. Demanding and taking,

"Now," she whispered against his mouth, fishing in his back pocket for a condom.

He palmed her knees apart and she purred her approval. Her fingers made fast work of his swim trunks, freeing his erection and sheathing him swiftly, surely.

She locked her legs around his waist and drew him in deeper. He drove into her again and again. She angled back, gripping the bar, bracelets sliding down to collect along her hand. He took in the beauty of her, her smooth skin, pert breasts, her head thrown back and hair swaying with every thrust. The boat rocked in a rhythm that matched theirs as his shouts of completion twined and mingled with hers, carried on the breeze.

In that moment she felt connected to him more than physically. She identified with him, overwhelmed by an understanding of him being as alone in the world as her. But also hammered by a powerlessness to change that. His vision and walls were as strong as hers, always had been. Maybe more so.

What a time to figure out she might have sacrificed too much for her work—only realizing that now, as she fell for a man who would sacrifice anything for *his*.

The taste of the sea, sweat and Mari still clinging to his skin, Rowan opened the door to their suite the next morning, praying the return to land and real life wouldn't bring on the crushing sense of loss. He'd hoped to distract her from Issa—and also find some way to carve out a future for them. They were both dedicated to their work. They could share that, even in their disagreements. They could use that as a springboard to work out solutions. Together. His time with her overnight on the sailboat had only affirmed that for him.

He just hoped he'd made a good start in persuading Mari of the same thing.

Guiding her into the suite with a hand low on her spine, he stepped deeper into the room. Only to stop short. His senses went on alert. There was someone here.

Damn it, there was more traffic through this supposedly secure room than through the lobby. Which of course meant it was one of his friends.

Elliot Starc rose from the sofa and from Mari's gasp beside him, clearly she recognized the world-famous race-car driver...and underwear model.

Rowan swallowed a curse. "Good morning, Elliot. Did you get booted out of your own room?"

Laughing, Elliot took Mari's hand lightly and ignored Rowan's question. "Princess, it's an honor to meet you."

"Mr. Starc, you're one of Rowan's Brotherhood friends, I assume."

Elliot's eyebrows shot up. "You told her?"

"We talk." Among other things.

"Well, color me stunned. That baby was lucky to have landed in Rowan's room. Our Interpol connections kept all of you safe while bringing this to a speedy conclusion."

Crap. The mention of Interpol hung in the air, Mari's eyes darting to his.

Oblivious to the gaffe, Elliot continued, "Which brings me to my reason for being here. I've emailed a summary of the existing security detail, but I need to get back to training, get my mind back in the game so I don't set more than my hair on fire."

Rowan pulled a tight smile. "Thanks, buddy."

Mari frowned. "Interpol?"

Elliot turned sharply to Rowan. "You said you told her about the Brotherhood."

"Classmates. I told her we're classmates." He didn't doubt she would keep his secret safe, but knowing wouldn't help her and anything that didn't help was harmful. "You, my friend, made a mighty big assumption for someone who should know better."

"She's a princess. You've been guarding her." Elliot scratched his sheared hair. "I thought… Ah, hell. Just…" Throwing his hands out and swiping the air as if that explained it all, Elliot spun on his heel and walked out the door.

Mari sat hard, sinking like a stone on the edge of the sofa. "You're with Interpol?" She huffed on a long sigh. "Of course you're with Interpol."

"I'm a physician. That's my primary goal, my mission in life." He paused, unable to dodge the truth as he kneeled in front of her. "But yes, I help out Interpol on occasion with freelance work in the area. No one thinks twice about someone like me wandering around wealthy fundraisers or traveling to remote countries."

He could see her closing down, pulling away.

"Mari?"

"It's your job. I understand."

"Are you angry with me for not telling you?"

"Why would you? It's not my secret to know. Your friend…he assumed more about us than he should. But you know I won't say a word. I understand well what it's like to be married to your work."

Her words came out measured and even, her body still, her spine taking on that regal "back off" air that shouted of generations of royalty. "Mari, this doesn't have to mean things change between us. If anything we can work together."

"Work, right…" Her amber eyes flickered with something he couldn't quite pin down.

"Are you all right?"

"I'll be fine. It's all just a lot to process, this today. Issa yesterday."

He cradled her shoulders in his hands. She eased away.

"Mari, it's okay to shout at me if you're mad. Or to cry about Issa. I'm here for you," he said, searching for the right way to approach her.

"Fine. You want me to talk? To yell? You've got it. I would appreciate your acting like we're equal rather than stepping into your benevolent physician shoes because no one would dare to contradict the man who does so much for the world." She shrugged free of his grip.

"Excuse me for trying to be a nice guy." He held up his hands.

"You're always the nice guy." She shot to her feet. "The saint. Giving out comfort, saving the world, using that as a wall between you and other people."

"What the hell are you talking about?" He stood warily, watching her pace.

"There you go. Get mad at me." She stopped in front of him, crossing her arms over her chest. "At least real emotions put us on an even footing. Oh, wait, we're not even. You're the suave doctor/secret agent. I'm the awkward genius who locks herself away in a lab."

"Are we really returning to the old antagonistic back-and-forth way of communicating?" he asked. Her words felt damn unfair when he was working his tail off to help her through a rough time. "I thought we'd moved past that."

"That's not what I'm talking about and you know it. You're a smart man."

"Actually, you're the certified genius here. How about you explain it to me."

"You want me to cry and grieve and open myself up to you." She jabbed his chest with one finger, her voice rising with every word. "But what about you? When do you open up to me? When are you going to give me something besides the saintly work side of your life?"

"I've told you things about my past," he answered defensively.

"To be fair, yes you have," she conceded without backing down. "Some things. Certainly not everything. And when have you let me in? You're fine with things as long as you're the one doling out comfort. But accepting it? No way. Like now. You have every reason to grieve for Issa."

"She's in good hands, well cared for," he said through gritted teeth.

"See? There you go doing just what I said. You want me to cry and be emotional, but you—" she waved a hand "—you're just fine. Did you even allow yourself to grieve for your brother?"

His head snapped back, her words smacking him even as she kept her hands fisted at her sides. "Don't you dare use my brother against me. That has nothing to do with what we're discussing now."

"It has everything to do with what we're talking about. But if I'm mistaken, then explain it to me. Explain what you're feeling."

She waited while he searched for the right words, but everything he'd offered her so far hadn't worked. He didn't have a clue what to say to reassure her. And apparently he waited too long.

"That's what I thought." She shook her head sadly, backing away from him step by step. "I'm returning to my old room. There's no reason for me to be here anymore."

She spun away, the hem of her sarong fluttering as she raced into her room and slammed the door. He could hear her tossing her suitcase on the bed. Heard her muffled sobs. And heard the click of the lock that spoke loud and clear.

He'd blown it. Royally, so to speak. He might be confused about a lot of things. But one was crystal clear.

He was no longer welcome in Mari's life.

Twelve

The conference was over. Her week with Rowan was done.

Mari stood in front of the mirrored vanity and tucked the final pin into her hair, which was swept back in a sleek bun. Tonight's ball signified an official end to their time together. There was no dodging the event without being conspicuous and stirring up more talk in the press.

As if there wasn't enough talk already. At least all reports from the media—and from Rowan's Interpol friends—indicated that Issa was adapting well in her new home after only a couple of days. Something to be eternally grateful for. A blessing in this heartbreaking week.

Her pride demanded she finish with her head held high.

After her confrontation with Rowan, she'd waited the

remainder of her stay, hoping he would fight for her as hard as he fought for his work, for every person who walked through those clinic doors. But she hadn't heard a word from him since she'd stormed from his room and she'd gone back to her simple room a floor below. How easily he'd let her go, and in doing so, broken her heart.

But his ability to disconnect with her also filled her with resolve.

She wouldn't be like him anymore, hiding from the world. She was through staying in the shadows for fear of disappointing people.

Mari smoothed her hands down the shimmering red strapless dress, black swirls through the fabric giving the impression of phantom roses. The dress hugged her upper body, fitted past her hips then swept to the ground with a short train. It was a magnificent gown. She'd never worn anything like it. She would have called it a Cinderella moment except she didn't want to be some delicate princess at the ball. She was a one-day queen, boldly stepping into her own.

Her hands fell to the small tiara, diamonds refracting the vanity lights. Carefully, she tucked the crown— symbolic of so much more—on her head.

Stepping from her room, she checked the halls and, how ironic, for once the corridor was empty. No fans to carefully maneuver. She could make her way to the brass-plated elevator in peace.

Jabbing the elevator button, she curled her toes in her silken ballet slippers. Her stomach churned with nerves over facing the crowd downstairs alone, even more than that, over facing Rowan again. But she powered on, one leather-clad foot at a time. While she was ready to meet the world head-on in her red Vera Wang, she wasn't prepared to do so wearing high heels that would likely send her stumbling down the stairs.

She was bold, but practical.

Finally, the elevator doors slid open, except the elevator wasn't empty. Her stomach dropped in shock faster than a cart on a roller-coaster ride.

"Papa?" She stared at her father, her royal father.

But even more surprising, her mother stood beside him. "Going down, dear?"

Stunned numb, she stepped into the elevator car, brass doors sliding closed behind her.

"Mother, why are you and Papa here? *Together?*" she squeaked as her mom hugged her fast and tight.

The familiar scent of her mom's perfume enveloped her, like a bower of gardenias. And her mom wasn't dressed for a simple visit. Susan Mandara was decked out for the ball in a Christmas-green gown, her blond hair piled on top of her head. Familiar, yet so unusual, since Mari couldn't remember the last time she'd seen Adeen and Susan Mandara standing side by side in anything other than old pictures.

Her father kissed her on the forehead. "Happy Christmas, little princess."

She clutched her daddy's forearms, the same arms that used to toss her high in the air as a child. Always catching her.

Tonight, her father wore a tuxedo with a crimson tribal robe over it, trimmed in gold. As a child, she used to sneak his robes out to wear for dress-up with her parents laughing, her mother affectionately calling him Deen, her nickname for him. She'd forgotten that happy memory until just now.

Her mother smoothed cool hands over her daughter's face. "Your father and I have a child together." She gave

Mari's face a final pat. "Deen and I are bonded for life, *by* life, through you. We came to offer support and help you with all the press scrutiny."

Did they expect her to fail? She couldn't resist saying, "Some of this togetherness would have been welcome when I was younger."

"We've mellowed with age." Susan stroked her daughter's forehead. "I wish we could have given you a simpler path. We certainly wanted to."

If her mother had wanted to keep things simple, marrying a prince was surely a weird way to go about it.

Her father nodded his head. "You look magnificent. You are everything I wanted my princess to grow up to be."

"You're just saying that because I'm decked out in something other than a sack," she teased him, even though her heart ached with the cost of her newfound confidence. "But I can assure you, I still detest ribbon cuttings and state dinners."

"And you still care about the people. You'll make your mark in a different manner than I did. That's good." He held out both elbows as the elevator doors slid open on the ground floor. "Ladies? Shall we?"

Decorations in the hallway had doubled since she went upstairs to change after the final presentation of the day. Mari strode past oil palm trees decorated with bells. Music drifted from the ballroom, a live band played carols on flutes, harps and drums.

The sounds of Christmas. The sounds of home. Tables laden with food. She could almost taste the sweet cookies and the meats marinated in *chakalaka*.

A few steps later, she stood on the marble threshold of the grand ballroom. All eyes turned to her and for a moment her feet stayed rooted to the floor. Cameras clicked and she didn't so much as flinch or cringe. She wasn't sure what to do next as she swept the room with her eyes, taking in the ballroom full of medical professionals decked out in all their finery, with local bigwigs in attendance, as well.

Then her gaze hitched on Rowan, wearing a traditional tuxedo, so handsome he took her breath away.

His hair was swept back, just brushing his collar, his eyes blue flames that singed her even from across the room. She expected him to continue ignoring her. But he surprised her by striding straight toward her. All eyes followed him, and her heart leaped into her throat.

Rowan stopped in front of them and nodded to her father. "Sir, I believe your daughter and I owe the media a dance."

Owe the media?

What about what they owed each other?

And how could he just stand there as if nothing had happened between them, as if they hadn't bared their bodies and souls to each other? She had a gloriously undignified moment of wanting to kick him. But this was her time to shine and she refused to let him wreck it. She stepped into his arms, and he gestured to the band. They segued into a rendition of "Ave Maria," with a soloist singing.

Her heart took hope that he'd chosen the piece for her. He led her to the middle of the dance floor. Other couples melted away and into the crowd, leaving them alone, at the mercy of curious eyes and cameras.

As she allowed herself to be swept into his arms—into the music—she searched for something to say. "I appreciate the lovely song choice."

"It fits," he answered, but his face was still creased in a scowl, his eyes roving over her.

"Don't you like the dress?"

"I like the woman in the dress," he said hoarsely. "If you'd been paying attention, you would have realized my eyes have been saying that for a long time before you changed up your wardrobe."

"So why are you scowling?"

"Because I want this whole farce of a week to be over."

"Oh," she said simply, too aware of his hand on her waist, his other clasping her fingers.

"Do you believe me? About the dress, I mean." His feet moved in synch with hers, their bodies as fluid on the dance floor as they'd been making love.

"We've exchanged jabs in the past, insults even, but you've always been honest."

"Then why are you still sleeping on another floor of the hotel?"

"Oh, Rowan," she said bittersweetly. "Sex isn't the problem between us."

"Remind me what is?"

"The way you close people—me—out. It took me a long time to realize I'm deserving of everything. And so are you."

"I guess there's nothing left to say then."

The music faded away, and with a final sweep across the floor he stopped in front of her parents.

Rowan passed her hand back to her father. "With all due respect, sir, take better care of her."

Her mother smothered a laugh.

Her father arched a royal eyebrow. "I beg your pardon."

"More security detail. She's a princess. She deserves to be cared for and protected like one."

With a final nod, Rowan turned away and melted into the crowd and out of her life.

Five hours later, Mari hugged her pillow to her chest, watching her mom settle into the other double bed in the darkened room. "Mother, aren't we wealthy enough for you to have a suite or at least a room of your own?"

Susan rolled to her side, facing her daughter in the shadowy room lit only by moonlight streaming in. "I honestly thought you would be staying with Dr. Boothe even though this room was still booked in your name. And even with the show of good faith your father and I have given, we're not back to sharing a room."

Curtains rustled with the night ocean breeze and sounds of a steel-drum band playing on the beach for some late-night partiers.

"Rowan and I aren't a couple anymore." Although the haunting beauty of that dance still whispered through her, making her wonder what more she could have done. "It was just a…fling."

The most incredible few days of her life.

"Mari dear, you are not the fling sort," her mother reminded her affectionately. "So why are you walking away from him?"

Tears clogged her throat. "I'm honestly too upset to talk about this." She flipped onto her back, clenching her fists against the memory of his tuxedoed shoulders under her hands.

The covers rustled across the room as her mother sat up. "I made the biggest mistake of my life when I was about your age."

"Marrying my father. Yeah, I got that." Was it in her DNA to fail at relationships? Her parents had both been divorced twice.

"No, marrying the man I loved—your father—was the right move. Thinking I could change him? I screwed up there." She hugged her knees to her chest, her graying blond hair trailing down her back. "Before you think I'm taking all the blame here, he thought I would change, as well. So the divorce truly was a fifty-fifty screw-up on our part. He should have realized my free spirit is what he fell in love with and I should have recognized how drawn I was to his devotion to his country."

What was her mother trying to tell her? She wanted to understand, to step outside of the awkwardness in more ways than just being comfortable in a killer red dress. Except her mom was talking about not changing at all.

"You're going to have to spell it out for me more clearly."

"Your father and I weren't a good couple. We weren't even particularly good at being parents. But, God, you sure turned out amazing," her mother said with an unmistakable pride, soothing years of feeling like a disappointment. "Deen and I did some things right, and maybe if we'd focused more on the things we did right, we might have lasted."

Mari ached to pour out all the details of her fight with Rowan, how she needed him to open up. And how ironic was it that he accused her of not venting her emotions? Her thoughts jumbled together until she blurted out in frustration, "Do you know how difficult it is to love a saint?"

Her mother reached out in the dark, across the divide between their beds. "You love him?"

Mari reached back and clasped her mother's hand.

"Of course I do. I just don't know how to get through to him."

"You two have been a couple for—what?—a week? Seems to me like you're giving up awful fast."

Mari bristled defensively. "I've known him for years. And it's been an intense week."

"And you're giving that up? I'd so hoped you would be smarter than I was." Her mom gave her hand a final squeeze. "Think about it. Good night, Mari."

Long into the night, Mari stared out the window at the shoreline twinkling with lighted palm trees. The rolling waves crashed a steady reminder of her day sailing with Rowan. He'd done so much to comfort her. Not just with words, but with actions, by planning the day away from the hotel and painful memories.

What had she done for him?

Nothing.

She'd simply demanded her expectations for him rather than accepting him as he was. He'd accepted and appreciated her long before a ball gown. Even when he disagreed with her, he'd respected her opinion.

Damn it all, she *was* smarter than this. Of course Rowan had built walls around himself. Every person in his family had let him down—his parents and his brother. None of them had ever put him or his well-being first. Sure, he'd made friends with his schoolmates, but he'd even admitted to feeling different from them.

Now she'd let him down, as well. He'd reached out to her as best he could and she'd told him what he offered wasn't good enough, maybe because she'd been scared of not being enough for him.

But she knew better than that now. A confidence flowed through her like a calming breeze blowing in

off the ocean. With that calm came the surety of what
to do next.

It was time to fight for the man she loved, a man she
loved for his every saintly imperfection.

Rowan had always been glad to return to his clinic
on the mainland. He'd spent every Christmas here in
surgical scrubs taking care of patients since moving to
Africa. He welcomed the work, leaving holiday celebrations to people with families.

Yet, for some reason, the CD of Christmas carols
and a pre-lit tree in the corner didn't stir much in the
way of festive feelings this year. A few gifts remained
for the patients still in the hospital, the other presents
having been passed out earlier, each box a reminder of
shopping with Mari.

So he buried himself in work.

Phone tucked under his chin, he listened to Elliot's
positive update on Issa, followed by a rambling re-
counting of his Australian Christmas vacation. Rowan
cranked back in a chair behind his desk, scanning a
computer file record on a new mother and infant due
to be discharged first thing in the morning.

One wing of the facility held a thirty-bed hospital
unit and the other wing housed a clinic. Not overly
large, but all top-of-the-line and designed for efficiency.
They doled out anything from vaccinations to prenatal
care to HIV/AIDS treatment.

The most gut-wrenching of all? The patients who
came for both prenatal care and HIV treatment. There
was a desperate need here and he couldn't help everyone, but one at a time, he was doing his damnedest.

The antibacterial scent saturated each breath he took.
Two nurses chatted with another doctor at the station

across the hall. Other than that, the place was quiet as a church mouse this late at night.

"Elliot, if you've got a point here, make it. I've got a Christmas Eve dinner to eat."

Really, just a plate to warm in the microwave but he wasn't particularly hungry anyhow. Visions of Mari in that red gown, cloaked in total confidence, still haunted his every waking and sleeping thought. He'd meant what he'd said when he told her it didn't matter to him what clothes she wore. But he was damn proud of the peace she seemed to have found with being in the spotlight. Too bad he couldn't really be a part of it.

"Ah, Rowan, I really thought you were smarter than me, brother," Elliot teased over the phone from his Australian holiday. The background echoed with drunken carolers belting out a raucous version of "The Twelve Days of Christmas."

"As I recall, our grades were fairly on par with each other back in the day."

"Sure, but I've had about four concussions since then, not to mention getting set on fire."

A reluctant smile tugged at Rowan. "Your point?"

"Why in the hell did you let that woman go?" Elliot asked, the sounds of laughter and splashing behind him. "You're clearly crazy about her and she's nuts about you. And the chemistry… Every time you looked at each other, it was all I could do not to shout at you two to get a room."

"She doesn't want me in her life." The slice of her rejection still cut so much deeper than any other.

"Did she tell you that?"

"Very clearly," he said tightly, not enjoying in the least reliving the moment. "I think her words were along the lines of 'have a nice life.'"

"You've never been particularly self-aware."

He winced, closing down the computer file on his new maternity patient. "That's what she said."

"So are you going to continue to be a miserable ass or are you going to go out and meet Mari at the clinic gate?"

At the gate? He creaked upright in his chair, swinging his feet to the floor. "What the hell are you talking about? You're in Australia."

But he stormed over to look out his office window anyway.

"Sure, but you tasked me with her security and I figured some follow-up was in order. I've been keeping track of her with a combo of guards and a good old-fashioned GPS on her rental car. If my satellite connection is any good, she should be arriving right about… now."

Rowan spotted an SUV rounding the corner into sight, headlights sweeping the road as the vehicle drove toward the clinic. Could it really be Mari? Here? Suddenly, Elliot's call made perfect sense. He'd been stringing Rowan along on the line until just the right moment.

"And Rowan," Elliot continued, "be sure you're the one to say the whole 'love you' part first since she came to you. Merry Christmas, brother."

Love her?

Of course he loved her. Wanted her. Admired her. Desired her. Always had, and why he hadn't thought to tell her before now was incomprehensible to him. Thank God for his friends, who knew him well enough to boot him in the tail when he needed that nudge most.

Thank God for Mari, who hadn't given up on him. She challenged him. Disagreed with him. But yet here she was, for him.

The line disconnected as he was already out the door and sprinting down the hall, hand over his pager to keep it from dislodging from his scrubs in his haste. His gym shoes squeaked against the tiles as he turned the corner and burst out through the front door, into the starlit night. The brisk wind rippled his surgical scrubs.

The tan SUV parked beside the clinic's ambulance under a sprawling shea butter tree. The vehicle's dome light flicked on, and Merry Christmas to him, he saw Mari's beautiful face inside. She stepped out, one incredibly long leg at a time, wearing flowing silk pants and a tunic. The fabric glided along her skin the way his hands ached to do again.

Her appearance here gave him the first hope in nearly a week that he would get to do just that.

"You came," he said simply.

"Of course. It's Christmas." She walked toward him, the African night sky almost as magnificent as his princess. She wore the bracelets he'd given her, the bangles chiming against each other. Toe-to-toe, she stopped in front of him, the sweet scent and heat of her reaching out to him. "Where else would I be but with the man I l—"

He pressed a finger against her lips. "Wait, hold that thought. I have something I need to say first. I love you, Mariama Mandara. I've wanted you and yes, loved you, for longer than I can remember. And I will do whatever it takes to be worthy of your love in return."

"Ah, Rowan, don't you know? You're already exactly what I need and everything I want. God knows, if you get any more saintly you're likely to be raptured and I would miss you so very much. I love you, too."

Relief flooded him, his heart soaking up every word like the parched ground around him absorbing a rain shower. Unable to wait another second, he hauled her to his chest and kissed her, deeply, intensely, hoping she really understood just how much he meant those words. He loved her. The truth of that sang through him as tangibly as the carols carrying gently through an open window.

Ending the kiss with a nip to his bottom lip, Mari smiled up at him. "I had a far more eloquent speech planned. I even practiced saying it on the way over because I wanted the words to be as special as what we've shared together."

"I hope you trust I love you, too." He only wished he had a more romantic way of telling her.

"I do. You showed me." She tugged the ends of the stethoscope draped around his neck, her bracelets sliding along her arm. "I just needed to stop long enough to listen with my heart. And my heart says we're perfect for each other. That we're meant to be together."

"Then why did we give each other such a hard time all these years?"

"We are both smart, dedicated people with a lot to offer, but we should be challenged. It makes us better at what we do." She tugged his face closer, punctuating the words with a quick kiss. "And if I have my way, I'm going to challenge you every day for the rest of my life."

"You have mesmerized me since the moment I first saw you." Desire and love interlocked inside him, each spiking the other to a higher level.

"That's one of the things I love most about you." She toyed with his hair, which just brushed the collar of his scrubs.

"What would that be?" He looped his arms low around her waist.

"You think my baggy, wrinkled wardrobe is sexy."

"Actually, I think peeling the clothes off of you is life's most perfect pleasure." He brought them closer together, grateful to have her in his arms, determined never to let this woman slip away from him again.

"Well, then, Dr. Boothe, let's find somewhere private to go so you can unwrap your Christmas present."

* * * * *

A sneaky peek at next month...

PASSIONATE AND DRAMATIC LOVE STORIES

My wish list for next month's titles...

In stores from 15th November 2013:

❏ It Happened One Night — Kathie DeNosky

& The Diplomat's Pregnant Bride

— Merline Lovelace

2 stories in each book - only £5.49!

❏ Her Return to King's Bed — Maureen Child

& A Billionaire for Christmas — Janice Maynard

❏ The High Price of Secrets — Yvonne Lindsay

& Second-Chance Seduction — Kate Carlisle

Available at WHSmith, Tesco, Asda, Eason, Amazon and Apple

Just can't wait?

Visit us Online

You can buy our books online a month before they hit the shops!

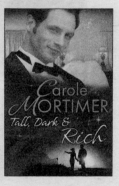

Meet The Sullivans...

Join the Mills & Boon Book Club

Subscribe to **Desire**™ today for
3, 6 or 12 months and you could
save over £30!

We'll also treat you to these fabulous extras:

- **FREE L'Occitane gift set worth £10**

- **FREE home delivery**

- **Rewards scheme, exclusive offers…and much more!**

Subscribe now and save over £30
www.millsandboon.co.uk/subscribeme